just one look at you

By Jill Mansell

Just One Look at You
An Almost Perfect Summer
The Wedding of the Year
Promise Me
Should I Tell You?
And Now You're Back
It Started With a Secret
Maybe This Time
This Could Change Everything
Meet Me at Beachcomber Bay
You and Me, Always
Three Amazing Things About You
The Unpredictable Consequences of Love
Don't Want to Miss a Thing
A Walk in the Park
To the Moon and Back
Take a Chance on Me
Rumour Has It
An Offer You Can't Refuse
Thinking of You
Making Your Mind Up
The One You Really Want
Falling For You
Nadia Knows Best
Staying at Daisy's
Millie's Fling
Good at Games
Miranda's Big Mistake
Head Over Heels
Mixed Doubles
Perfect Timing
Fast Friends
Solo
Kiss
Sheer Mischief
Open House
Two's Company

Jill Mansell
just one look at you

REVIEW

Copyright © 2026 Jill Mansell

The right of Jill Mansell to be identified as the Author of the Work has been asserted by her in accordance with the Copyright, Designs and Patents Act 1988.

First published in 2026 by Headline Review
An imprint of Headline Publishing Group Limited

1

Apart from any use permitted under UK copyright law, this publication may only be reproduced, stored, or transmitted, in any form, or by any means, with prior permission in writing of the publishers or, in the case of reprographic production, in accordance with the terms of licences issued by the Copyright Licensing Agency.

All characters in this publication are fictitious and any resemblance to real persons, living or dead, is purely coincidental.

Cataloguing in Publication Data is available from the British Library

Hardback ISBN 978 1 0354 1003 3
Trade Paperback ISBN 978 1 0354 1004 0

Map illustration by Laura Hall

Typeset in Bembo Std by Palimpsest Book Production Limited, Falkirk, Stirlingshire

Printed and bound in Great Britain by Clays Ltd, Elcograf S.p.A.

Headline's policy is to use papers that are natural, renewable and recyclable products and made from wood grown in sustainable forests. The logging and manufacturing processes are expected to conform to the environmental regulations of the country of origin.

Headline Publishing Group Limited
An Hachette UK Company
Carmelite House
50 Victoria Embankment
London EC4Y 0DZ

The authorised representative in the EEA is Hachette Ireland, 8 Castlecourt Centre, Dublin 15, D15 XTP3, Ireland (email: info@hbgi.ie)

www.headline.co.uk
www.hachette.co.uk

This book is dedicated to the memory of Jerry Lynden – a wonderful friend, gone far too soon and much missed by all who knew him.

With love to his wife, Sheonagh, and the rest of Jerry's family, especially his children, Emilia and Chris.

Chapter 1

Bristol

Disa O'Toole flipped the switch and flooded the garage with light. What a mess; she should probably be ashamed of herself at having left it like this for so long.

But time really did fly when there was a job needing to be done that you didn't want to do. Plus, knowing her luck, there were spiders the size of Pringles waiting to leap out at her the moment she started prising open boxes and sorting through the contents.

The air was dry, dusty and tinged with the scents of motor oil and household paint. It had been twelve years since her husband's death and life as she'd known it had screeched to a halt. Having promised never to leave her, after nearly forty years of marriage Declan had skied down a mountainside and crashed at high speed into a tree, doing just that. One broken promise, one bereft widow and a house full of stuff she'd had no idea what to do with meant she'd hired a man to pack everything away into storage boxes and stack them up out here in the double garage, to be dealt with when she eventually felt up to it.

And at long last, today was the day. Disa wiped her hands down the sides of her jeans and prepared herself to begin the world's most tedious task. She tore the strip of packing tape off the lid of the first box with a satisfying *rrrrrrrrrip* and a flourish, sending a fine spray of dust into the air. This one contained books, chiefly non-fiction, nothing she would ever want to read. The whole lot could go to the charity shop.

Next.

Two hours later, ploughing through the assorted contents of yet another crate, she came to a fat padded envelope with *Income Tax Receipts 2009* written across it in Declan's instantly recognisable scrawl.

Since the charity shop was unlikely to welcome these with open arms, Disa chucked the envelope onto the bonfire pile, then reached over and retrieved it, because while HMRC stuff might be deadly dull, she didn't want to destroy anything that might be important. And what if there was something vital tucked away in there, like long-forgotten Premium Bonds or share certificates?

But opening the padded envelope revealed neither share certificates nor income tax receipts. Instead, it held a sizeable collection of letters all addressed in the same flowing handwriting to Declan at the office where he'd worked.

A slow drumbeat of foreboding began to bump against Disa's chest. The envelopes were yellowed with age, as were the letters inside. It was midday, time for a break. Carrying the package into the house, she switched on the kettle and dropped a tea bag into a mug, then thought better of it and poured herself a tumbler of gin, tonic and ice instead.

Something told her she might need it.

Outside in the garden, the spring sunshine was bright, and clusters of daffodils dotted the lawn. She took a swallow of gin and sat down on the bench in the shade of the cherry tree whose cherries were always snaffled by birds before they had a chance to properly ripen and be picked.

The first letter, written in turquoise ink, began: *My darling, every day without you is . . .*

Oh, Declan, no.

Again?

When she'd first found out, all those years ago, she'd yelled at him and hurled expensive plates at the wall, smashing them one after the other until the living room had been awash with shards of silver-and-blue bone china that had taken for ever to completely clear up.

This time, she had no one to yell at, no one to see their favourite dinner plates being shattered and no one to apologise over and over, desperate to reassure her that she was the only one he loved.

Which was the most infuriating realisation of all.

Leon was busy causing havoc in the kitchen, sliding across the tiled floor in his socks and singing along to Taylor Swift while making cheese on toast in his usual slapdash way.

'Hey, Nigella.' Jamie marvelled at the spectacular amount of mess he was creating. 'Second week in May. What are you up to?'

Sending crumbs flying over the marble worktop as he sawed the toast into uneven triangles – always triangles – Leon said, 'Pretty sure I'm free. Why?'

'I need a wingman.'

'Of course you do. To give you a helping hand with the ladies.

Mate, you're about the last person in the world to need one of those.'

'OK, wingman slash bodyguard.' Heading for the fridge, Jamie took out a can of lager and cracked it open. 'My agent's confirmed me for the Venice trip and he thinks it's definitely a good idea to take someone with me. I don't mind socialising with the guests, but if I'm on my own, it could get a bit much.'

'Is this the river cruise thing?' Leon didn't look enthused. 'Full of geriatrics?'

'Apparently not. It's a mix of ages. OK,' Jamie admitted, 'it's not eighteen-to-thirty. But we'll be on a five-star ship. And it's Venice.' He pinched one of the triangles of cheese on toast. 'In the city of luuurve.'

'I've never been.'

'Nor me. We can be Venice virgins together.'

'But why are you asking me?' Leon made a token effort to brush the crumbs off the worktop and into the sink. 'If it's the city of love, shouldn't you be taking Zoe?'

It was Jamie's turn to pull a face. 'We're talking two months from now.' When it came to dating, two months was a long time.

'Fair enough.' Leon nodded in agreement, then broke into a grin. 'But you'll still love me.'

And in a funny kind of way, he did. They'd met on their first day of university, having been randomly allocated adjoining rooms in the same hall of residence. Bouncing off each other from day one, they had become almost inseparable within weeks, despite being unalike in almost every way. Jamie, the son of a loving single mother who worked as a nursing assistant, had grown up on a small council estate on the outskirts of Southampton. Leon Spencer-Carr was the product of wealthy parents who lived in a Georgian mansion not far from Wotton-under-Edge in Gloucestershire. Clever but distractable and not excelling at sports, Leon was as clumsy and overenthusiastic as a Labrador puppy, permanently upbeat, and prone to falling head over heels for the kind of women who adored having him as a friend but that was as far as it went because they preferred men with chiselled cheekbones and irresistible mouths who treated them as if they couldn't matter less.

Which was, coincidentally, the reason Jamie was such a hit with the opposite sex, even though he never planned for it to be that way. It absolutely wasn't deliberate, just something that happened inside him, like the childhood sensation of being on a see-saw. The more emotionally involved the women in his life became, the more he found himself losing interest and backing off, feeling the need to slide away. And he didn't even want to be like this. It felt like a kind of Pavlovian reaction, and a failing on his part. Which was another reason he was so glad to have a friend like Leon in his life, because women might come and go, but a best friend was for ever. It was just a shame this best friend was so messy; if Leon ever learned how to clear up after himself and occasionally unload the dishwasher, he might actually be perfect.

Jamie made a grab for a second piece of toast, but Leon intercepted the move and whisked it out of reach. 'Would we have to share a room?'

'They call them cabins on a ship. And no, JD wangled an extra one. If you want it,' Jamie added. 'If you can't make the trip, I'll ask Bruno or Drew.'

'Hold your horses, give me the exact dates.' Whipping out his phone, Leon checked his calendar and appointments diary. 'All good, nothing I can't switch around. We're on.' He high-fived

Jamie, then did a triumphant sock-slide across the kitchen. 'This is going to be so cool, you and me in a couple of gondolas racing each other down the Grand Canal.'

Jamie grinned. 'Like the time we borrowed those canoes and almost got ourselves arrested? Maybe not. The gondoliers might not be too thrilled.'

Undeterred, Leon said, 'We'll do it at night when they're asleep. Except they wear hats, don't they? Damn, I'd look a right wally in a hat. Unlike you, of course.' He pretended to smoulder and struck a model pose. 'I can see it now.'

'Don't.' When Jamie viewed himself in a mirror, it never occurred to him that he was good-looking; it was his face and he was used to it. Yet he also knew it had opened doors for him that otherwise might have remained closed; a successful career playing rugby for England was all very well, but it had been his physical appearance that had caught the attention of viewers on TV, opening up opportunities that hadn't been made available to others in the team. Signed by one of the top agents in the field, he'd found himself in demand for personal appearances, ad campaigns and panel shows on TV because his quick wit and ability to poke fun at himself while also making others laugh had brought him millions of new fans. According to JD Templeton, women fancied the pants off him and men wanted to be him, which basically made him a hot property. For now, at least. Until the looks faded along with his wit, and he drifted into obscurity once more.

When he'd made a comment along these lines recently, Leon had said, 'Mate, I'll still love you when you're ugly and boring. Don't worry, you'll always have me.'

Chapter 2

Oxford

'There you are!' Hattie was in the process of placing the more valuable jewellery in the safe and closing up for the night when Kayla burst into the antiques shop, her spiky red and gold hair making her look like a cockatiel on high alert. Right now she was actually hyperventilating. 'I hate it when your phone's switched off. Guess what's happened? You'll never guess!'

Hattie gave it her best shot. 'George Clooney turned up at your front door and you've got him tied to your bed. There's no escape.'

'What am I, *sixty*? I'm over George now, he's too old. Wouldn't say no to a Hemsworth, mind you. Anyway, you didn't guess, so I'll tell you. I've won a competition!'

Hattie blinked, taken aback. 'You never enter competitions.'

'I did today. And I only went and bloody won, didn't I? I still can't believe it.' Kayla fanned herself vigorously. 'I think I'm in shock.'

Kayla had a history of believing everything she was told. If a man said he'd definitely call her again after a first date, she was always surprised when it didn't happen. If a bizarre fad diet guaranteed the loss of ten kilos in a week, Kayla would launch into it with gusto. Taking a deep breath, Hattie said cautiously, 'How did it happen? Did someone call you out of the blue?' If it was con artists, she prayed Kayla hadn't handed over her bank details so they could – allegedly – send her the prize money.

'Look at you, being all suspicious! I'm not completely stupid . . . I haven't fallen for some scammer. I called into the radio station and got picked to enter, so I was live on air and they asked me a question about rugby, and God knows I have *no* clue about rugby, but it was about how many points were scored in the last season, so I blurted out a random number.' Clutching at Hattie's elbows, she yelped, 'And I only went and got it bang on!'

Hattie gasped. 'That is *mad*.'

'I know! The only thing I've ever won before in my life was a bag of dog biscuits in the hospital Christmas raffle, and I didn't even have a dog.'

'What's the prize?' Something rugby-related, at a guess. But even if it was only tickets to a match, Kayla could sell them, and from her reaction, it might even be season tickets. At any rate, it was better than dog biscuits.

'Nothing much . . . only a week's holiday on a five-star cruise ship sailing around the Venetian islands. *Waaahhh!*' Kayla shrieked, jumping up and down. 'I've always wanted to visit Venice and now it's actually going to happen. Honestly, my heart's still going like the clappers. It hasn't sunk in yet.'

A holiday? Hattie's jaw dropped. And if it was a radio competition, it had to be genuine.

She and Kayla had been friends for eight years now, since

first meeting by chance at a yoga class that had turned out to be run by a sadist and not their sort of thing at all. Having got chatting during the half-time break, they'd promptly escaped to the nearest wine bar and discovered they got on like a house on fire. At the age of thirty, Kayla had been almost exactly two years older than Hattie. They found other classes to go to, enjoyed each other's company, always had fun together and never argued. Eighteen months after that fortuitous initial meeting, Hattie's marriage to Guy had bitten the dust and Kayla, happily divorced herself and living her best life, had been an absolute rock during the ensuing difficult months. Their friendship had been further cemented when Kayla's mother and Hattie's father had died within weeks of each other.

If anyone deserved to win a fabulous holiday, it was Kayla. Hattie gave her a massive hug. 'I'm so happy for you. And don't worry about Bandit, I can pop in twice a day and feed him, make sure he's OK.'

Kayla hesitated, then pulled a face. 'Thanks, but I'll probably ask Tony from over the road to look after Bandit.'

'OK.' Hattie was confused; did Kayla not trust her to take proper care of her beloved cat?

'Come on.' Kayla burst out laughing. 'Don't you get it? I've won a trip for two people. How can you look after Bandit when you're going to be in Venice with me?'

It took a long moment to sink in. Hattie stared at her in disbelief. 'Are you serious?'

'Why wouldn't I be?' Kayla's spiky hair swayed as she shook her head. 'Who else would I want with me? We have to share a cabin, but that's no problem and you know I don't snore. So let's do it. Unless you'd really rather stay behind and feed my fussy cat instead.'

What a choice. Her last holiday had been a long weekend spent in a musty-smelling caravan in Dorset, made longer by the rain that had fallen non-stop. Giddy with joy, Hattie said, 'We'll send Bandit a postcard. He'll be fine.'

Bristol

Was there a more stylish woman in this city than Disa O'Toole? If there was, Fen hadn't met them yet. To spend time with her grandmother was simultaneously blissful – because she loved her to bits – and a tiny bit daunting, because you always felt scruffy by comparison.

Toot toot went the horn of Disa's beloved white soft-top Mercedes as she pulled up at the kerb, and Fen marvelled at today's outfit. The silver-blonde hair, courtesy of her Dutch heritage and cut into a long choppy bob, fell in precisely the right way to her shoulders, the colour exactly matching her high-collared shirt, loose jersey top and slender cigarette pants. There were long strings of pearls around her neck, her eye make-up was dark and her lipstick pale, and diamonds flashed in the sunlight as she tapped her fingers on the steering wheel.

Leaving her flat, Fen ran down to the pavement and jumped into the passenger seat. Leaning over, she planted a kiss on her grandmother's velvety cheek. 'You look fantastic.' But what was new? Even when Disa was up a ladder, energetically painting a ceiling while wearing faded jeans and an emulsion-splashed overshirt, she still managed to look elegant.

'Darling, so do you.' Disa waved at a middle-aged man across the street, put the car into gear and accelerated up the road.

'Did you know that guy?'

'Don't think so. I just waved in case he knew me.' She was accustomed to being stared at by strangers.

They reached the restaurant Disa had booked for lunch and were shown to their table. 'So,' Disa announced, once they'd sat down. 'I'm booking a trip to Venice and wondered if you'd like to come with me?'

'Oh my God, are you serious?' Fen almost knocked over the tumbler of water she'd been about to pick up. 'That sounds incredible. When?'

'In three weeks. Sunday the twelfth of May, back on the nineteenth. If you can make those dates?'

Fen thought for a moment, then nodded. Working online and having the ability to be flexible definitely had its advantages. 'Yes, I can do that. Thank you so much, it sounds fantastic. What's brought this on?'

'Well, I've been to plenty of places in my life, but never Venice. And neither have you. I watched a documentary about it the other evening and it reminded me that I'd always planned to visit. Then last night I happened to come across this advert online.' Disa took out her phone, clicked on the bookmarked page and showed it to Fen. The holiday was a luxury river cruise aboard the SS *La Violetta*, mooring within a short walk of St Mark's Square for most of the week while also visiting the islands of Torcello, Murano, Burano and Chioggia. A brief video of the ship showed it to be small but wildly glamorous, capable of carrying a hundred and twenty-five guests and with every last aspect, from the glittering Murano glass chandeliers to the luxurious Italianate furnishings, like a fabulous five-star hotel.

The prices included everything, but they still made Fen blanch when she saw them.

Observant as always, Disa said crisply, 'Don't even think about it. I'm inviting you, not asking you to go halves. This is my treat.'

'Really? Are you sure?' As if she could have afforded it otherwise. But still, what a relief.

'I spoke to the travel agent this morning. There are two adjoining cabins left. Are you up for it?'

'Definitely, I'd love to. Thank you so much.' What a trip to be able to look forward to. 'We'll have the best time.'

'Right, give me five minutes. I'll make the call and book it now.' Taking back her phone and rising from her chair, Disa left the restaurant. To pass the time, Fen took out her own phone and looked up the same website. This time, scrolling further down the page, she saw that the cruise ran weekly from late March to early November, and once a month there would be a celebrity guest on board to enhance the experience – maybe a famous chef, a popular TV presenter or an actor, that kind of thing.

Scrolling down further still to the list of upcoming dates with accompanying headshots, Fen recognised a gardening expert with an impressive handlebar moustache, the shouty host of a TV show about cars, and a successful thriller writer who'd been married six times.

The next photo stopped her in her tracks, because this time it was someone she knew. OK, not actually knew. But he lived here in Bristol, in the same part of the city that she did, and she'd seen him in person. Twice.

Then again, Jamie Hamilton was someone you couldn't help noticing; he was never going to slip under the radar. Even if he didn't have those striking good looks, the body alone would be enough to attract anyone's attention. Fen wasn't a fan of rugby, but she knew of him through his appearances on TV, on comedy panels and chat shows. The first time she'd encountered him in the flesh – so to speak – he'd been standing behind her in the queue at the local deli as she waited to pay for her Scotch egg. Unaccustomed to being inches away from someone off the telly, she'd been hyper aware of his presence, the just-showered smell of him and the mintiness of his breath on the back of her neck. Paying the cashier, she'd wished she was buying something more exotic than a Scotch egg. Then, taking a bit longer than entirely necessary to slide her credit card back into her purse while it was his turn to pay, she'd seen that he was buying two bundles of asparagus, a bottle of aged balsamic vinegar, a wedge of Brie and a ribbon-wrapped box of macarons that she knew for a fact had a price tag of twenty-six pounds fifty.

Loitering on the pavement outside, she'd watched as he emerged from the deli and strode across the street to the silver sports car parked directly opposite. Evidently when you were Jamie Hamilton, parking spaces magically made themselves available, while she'd had to drive around Clifton for ages before finally managing to leave her car down a narrow side street nearly half a mile away.

It must be a nice skill to possess.

The second time she'd seen him, he'd done something that hadn't been terrible, but it wasn't great either, which was the downside of being recognisable. She'd been at a friend-of-a-friend's party at a bar on Whiteladies Road, and Amanda, the birthday girl, had been gleefully telling everyone that Jamie Hamilton would be arriving soon because she'd met him at a works event the other evening and invited him to join them tonight.

It was stiflingly hot in the bar, and after an hour, Fen slipped outside to get some fresh air. When a taxi drew up and a group of men emerged, she spotted Jamie Hamilton and felt relieved on Amanda's behalf that he'd turned up.

The next moment, glancing at the brightly lit name of the bar above the entrance, Jamie said, 'Hang on, I've just remembered something. We don't want to go to this one.'

One of his friends said, 'Why not? I was in there the other week. It's fine.'

But Jamie was shaking his head. 'There's a party on tonight. I was invited to it by this girl. She was pretty full-on, and I know what it'll be like if we go in.'

Another friend said, 'No bother, there's plenty more bars to choose from.'

Fen, leaning against the wall, hidden in the shadows, pictured Amanda's disappointment and heard herself say, 'She's expecting you to be there.'

She was glad of the darkness enveloping her when they all turned to look in her direction.

The first friend laughed. 'They always do.'

'Look, I'm sorry.' This was from Jamie. 'But I can't even remember her name. We're out tonight for a few drinks and a catch-up.'

'It's her birthday,' Fen reminded him.

'I know, she kept telling me. She was quite . . . pushy.'

'Come on,' said his mate, 'we'll find somewhere else further up the road.' He clapped Jamie on the shoulder and made to leave, but Jamie turned back and looked at Fen, still in shadow. 'I really am sorry about your friend. But it might be kinder if you don't mention any of this.' He gestured vaguely.

It would be kinder if you popped in and wished her a happy birthday. Fen didn't say it. At least he was feeling guilty. She shrugged. 'Don't worry, I won't tell her you were here. Her name's Amanda, by the way.'

'That's it.' He nodded. 'Thanks.'

When he'd left, she'd headed back inside to rejoin the party and hadn't mentioned her brief encounter with Jamie Hamilton to anyone, either then or at any time since. Whereas he'd doubtless forgotten it completely, she'd remembered every detail of their brief exchange.

And now here he was again, grinning up at her unrepentantly from her phone, due to be on board the SS *La Violetta* the exact same week she'd be cruising on it with Disa.

What were the chances?

Still, at least he wouldn't recognise her.

Here came her grandmother now, attracting attention from other diners as she threaded her way between the tables. When it came to slinking, Disa could out-slink Naomi Campbell. Taking her seat, she said, 'All sorted. The travel agent's booked everything, including the flights.'

'There's going to be a famous rugby player on board with us.' Fen showed her the page on her phone.

'I saw that. No idea who he is, though.' Disa wasn't a fan of the sport either.

'He lives here in Bristol.'

'Does he? Rugby's so muddy, not my kind of thing. Quite pretty, though,' Disa added with a mischievous smile. 'You might like him.'

Fen briefly wondered how Jamie Hamilton would feel being called *quite pretty*. Firmly, she said, 'Not my kind of thing either.'

'We'll have fun anyway.' Disa caught the sommelier's eye. 'Now, shall we order some wine, darling? Maybe Prosecco to celebrate? And let's take a look at this menu.'

Being taken out like this was a treat Fen always looked forward to. Because she worked from home, as a remote PA, designated breaks weren't a thing, and lunches consisted of whatever was left in the fridge being eaten in front of her laptop. It was the self-employed way. But today there were seared scallops, shiitake mushrooms in a white wine sauce and a spring vegetable risotto on offer. She was definitely having those.

When they'd ordered, and their drinks had been poured, they clinked glasses. Fen said, 'I'm so lucky to have you. And I can't wait for us to explore Venice.'

'I'm glad you're coming with me. There's something I need to do while we're over there and it'll be good to have your support.'

Fen raised her eyebrows. 'What kind of something?'

But Disa was already shaking her head. 'I shouldn't have said that.' She took a tiny sip of Prosecco. 'Let's leave it until we get there.'

'But . . . support? Is it something I should be worrying about?'

'No, sweetheart. Not at all.'

'Is it something nice?'

'Until it happens, *if* it even happens, we won't know. Maybe not, but hopefully yes. And that's enough for now.'

Fen adored feel-good romantic movies. She gasped and exclaimed, 'Oh my God, have you tracked down an old boyfriend from years ago? Or has one of them contacted you and wants to meet up? Disa, is that what this is all about?'

'Shh.' Disa was smiling her mysterious smile. 'Not another word. You'll have to wait and see.'

Chapter 3

Three weeks later, Fen blinked as a Scotch egg encased in its cellophane wrapper came bouncing down the escalator towards her. Seriously, what were the odds when you were as big a fan of Scotch eggs as she was?

But no, only a bad person would snatch it up and keep it for themselves. She wasn't that heartless.

Besides, she'd been seen.

'Well held,' shouted a male voice from the top of the escalator, as, having switched her carry-on case to her left hand, she caught the Scotch egg in her right. Waiting for her to reach him, he applauded her dexterity. 'You saved my snack, and that makes you my hero.'

Sometimes you saw someone and instinctively liked them at first sight. He had unbrushed light brown hair, merry dark brown eyes and an engaging smile, and was wearing a stripy blue and white shirt with ancient blue jeans and trainers.

'All in a morning's work.' Fen gently tossed the snack towards him, and watched in disbelief as he fumbled the catch.

'Nooo!' He clapped his hands to his head as it landed on the top step of the escalator and began to roll down all over again. 'Hang on.' Dropping his bag at her feet, he careered down the staircase running alongside the escalator and reached the ground floor just as the Scotch egg ricocheted off the side of an elderly woman's wheelie case. Retrieving it, he raced back up the stairs.

'Not very well held,' said Fen.

'What can I say? I'm a klutz. But thank you.'

'Some things are worth rescuing. Food of the gods. I might have to buy one for myself now.'

His face lit up. 'A fellow gastronome, that's what I like to see. Has your flight been called?'

'Not yet. Why?'

'This one's still edible. If you want, we could share it.'

There was an offer to brighten any day. Disa had made herself at home in the airport's private lounge and was currently reading the papers while enjoying a leisurely late breakfast. They weren't due to board for another forty minutes. And this funny, charming stranger was now waving his Scotch egg tantalisingly in front of her like a hypnotist. To entice her further, he said, 'If it helps, I have a bottle of orange Fanta too.'

He knew how to win a girl over. Fen said, 'In that case, how can I refuse?'

Leon was having possibly the best morning of his life; he'd met someone amazing and had instantly clicked with her. Better still, she was showing every sign of liking him too. And OK, this was an airport, so they were both heading off somewhere away from Bristol, but hopefully they'd both be returning before long and could meet up again. He already knew he wanted this to happen. Her name was Fenna – it was Dutch, apparently – but everyone called her Fen, and she had the kind of face he thought he'd never tire of looking at. She was gorgeous, for a start, but not in an intimidating way. Her curly blonde hair bounced around her shoulders, her skin was flawless and there was an adorable scattering of tiny freckles across her nose. She also had long-lashed wide grey eyes and a mischievous mouth that was born to smile. Best of all, she was funny. As far as Leon was concerned, anyone lacking a sense of humour held no attraction for him.

But Fenna – *Fen* – did, big time. Here they were, perching opposite each other on wildly uncomfortable high stools, and he'd never felt more at ease with a female in his life. A bonus was that Jamie was safely out of the way in the private lounge, which meant Leon had her undivided attention. If Jamie were sitting with them, she would be sneaking glances at him and finding him infinitely more fascinating as time went by. Leon didn't resent his friend for this, not one bit. He was used to it by now. And it was hardly Jamie's fault after all. But today it was nice to be enjoying this time with Fen without worrying about the competition.

'So here we are,' he announced, 'sharing an exceptional Scotch egg, and I haven't even introduced myself properly yet. How rude.' Solemnly he extended his hand across the table. 'Leon Spencer-Carr.'

She shook it. 'Very nice to meet you. Fen Madden.'

It was a good name. He wanted to know everything about her. 'And do you live near here?'

'I do. In Bristol. Off Whiteladies Road.'

His heart lifted; better and better. 'I'm in Clifton. We're practically neighbours.'

'And this trip.' Fen mimed a plane taking off. 'Business or pleasure?'

'Pleasure. A week in Venice.'

She spluttered with laughter. 'You're kidding. Me too.'

They stared at each other in delight. Leon experienced an adrenalin rush that made his skin tingle all over. 'We're staying on a small ship, cruising around the different islands and—'

'OH MY GOD!' Fen shouted, almost rocking back on her high stool. '*La Violetta?*'

On the one hand, this was amazing news. On the other, did that mean she was one of Jamie's super-keen superfans? Because that wouldn't be amazing at all. Feeling a bit sick, he said, 'Keen on rugby, are you?'

She pulled a face. 'Urgh, *no*. More of a tennis fan.'

That was something, at least.

Twenty minutes later, when they'd made their way to the private lounge – another coincidence – there was Jamie, chatting to a glamorous woman swathed in a cream pashmina while a member of staff topped up their drinks.

Shaking her head, Fen said, 'Why am I not surprised? Time for you to meet my grandmother.'

'Darling, there you are!' the woman exclaimed. 'We're ahead of you. This is the young man whose boring talks about rugby we'll be avoiding like the plague. But I've already told him, and he promises he doesn't mind.'

'Not a bit.' Jamie grinned. 'Although I should warn you, I won't only be talking boringly about rugby; there'll be other subjects too. You must be Fenna. I've been hearing all about you.' Indicating Leon at her side, he went on, 'And I guess you've probably been hearing a bit about me as well.'

Leon might appear calm on the outside, but inwardly he was bracing himself for Fen's reaction to meeting Jamie. This was a situation he'd witnessed countless times over the years, and it had never bothered him before, but this time was different. It mattered.

'Hi.' Seemingly unfazed, Fen briefly shook Jamie's hand. 'Actually, all I know is that you and Leon share a flat. We've been too busy talking about other things.'

'You have? Excellent. Like what?' Jamie observed her with interest.

'Orangina versus Tango.' She shrugged as if it was obvious.

'Tango.'

'Sorry, you're wrong.'

'All the bones we've ever broken,' Leon chimed in. He'd won that one, having broken a *lot*.

'Men in socks and sandals.' Fen grimaced. 'Also, men in *no* socks and sandals.'

'Tattoos, good and bad,' said Leon.

'Shoplifting,' said Fen.

'Monsters under the bed when we were little kids.' Fen's monster had been black with tentacles, while his had been green with fangs and hairy arms.

'And of course,' Fen concluded, 'the surprising bounceability of particular brands of Scotch egg.'

'This is getting the week off to an interesting start,' Jamie remarked once they'd paid attention to the safety instructions and the plane had finished taxiing to the main runway in preparation for take-off.

Leon checked his watch; no matter how many flights he'd taken over the years, it never failed to amaze him that in an hour or two you could land in another European country. 'I know. We'll be there by one.'

'Not what I meant.'

'What then?'

'You and Fenna. You're like that emoji with hearts for eyes.'

'I'm not, am I?' Leon felt his face heat up.

'Just a bit.'

'D'you think she noticed?' He twisted in his seat and glanced back, checking that Fen and her grandmother were far enough behind them not to have heard.

Jamie shook his head. 'You're safe. It's only because I know you so well.'

Leon lowered his voice anyway. 'Do you think she likes me?'

'I'd say it's on the cards. Could be your lucky week. Who knows what might happen?'

What indeed? The engines began to roar now as the plane suddenly accelerated, the g-force pressing them back into their seats. Watching the ground disappear beneath them as they took off, Leon tried to imagine what this coming holiday might hold if the sense of anticipation building inside him like a giant helium balloon didn't get crushed along the way. The last hour had been something of a revelation. What if – for once in his life – nothing went wrong and everything went right?

Realising Jamie had said something, he leaned across. 'What was that?'

'You've got this. She seems great.' Jamie gave his arm an encouraging nudge. 'I think you should go for it.'

Chapter 4

Venice

They'd chosen a good day for it, soaring through a cloudless sky across France and over the snow-capped Alps into Italy, before gazing down at Venice and the lagoon below them, then finally landing at Marco Polo airport. Having made their way through passport control and retrieved their cases from the carousel, Fen and Disa headed out to Arrivals to be greeted by a woman with a clipboard, who directed them out to the waiting taxis.

'Shall we wait for the boys?' said Disa.

Boys. Then again, she was seventy-two, she was allowed to call them that.

'No.' While they'd been queuing to have their passports checked, Fen had seen Jamie and Leon behind them being engaged in conversation by a group of women clearly delighted to be meeting them. The last thing she wanted was to look like a fangirl. Besides, they were here now, and she wanted to be able to concentrate on taking in her first sight of Venice without being distracted.

It took no longer than twenty minutes to leave the airport

on the mainland behind them, travel across the high road that took them over the water to the island itself, and arrive at San Basilio, where their home for the next seven days waited for them, white and gleaming in the sunshine.

The short gangway led up to the reception area, all plush jewel-toned wallpaper, glamorous Italianate lighting, exotic potted plants and highly polished wooden flooring.

Disa pushed her dark glasses to the top of her head. 'Not too shabby. I think I can cope with this.'

'Good,' said Fen. 'I'm glad we don't have to catch the next flight home.'

Once they had checked in at the front desk, they made their way up a small flight of stairs to their cabins. Since these were identical, they explored Fen's together.

'Smaller than a hotel room,' Disa observed, 'but every bit as luxurious.' She ran her fingertips lightly over the silky coffee-and-cream fabric that covered the walls and ceiling, and the matching curtain blinds pulled up to reveal the glorious view through the picture window, of glittering turquoise water lapping against the side of the ship, and the spectacular buildings hundreds of metres away, on the opposite bank of the Giudecca Canal.

'Fabulous bed,' Fen exclaimed, throwing herself onto it and spreading out like a starfish.

'Plenty of storage space.' Disa nodded with approval, opening and closing wardrobe doors.

There was a TV on the wall. A velvet-soft white robe. A dressing table and chair, although Fen had never once in her life sat on a chair in order to do her hair and make-up. Presumably some people did. Bouncing off the bed, she opened the door to the bathroom, again small but well appointed, and containing everything you could need.

At that moment they heard high-pitched shrieks of delight in the corridor outside the cabin. A female voice exclaimed, 'Can you believe it? We're in Venice, we're actually *here*.'

'This ship is bougie.' A second woman sounded even more excited. 'First things first, let's get to the bar and see if that fit guy's arrived yet.'

Wryly, Disa said, 'I think we'll leave them to it. Unpack first, then explore the rest of the ship and have a drink later.'

Hattie heard his voice before she saw him, but because it couldn't possibly be *his* voice, she ignored it. There were other guests up here on the top deck of the ship, enjoying the sunshine and the magical view, but she was currently alone. Having failed to track down the good-looking rugby guy in the bar at the front of the ship, Kayla had consoled herself with three cocktails on an empty stomach and was currently sleeping them off in their cabin.

Shielding her eyes from the sun, Hattie watched as a noisy flock of birds flew squawking overhead, their beaks and necks elongated. Were they herons maybe? Or storks?

Then, coming up the steps behind her, she heard a woman say, 'Guy, stop it!' and almost tipped over backwards, because that was a similarity too far.

Spinning round and banging the side of her leg painfully against one of the wooden sunloungers, she saw a slender brunette in a racerback white Lycra vest and leggings, followed a couple of seconds later by a rather more overweight man in his forties.

A mind-bogglingly familiar man, at that.

She had been married to him for seven years. It made him difficult to forget.

But what on earth – assuming he wasn't a hallucination – was he doing on this ship?

Was this some kind of bizarre joke?

'Will you look at that?' Guy was marvelling at the deck, walking on the spot. 'I thought it was wooden planks, but it's actually carpet. Isn't that wild? It looks exactly like—' His gaze met Hattie's and he stopped dead.

A pigeon flew low overhead and the woman with him said, 'What's wrong?'

'I don't believe it.' He looked as stunned as Hattie felt. 'This is . . . crazy.'

His hand was pressed to his chest. Hattie said, 'Are you OK?'

'What?' He shook his head. 'Yes, of course. But I could be in shock. What are you doing here? Did you know we were going to be on this ship?'

She blinked. 'Does this look like the face of someone who knew you were going to be on this ship?'

Guy was frowning now. 'So you didn't book the same holiday on purpose?'

'Are you serious? Why would I *do* that?' Was he actually trying to make her out to be some kind of stalker? 'No,' she said firmly, 'of course I didn't. That's the last thing in the world I'd do, and you know it.'

Guy broke into his trademark broad smile. It seemed she'd convinced him. Moving towards her, he held out both arms. 'In that case, it's one of those crazy coincidences. Come here, Hattie, it's good to see you. You're looking wonderful.'

'*Hattie?*' echoed the woman in Lycra. 'You mean this is your ex-wife?'

'The very same.' He kissed Hattie on both cheeks, then stepped back and said cheerfully, 'Let me introduce you. Suzanne, meet Hattie. Hats, this is Suzanne.'

Whose name he hadn't shortened, Hattie noted. It might have been a couple of years since they'd last seen each other, but there was no way Guy could have forgotten how irritating she'd always found it when he called her Hats. Nevertheless, she did the polite thing and said a friendly hello to Suzanne. Because it was easier all round than getting snippy with Guy within ninety seconds of bumping into him again.

'How long have you been divorced?' Suzanne's own smile was fleeting.

'A while, I suppose.' Guy gestured vaguely. 'A few years?'

'Six years separated,' Hattie reminded him. 'Divorced for five.'

'And why did you break up?' The woman had quite an intense gaze, like a bird of prey. You had to have chutzpah to come out and ask a question like that.

'We just drifted apart, didn't we, Hats? *Hattie*,' Guy hastily amended when she shot him an intense look of her own.

'That's it.' She shrugged. 'Just one of those things.' It was easier not to elaborate, and not really that interesting, with hindsight. They'd turned out not to be as well suited to marriage as they'd thought, that was all. Guy especially hadn't.

'And who are you here with?' He glanced across at the cluster of guests at the other end of the boat. 'Got yourself a new chap, I'm guessing. Or have you come on your own?'

'I'm here with Kayla.'

'Really? Wouldn't have thought this was her kind of holiday.'

Kayla's neighbour had advised her not to tell everyone she'd won the cruise in a competition, because other guests who'd paid full whack might resent her for it. Hattie said, 'It is. I wouldn't have thought it would be your sort of thing either.'

Guy looked surprised. 'Why ever not? I've always wanted to visit Venice. Suze and I found this trip online, didn't we? By sheer chance, a chap at work was raving about river cruises, banging on about how amazing they are. Then I saw that this one had Jamie Hamilton on board, and that was it, I was sold. So here we both are. Wild. It's like that time we were on holiday in Portugal, d'you remember? Sitting outside one of the bars in Albufeira, and who should walk by? Only Stu and Josie from the cricket club! Crazy how these things happen.'

'You're kidding!' Instantly wide awake, Kayla sat bolt upright in bed.

'I wish I was.' Hattie sprayed her face and cleavage with sunscreen. 'It was weird enough seeing him again, let alone here, of all places. We're going to be bumping into them the whole time.'

'Is it going to ruin your holiday?'

'No, of course not. I can cope. It was a shock, that's all.'

'What's the girlfriend like?'

'Younger than me. Model figure. Asked me why we'd broken up.'

'Did you tell her?'

'That her boyfriend never got his head around the basic rules of being married? That it meant preferably *not* going out with his mates all the time and actually staying at home with his wife every so often? No, I'd only have sounded like a bitter ex.'

'You're allowed to be bitter.' Kayla unscrewed the cap on the bottle of water next to her bed and gulped half of it down. 'I might casually mention it to her.'

'Let's not. We'll just try to keep away from them. I mean, they're not going to want to bump into us either, are they?

What are you doing?' Hattie stared as Kayla hopped out of bed and began stripping off her clothes.

'I'm going to jump in the shower.'

'Curtains are open!'

'Hello?' Kayla turned to gesture at the vast expanse of water separating them from the buildings on the other side of the canal. 'No one's going to see me from all the way over there.'

The next moment, just as she unfastened her bra, a boat full of camera-snapping tourists chugged past the window a few metres away. Hattie let out a squeak of alarm, but Kayla, undaunted, gave them a wave and a jaunty boob-jiggle.

'Kayla!'

'Oh, come on, they're on holiday, don't they deserve a little treat?'

From where their boat was berthed at San Basilio, it was only a few minutes' walk along narrow streets and up and over tiny bridges before Disa and Fen came to the larger wood and metal Ponte dell'Accademia, which crossed the Grand Canal.

By the time they reached it, Fen had already stopped at least fifty times to point her phone and take photos. At the highest section of the bridge, she was proving impossible to drag away.

'One more,' she protested, leaning over the balustrade and taking another dozen at least, as various boats and gondolas emerged from the shadows beneath the arch into bright sunshine.

Disa finally managed to lure her down the steps on the other side of the canal. Her heart began to clamour in her chest as she led the way, without appearing to be leading the way. Following the route she'd so carefully mapped out in her head, she was forced to pause every thirty seconds or so while Fen stopped to take yet another photo of a stone gargoyle, a slinking cat, a reflection in the water, or a class of tiny chattering children in matching yellow caps being guided by their teachers over a bridge. Nearly there now; a bit further along the side of this narrow canal, then next left and round the corner to the right.

And here it was, exactly as it had looked in all the photos she had pored over online. A pair of ornate iron gates stood open, surrounded by a profusion of greenery and leading into what looked like a secret garden. To the right of the gates was a board bearing a handwritten menu, and outside the ivy-clad building were tables and chairs occupied by people eating and drinking, because this was La Lanterna di Rosa, even if the name on the sign was obscured from view by the low-hanging branches of the tree at the entrance.

'Look at that,' Fen exclaimed, catching up with her and – surprise, surprise – taking five or six more photos. 'Gorgeous!'

'Doesn't it look nice?' Having always prided herself on being an effortless liar, Disa was belatedly discovering it rather depended on the importance of the lie. It was a wonder Fen couldn't hear her heart thudding. She pretended to peer at the menu, despite not being able to see it without her reading glasses, and said casually, 'Shall we stop for a rest, have something to eat?'

Fen gave her a puzzled look. 'We only ate on the ship an hour ago. And we're having dinner at seven.'

'I know, but I thought you might be peckish. They do small plates here. Or we could have a drink? Are you thirsty? I'm quite thirsty.' *For goodness' sake, woman, stop babbling.* Her voice was sounding weird now, higher-pitched than usual. She should have done this alone, but Fen had been keen to come ashore with her and explore.

'Fine, we'll have a drink,' said Fen. 'Quick, those men are leaving, let's grab their table.'

They were here. Too late to back out now.

A young waiter speedily cleared the table and invited them to sit. The waitress emerging from the restaurant with a tray of drinks was in her forties and Italian. Disa began to breathe more easily and ordered a couple of glasses of orange juice. After all this pent-up anticipation, today clearly wasn't the day after all.

'Excellent tablecloths.' She stroked the crimson linen, then admired the many lanterns hanging outside the restaurant and in the trees surrounding them. 'I bet this place looks magical at night.'

'We could come here for dinner tomorrow evening,' said Fen. 'If you want.'

'Maybe.' Disa gave an offhand shrug. 'We don't always have to eat on the ship, do we? Let's see how things go.'

The dining room on deck three opened at seven in the evening, and guests were welcome to sit anywhere they liked. Two middle-aged couples, Fen saw, had bagged seats at Jamie and Leon's table and the men were engaged in a lively conversation about rugby. Her stomach did a little flip when Leon caught her eye as she and Disa passed by on their way to the other side of the restaurant.

What she was rapidly discovering was how sociable this trip was already proving to be. Having returned from their brief exploration of the San Marco neighbourhood of Venice, they'd chatted on the sun deck to fellow guests from Australia, Brazil, California – and Slough. Everyone was eager to get to know everyone else. At pre-dinner drinks they'd met a couple of women who'd been best friends since they were eight years old. Now in their late seventies, they'd been taking holidays together for almost half a century.

At dinner, they sat with a lively woman called Helena who was celebrating her recent divorce, a man called Horgan from New York whose husband had died two years ago, and Jeff and Gina, both teachers, who had been on many cruises all over the world and had first met at Paddington station, when they'd accidentally been allocated the same seat on a jam-packed train heading down from London to Penzance.

'We had a huge row about it,' said Gina.

'She threatened to sit on my lap,' said Jeff.

'I needed the seat. I had a shocker of a hangover.'

Jeff said, 'I had a broken foot!'

Disa was enthralled. 'So what happened?'

'By Reading, I'd decided I quite liked him,' said Gina.

Jeff shrugged. 'By Swindon, I thought maybe she was OK after all.'

'By Bristol, I fancied him rotten.'

'By the time we reached Penzance, I knew I wanted to marry her,' said Jeff.

'And I knew he had bony knees,' Gina added, 'because I was sitting on his lap. But we got married anyway, seven months later. All thanks to a ticket mix-up.'

Jeff winked at her. 'Best ticket mix-up of my life.'

The food was superb, the wine magnificent. Earlier, Fen had seen Leon swivel round in his chair as if searching for someone, then break into a grin when she caught his eye. Helena and Disa, having discovered a mutual passion for art, were making plans to meet up and visit the Peggy Guggenheim Collection.

The next moment, a hand came to rest on her shoulder. She looked up, and there was Leon, bending to murmur in her ear. 'I'm not usually one for being forward, but if you fancy joining me for a drink on the top deck after dinner, I'll be heading up there in a few minutes.' He paused, took a breath. 'And if you don't, that's absolutely fine, please forget I even mentioned it.'

The touch of his fingertips on her bare shoulder made Fen want to squirm with delight. Did he really think she'd say no? It was crazy; when she'd woken up this morning, she hadn't known he existed, yet now he was starting to feel like one of the most important people in her life. Then again, look at Gina and Jeff.

Who were in turn observing her and Leon with interest.

Disa said, 'Darling, don't worry about me. Helena and I are going to be in the bar discussing the life of the fabulous Peggy.'

'Peggy Mitchell? From *EastEnders*?' Leon winked. 'Wasn't she great?'

True to his word, he was up on deck waiting for her when she arrived ten minutes later. Pausing at the top of the staircase, Fen drank in the sight of him in profile as he surveyed the view, and marvelled at the zing of pleasure coursing through her veins. The sun was setting in the west, turning the sky a dozen deepening shades of apricot, and the first lights had started to come on in the buildings over on Giudecca Island. Pulling out her phone, she took a few photos and made sure to include Leon in all of them. Maybe once this holiday was over, she might choose one of them as her screensaver.

Without turning round, Leon said, 'My ears are burning.'

She smiled, loving the sound of his voice. 'I didn't say anything, I was just thinking it.'

'What were you thinking? Hope it wasn't, "Oh, no, not him again."'

Fen said, 'I wasn't thinking that.'

He turned, and her heart skipped a beat. She joined him on

the blue and white striped two-seater sofa and he handed her one of the matching pair of drinks on the table in front of them. 'Aperol spritz,' he said. 'I've never had one before, but apparently it's a thing in Venice.'

'I love an Aperol spritz.'

He touched his glass to hers, then took a sip and pulled a face. 'God, that's horrendous.'

'I'll have both of them.'

He shook his head, still grimacing. 'I'll order a beer in a bit. So, what's the verdict so far?'

'On Venice? Or the boat? Or you?' The wine at dinner had loosened her tongue.

'Whichever.'

'All good.' In case she was sounding like one of his friend Jamie's fans, Fen said, 'Dinner was excellent. Apart from no Scotch eggs, obviously.'

Leon laughed. 'Shame we couldn't have shared a table. Never mind, we're here now. And I want to know more about you.'

The sky was darkening, the shades of vivid orange fading and blending with translucent greys as the sun disappeared.

'What kind of stuff?'

'Everything. All there is to know. Family. Death-row meal. Best friends growing up. Worst ever public humiliation. Most impressive party trick.'

So she told him about losing her mum to cancer seven years ago, followed by the departure of her dad a couple of years after that to a new life in Cape Town. She confided her all-consuming love for tomato-ketchup-flavoured crisps, especially in sandwiches, although sandwiches made with plain crisps and tomato ketchup were the *worst*. Then she told him about her best friend, Tonia, who'd kept her going through the hard times, taught her how to dance, cook and apply false lashes, and had all but broken her heart when she'd moved to Amsterdam.

'Your friend moving away was more traumatic than your father leaving to live in South Africa?'

'We never had that much to do with him.' Fen shrugged. 'He wasn't cut out for family life. Mum held everything together until she got ill. She was incredible, and pretty much raised me single-handed. Until it was my turn to look after her.'

Leon's gaze was sympathetic. 'You've been through a lot.'

'Others have it worse. I'm fine. I have Disa. Her husband died twelve years ago, but he was wonderful too. I loved them both so much.'

'That's good.' Leon nodded and brushed an insect from her arm, causing her skin to tingle. 'And you and Tonia are still friends?'

'We are. We visit each other a couple of times a year. She's married now, to Hendrik, and has a toddler, Sebastian, with another baby on the way. Works in a fancy art gallery in the centre of Amsterdam three days a week. Charming husband, big house, dream life.'

'Do you envy her?'

May as well be honest. Fen took a sip of her drink. 'Sometimes, yes. She has it all, including silky-smooth hair. Even her parents are the best.'

Leon tilted his head and studied her. 'Sometimes life isn't fair. But right now, you're in Venice, drinking some bizarre drink that tastes completely repulsive if you ask me but for some reason you like it. You're up here on deck after a five-star dinner, watching the world go by.' He gestured to the vaporetto chugging its way past their mooring, and the speedboats bouncing over the darkening surface of the water. 'Plus, you're sitting next to someone who's really glad he met you today. He also happens to think you're looking incredible. So maybe this evening plenty of people would envy *you*.'

He stopped himself, then smacked his forehead with the palm of his hand. 'God, sorry, sometimes I say stuff and it comes out all wrong. I'm such an idiot. Jamie's the smooth talker, the one who always knows how to get it right. I just . . .' He shook his head, took a distracted gulp of Aperol and pulled a face once more.

'You just what?' Fen held her breath.

'Urgh, this stuff is *so* gross.' He coughed and swallowed. 'OK, I was going to say I feel as if I've known you for ever. I keep forgetting I haven't and you probably think I'm barking mad.'

'I'm not thinking that. And I'm glad I've met you.' If he could be honest, so could she. 'I was looking forward to this holiday anyway, but now I'm going to enjoy it even more.'

'You could be bored with me by tomorrow.'

'Pretty sure that isn't going to happen.' A waiter had appeared; Fen waited until he'd taken Leon's request for a Peroni. Longing to discover more about him, she said, 'And now it's your turn to tell me everything about you.'

Chapter 5

Leon reached up and rubbed his hand over his already ruffled hair. 'I'm not that interesting.'

I beg to differ.

Aloud, Fen said, 'Try me.'

An hour later, she'd learned a lot. Other guests had come up on deck to enjoy the warm breeze and the view of Venice at night, but it was as if there was an invisible force-field around the two of them; after glancing over and seeing them engrossed in conversation, they'd moved on, leaving them to continue getting to know each other without interruption.

What she hadn't expected to discover was that Leon's family were wealthy. Growing up in the Cotswolds, he'd been packed off to boarding school at the age of eight and had battled his way through homesickness by dreaming of one day running away to join the circus.

'As?'

'A lion-tamer. Until my friend told me there weren't any lions in circuses any more, so I decided to become a fire-eating acrobat instead.'

Fen nodded sagely. 'Much safer.'

'I also planned to train puppies to do tricks on trampolines. Because, you know, who doesn't love a somersaulting puppy?'

'Is this what you do now? Because if it's your actual career, I *will* burst with jealousy. This is your ten-second warning.'

'It's even more exciting than that,' said Leon. 'I'm a financial adviser.'

She gasped and clutched her chest. 'For real?'

'I know, it's hard to take in. I look so ordinary on the outside.'

'What's your hidden superpower?'

'Take your pick. I'm an excellent hula-hooper. I can make shadow puppets with my hands.' He flapped them like a bird taking off. 'And I do the best Hugh Grant impression you ever heard.'

'Hit me with it. I'm ready.'

'Sorry, not tonight. I need to hold something back to impress you with tomorrow.'

Her heart swelled. 'Anything else?'

'I can gargle "The Winner Takes It All".'

'While riding a unicycle?'

'Not while riding a unicycle.'

'Damn, that's a shame.'

'Give me time. I'll learn.'

Fen rested her head against the back of the sofa and looked up. The stars were out now, dazzling pinpricks of light in a black velvet sky. The chatter of the other guests had faded into the background, and it felt like a night filled with infinite possibilities. Since this wasn't the place for public affection, she was enjoying the wait, the indescribable sense of anticipation. Because it was going to happen, no doubt about it. Just not yet.

'Show me some photos,' she said, and the ploy to lean more

closely against him worked as well as she'd hoped. Leon's tanned forearm rested against hers as he angled his phone so they both had a good view of the screen.

'What would you like to see?'

'Photos of you.'

'Not of me and Jamie?'

She gave him a look. 'No. Why?'

'It's usually what most people want.' His tone was wry, and it occurred to her that the price he paid for being Jamie Hamilton's best friend was always being regarded as the less interesting of the two of them.

'Show me your family.'

He scrolled through the relevant folder and kept up a running commentary, introducing her to his parents, Hilary and Greville Spencer-Carr.

'They look nice!' In reality, they looked faintly intimidating, but she could hardly say that.

'And this is us taken last summer.' He showed her another photo of the three of them, standing together on a flight of stone steps in front of a spectacular Cotswold-stone property.

'Were you visiting a stately home?' Inwardly she wondered if he wasn't a bit old to be going on day trips with his parents, but maybe it was a country house hotel and they'd all been invited to a wedding.

'It's our house. I know,' Leon sounded embarrassed, 'it's a bit big.'

Fen was taken aback. The house was enormous, and surrounded by what looked like acres of parkland. 'It's quite intimidating.'

'Why?'

'Because I don't know anyone who lives in a place like that.'

'You do. You know me. And I'm not intimidating, am I?'

'I'm not sure any more. Are you related to royalty?'

'Not really, they're just cousins.'

'*What?*'

He laughed. 'That was a joke. No, not remotely related to royalty. My great-grandfather made his money in bathroom fittings. Our toilets have been used by VIPs all over the world. My mother can't stand me saying that, but it's true. And it's given her an enviable lifestyle. You're still looking shocked.'

A degree of happiness had leaked out of the evening. 'My flat's tiny. It'd probably fit into one of your downstairs loos.'

'And?'

'I don't know. It's like you're a different person now.'

'I'm still me. Usually girls' eyes light up – *ding dinggg* – when they see the house.' Leon saw the expression on her face. 'If you think it's going to put you off me, I'll never set foot in the house or see my family again.'

She mustn't overreact. 'I won't let it put me off you.'

'Good.' He hesitated, then rested his hand on hers, his fingers overlapping her smaller ones. The simple physical contact felt . . . gosh, it was indescribable.

For several seconds, they stayed like that, in silence. Then Leon said, 'This could be the best night of my life. And I can't believe I'm saying it out loud, but I really think you could be my perfect ten.'

'The Australian couple keep looking over at us,' Fen murmured. 'They're nudging each other.'

'I think we're the star attraction. Those people over there have been watching us too. This must be what it's like being Jamie. If you want, we could go and . . .'

And? *And?* But Leon was raising a hand in greeting, saying,

'Speak of the devil,' and here came Jamie now, making his way across the deck towards them.

'You two OK? Sorry, am I interrupting?'

Yes. And yes, you are. But since she couldn't say that, Fen smiled and shook her head. Leon, who evidently could say it, replied cheerfully, 'Of course you're interrupting, but we'll let you off. Been having fun?'

Jamie pulled up a chair. 'There's a band playing, down in the bar. A redhead called Kayla keeps dragging me onto the dance floor and telling her friend to take photos of the two of us.'

'You could say no,' Fen suggested.

He shrugged. 'I could. But it was easier to make a strategic escape. I try to be nice to people when I can.'

Hmm, not always. But now wasn't the time to remind him of their previous encounter.

'Which one is she?' said Leon.

'Spiky red and gold hair. Pink dress.'

'Ah yes, I know the one you mean.' Leon nodded, then pointed to the left. 'And here comes another troublemaker.'

This time it was Disa, shimmering towards them in her ivory crêpe dress, with a navy silk shawl covering her bare shoulders.

'Darling, there you are.' She rested a hand lightly on Fen's shoulder. 'It's been a wonderful evening, but we do need to be up early tomorrow. I think it's time we headed back to our cabins now, don't you?'

What? It was only ten thirty. Fen looked up at her, ready to protest that she wasn't tired, but Disa increased the pressure of her fingertips and said, 'Come along, let's say goodnight.' She turned to Jamie and Leon. 'It's been so nice to meet you. Maybe we'll bump into you tomorrow.'

Disa had paid for the holiday. She was the boss. Fen shrugged at Leon, then rose to her feet and followed Disa, because what else could she do? As they made their way down the stairs, she said, 'Do you need a hand with anything?'

'You mean why did I drag you away when you were having a good time?'

The very best time. 'Yes.'

'Do you like him?'

'Yes.'

'A lot?'

'Yes.' OK, starting to sound like a parrot now.

'Sweetheart, then that's the best time to leave.'

'But . . . why?'

They'd reached their cabins. Disa produced her key and gestured for Fen to follow her inside. When the door had closed behind them, she said, 'Basic rule number one: always leave them wanting more. I can see you're smitten. And since the two of you have been up on deck for the last couple of hours, it's time to make him miss you.'

'Really?'

'Trust me, sweetheart. I'm old and I've seen it all, heard it all. This way, he'll spend the rest of the evening looking forward to seeing you again tomorrow.'

'But we're going on a trip to a winery straight after breakfast.'

'So? If Leon wants to join us, he can.' Removing the silver combs from her hair and taking out her earrings, Disa turned to look at her. 'You'll both enjoy it all the more.'

'Hmm.' *But that's twelve whole hours away.*

'OK, that's my advice.' Disa swiftly brushed the Elnett out of her hair. 'We both know I can't force you to take it. If you want to head back up on deck, you can. I'm sure he'll be thrilled. If you decide you want to spend the night in his cabin . . . he'll be even happier.'

'Gran!'

'Sweetheart, I do know what goes on in the world. Sometimes two people meet and have sex on the first night, and they end up staying together for ever. Other times – and rather more often – they don't. I'm not saying you mustn't sleep with him. I just think it might be nicer for both of you to spend a little more time looking forward to it.'

'I get the message.' Fen's smile was rueful. It would be interesting to know how long Disa had made the men in her life wait, but she was her grandmother, so she wasn't going to ask. Also, the answer might be something horrendous, like three years. 'I'll go to my room, have an early night.'

Chapter 6

Waking early the next morning, Disa raised the electric blinds at the window. An ethereal veil of mist was hovering above the silver-blue water, in the process of being burned off by an already bright sun. A family of ducks swam by, bobbing in the wake of a just-passed motorboat. It was going to be a stunning day.

With her trusty iPad on her lap, Disa checked her emails first, then moved on to Wordle, followed by a scroll through her WhatsApp groups. She sent a photo of the spectacular view from her bed and let her various friends around the world know she was having a wonderful time.

Only when that was done did she go to the bookmarked website, mentally crossing her fingers in the hope that the blog she'd been following had been updated.

And hooray, yes, it had!

The post was only short, but that was OK. Avidly, she read:

Hi, all! Wow, what a special day yesterday was, celebrating the wedding of dear friends Julietta and Stefano! They both looked so beautiful, as did the little bridesmaids in the embroidered dresses made for them by Julietta's clever mum. The church was full of flowers, and the reception was the best fun. I'll post more photos tonight once I've had time to sort through them, but here's one of me looking hot and frazzled because we'd been dancing!

And now I have to rush off to work, so bye, all, have a great day! Xxx

She'd only posted the update a few minutes ago. The unfiltered photo was endearingly unflattering, showing her with her hair falling down on one side and her face shiny in the heat, although the happy smile was as infectious as ever. She was wearing a pomegranate-pink dress that cinched in at the waist and flared out below the knee, and had evidently kicked off her shoes to dance. She seemed lovely; who wouldn't want to be friends with a girl like that? But that was the thing about posting words and photos on the internet; Disa had seen enough instances of people appearing charming and entirely genuine then being found out to be the opposite. Online, they made themselves seem like a catch in every way. She preferred to discover for herself just how accurate their portrayal of themselves was in reality.

Especially now.

She closed the page and finished her glass of water. Maybe today would be the day she'd be able to make a start. Outside the window, a duck quacked in noisy agreement.

'I know,' she told it. 'I hope so too.'

By nine thirty, breakfast had been eaten in the restaurant and everyone heading out on the trip to the winery was gathering in the reception area.

And here came Leon, clearly delighted to be joining them.

Disa saw Fen's face light up at the sight of him. In a couple of minutes she would make her excuses and leave them to it.

'Morning!' she greeted him. 'Is your friend not coming along too?'

'Jamie? He's being interviewed by a journalist, then photographed for a magazine. Poor guy,' said Leon. 'It's torture for him, what with him being so ugly.'

Better and better. Leon and Fen didn't need a third wheel to distract them from each other. Right, it looked as if the cruise manager was ready to lead everyone off the ship and round to where the coach was waiting for them to board. Disa straightened her spine and winced, but Fen hadn't noticed, so she did it again.

'Everything OK?' said Leon.

'I'm afraid not.' She heaved a sigh of disappointment. 'I hoped it would ease up a bit, but my back's still giving me trouble.' Really, her acting skills were superb; Fen was looking concerned. 'Sorry, it started last night. Probably only a muscle spasm, but walking around a vineyard might be too much for me today. I think I'd be better off staying here and taking things easy.'

'Gran, that's such a shame.' Fen sounded disappointed, but maybe she was acting too. 'I had no idea your back was bad. Do you want me to stay with you? Should we call a doctor?'

'Goodness, no. No need for that. I'll be fine,' Disa assured her, before giving another tiny wince for good measure. 'I'll sit in the sunshine and read. You two must go and try all the wine on my behalf. Have a fun day together.'

'Are you sure?'

'Completely.' The other guests were disembarking around them.

'If you're going to be up on deck, you can watch Jamie having to endure his photo shoot,' said Leon. 'Pull faces at him, make him laugh when he's supposed to be looking moody. He loves it when I do that.'

Disa smiled. 'I'm afraid I'm going to be too busy reading my book.'

An hour later, she was attempting to do just that, but Jamie and the photographer were proving to be something of a distraction. Only indirectly; it was the woman on a nearby sunlounger who was being the most noticeably distracted.

'*Look* at him. Can you imagine how it felt, dancing with him last night? As soon as that photographer guy's finished with him, I'm going to get another selfie.'

It was the same woman Disa had seen yesterday evening, the one with the spiked-up red and gold hair. She was wearing crimson lipstick, sparkly eyeshadow and a lime-green bikini. Her tongue might not be actually hanging out, but it was nearly there. Luckily, she wasn't addressing Disa; the observations were being made to the friend next to her.

'You don't want to pester him.'

'I'm not pestering him, Hattie! It's only a selfie. And he already knows my name.'

'That's because it's on your necklace,' her friend pointed out. 'Plus, you keep telling him. You're going to scare him off.'

'I'm not scary, though. I'm just giving it my best shot, being friendly. Let's face it, I'm never going to have another chance like this.'

Unable to concentrate, Disa put her book down and looked over at Jamie. He clearly wasn't enjoying being photographed, but was doing as he was instructed with humour and good grace. She gathered her belongings together and left the deck; after a peaceful period of reading in her cabin, she would head out on her own and have lunch at the restaurant she'd visited yesterday.

An hour later, having changed into a floaty honey-coloured kaftan and narrow ivory trousers, she walked off the ship and began to make her way along the footpath. It was while she was pausing to take her sunglasses out of her bag that she heard the rap of knuckles on glass, and saw Jamie through a window, waving to catch her attention and mouthing something that looked like *Help*. That was when she saw he had indeed been buttonholed once more by the persistent redhead.

Amused, she rolled her eyes and tapped her wristwatch, and he moved across to a section of open window.

'Sorry, I know I'm late,' he called. 'I'm coming out now.'

'Hurry up then, I nearly went without you.' Disa watched as he excused himself and made his escape. Less than a minute later, the glass doors in the central reception area slid open and he appeared, hurrying down the gangway to catch her up.

'She's still watching you,' said Disa.

'She never stops watching me. I mean, it's fine, but it's starting to get a bit much. She keeps talking about star signs and telling me how well matched we are because Aquarians and Librans are the best pairing of all.'

'You lucky thing.'

'Plus, she told me she had a dream we were swimming together and I rescued her from almost drowning. Then she asked if I'd had the same dream about her, because apparently that happens sometimes and it means we have a special connection.' He shook his head. 'Anyway, never mind. Thanks for helping me to make my escape.'

'Any time,' said Disa.

'And don't worry, I'm not planning to inflict myself upon

you. As soon as we're round the corner and out of sight, we can go our separate ways.'

'I wasn't worried. Not unless you were about to start banging on about star signs.'

He laughed. 'I promise not to do that. So why didn't you go on the trip to the winery?'

'My back was playing up.' Another effortless lie. 'It's much better now. How did your interview go?'

'It was great. Less fun being photographed, but these things need to be done. All part of the job.' They crossed the first bridge, with the sunlight bouncing off the ripples on the water and the tethered boats swaying gently in unison. 'So are you randomly exploring the area, or do you have plans for today?'

'Just having a wander.' Disa adjusted her dark glasses. 'Thought I'd find somewhere to have a spot of lunch.'

'I've been recommended a place. A friend says it's excellent.' Taking out his phone, he began to scroll through a ream of messages.

'Actually, Fen and I stopped for a drink at a restaurant yesterday. Really pretty, lots of trees surrounding a little courtyard. I quite fancy going back and giving the food a try,' said Disa. 'It was called La Lanterna di Rosa.'

In a few seconds, he'd found it online. 'Sounds good. Were you wanting to eat alone, or could you tolerate some company? It's fine to say no if you'd rather be on your own, I just thought we could chat about my friend and your . . . *Oh.*' He was struck by a thought. 'Or maybe you have a hot date arranged with a handsome gentleman, an Italian count, perhaps, and the last thing you need is some galumphing ex-rugby player tagging along as a third wheel, ruining everything.'

'It's been years since I had a hot date with a handsome Italian count. And trust me, he was no gentleman.' She smiled. 'Also, you don't galumph.'

'That's a relief.' Jamie paused. 'So shall we try out this restaurant of yours?'

Why not? They'd got on well together yesterday while chatting in the private lounge at the airport. 'Let's do it,' said Disa.

When they reached La Lanterna di Rosa twenty minutes later, there was the girl whose photos she had seen online. She was wearing the all-black uniform of T-shirt and trousers, her wavy light brown hair was tied back in a high ponytail and she was chattering away in rapid Italian to a table of customers. When she glanced across at the new arrivals, Disa saw her clock Jamie immediately, then nod when he signalled to check that they could sit at the table they'd chosen in the courtyard.

Seriously attractive men had their uses. The girl came to greet them almost at once, smiling first at Disa, then – more lingeringly – at Jamie.

And who could blame her? His eyes were incredibly blue in this dappled sunlight, his teeth were white and there were glints of gold in his almost shoulder-length dark hair.

'*Buongiorno.*' Then she switched to her native English. 'Welcome to La Lanterna di Rosa.'

Jamie grinned. 'Thanks. Are you Rosa?'

'I wish! I'm Molly, I just work here, waiting tables. And I know who you are. Here on holiday, I'm guessing?'

He nodded. 'We're on the SS *La Violetta*, berthed at San Basilio. And what brought *you* to Venice?'

'The weather in the UK, mainly. I've been working here for almost a year now, and it's the best move I ever made. Now, let me get you some drinks. What would you like? And are you staying for lunch? I'll bring menus.'

Disa felt the tension in her body relax; when Molly looked at her, there was no flicker of recognition. She clearly had no idea who she was. Then again, up until the discovery she'd made in her garage two months ago, she hadn't been aware of Molly's existence either. And she wasn't ready yet to jump up and make the announcement out of the blue, not before she'd decided whether it was the right or appropriate thing to do.

Chapter 7

They decided to order a bottle of Brognoligo. Disa chose 'nduja arancini and burrata with honey and walnuts, and Jamie went for fritto misto, followed by tagliolini with asparagus and zucchine.

'Excellent choices.' Molly took down the order and headed to the kitchen.

'What are you thinking?' said Jamie when she'd disappeared inside.

'Nothing in particular. Why?'

'You kept looking at her.'

Disa shrugged. 'She's a pretty girl.'

Jamie raised an eyebrow. 'Sure?'

God, he really didn't miss a trick. But if he'd noticed, did that mean Molly had too? She'd tried so hard not to stare, but it had been almost impossible. And now she'd hesitated before answering, and he'd noticed that too.

Time for more fibbing.

'She seemed familiar, and I think I know why. Before we

booked this holiday, I was looking up articles about Venice online. I came across a blog written by an English girl who lived here, and I'm pretty sure it was her.'

Molly was returning, bringing them an ice bucket on a stand along with their bottle of Brognoligo.

'Do you have a blog?' Jamie asked her, as he signalled for her to go ahead and pour the wine she'd just expertly uncorked.

'Yes, I do!' She looked thrilled. 'Do you read it?'

'Not me.' He indicated Disa, who was beginning to wish she'd come on her own. Forcing herself to sound normal, she said, 'I kept thinking I knew you from somewhere, then realised it was from the photos on your blog.'

'Wow, it happens every now and again.' Molly nodded happily. 'Although I don't have thousands of followers. Have you ever messaged me? What's your name?'

'I didn't send any messages,' Disa said hastily. 'I just used to read the posts.'

'Ah, well, that's fine too. I hope you enjoyed them. There you are.' Molly finished filling their glasses. 'Let me know if there's anything else you need.'

When she'd left, Jamie tapped his glass against Disa's. 'Cheers. Here's to young love. I wonder how Leon and Fen are getting on without us?'

Less than five seconds later, a notification flashed up on Disa's phone, and she said, 'I think we're about to find out.'

The message from Fen said: *Hope you're feeling better. We're having the best time – this place is stupendous! See you soon.* The accompanying photograph was of Fen and Leon beaming into the camera with dozens of neat rows of vines stretching into the distance behind them.

Disa smiled; young love indeed. It might have been decades ago, but she still remembered how it felt, could imagine how her granddaughter was feeling right now.

Then again, Fen and Leon had only known each other for twenty-four hours. First impressions weren't always the most accurate, and crushing disappointments could lie ahead. In her time, she'd had experience of that too.

She showed the photo to Jamie, then placed the phone face-down on the red tablecloth and said, 'Tell me about Leon.'

'Ah, the inquisition.' He reached for his glass. 'You mean apart from the gambling problem, the cocaine addiction and that time he served three years in prison for financial fraud?'

'You haven't heard about Fen yet. Sounds like they're made for each other.'

Jamie laughed. 'He's one of the good guys. What you see is what you get. He's honest, loyal, terrific company and always up for an adventure. When we were at uni, he won a pickled-onion-eating competition. Six years ago, he gained his helicopter pilot's licence. One disappointment; he hates olives. I know, it's ridiculous.'

'Fen can't stand cucumber,' said Disa. 'And you can't hide it in any meal; she can sniff it out at fifty paces. Says it tastes *green*.'

'It's nice seeing the two of you together. You get on so well.'

Disa felt her heart expand, as it always did when she thought about Fen. 'I love her so much. She's my only grandchild. We've always been close.'

'That's good.'

'And now you're making me do the terrible proud-grandma thing and show you my favourite photo.' Unable to resist the ever-present temptation, she found it on her phone. 'This was one afternoon when I'd collected her from school. It had been snowing all day and you've never seen a more hyped-up six-year-old. We were heading home through Birdcage Walk in Clifton and Fen was twirling around, being a fairy, with snowflakes in her hair. She said she loved me to the moon and back and that this was the best day of her whole life.' Disa's eyes prickled with emotion at the joyful memory. 'Which made it the best day of *my* whole life too. And that's when I took this photo of the two of us.'

'I can see why it's your favourite.' Jamie studied their happy faces beneath the archway of metal framework and interwoven branches that made up Birdcage Walk, with snow blanketing the ancient, wonky gravestones of St Andrew's church beyond the iron railings on either side of the long tunnel of trees. 'It's a keeper.'

'OK, sorry, one more. Then I'll stop, I promise.'

On the surface, it was just another snap of the two of them laughing together, this time taken on a spring day on the hotel terrace overlooking the Avon Gorge, with the suspension bridge behind them.

'Been there, many times. When was this taken?' He was being polite, but was evidently wondering what made this one so special.

'Eleven years ago. Eighteen months after my husband died. We lost him in a skiing accident.' Disa took a sip of wine. 'A huge shock, obviously. I was devastated. So was Fen, of course. But I honestly don't know how I'd have got through it without her. The grief was awful, it was like being crushed under a lead blanket. I couldn't see it ever lifting, couldn't imagine ever feeling normal again. But Fen didn't give up on me. When I couldn't face leaving the house, she stayed in and kept me company. She was so patient, like an angel. Somehow I got through the first year. Then the next few months. A fortnight after that, I asked her what she'd like for her seventeenth birthday the following week. And Fen said, would I agree to go out with her for the day?'

She paused, shook her head. 'I wanted to say no, but how could I? I had to agree. She planned everything herself and put together an itinerary: breakfast in a favourite café, then a trip to the zoo we used to take her to as a child, then swimming at the Lido, followed by dinner and drinks on the terrace right here.' She tapped the photo on the screen. 'She also gave me a letter she'd written, telling me Declan wouldn't want me to waste the rest of my life being sad, that he'd want me to be happy again. Honestly, that girl, she was only seventeen, but it was the most incredible letter. Don't worry, I won't show you that too.'

She half smiled, lost in admiration. 'I'd heard it all before from friends, obviously. But this time it felt different. For once I believed it might actually be true. It was like a light being switched on in my head. More than a light,' she amended. 'A massive chandelier. So I ordered a bottle of Declan's favourite champagne, and we sat there for the next hour reminiscing, telling each other funny stories about him, and it was unbelievably *cathartic*. And when Fen took this photo of us, I knew I was on my way out of the darkness at last. I was feeling properly happy again, and there was no need to feel guilty about it. I was sixty-two years old, still alive, and from then on I decided I was going to make the most of every day. That was my big turning point.' She raised her glass and broke into a proper smile. 'All thanks to my gorgeous granddaughter.'

'You're lucky to have each other.' Jamie shook out his napkin and moved his water glass as Molly returned with their first courses.

'I almost didn't want to interrupt, you were so deep in

conversation.' She placed the oil-drizzled burrata in front of Disa. '*Buon appetito!*'

Over lunch, they chatted about Jamie's school days, and about Disa's career as an estate agent, then moved on to comparing the various types of holidays they'd taken over the years. At the end of the meal, Molly brought each of them a coffee and a *digestivo* and confided that she'd messaged a friend, who was wildly envious to hear she had Jamie Hamilton in her restaurant. 'You're lucky she's in Norfolk, or she'd be turning up here with her furry handcuffs.'

Clearly accustomed to such comments, he looked amused. 'I'm sorry to miss her.'

'I don't suppose I could bother you for a photo?'

'Of course, no problem.'

She produced her phone and passed it to Disa, who took a couple of snaps of the two of them together. Then Jamie excused himself to visit the men's room inside the restaurant, and Disa asked Molly for *il conto, per favore*. She might not know much Italian, but it was always nice to use the smattering she possessed.

It was less than two minutes later, while she was waiting for Molly to collect the small pile of notes she'd left on the saucer, that Jamie reappeared and said sternly, 'Disa! What d'you think you're doing? Put that money away.'

Disa jumped and gasped, her heart leaping into her throat, because here was Molly, and she'd heard him say her name. Would it mean anything to her?

They were about to find out. Mentally bracing herself, she met the girl's gaze and saw . . .

Nothing. No recognition whatsoever. Instead, she was wagging a reproving finger at Jamie. 'Now, now, no fighting on the premises. We don't allow arguments.'

Not so much as a flicker. Which was good news, for now at least.

'I wouldn't dream of arguing.' Rolling up the notes, he pushed them into the corner of Disa's still open handbag and showed Molly a credit card. 'I invited myself along, so I'm paying. I insist.'

'Thank you.' Disa felt the tension leave her body; she gave in with good grace and turned to Molly. 'I bet this place looks magical at night. I might have to come back one evening with my granddaughter.'

Holding out the machine so Jamie could use his card, Molly smiled at her. 'I hope you will. It'd be lovely to see you again. And thanks so much for reading my blog – I'm glad you liked it.'

'I did. And that dress you wore to the wedding yesterday was gorgeous,' Disa said cheerfully. 'It really suited you.'

To say something? Or not to say something? Jamie didn't want to pry, but on the other hand, he'd never been able to resist getting to the bottom of a mystery. While Disa disappeared to the ladies' room, he had a quick look at Molly's website. Then Disa returned and together they left the restaurant.

'Did you not want her to know your name?' He said it casually and observed her quick intake of breath. 'Sorry, just curious. And you said you *used* to read her blog, but you must have checked it this morning to see what she wore to yesterday's wedding.'

This time, Disa exhaled audibly. 'I realised that as soon as I'd said it. I blame the wine.' She gave him a wry look. 'You don't miss a trick, do you?'

'Sorry,' he repeated. 'It's just, once you've noticed one thing, you start paying more attention. But if you don't want to talk about it, I won't ask any more questions. And that's a promise.'

As they paused to allow a woman with a pushchair to pass them on the narrow footpath, Disa looked as if she was considering it. After a few seconds she said, 'If I tell you, how do I know you'll keep it to yourself?'

She was definitely tempted. Jamie said, 'You'd have my word.'

She returned his gaze, hesitated some more, then shook her head. 'No, I can't do it. I mustn't.'

Now it was even more of a mystery. 'OK.'

'It's not that I don't trust you. But it wouldn't be fair to tell you before Fen, and she doesn't know yet. She should be first.'

'Right.'

'But that'll happen at some stage this week. I'm almost sure it will. And if all goes according to plan, you'll hear about it then. How about that?'

'It's a deal.' He nodded.

'And in the meantime, I'd be grateful if you'd keep this to yourself. Don't mention it to Leon. Or to Fen, obviously.'

'Don't worry. I won't.' To reassure her, Jamie added, 'I'm very discreet.'

She looked relieved, then broke into a smile. 'I guess you have to be, what with you getting as much attention from women as you do.'

'Meaning?'

'I googled you this morning. Quite a high turnover in the girlfriend department.'

'Ouch.'

'I suppose it goes with the territory when you're sporty, good-looking and famous. Anyway, why wouldn't you make the most of being in demand?'

'I don't always,' he reminded her. 'You rescued me this morning.'

'Ah, but have you given her enough of a chance?' Disa's clear blue eyes glinted with mischief. 'If you really get to know her, maybe she could turn out to be the love of your life.'

He grinned. 'You never know.' They'd been making their way back towards the Ponte dell'Accademia, but Disa had come to a halt. 'Everything OK?'

'Everything's fine. Except I can't stop thinking about a handbag I spotted in a shop yesterday. I told myself I wasn't going to buy it, but I don't think myself is very happy with that decision. In fact, she's keen for me to change my mind, and I think she might be right. You go ahead, get back to the ship. I'm going to find that shop and take another look.'

'How will you feel if the bag's been sold?'

'I'll be devastated.'

'In that case,' Jamie told her, 'if it's still there, you'll know you have to buy it.'

She smiled. 'Of course. That's the rule.'

Chapter 8

Disa watched Jamie leave, then turned and retraced the route she and Fen had taken yesterday. When she reached the shop, yes, the bag was still there on display in the window, elegant in its simplicity and the perfect shade of ballet-slipper pink. Her heart leapt because not only had she genuinely admired it before, it was now providing her with an excellent reason to be back here, which made her love it even more.

But the church bells were chiming three o'clock, meaning she still had another hour to kill, so she took her time inside the shop, examining all the bags in all the colours to ensure hers was the absolute best. Having paid for it, she next visited another shop and chose a turquoise silk scarf for Fen, then a deep purple Murano glass necklace for Mary, the next-door neighbour back in Bristol who'd volunteered to water her garden while she was away.

Finally, at eight minutes to four, she returned to La Lanterna and loitered on the street outside, because in one of Molly's previous online posts, she'd explained that her early shifts at the restaurant ran from eight until four, while the later ones meant working from four until midnight.

The moment the girl emerged through the open iron gates, Disa began limping dramatically. All she could do was hope that karma wouldn't punish her for feigning two injuries in one day by causing her to trip and fall into the nearest canal.

'Hello! Oh no, what's happened?' Molly's gaze went to her foot, and Disa leaned against the wall to take the weight off it.

'I'm an idiot, so busy looking in shop windows that I didn't see the step and went over on my ankle. I broke it a few years back, so it's been a bit dodgy ever since.'

'You poor thing! Have you sprained it, do you think?'

'No, no, it's just sore. My own silly fault.'

'And where's your friend Jamie?'

'He's not here. I wanted to do some shopping on my own. It's OK, once I'm on the ship, I'll be fine.'

Molly looked concerned. 'I can't leave you here like this. Let me walk you back.'

'Oh no, I can't ask you to do that.'

'You didn't ask. I offered. Come on, lean on me. The last thing you need is to go over on it again and make things worse.'

'Are you sure? But haven't you just finished work?'

'I have, and of course I'm sure. It's not far. Here, take my arm. We'll have you back in no time.'

Disa allowed herself to be supported. How could she ever have doubted this young woman? But that was down to natural scepticism, born from decades of thinking the best of people. Molly had seemed lovely in her blog – but then who didn't? Everyone presented themselves in the best light and neglected to reveal any less attractive aspects of their personality. Similarly, working in a restaurant involved being charming and giving the customers excellent service.

But this was going above and beyond. Molly-in-Venice had

proved herself to be a genuinely kind person, volunteering to help an injured older woman out of the sheer goodness of her heart.

It was the result she'd very much hoped for.

'Tell me about your family back in England,' she said, remembering to maintain her limp as they made their way back to San Basilio. 'They must miss you, living over here.'

'Hang on.' Hattie frowned. 'What are you doing on Tinder when we aren't even at home?'

Kayla, out of the shower and preparing to do her make-up, said, 'Because being on holiday is the best time! There's no one I fancy on this boat – well, no one who fancies me back – so it makes sense to check out the local area, see if I can't rustle us up a couple of fit Venetians while we're here. You wouldn't say no, would you?'

'I'm not on Tinder.'

'And that's your first mistake. Haven't I been telling you for months to get yourself on there? Look, this one's an actual gondolier.' She showed Hattie a photo and waggled her eyebrows suggestively. 'Imagine having sex in a gondola!'

These days, Hattie was hard pushed imagining herself having sex anywhere at all. Life hadn't worked out the way she'd expected, and neither had her marriage to Guy. She'd been too young, she accepted that now; they'd met when she was twenty-one and had married two years later because it seemed to be the logical next step. And Guy had been great company, so it stood to reason they'd be happy together for ever.

Except he hadn't turned out to be the world's best husband. An inveterate extrovert, he had loved to be out and about as often as possible. He'd belonged to various clubs and social groups and had encouraged Hattie to go along to them with him, but she'd preferred spending time at home, and over the years the differences between them had grown more apparent. They'd had less and less in common, and other people had liked to point out that married couples were supposed to do things together.

There hadn't been one major rift at the end. Guy hadn't had an affair or anything like that. He had just been a bit selfish – OK, sometimes quite a lot selfish – and had carried on doing all the things he enjoyed doing, while she had initially nagged at him, then discovered she hated to nag so had given up trying to force him to change.

They'd loved each other, but in the end that hadn't been enough, and their relationship had run out of steam. Like a sparkler on Bonfire Night, it had simply ended up fizzling out.

Which had been disappointing, of course, but these things happened and Hattie knew she wasn't the only thirty-year-old with a failed marriage behind her. Plus she had Kayla and other friends to go out and about with, which was a bonus. After taking a while to get over the break-up, she had imagined she would start socialising again, making the most of being single, then within two or three years would find someone new to settle down with, someone more suitable this time than Guy.

Except six years on, life hadn't proceeded according to plan. There had been some false starts, but the right man hadn't come along and here she was, still single. Not that she was desperate, but it would've been nice if he could have been here by now. She had no idea who her eventual next partner might be, but he was definitely taking his time turning up.

Now, watching as Kayla slathered on primer, then reached for her bottle of foundation, she protested, 'Everyone here on the ship is really nice, though.'

'I know they're *nice*, but some are old and most of them are couples, and the only really good-looking guys are gay. Apart from Jamie, but I've pretty much offered myself up to him on a plate and he's obviously not interested.'

'I saw you talking to him in the bar earlier. What happened?'

'That was me doing the offering! I mean, he was being kind about it, but it was a definite no. And his mate Leon's pretty cute, but it looks like he's off the market now too. No point flogging a dead horse.' Kayla finished rubbing the foundation into her skin, then began energetically buffing blusher onto her cheeks. 'I gave it my best shot, so now it's time to move on to someone who will appreciate me for the total goddess I am. Like Angelo.'

Hattie studied the profile on the app. Angelo, the gondolier who'd matched with Kayla, was thirty-three years old and in his photo was wearing double denim and the kind of naughty grin that told you everything you needed to know about his personality.

'You're actually going to meet this guy? When?'

'Tonight! Want me to ask him if he has a friend he can bring along?'

'No, really. It isn't my kind of thing.'

'And *that* is the reason you're single.'

'So are you.'

'But I'm having more fun.' Kayla finished her eyeshadow and got busy with the mascara. 'You don't mind if I go, do you? Will you be all right here?'

'I'll be fine. You need to be careful, though. Meet him in public and don't go back to his place, whatever you do.'

'Yes, *Mum*.' Kayla batted her sooty lashes, then drew on lipstick and blew her a kiss. 'Now, big shirt and leggings? Or pink bandage dress?'

'Shirt and leggings, definitely.'

She pulled open her wardrobe door and triumphantly reached for the short pink dress. 'How did I know you were going to say that?'

Before dinner in the ship's restaurant, Jamie gave a talk about his sporting career and his subsequent move into TV. It was well attended and he was an entertaining host, joking with the audience and encouraging them to join in. Without having expected to, even Fen enjoyed it.

But really, today couldn't have gone any better. Spending time with Leon had been so giddy-making, she was starting to panic inwardly, convinced something was about to happen that would bring it all down. After dinner, they all headed up on deck, with groups of guests forming and re-forming as they got to know each other better. Music drifted up from the band playing in the bar downstairs, lemon drop martinis were recommended by a lively octogenarian and discovered to be unbelievably delicious, and laughter rang out as the chatter grew noisier and more drinks were served.

'Nice photo.' Leon, who was following the ship's account on Instagram, showed Fen one of her and Disa taken last night. Then he scrolled to the next, of the excitable guest with spiky red and gold hair dancing with Jamie and evidently having the time of her life. Holding up his phone, he addressed her companion as she walked past: 'Has your friend seen this? Looks like she was enjoying herself. I don't think I've seen her on the boat this evening. Is she around?'

'Gone out on a hot date with a gondolier tonight. Look, sorry if Kayla was a bit OTT.' The woman, whose name Fen belatedly remembered was Hattie, shook her head. 'She gets carried away sometimes.'

'Hey, don't worry, Jamie's used to it.' Leon grinned. 'Last week he was filling up his car at the petrol station and a woman wanted him to autograph her chest.'

Across the deck, a pair of burly rugby enthusiasts were talking to Jamie. Nodding in their direction, Hattie said, 'Let's hope those two don't ask him to do that.'

Fen was intrigued. 'How did she meet the gondolier? Did he take you for a ride earlier and ask her out?'

'No, Tinder. I just hope he's legit. He's a few years younger than she is. I warned her to be careful, even offered to go with her, but she turned me down, said she didn't need a chaperone.'

Fen pulled a sympathetic face. 'Fingers crossed it's OK.'

'All good so far.' Taking out her phone, Hattie showed them a video of her friend. 'Here she is, sitting in a gondola being serenaded by her date. Having a whale of a time.'

'And you're left here on your own? If you want to join us, pull up a chair.' But even as Fen said it, one of the other guests was approaching them, tapping Hattie on the shoulder and making her jump.

'Hi there, can I borrow you?' He was in his forties at a guess, a tad overweight but attractive, with a genial manner and a winning twinkle in his eye. Fen had seen him around the ship with an elegant younger woman who looked like a cross between a ravishing eagle and a hardcore fitness instructor.

'Me?' Hattie looked surprised. 'Why? Where's Suzanne?'

'In the cabin. On the phone to her daughters, reading them a bedtime story. And I'd love it if we could have a quick word.'

'Fire away.'

'Maybe somewhere quieter?'

She hesitated for a moment, then shrugged. 'OK.'

'It's all right, we've met before.' Having noticed the interested looks from Fen and Leon, the man said cheerfully, 'She's my ex-wife.'

'Go on then,' Hattie prompted when Guy had led her down to the secluded section at the very front of the ship. 'What's this about?'

'Enjoying the holiday so far?'

'Of course.' It was five-star luxury in Venice. And it was free; who could ask for more?

'Hattie, can I just say, you're looking incredible. Really good.'

She narrowed her eyes at him. Something was up. 'And?'

'I have a tiny confession to make.' He returned her look of suspicion with the kind of playful half-smile that rang a familiar bell. When they'd been together, it had been the method he'd tended to employ in order to excuse any behaviour he'd known she wouldn't like, such as staying out late, or forgetting to mention that he'd booked a golfing weekend away with his friends, or had bought a new car simply because he fancied a change. When Guy decided he wanted to do something, he did it first and confessed afterwards.

'Go on,' Hattie prompted. Once, he'd gone out to buy her a birthday present and had come home with a slim silver bangle for her plus a Breitling watch for himself. OK, that wasn't fair; he hadn't been ungenerous, and had more than made up for it a month later with a wonderful trip to Paris. He'd just happened to fall in love with that expensive watch on that particular shopping trip and been unable to resist buying it. If her impulsive ex-husband wanted something, he didn't like to wait; he was very much a fan of instant gratification.

Guy said, 'I kind of knew you were going to be on this trip.'

Chapter 9

There it was again, the I've-been-a-bit-naughty smile that had got him out of trouble on so many occasions over the years.

Hattie raised an eyebrow. 'How did you *kind* of know?'

'Pete from the cricket team told me.' Guy shrugged, as if it were obvious. 'His wife used to work at the hospital with Kayla and they're still friends on Facebook. This afternoon, Kayla posted about the coincidence of you being on this cruise and me turning up on the ship too.'

Slowly nodding, Hattie discovered she wasn't actually that surprised. It *had* been too much of a coincidence. 'And you're telling me now because . . .?'

'I thought I should come clean.'

'You mean Pete called to warn you that his wife was going to tell Kayla, who'd then obviously tell me. So you thought you'd get in first.'

'Hattie, it was just one of those things. As soon as I heard about this cruise, I thought it sounded right up my street. And yes, we could have booked a different date, but this was the week that suited us best. Plus, it had Jamie Hamilton on board, which was a massive bonus. And honestly? I thought it'd be great to see you again, and it *is* great. There's no reason why we can't be friends, is there? You have no idea how often I think about you.' He paused. 'Or how much I miss you.'

All those years, all those happy times, followed by less happy times, and finally the failure of their marriage. Despite everything, Hattie felt her stomach flip, as hearing Guy say those words brought a million memories flooding back. Because there had been love there, on both sides.

Then again, she'd had plenty of time to get him out of her system. She was older and more mature now.

Also, less gullible.

'And how does Suzanne feel about this?'

He watched as a speedboat swooshed past, bounce-bounce-bouncing over the surface of the water, then turned back to meet her steady gaze. 'She doesn't know. Hattie, seeing you again has honestly knocked me for six. I had no idea it was going to have this much of an effect on me. But it has.' He paused. 'It really has.'

'That'll be the force of my flawless looks and irresistible personality.' What else could she do but be flippant?

'You're joking,' said Guy. 'But I mean it.'

'Poor Suzanne.'

'There's nothing poor about Suzanne. You've seen what she looks like.'

'I have.' Hattie nodded in agreement.

'She's stunning.'

'Absolutely.' Curiosity compelled her to ask, 'Is she the one, do you think?'

'It's still early days. A couple of little things need ironing out.' Guy pulled a face and said wryly, 'She does keep trying to teach me yoga.'

Hattie managed to keep a straight face. 'Do you wear a leotard for that?'

'I do not, and don't you dare laugh. She also wants me to eat more healthily. Tells me my arteries will clog up if I have too much fried food, and I'll have a heart attack.'

'Which is true, that could happen. She wants you to be healthier for your own sake as well as hers,' Hattie pointed out. 'That's fair enough, isn't it?'

'She wants me to jog,' Guy said mournfully.

'I'd pay good money to see that. Double if you're in a leotard.'

'Sounds like you're on her side.'

'I'm not on anyone's side. But it does seem as if you've met your match. Which can only be a good thing. Has she been married before?'

'Yes. Her ex-husband's a triathlete. It was an amicable divorce,' said Guy. 'He's back in the UK taking care of the kids while she's over here with me. They're sweet girls, six and four. When he dropped them off with us a couple of weeks ago, he asked me what my BMI was.'

'He did? What did you say?'

'I told him I didn't have one, I drove a Porsche.'

Hattie laughed, and Guy smiled too. 'He's a nice enough chap, but now he probably thinks I'm fat *and* stupid.'

'You aren't that fat. Only a few kilos overweight.'

'Compared with them, I'm a sumo wrestler.' He glanced past her. 'Story time's over. Here she comes. Anyway, it's been great chatting with you. I hope we can all enjoy our holiday. And I meant it when I said you're looking fantastic.'

Not nearly as fantastic as lithe, snake-hipped Suzanne, though, in her short primrose-yellow Lycra dress and silver sandals. Who could begin to compete with someone as physically flawless as that?

Catching the eye of the friendly New Yorkers she'd been talking to earlier, Hattie said, 'Enjoy your evening. I'm going to grab a drink and catch up with Bill and Janey.'

But as she was walking away, she heard Suzanne behind her say with amusement, 'Were you just being chatted up by your ex-wife?'

Having escaped at last from a group of enthusiastic rugby fans in the bar, Jamie headed up on deck to find Leon and Fen. When he reached them, Leon was on his phone, in the process of ending a call.

'I'm going to have to sort this out in the cabin.' Leon looked resigned. 'It's a client in Singapore having a panic attack about his finances. I need to set up a Zoom and go through all his files on my laptop.'

As he rose to his feet, Jamie slid onto the space on the sofa he'd vacated. 'That's OK, we'll talk about you behind your back. I'll tell Fen all the stories you don't want her to hear.'

'Don't listen to him,' Leon instructed Fen. 'Whatever he says, none of it's true. It's a pretty complicated situation,' he went on, indicating his phone. 'I could be gone for some time.'

Jamie sat back. 'Just as well. It'll take me a while to tell her everything.'

'Go on then,' said Fen when Leon had left. 'Break it to me gently. He's married.'

'Two wives. Four kids. Treats them all *very* badly indeed. Kicks dogs too.'

'OK, now the really important stuff. Does he give away the endings of thrillers?'

'Always.' Jamie nodded. 'You've dripped some of your drink onto your top, by the way.'

She examined the purple stain on her lilac vest, gave it an experimental prod with one finger, then said comfortably, 'No worries, I'm sure it'll wash out,' and took another sip of her drink. 'This cocktail's so delicious it's worth it.'

He liked the way she didn't fly into a panic, but took the minor setback in her stride. As if reading his mind, Fen said, 'I'm never going to be as stylish as Disa. She doesn't spill stuff down herself like I do.'

Jamie said, 'It's funny to think you live in Redland and we're only a mile away in Clifton but you and Leon had never bumped into each other before. I bet you went to the same restaurants, pubs, shops.'

'We probably did, we just didn't notice each other.'

'He told me he'd have recognised you if he had. And I believe him. I reckon you're exactly his type.'

'Really?' Smiling, she plucked at her stained top then twanged one of her springy curls. 'Messy and accident-prone with mad hair?'

Jamie laughed and turned towards her, pretending to study her in detail. 'Your hair isn't mad, it's great.' It was that shade of natural white-blonde that displayed her heritage, but her brows and lashes were dark brown. Her eyes were a clear silvery grey and there was a small scar beneath the left one, as well as a dusting of freckles across her nose. She'd been wearing lipstick earlier but it had all worn off now, courtesy of eating, drinking and – more than likely – kissing Leon. During the years they'd known each other, Leon's girlfriends had been an eclectic mix ranging from skinny to curvy, sporty to nerdy, city to countryside.

'You know, I'd say up until now he never really had a type. But maybe that was because he hadn't met you.' He paused, then added slowly, 'But now he has. And it turns out you're it.'

All around them, people were chatting, laughing and getting to know each other. For several seconds, Fen didn't move and remained silent. Finally, she said, 'Are you joking?'

He shook his head. 'Not at all. Deadly serious.'

'Oh my God, I can't believe you said that.'

'Me neither.' He didn't make a habit of being serious, particularly when it came to emotions, and *especially* emotions of a romantic nature. It wasn't his thing. Life was easier if you joked your way through it. As far as his own dating history was concerned, women had tended not to criticise him, but if they did, it was to point out that he wasn't taking their relationship seriously enough, preferring to play it for fun and laughs rather than getting more deep and meaningful.

But they were talking about Leon now. And Jamie knew instinctively that Leon felt differently about Fen from how he'd felt about any of his previous girlfriends. This really could be it for his best friend, and since Jamie liked Fen too, he couldn't be happier.

'I know it's early days,' Fen said now. 'Like, *really* early. But I hope you're right.'

Jamie smiled, charmed by her honesty and lack of guile. 'It's still wild, thinking of the two of you going around Clifton, dipping in and out of shops and bars, never managing to meet each other.'

She nodded in agreement. 'I know, it's all so random.'

'And I'd say I have a good memory for faces,' he went on. 'If I'd seen you before, I'm sure I'd have remembered you too.'

A slow smile lifted the corners of her mouth. 'Except we have met before.'

'We have?'

Fen nodded. 'Oh yes.'

What did *that* mean? There hadn't been any mention of it before now. What had happened? Had they danced together? Kissed? Surely not more than that.

'Don't look so panicky.' Fen was entertained. 'It wasn't terrible.'

Thank God.

'That's a relief.'

'You just did something a bit bad and I told you off.'

This wasn't good. 'I did something bad to *you*?'

'Not me. You'd been invited to a birthday party at a bar on Whiteladies Road. And the girl whose birthday it was, she really thought you'd turn up. But you didn't.'

The memory of that evening came flooding back. Jamie did a double-take. 'You were the one outside who gave me the lecture?'

'I was.'

'Over by the wall, in the shadows?'

'Yep.'

'That was really you?' He started to laugh, partly with relief that it hadn't been anything more physical, because that would have been acutely embarrassing. And partly because he'd had a sneaking admiration at the time for the owner of the voice, who'd pointed out calmly but firmly that what he was doing was a bit unkind.

'It was me.' Fen nodded.

'You called me out. She was so insistent when she asked me, I couldn't get away until I said I'd go. But I didn't expect her to believe me. I felt awful about it afterwards, when you told me.'

'That was the plan.'

'I did apologise to her.'

It was her turn to look surprised. 'You did? How?'

'She'd messaged me on Instagram. I said I was really sorry I hadn't been able to make it, and arranged for flowers to be sent to her place of work.'

'I didn't know that.'

'It's on her Instagram page. She tagged me in the post.'

Fen opened her phone, found Amanda and searched her grid. And yes, there she was, clutching a bouquet and beaming like a competition winner. Beneath the photo, she'd posted: *Day made!!! Look what was just delivered to my office, only the most fabulous flowers from Jamie Hamilton himself to say sorry he couldn't make it to my birthday party! Apology very much accepted, Jamie, feel free to slide into my DMs any time, and thank you!!! Xxxxxxx*

'I didn't see this,' Fen marvelled. She turned to look at him. 'That was a nice thing to do.'

'Thanks to you making me feel guilty.'

'And did you? Slide into her DMs?' Her eyes were bright with mischief.

'No. But I'm glad I sent the flowers. It made me feel like a better person.'

'Now I'm glad I told you off.' She tapped her glass against his. 'Cheers to both of us.'

'Cheers.' He tapped back, his wrist making contact with the side of her hand.

'There's a couple of men to our left looking over. I think they're hoping to talk rugby with you. If you want to go off and have a chat with them, don't worry about me. I'm fine here.'

It was the two Glaswegians he'd spent forty minutes with before dinner. Feeling he'd done enough for one evening, Jamie said, 'I'd rather stay and talk to you.'

★

'All done,' Leon announced just over an hour later, appearing before them with his hair ruffled and a bottle of Peroni in his hand. 'Panic over, problem sorted, time to relax. Did you miss me?'

'With every beat of my heart. Here, you can have your seat back.' Jamie moved over from the sofa to the chair opposite, so Leon could rejoin Fen.

'What have you two been talking about while I was gone?'

'All sorts. The way all our paths have crossed without knowing it. We go to the same deli.'

'The one that sells the best Scotch eggs,' said Fen. 'Obviously.'

'And every time Fen goes for a walk across the suspension bridge and back, she passes our flat.'

'And I always admire your blue front door,' Fen chipped in. 'But my number one favourite is the bright red one further down the hill.'

'We both used to play on the grabber machines at Weston Pier. I won a green toy monkey,' said Jamie.

'I won a purple lion with a wonky eye and no tail.'

'And we get our Indian takeaways from the same restaurant. We're practically twins.'

'I'd struggle to tell you apart,' said Leon.

'Plus, remember that time I was out with a couple of guys from the rugby club and got told off by a woman because I'd been invited to her friend's birthday party but didn't want to go?'

Leon nodded. 'She made you feel guilty, so you ended up sending flowers to the friend. That one?'

'That one.' Jamie pointed at Fen.

'It was you?' Leon applauded. 'Excellent! Not many people have the nerve to tell him off.' He drew her against him and gave her a congratulatory squeeze. 'Well done, you.'

'Here comes Disa.' Jamie nodded as she appeared at the top of the steps and made her way towards them in a swirl of turquoise silk. Jokingly, he said, 'Let's hope she hasn't come to whisk Fen away again like last night.'

But when Disa reached them, she didn't take the seat he'd drawn up for her. She looked at Fen and said, 'Sweetheart, is it OK if we go downstairs for a chat?'

'Really?' The joke was turning out not to be a joke after all. With a trace of suspicion, Fen said, 'Will it take long?'

For a split second, Jamie's gaze met Disa's and he wondered if it had something to do with Molly from the restaurant.

'I can't really say. And I'm sorry to be dragging you away, but this is something we need to talk about.'

'Starting to think Disa hates me.' Leon's tone was rueful as he watched them leave.

Someone else watching them leave was another mad-keen rugby fan, who promptly arrived at their table, plonked himself down opposite Jamie and blurted out, 'I've been waiting for the chance to talk to you about that try you scored in the last minute at Twickenham three years ago. Tell me, was that the best match of your career, or would you say it was the time you scored fifteen points against the All Blacks?'

Jamie exchanged a fleeting glance with Leon, who was accustomed to such interruptions, then turned back to the eager rugby fan. 'That's a great question,' he said with a nod. 'But I guess it had to be that final minute at Twickenham.'

'I was there!' the man exclaimed. 'I could hardly breathe!'

'But I got there in the end.' Jamie smiled at him. 'And it was worth the wait.'

Chapter 10

'I haven't been completely honest with you.' Disa settled herself onto one of the chairs in her cabin and indicated that Fen should take the other. 'There was a reason I wanted to come to Venice. Remember when I said I could do with your support?'

She was looking serious. Alarmed, Fen said, 'Is something wrong? Are you ill?'

But Disa was already shaking her head. 'No, no, I'm not ill. Nothing like that. It's to do with . . . well, family, I suppose. You know how a couple of months ago I cleared out the garage? I found some letters I was never supposed to see.'

'Letters? Who from? Were they sent to you and you've only just found them?'

Another shake. 'They'd been sent to your grandfather, at his office. And he'd kept them well hidden. In an old envelope labelled "Income Tax Receipts",' Disa elaborated drily. 'Because who in their right mind would look at ancient tax documents?'

The gentle slosh of water against the side of the ship increased as a motorboat chugged past. The air-conditioned cabin smelled of the signature perfume Disa always wore, a mix of peony and rose. Fen realised she was deliberately concentrating on these scents and sounds to avoid thinking about what the letters might contain.

'I loved your grandfather very much,' Disa continued. 'So much so that I married him even though I'd found out a few weeks before the wedding that he was still secretly seeing his previous girlfriend.'

'*No.*' Fen was genuinely shocked. 'How did you find out?'

'A friend saw them together and told me. She thought I should call off the wedding. Which I almost did, because obviously I was devastated. I lost it with Declan, went berserk and threw plates at the wall, all sorts. But he kept telling me he was sorry, he begged me to forgive him, and the truth was, I still loved him, still wanted to marry him.' Disa paused. 'He swore it was all over, he promised he'd never see the woman again. So we went ahead and got married, with no one else having any idea what had happened.'

Fen was still struggling to take it in. 'That must have been so hard for you.'

'It was. But at least nobody else knew. I'm sure people back then wouldn't have thought I was the type to put up with being cheated on, but it turned out I was, so long as it was just the once. For the next couple of years, I really struggled to believe he was wherever he said he was, but he was so sorry he'd hurt me, and desperate to make it up to me, that over time I grew to trust him again. We were happy and we had a fantastic life together.'

'You did,' Fen insisted. 'I used to love coming to your house. You were both always laughing and having fun.' But her mouth was dry, because the story wasn't finished and she still didn't know what was coming next. 'You were *so* happy.'

Disa nodded in agreement, then reached sideways and pulled a large tattered envelope out of the long drawer beneath the marble-topped dressing table.

Fen pulled a face. 'Are those the letters?'

'They are. Don't worry, you don't have to read them.'

'From her?'

'From her. Yvette.' Disa nodded and poured herself a glass of water from the carafe on the table. 'Not written back then, though. After our wedding, she went to live and work as an au pair in Paris, and they lost touch. From the letters, it seemed they had no contact for twenty years. Then she came back to Bristol, bumped into Declan, and they started seeing each other again.' She exhaled. 'Which goes to show how clever some people can be. They were secretly meeting up and I had no idea.'

Fen shook her head. 'It's so unfair.'

'It was. And that wasn't all,' said Disa. 'Within months, she was pregnant.'

Fen's hands flew to her mouth. '*What?*'

'I know. Sorry, I've had a couple of months to get used to it.'

'She sent the letters to Declan. So he knew. This is mind-blowing. Hang on,' said Fen. 'Twenty years after the affair first started?'

'I was twenty-one when we got married. Declan was twenty-three. People often settled down earlier in those days. And Yvette, it turns out, was the same age as me. When she gave birth, she was forty-two years old.'

'But you still had no idea that Declan had a secret family. My mum had a half-brother or half-sister and never knew.'

'All I have are Yvette's letters, but they're very detailed. She obviously adored him,' said Disa. 'And according to her, he loved her too, but he always told her he couldn't leave me.'

'Because he loved you more. He couldn't bear to lose you.' God, this was like a TV soap, except it had really happened. 'But why would he have run the risk of having an affair in the first place?'

'I suppose because he was a risk-taker. When it comes to affairs, some people can't resist that gamble, because if they don't get found out, it counts as a win.' Disa shrugged. 'And Declan didn't get found out, did he? He had a happy life with me – and it really *was* happy – as well as the extra thrill of a secret affair with Yvette.'

Fen was twisting one of her curls around her index finger, struggling to compare this less-than-flattering version of Declan with the grandfather she'd known and adored. 'I still can't believe he did it.'

'Nor could I, at first. But these things do happen. Please don't hate him for it; everyone makes mistakes. And it wasn't all fun and games for him, being torn between two families. From what she wrote, it was obvious he felt a huge amount of guilt for what he was doing to me, and to them. He loved them but wasn't able to visit as often as he wanted. That can't have been easy. If you do decide to read the letters, you'll see that for yourself. Some of it's quite heartbreaking. And Yvette struggled terribly too. She wanted a proper life with Declan but couldn't have that. In the end, she moved away from Bristol and found someone else. Declan tried to maintain a relationship with his daughter, but Yvette told him it would only confuse and upset her. Apparently the little girl was already calling the new partner Dad.' Disa took another sip of water. 'Basically, Yvette stopped any further contact and remarried.'

Fen took a deep breath. 'And where does Venice come in?'

Disa smiled. 'I wondered when you'd get to that. The daughter lives here. I did a little light investigating, out of curiosity, and found her online.'

'What? Are you going to make contact? Do you want to meet her?'

'I did, today.'

'*What?*' This was becoming more surreal by the second. 'How? Where?'

'She works at that restaurant, La Lanterna di Rosa.'

Fen's jaw dropped. 'You're kidding!'

'She wasn't working yesterday when you and I went there.'

'So this time you took Jamie instead of me.'

'I hadn't planned to take Jamie, it was just the way it happened. And she doesn't know who I am yet. I couldn't do that to her without any warning, not while she was in the middle of her shift. I wanted to see her, speak to her, get an idea of what she was like.' Disa twisted the hexagonal gold bangle on her wrist. 'If I didn't like her, that might be enough and I wouldn't feel any need to introduce myself.'

'Which means you did like her,' said Fen.

'I did. Anyone would. She's a lovely girl.'

'What's her name?'

'Molly.'

'What does she look like?'

'That's the extraordinary thing. She looks a lot like Declan. I mean, she's his daughter, so it's hardly surprising. But seeing her in the flesh felt almost like seeing him again. Your mum took after me – well, you already know that. But this girl has Declan's eyes, and his smile . . . it's incredible. She even laughs like him.'

'How old is she?'

'I worked it out from the letters. Thirty-one.'

'Three years older than me.'

'Do you want to see photos of her?'

'You took sneaky photos in the restaurant? Like a *spy*?'

'I would have liked to,' Disa admitted with a smile, 'but I didn't. She has a blog.' Twisting round on her chair, she reached behind her for the iPad resting on the wide window ledge.

'You didn't really have a bad back this morning,' Fen realised.

'No.'

'You could have asked me to go with you today.'

Disa gave her a fond look. 'And if you hadn't met your lovely man, I might have done. But I couldn't do that to you, sweetheart. You wouldn't have wanted me to drag you away from Leon again.'

Like you did this evening. Fen didn't say it aloud, but Disa saw her raised eyebrows and the playful smile on her face.

'I know, sorry about that, but I needed to tell you. I sent her an email earlier and she's replied. Actually, you should read the emails first.' Disa passed the iPad over to her so she could see.

Hi Molly,

It was so lovely to chat to you in the restaurant today – I came in with Jamie Hamilton at lunchtime and you very kindly helped me back to the ship when I hurt my ankle.

Time for me to come clean now. I wanted to meet you because we have someone in common. My name is Disa O'Toole, and my husband was Declan, your father. I'm sure this will come as a huge shock, but I promise I feel no ill will towards you.

I'm here in Venice with my granddaughter and would love it if we could meet up properly. There's lots to talk about, and I will also bring some personal effects you and your mum might like to have. Whenever and wherever suits you, just let me know, and apologies for the subterfuge earlier!

Best,

Disa

Fen's gaze switched to Molly's reply, which had arrived twenty minutes ago and was shorter.

Oh, wow. I mean, WOW. This is wild. I was just telling one of my friends earlier about meeting you and Jamie Hamilton today, and how nice you both were – and now this! But yes, it'd be great to meet up properly. I'm free tomorrow morning if that's convenient for you? Let me know and I'll think of a good place. Gosh, I can't concentrate at the moment, my mind's in a whirl.

'So it's happening,' said Disa. 'Will you come with me tomorrow to meet her?'

'Of course I will!' Fen nodded vigorously. 'And I would have gone with you to that restaurant today as well.'

'I know. But it might actually have worked out better, having Jamie there. I think Molly was quite taken with him, which meant she spent more time chatting with us at our table. Anyway, now you know.' Disa took back the iPad. 'And if you want to find out more about her, her website is called "Molly in Venice".'

An hour later, Fen was sitting up in her own bed with her laptop balanced on her knees, still reading Molly's blog. There had been too much going on in her head for her to return to the top deck and find Leon; this had obviously taken precedence. She'd messaged him, though, and explained that tomorrow morning she'd be going out with Disa but hopefully they could meet up later in the day. It didn't seem right to blurt out all the details just yet, before they'd had their first proper meeting with Molly.

Luckily, Leon understood, as she'd known he would. He really was the best.

But it had been a long day and, compounded with the bombshell surprise, an exhausting one.

Eventually her eyelids had begun to droop, and by midnight she was fast asleep.

Chapter 11

'Finally! Thank goodness you're back.' Hattie had been far too wound up to be able to sleep. When the cabin door opened after midnight, she jerked into a sitting position. 'Your phone's switched off. I didn't know where you were. I thought you were *dead*.'

'What are you, my mum?' Kayla threw herself onto her own bed and kicked her legs in the air. 'I turned off my phone because the battery was nearly flat. And I'm not dead. I've had the best-best-best first date ever!'

She was looking flushed and ridiculously happy. Hattie said, 'Tell me everything.'

'He's gorgeous. He pays me compliments and tells me I'm beautiful. He sang to me, too. What a voice,' Kayla said dreamily. 'And you should see his abs.'

'He showed you his abs?'

'I saw everything. He's brilliant in bed.'

'You *slept* with him?'

'No sleeping involved. We were far too busy having sex.'

'Oh my God, what did I tell you about not going back to his place?'

'What else could we do? I wasn't allowed to bring him here, was I? We went for dinner in a dear little trattoria, but he forgot to bring his wallet so I used my card, then we went to his so he could pay me back. Except it turned out he was out of cash, but that's OK, it just means we have to meet up again tomorrow night, yay, can't wait!'

Talk about a recipe for disaster. And here was Kayla blithely thinking she'd found the love of her life at last. Inwardly wincing, Hattie shook her head. 'It's not going to happen, though, is it?'

'Of course it is. He's meeting me in St Mark's Square at seven on the dot, then taking me on a romantic walk, then probably back to his place for more top-class bed action. This is going to do wonders for my figure.' Kayla patted her stomach and did another happy foot-waggle. 'And don't look at me like that. I gave it my best shot with Jamie Hamilton, but he wasn't interested, was he? And now I'm glad, because who wouldn't prefer an actual Italian with his very own gondola?' She twisted onto her side and looked at Hattie. 'I do feel a bit bad, though, about leaving you here on your own again. Are you sure you don't want me to ask him if he has a friend he can bring along? We could all go out together.'

'No need,' Hattie said quickly. 'It's fine. I like being here on the ship anyway. I'm really enjoying getting to know the other guests.'

If the money-borrower with his tragically empty wallet turned up at seven to meet Kayla tomorrow night, she'd be amazed. By eight o'clock, she very much hoped, her friend would have learned all she needed to learn about the nefarious ways of handsome and much younger Venetians with an eye to the main chance. And washboard abs.

★

Very rarely, Jamie experienced a lucid dream. It was happening now. He knew he was dreaming, and was aware that he could – to a lesser or greater extent – control what happened next. If he wanted it to stop, all he needed to do was open his eyes and wake up.

Which was what he should be doing, except he really didn't want to, because in his dream he was walking over a deserted Ponte dell'Accademia at night with Fen Madden. The stars were out and the connection between them was absolutely electric. At the highest point of the bridge, they stopped and turned to face each other, then Fen reached up and lightly touched the side of his cheek, causing his pulse rate to rocket. And now she was searching his face, her breath quickening. Apart from the sound of water lapping quietly around the boats moored below, they were surrounded by stillness and silence.

Fen murmured, 'What would you say if I told you I wanted to kiss you?'

It was taking all his self-control not to tell her the same, despite the chemistry between them being off the scale. But she didn't belong to him, so it mustn't happen. This was the girl who had stolen his best friend's heart, practically at first sight, and there was no way he could give in to temptation, because what if it made him realise he couldn't give her up, that there would be no going back?

What if that one kiss proved to be life-changing and meant losing Leon's friendship for ever?

Fen was still gazing up at him, waiting for him to react.

There was only one way to go, even though it was the very last thing he wanted to happen.

He stepped away and said, 'Sorry.'

Then he forced himself to open his eyes, and the dream

disappeared. He could see it dissolving into nothingness around him, leaving Fen standing alone on the bridge, tragically unkissed.

Jamie took a steadying breath, gazed up at the ceiling and wondered if he'd ever done anything more heroic in his life.

Or more idiotic, because it was only a dream after all. And God knows, it was what he'd wanted to do more than anything.

Except that was why he'd known he mustn't allow it to happen.

But since there was no one he could tell, *especially not Leon*, at least no one else would ever find out.

He closed his eyes and willed himself to get back to sleep. Preferably a sleep not punctuated by ethically troublesome dreams.

Or by the creeping realisation that if Leon hadn't been the one to stake his claim first, he wouldn't have hesitated for one second before making a move of his own on Fen Madden.

Breakfast in the restaurant was served buffet style. Making her way towards a free table, Hattie found herself being waylaid by Guy, seated by the window to her left.

'Morning! Care to join me?'

He was alone at a table for two. As she hesitated, a Canadian couple beat her to the other one.

'Is Suzanne not with you?'

'She's up on deck, saluting the sun. Yoga, then Pilates.' He gave a good-natured shake of his head. 'Followed by meditation. She doesn't eat breakfast.'

The restaurant was busy. Hattie put down her bowl of fresh fruit and plate of eggs Benedict and sat opposite him. Guy was tucking into a full English, which came as no surprise at all.

'Scrambled eggs *and* a fried egg?' Not to mention the bacon, sautéed potatoes and one of each kind of sausage.

He winked. 'Don't tell Suze. What she doesn't know won't kill her.'

'Might kill you.'

'Me? I'm indestructible.' He patted his stomach, then speared a mushroom and a cherry tomato. 'There, that's two of my five-a-day. Are you doing the trip to Vicenza later?'

A coach was taking anyone who wanted to go on a visit to Vicenza for tours of the Basilica Palladiana and the Olympic theatre. Hattie shook her head. 'No, Kayla's staying on the ship to sunbathe and I want to see more of Venice.'

'Me too!' His face brightened. 'Suze is catching the coach and meeting up with an old college friend who lives in Vicenza. We can explore together.'

One of the waiters filled their cups with fresh coffee. Hattie thanked him, then turned back to Guy. 'Wouldn't Suzanne find that a bit weird?'

No way could she bring herself to call her *Suze*.

'It wouldn't bother her at all. She isn't the jealous type.'

Or maybe she wasn't the jealous type when she was absolutely sure Guy's ex-wife was zero competition. Remembering the comment Suzanne had made about her last night, Hattie said drily, 'She thinks you'll be safe with me.'

'You could be right.' The twinkle was back in his eye. 'The question is, will I?'

It was moments like this that reminded her of the good times they'd spent together. When he was on playful, flirtatious form, Guy had been the best company. She took a sip of coffee, then said primly, 'I guess you'll have to wait and find out.'

Chapter 12

'There she is,' said Disa as they rounded a bend in the narrow path running alongside the canal.

Fen saw her at once, sitting at an aluminium-topped table outside a bar, wearing an orange shirt, denim shorts and white flip-flops. Having read her way through Molly's blog, she'd seen plenty of photos depicting all aspects of her life here in Venice. It was thanks to Molly that she'd learned that cafés in Italy were called bars. Her wavy brown hair was tied up in a casual topknot and there were silver bangles on her left arm, glinting in the sunlight as she checked her watch, then looked to the left and spotted them making their way towards her.

She was on her feet when they reached her, looking faintly apprehensive.

Disa said, 'Thank you for this. I know it must have come as a shock to you. And sorry for the subterfuge yesterday. But it's good to properly meet you.'

'Thanks.' Molly turned. 'And you must be Fenna. I gather you've only just found out about all this as well.'

Fen smiled. 'It's been a bit of a bolt from the blue.' But it was exciting, too. A brand-new relative, appearing out of nowhere, and she seemed nice.

'Who knew this was how I'd be spending my morning off?' Molly returned the smile. 'Are you OK, though?'

This pretty brunette, only three years her senior, was her aunt. Her mother's half-sister. Her grandfather's other daughter. Fen could barely tear her eyes away from her, because seeing her in those online photos was one thing, but recognising the filial similarities with her own mum was an emotional experience. Their colouring might be different, but they shared the same straight eyebrows, rounded cheeks and neat jawlines. The likeness was even more striking when it became apparent that both of them had inherited their unmistakable smile from Declan.

'You're seeing it as well, aren't you?' said Disa. 'It's the strangest sensation.'

Molly's straight eyebrows slanted with concern. 'In a bad way?'

'Not at all, just strange-strange, seeing hints of Declan in you.' As they pulled out chairs and sat down, Disa rested a hand on Molly's arm. 'It all happened many years ago. It's lovely to be able to meet you.'

'It probably sounds silly, but I can't help feeling a bit guilty. Before he died, it always felt like we'd been stealing a bit of him away from his real family.'

'You absolutely mustn't feel guilty. And you lost your birth father. That can't have been easy, even if you hadn't seen him for years.'

Molly looked at Fen. 'And you lost your mum. I'm so sorry.' She turned to Disa. 'For you too. It must have been unbearable.'

'It was. But we get through these things because we have to.' Disa nodded. 'We don't have a choice.'

They ordered from the waiter, then Molly glanced down at

the large canvas carrier bag on the ground next to Disa's chair. 'The things you mentioned bringing with you. Are they in that bag?'

'They are. Everything I found is in here.' Leaning sideways, Disa lifted it onto her lap. 'I didn't know if you'd want the photos of you with your dad, but—'

'*Yes*,' Molly blurted out, 'I really do. Please. We lost all our photo albums when a frozen pipe burst in the loft and flooded our flat, so I have hardly any pictures of him. Or of us together.'

'In that case, I'm glad I brought them with me.'

'Me too. It's so kind of you to do this. I really loved him.' Watching as Disa drew out the first packet of photographs, Molly's eyes sheened over. She blinked and surreptitiously wiped at them with her thumb.

When the waiter had brought their drinks and departed, Disa said, 'Your mother loved him too.'

'Are you angry with her?'

'Honestly? I don't know. Sometimes I am, other times it's easier. Then I find myself feeling sorry for her, because she never did get what she wanted.' Disa took a sip of her caffè macchiato. 'And it might be bad manners to read someone else's private correspondence, but when it's from your husband's mistress, I think it's allowed. Of course I read every letter.' She pulled out the padded envelope, then dropped it back into the bag. 'But I don't know if you should. Some of them are very emotional. Handing over the photos is the reason I'm here. If your mother would like to have her letters back, I can post them to her.'

'You'd do that?' Molly looked surprised.

'Why not? It all happened many years ago. Declan's no longer here for any of us. Ask her,' said Disa. 'If she doesn't want them,

I'll burn them myself. Anyway, there are plenty of photos for you to be going on with. He always did love taking them.'

Having watched Molly as she spread the photographs out over the table, Fen said suddenly, 'Mum used to do that!'

Molly looked up, confused. 'What, take lots of photos?'

'No, that thing with your hand.' As she'd been leaning in, studying the photographs and touching the corner of each one with her right hand, Molly had been rapidly tapping the second finger and thumb of her left hand together. 'It's exactly what she always did when she was concentrating on something.'

'You're right,' Disa exclaimed. 'She did!'

'That's so weird. It's a habit, something I've always done.' Molly was now gazing in fascination at her own left hand. 'Maybe we copied it from Dad.'

'Except I don't remember him ever doing it. But the more I look at you, the more similarities I'm seeing,' Disa marvelled. 'It's uncanny.'

Molly beamed and showed them a photo. 'I love this one.'

It was an informal snap, presumably taken by her mother, of Declan and Molly kicking their way through a mound of autumn leaves. He was laughing at her as she clutched handfuls of orange and crimson horse chestnut leaves and waved her arms in the air. Molly was around the age Fen had been when Disa had taken that photo of them together in the snow as they'd made their way home from school through Birdcage Walk. Pulling out her phone, Fen found it and showed Molly, who exclaimed, 'That's so brilliant! We both look so happy.' She paused, then added impulsively, 'I know we don't know each other at all, but meeting you today, it does kind of feel like we could be sisters.'

Fen looked at her and nodded. Yes, Molly was her aunt, but

it really did feel that way. Reaching for her hand, she gave it a squeeze. 'It does.'

'My goodness. You girls.' Disa dabbed at her eyes with a serviette. 'I'm so glad we found you.'

'Not as glad as I am.' Molly picked up another photo, the second finger and thumb still tap-tapping together as she studied it. Leaning sideways, Fen saw that this was one of Molly on her own, in a little red Santa suit, opening presents in front of a Christmas tree.

'Obviously we never saw Dad on Christmas Day. He usually came the week before, to drop off presents,' Molly explained. 'This must have been one of the last times I saw him. Mum wasn't happy about us being his dirty little secret, and she hated seeing me get so upset every time he left. She'd met Harry by then, and things had turned serious, so she told Dad it would be better if he didn't visit us any more. She wanted me to have a proper father figure, so we could live together like a normal family. I think those years of being a single parent were pretty hard for her.'

Disa nodded. 'They were. It's all there in the letters she sent him.'

'It can't have been easy for Dad either.' Molly shook her head. 'He couldn't split himself in two. Mum was doing what she thought was best for us. And I did like Harry; it was much better having him around all the time. As the years went by, although I still missed Dad, I suppose I got used to not seeing him any more. Plus, it wasn't as if I had a choice.'

'That's sad,' said Disa.

'My plan was always to get back in touch with him once I turned eighteen. But Harry was never keen on that idea, and I didn't want to upset him, so I ended up putting it off for a bit longer. But I told myself that was OK, because we had all the time in the world to get back together.' Molly gazed down at the photo in her right hand and took a slow breath. 'Except it turned out we didn't.'

Disa looked desolate. 'How did you find out?'

'Mum had always kept him updated about me. She wondered why he hadn't replied to her last letter, because he always did reply. She wrote again, and still nothing. That was when she called his office. They assumed she was a business client and told her he'd died three weeks earlier.'

'I can't imagine. Such a terrible shock.'

'It was. We looked his name up online and read about the accident. I was devastated, but I also felt so guilty, because I should have tried harder to see him again. And Mum was in pieces too.' Molly turned to Disa. 'Luckily you hadn't been into the office yet to collect his belongings. Mum contacted his secretary and asked her to destroy the letters she'd sent him after he'd died.'

'Margaret.' Fen remembered the name of her grandfather's long-standing secretary. 'So does that mean she knew about you and your mum?'

'I think so. Apparently she was very loyal to him. But the reason Mum did that was so you wouldn't find out about us.' Molly addressed Disa again. 'She didn't want to cause you any more grief than you were already going through.'

'That was good of her.' Disa nodded. 'I wondered if she expected to be left anything in his will.'

'No. Dad made monthly payments to her up until we moved in with Harry. She said he would have carried on, but Harry wanted to take over after that. And since she didn't want Dad to see me any more, she thought it was unfair to take his money. So that was when it stopped.'

Fen looked at Disa. 'But you never knew he was making regular payments?'

'He owned his own successful company. And I owned mine.' Disa shrugged. 'We kept separate bank accounts. Even if I'd wanted to examine his statements, which I didn't, he could have covered his tracks easily enough. If we'd been living on the breadline, it would have been a different matter, of course. But we weren't. Sweetheart, are you all right?' Concerned, she noticed Molly blinking back tears as she gazed at another photo.

'I'm OK.' Molly hastily wiped her eyes. 'It's . . . a lot. All the old memories are flooding back. I've just remembered he gave me a toy dog called Binky and used to call me Pinky. And when I knew he was coming to visit us, I'd stand at the bedroom window, waiting for his car to pull up outside. I was always bursting with excitement, knowing I was about to see him again. I really did love him, so much.'

'And he obviously loved you too. We can tell you more about him. We're here all week,' Disa reminded her. 'I tell you what, we've arranged to go out to dinner with Leon and Jamie tomorrow evening, at a little place behind the Ponte delle Guglie that's been recommended. If you're free, why don't you join us?' She shrugged. 'If you can't make it, we can arrange something for another night.'

'I'm working an early shift tomorrow, so that'd be perfect. And I've heard about that restaurant but never been there. It sounds fantastic.' Molly's eyes shone. 'Jamie's really nice, isn't he? It'd be fab to see him again.'

'Of course it would. Now we all know each other, why not make a party of it?'

Fen smiled, because this was Disa all over; collecting new friends and getting everyone together was what she loved to do, and by widening the circle, it might make tomorrow evening less intense, more relaxed and fun. Over the years, too, she'd shown a flair for matchmaking, and had gained a reputation for introducing people to each other who'd ended up becoming bona fide couples.

Glancing across at Molly, Fen wondered if her grandmother was about to add to that number. That was the thing about chemistry: you never could tell. Who knew when that elusive mutual spark between strangers might strike?

And was it more likely to happen when you were in one of the most romantic cities in the world?

Chapter 13

'I like you,' said Leon.

Fen nodded. 'I like you too.'

'I mean, really like you. A lot.'

'Same.'

They were lying side by side on a pair of adjoining sunloungers on the top deck of the ship, facing each other and keeping their voices low because there were other guests probably within earshot. Their hands were touching, their little fingers secretly entwined.

'I can't say the next thing,' Leon went on. 'Because it's too soon. I know that.' He curled his little finger more tightly around hers. 'But if it wasn't too soon, I'd definitely be saying it.'

'You mean you're really hungry but it's still another hour before dinner.'

He smiled. 'I'm talking about something even more important than food.'

She knew. Of course she knew. Every time she saw him, her own feelings towards him grew at what felt like an exponential rate.

'Anyway,' said Leon, 'when we get home, will you come with me to Hetherton? Meet the family?'

A sensation like warm honey pooled in her chest; it was the inevitable next step. 'If you want me to.'

'I do.'

'Will they like me?'

'They'd be mad not to. My friend Arabella has seen a photo of you.'

'How? Where?'

'She follows Jamie online. Someone tagged him in a pic down in the bar, and we're there in the background. Apparently I was looking a bit . . . smitten, so they've been bombarding me with questions.'

'And what did you tell them?'

His brown eyes glinted with mischief. 'That I'd met the like of my life.'

At this rate, she was going to have to hope she didn't run out of heartbeats. Giddy with happiness, Fen said, 'Let's hope you're right.'

Guy was hovering in the reception area when Hattie left the restaurant after dinner. Breaking into that familiar playful smile when he saw her, he said, 'Fancy a stroll?'

They'd already spent the day together, exploring the city, while Suzanne had been visiting her old university friend in Vicenza. It had been so like old times – the old *good* times – that she'd half wondered if he might be about to make a move on her.

But that hadn't happened. Of course it hadn't; he was with Suzanne now. Instead, he'd been an entertaining companion and an absolute gentleman, accompanying her around the antiques and vintage jewellery shops he knew she loved to explore, treating her to lunch, making her laugh and reminding her of the way they used to people-watch together in restaurants and make up stories about the other diners around them. In fact today had been one of the nicest days she'd had in years, until, on her way into the restaurant earlier, a voice behind her had called out, 'Stop,' and the voice had belonged to Suzanne.

'What is it?' Turning, Hattie had felt her heart skip a beat. Was she about to be roundly told off for spending the day with Guy?

But Suzanne only said, 'The label's sticking out the top of your dress.'

'Oh, thanks.'

'Don't mention it.' She tucked it back in. 'Goodness, it says size sixteen. You should probably cut that out so people don't see it.'

It hadn't even been said snidely. The words had been uttered in a concerned, *caring* way.

Now, two hours later, Hattie said to Guy, 'Where's Suzanne?'

The angelic, fat-shaming assassin.

'Bedtime story.'

'OK.'

They walked off the ship together and were soon away from the busy waterfront, melting instead into the maze of back streets and canals behind it. The sun had set and the ornate pink-tinted glass of the street lamps cast rose-gold pools of light onto the paving stones below, the warm night air enveloping them like silk.

She knew what was coming next, had been expecting it all day. It hadn't happened then, but of course with fewer people around and under cover of darkness, it was about to.

As they approached one of the tiny stone bridges crossing a narrow canal, Guy reached for her hand and slowed to a halt.

'What?' said Hattie.

'Look up.'

Following the direction of his pointing finger, she saw, in the gap between the high buildings on either side of them, a gleaming full moon.

'*La bella luna,*' he proclaimed with a sweeping gesture of his left arm, and she laughed because he was quoting from *Moonstruck*, the movie starring Cher that had been her favourite for so many years. Maybe it still was; she hadn't seen it since their break-up. But it had been something they'd both loved to watch, lying in bed together and reciting all the best lines as they appeared on the screen.

'*La bella luna!*' Hattie echoed.

Then Guy said, 'I'm in love with you,' and she laughed again, because this was Nicolas Cage's line. In the film, Cher responded by slapping him across the cheek and telling him to snap out of it. Hattie did the pretend slaps – first one side, then the other – and was about to utter Cher's immortal line when Guy reached up and clasped her hand.

'I'm not joking. I am still in love with you. And no, I can't snap out of it.'

She'd been expecting something, but not this. Definitely not this.

'I thought you were going to try and kiss me. To see if you could.'

'And I'd like to. But I want you to know it's more serious than that.'

'You're here on holiday with another woman. Who, by the way, thinks I'm the size of a house.'

'She worries about other people's weight,' said Guy.

'I'm not that overweight! I'm comfortable—'

'I know, I remember.' The twinkle was back in his eye.

'I'm comfortable in my own body, you moron,' said Hattie.

He flashed a grin. 'I remember that too. And I'm sorry, I know it isn't ideal, her being here, this happening now. But what can I do? I need you to know how I feel. I had no idea that seeing you again was going to affect me this much. It really did, though. I don't know if you even realise it, but our divorce broke me.'

He was saying it as if he meant it. She stared at him in disbelief. 'The reason we got divorced was because you very nearly broke *me*. You weren't exactly husband of the year.'

'I know that now. And I'm so sorry. Looking back, it was entirely my fault. When you said you'd had enough and the marriage was over, I should have fallen to my knees and begged for another chance, but my stupid pride got in the way. I was ashamed of how I'd behaved, but you'd made up your mind and I was sure you wouldn't let me change it. I made a massive mistake, the stupidest mistake of my life.' He took a step closer, reached for her hands. 'But I've learned from it, too. I really think I'm a better person now.'

'Except you're here on holiday with your girlfriend and telling another woman you still love her.'

'It sounds bad when you put it that way.'

'Because it *is* bad, Guy!'

'OK.' He sighed. 'I'm sorry. All I wanted to do was tell you how I felt . . . how I feel about you. I know I made mistakes in the past, I take full responsibility for that. But I've grown up since then, I promise. I lost you, and that was all down to me. But . . . Oh, forget I said any of this. I was right about you never changing your mind. You've built a new life for yourself, and that's a good thing. I'm happy for you. Come on, let's get back to the ship. I won't bother you again, I promise.'

Hattie felt her stomach drop; it was like walking past a bakery, spotting a single immaculate cupcake in the window and wondering idly whether to treat yourself, then seeing it being bought by someone else. What had been mildly tempting thirty seconds ago suddenly became the cake you wanted more than anything else in the world.

Guy had turned and was starting to make his way back along the footpath. Glancing up, she saw the velvet-dark sky and that glowing full moon again.

La bella luna, shining down on them, bringing back memories of happier times.

She was only human, after all.

And what was wrong with being a size sixteen anyway?

Catching up with Guy, she reached for his arm and swung him round to face her.

'I've given you my word,' said Guy. 'I'm not going to pester you.'

'One kiss,' said Hattie. 'Just the one. For old times' sake.'

She saw his quick intake of breath. But he didn't hesitate. She closed her eyes, drowning in the sense of delicious, never-forgotten familiarity, because kisses were as individual as fingerprints, and this was something Guy had always been good at.

He hadn't lost his touch.

Flushed with success, she drew away after thirty seconds or so. Perhaps forty. Maybe a minute.

'Hattie.' He tried to pull her back for more.

'That's it.' She shook her head. 'Done. Now we need to get back to the ship.'

'You're killing me.'

She was glad that he couldn't see her smiling in the darkness. 'Good.'

★

A couple of hours later, Hattie was happily chatting with a professional portrait artist called Marla when Suzanne appeared in the bar in front of her.

'I found something I think belongs to you.' As she said it, she was digging in her handbag, and Hattie's guilt knew no bounds, because even if it was a completely impossible scenario, what if she pulled out a pair of size sixteen lacy knickers? What if she had followed them off the ship and had been spying on them when she'd initiated that kiss? Oh God, karma was out to get her; what had she been *thinking*?

Suzanne said, 'These are yours, aren't they?' and held up a pair of sunglasses.

The relief.

'Yes! I thought I'd lost them.' They were her favourite pair, a massive bargain from TK Maxx, three years old now but still in one piece and miraculously unscratched.

'You left them on a sunlounger up on deck. I managed to rescue them in time before one of those Texans sat on them.'

'Thank you so much.' Hattie clutched them to her chest and felt even more guilty. Suzanne was a good person after all. Maybe they could be friends and—

'If you don't mind me saying so, they don't do you any favours. When you have such a round face, that style of frame is the last thing you should go for. Here, try these on and I'll show you what I mean.' Suzanne produced her own dark glasses from her bag and passed them over.

Dumbfounded, Hattie put them on.

After studying her from all angles, Suzanne shook her head sorrowfully. 'Oh dear no, take them off, those don't suit you either. They make you look even worse.'

Chapter 14

'You know when you've been looking forward to something so much that you know it's going to be disappointing when it finally happens?'

'Like when you're a kid and you dream of getting a PlayStation for Christmas,' said Leon, 'and you end up with a new winter anorak instead?'

Lying in his arms in bed, Fen nodded. 'Exactly like that.'

'Go on then, break it to me. Am I the PlayStation or the anorak?'

She grinned, because they both knew the answer to that. Having waited long enough, they'd snuck away from everyone else shortly after dinner and come to Leon's cabin. She'd never known it was possible for an evening to be so completely perfect.

And it wasn't over yet.

'You're no anorak, put it that way. In fact, I'd say you're pretty stupendous.' She ran her bare foot over his kneecap, along his shin and down to his toes. Naked, he had an excellent body, tanned and finely muscled. But even if it hadn't been excellent, she knew she would still have just had the best sex of her life, because this was Leon and he was all she wanted. With him, there were no inhibitions and no tension. She was hot, naked and as happy and relaxed as it was possible to be with another person, which was what made the experience so extra-special.

'You're everything I've ever dreamt of.' He kissed her shoulder as her fingers danced across his chest. 'And I know that sounds OTT, but it's true. All these years I've been waiting to meet the right person, and now I have. You're the one.'

'What a coincidence. So are you.' She curled her arm around the back of his neck and pulled him in for another kiss.

'I always hoped it would happen. But after a while, you start to wonder if it ever will.'

Gently, she bit his bottom lip. 'You do.'

'I guess I owe it all to Jamie for bringing me along with him on this trip.'

'And Disa brought me.'

Leon slowly shook his head, brown eyes full of wonder. 'What if they hadn't? What if we'd never met? It doesn't bear thinking about.'

'But we don't have to think about it. We've found each other. We're here.'

They lay together in silence for a long moment. Outside, the water lapped gently against the side of the ship. Church bells began to chime, ringing in the hour. Leon kissed her on the temple and murmured, 'This, right here, is my favourite place in the world. This bed. This city. Everything about it is perfect. When I die, I want my ashes scattered here.'

Fen wrinkled her nose. 'In this bed? Won't someone else be sleeping in it?'

He laughed. 'In the water, then. The Venetian lagoon. Will you make sure that happens?'

'Me?'

He shrugged and stroked a strand of curly blonde hair out of her eye. 'Well, I'm planning on living until I'm eighty-five, so we've got a while to go. We'll have been married for over fifty years by then. You'd do that for me, wouldn't you?'

Married! Of course he was saying it in a jokey way, but just the fact that he'd uttered the word made her quiver inwardly with delight. There was no harm in picturing it, was there? And what would he look like at eighty-five? He might have lost all his hair and gained a lifetime of wrinkles, but he'd still be Leon. And hopefully she'd still love him. She couldn't imagine not doing so. She pulled him closer. 'If it's what you want, of course I will.'

'He's so fit,' Kayla sighed. 'He's out of this world. And he has the best arms I've ever seen.'

'Did he pay you back the money he owed you?'

'Not yet. But he will.'

'Did you ask him?'

'Yes, because that's the best way to make a man fall for you and want to see you again. Always a good look, nagging and complaining like an old fishwife.'

Hattie gave up. It was seven in the morning and Kayla had just floated into the cabin after spending a second night with Angelo the gondolier. At least this time she'd messaged Hattie at midnight to let her know.

'I think you're jealous because you don't have anyone.' Kayla stretched like a cat and yawned happily. 'You were OK here, though, were you? Anything exciting happen?'

'Just had a quiet evening.' Hattie kept her tone casual. 'There was a singer in the bar, he was really good.'

'Did you have wild sex with him?'

'Funnily enough, no.'

'You should try it sometime. It's fun!'

Yes, but I snogged my ex . . .

She didn't say it, couldn't take the risk. Kayla would never deliberately cause trouble, but sometimes words spilled out before she'd had time to wonder if it might be a better idea to keep some thrilling bit of newly discovered gossip to herself.

'The singer's wife was with him,' Hattie said. 'And he was at least seventy.'

Kayla yawned. 'All this sex is exhausting. Will you be OK on your own today?'

Hattie nodded. This might not be turning out to be the holiday she'd been expecting, but Venice had captured her heart nonetheless. 'I'll be fine, don't worry about me. The private tour of the Doge's Palace starts at nine.'

'Wow.' Another noisy yawn while Kayla shed her clothes. 'So much excitement, I can't believe I'm going to miss it. Give my love to the Doge, won't you? Whatever a Doge might be.'

'It's going to be so interesting.' Hattie had been reading up on the history of the city. 'The palace sounds stunning, and we get to visit the prison too, connected to it by the Bridge of Sighs. It's called that because men sentenced for execution would glimpse the lagoon through the stone windows and know it was the last time they'd ever be able to see the city they loved.'

'Fascinating.' Spread-eagled face down on her bed, Kayla spoke in a muffled voice. 'Absolutely riveting, but could you shush now, I have to sleep.'

The sun was setting in an apricot sky, the warm evening air in central Venice was heavy with garlicky cooking smells, and the sounds of an orchestra playing Vivaldi's *Four Seasons* drifted out from a nearby church. The five of them were seated around an oval table outside the restaurant, in a small square lined with bars and shops and buzzing with tourists and locals alike.

Despite slathering on suncream during their afternoon on the island of Torcello, Fen could feel the heat blooming on her bare shoulders and see the veil of pinkness that would hopefully fade to brown by tomorrow. Out of sight beneath the tabletop, Leon was holding her hand, slowly stroking her knuckles with his thumb while simultaneously resting the outside of his thigh against her own bare leg. It was like the most delicious secret, because no one else had any idea it was going on, which made it even more of a thrill. Until the waiter arrived with their main courses, and while everyone else's attention was diverted, Jamie caught her eye across the table and murmured, 'Sure you're going to be able to concentrate on the food?'

The low sun was shining directly into his sapphire-blue eyes as he observed her with amusement; the secret evidently wasn't so secret after all. Determined not to blush, Fen glanced at Molly, sitting to his right, then back at Jamie, and drawled with matching sangfroid, 'Are you?'

If he was making fun of her, she could make fun right back. Because at this moment Molly might be comparing her food with Disa's, but for the last forty-five minutes she'd evidently been finding it hard to tear her attention away from Jamie. Seeing him again this evening had caused her face to visibly light up; her interest in him was unmistakable. Now, as she turned to bring him into the conversation, lightly touching his arm as she did so, Fen watched and wondered if Jamie was as attracted to her as Molly was to him. In a few days, this holiday would be over and he'd be flying back to the UK.

Thank goodness she and Leon would be heading back together.

Having also noticed the goings-on across the table, Leon gave her knee a squeeze.

Jamie was telling Disa he wanted to buy a Murano glass necklace for his mother. Clasping his wrist, Molly exclaimed, 'I can definitely help you with that – I know all the best shops. There's one a couple of streets from here that has the most fantastic designs, and the owner doesn't rip you off – I can show you where it is before it closes!'

The rest of the food was arriving at their table, looking and smelling as superb as the online reviews had promised.

'Sounds like a plan,' said Jamie.

An hour later, the next two courses had been eaten and cleared away. Wine and espressos were still being enjoyed and Disa had charmed their waiter into taking photos of the five of them as reminders of the evening. Molly looked at Jamie's watch and said, 'That jewellery shop will be closing soon. We should shoot over there now.'

'I haven't finished my drink.' Disa raised her slender glass of Strega, the clear yellow liqueur gleaming like a tiger's eye in the candlelight. 'You two go. We'll wait here for you.'

'Won't be long.' Jamie rose to his feet and Molly jumped up too.

'We'll find your mum something fabulous,' she promised, looping her arm through his.

They disappeared together into one of the narrow streets leading off the square, and Disa said wryly, 'So much for my matchmaking talents. I didn't expect this to happen.'

'Jamie's like one of those giant magnets,' Leon said cheerfully. 'All he has to do is look at a woman, and *donkkk*, she superglues herself to him.'

'Not *every* woman.' Disa indicated Fen at his side.

'Not every woman,' he agreed, giving Fen's waist a squeeze. 'Thank goodness. But it happens pretty much all the time. You should see the way they—'.

'NOOOO!' A panicky shout rang out behind them, and they swivelled round to see an older woman, another customer of the restaurant, grappling with a teenage boy who'd lunged at the expensive-looking leather shoulder bag she'd left hanging over the back of her chair.

'Get off, *get off.*' The woman, who was American, was fighting a losing battle, and her husband, also yelling, was too frail to help. But Leon was already on his feet, his chair falling back with a clatter as he shot over to them, just as the teenager won the struggle for the bag and began to race away. Leon took off after him like a bullet, scattering a group of pigeons, which flew up in alarm. Everyone in the vicinity was watching them now, and a few people were shouting at the thief to stop, but no one else had joined the chase, possibly because Leon was gaining ground.

As the boy reached the edge of the square and was about to disappear down a narrow alleyway, Leon caught up with him and managed to grab the strap of the woman's bag. A brief furious tussle ensued, and the boy swung him round, slamming him into the wall with such force that Leon let out a gasp of pain and collapsed to the ground. But he still had the bag clutched to his chest. The boy began frenziedly kicking at him to release it, but Leon refused to let go. The next moment, twisting round and kicking out himself, he made contact with the teenager's leg, causing the thief to yelp, curse and abandon his hold on the strap. The boy spun round and raced off down the alleyway, vanishing in less than a second.

Chapter 15

Still out of breath, Leon returned the bag to the grateful American woman, then came and sat back down next to Fen.

'Are you hurt?' Her own heart was racing.

He shrugged. 'I'm OK.'

'You were amazing. Like Superman. Except that boy could have had a knife.'

'But he didn't. I'm fine.'

Other people around them had applauded and congratulated him as he'd come back with the bag, limping slightly but visibly embarrassed by the attention. He wasn't fine, but clearly he didn't want a fuss made, so Fen let it go.

Less than three minutes later, Jamie and Molly returned from their trip to the jeweller's.

'Would you believe it? They closed early tonight.' Molly was indignant. 'Typical! Never mind.' She beamed at Jamie, next to her. 'I'll take you back there tomorrow when they're open.'

'You don't need to,' he told her. 'I know where it is now. I can go by myself.'

'I think I should be with you, though. You'll get a better price.'

'You missed Leon being a total hero,' Disa chimed in, and promptly launched into the story, interrupted only by the American couple stopping by to thank him again for his actions before leaving the restaurant. If he was ever in Texas, they told him, he was welcome to come and stay with them on their family ranch for as long as he liked.

When the pair had left, Jamie exclaimed, 'Hey, good for you,' and clapped him on the back, causing Leon to say mildly, 'Ow.'

'Sorry. But if you will keep swooping in to the rescue, it's going to happen.' He turned to the others. 'This isn't his first time, you know. When we were at uni, he rescued a lad who'd got into difficulty swimming in the river. Saved his life. And another time he climbed up a tree to help a kid who'd got stuck and was panicking.'

'OK,' said Disa, 'that makes you a superhero.'

'What he hasn't mentioned is that I'd had a few beers before the tree thing.' Leon pulled a face. 'I managed to get the kid down far enough for Jamie to catch him, then lost my balance and fell off the last branch. Landed flat on my back in a patch of nettles.'

'I still have the video of that,' said Jamie. 'It was hilarious.'

'You could have really hurt yourself,' Disa protested.

Jamie was still laughing. 'It was just his pride. And those nettle stings all over his arms. We're never going to let him forget it.'

Dinner was over. As they prepared to leave, Molly turned to Jamie. 'If you fancy staying out for another drink, I know a brilliant little bar behind the Piazza San Marco.' Then, when he hesitated for a moment, she amended hastily, 'I don't just mean you and me. We could all go.'

'Not for me, thanks.' Disa shook her head. 'I'm going to head back to the ship.'

'I think we will too.' Leon checked with Fen. 'If that's all right with you?'

'It's fine.' He was limping while trying not to; Fen could see he was in pain. 'I'm happy to go back.'

'You can't turn me down too.' Molly gave Jamie a pleading look. 'It's not that late.'

He hesitated, then said, 'OK, let's go.'

'Yay!' Molly hugged the rest of them. 'It's been so lovely. See you again soon.'

'She really likes him,' Disa observed, watching Molly and Jamie set off towards the Piazza San Marco. 'Oh dear, let's hope he doesn't break her heart.'

Leon gave Fen's hand another secret squeeze and murmured, 'He probably will.'

Once back on the ship, Disa was swiftly commandeered by a handsome Danish architect and borne off to the top deck for dancing and cocktails.

Fen and Leon retired to his cabin and made love with care because his torso and legs were already coming out in prominent bruises from the vicious kicking he'd received and there was a nasty graze on his back.

'Be gentle with me,' he whispered into her ear. Then, a couple of minutes later, 'Not as gentle as that.'

Afterwards, he swilled a couple of painkillers down with iced water and they lay in each other's arms.

'That was a brave thing you did this evening,' Fen told him.

He smiled. 'Were you impressed? Does it make you like me more?'

'I think it does. It's a shame Jamie and Molly missed it. They'd have been impressed too.'

'Honestly? I'll let you into a secret. Jamie's fitter and faster than me. If he'd been there, he'd have beaten me to it and got all the praise. And maybe then you'd have decided you preferred him to me.'

She shook her head. 'I wouldn't.'

'You might. He would have caught the guy and marched him off to the nearest police station. Not let him get away.'

'Hey, there were dozens of people in that square when it happened. You were the only one who did anything. And now you have two new best friends in Texas.' She kissed him. 'And I definitely prefer you. Which is why I'm here with you now. I don't spend the night in just anybody's cabin, you know.'

'Glad to hear that.' He returned the kiss. 'Mind you, if you spend tonight in Jamie's cabin, I'm guessing you'll be on your own, because he'll be over at Molly's place with her.'

Echoing Disa's comment earlier, Fen said, 'I hope she doesn't end up getting hurt.'

'You never know.' Leon shrugged. 'One day Jamie's going to find the woman of his dreams. It has to happen sooner or later, and maybe it's Molly. She could turn out to be the one he's been waiting to meet all his life.'

'You can come in for a drink if you like.' Molly's tone had been casual, but hope shone in her hazel eyes.

Jamie shook his head. 'Thanks, but I've had enough.' They'd spent the last hour and a half in her favourite bar and he'd walked her back to her apartment in Cannaregio.

'Coffee, then?' She'd gazed up at him. If he agreed, he knew what would happen next.

'Best not. I should get back.'

'Well, that's a shame.' Her flirtatious smile wasn't giving up yet. 'If you want to, you're welcome to stay. And not because you're famous. Nothing to do with that. It just feels as if we have, you know, a good connection.'

For a long moment he'd almost been tempted, because why not? Where was the harm? But no, he'd made his polite excuses and left, returning to the ship and joining a group of rugby enthusiasts up on deck because Leon and Fen had retired to Leon's cabin and he knew only too well what they would be getting up to.

Anyway, that had been last night, seventeen hours ago. He'd slept well, and alone, and had woken early, not regretting his decision at all but at the same time still somewhat intrigued by the fact that he'd made it. At the grand old age of thirty-one, was this nature's way of letting him know that it was time to grow up and settle down?

It was now Thursday afternoon and the ship had sailed across the Venetian lagoon earlier, bringing them to Burano. Along with almost all the other guests on board, they had gone ashore and explored the small but staggeringly picturesque island. What it lacked in gondolas it more than made up for with its uniquely colourful and photogenic buildings and air of celebration.

Exploring the shops along with Leon and Fen, Jamie chose a striking cranberry glass pendant for his mother while Leon bought a set of multicoloured tumblers and a hand-made lace tablecloth for his parents, as well as an iridescent peacock-blue silk kaftan for Fen. Then it was time to set sail once more, back to Venice, taking photos and videos all the way.

Once they were moored alongside Riva dei Sette Martiri, Jamie left Leon and Fen to it – *it* undoubtedly being more sex

– and returned to his own cabin to shower and change before his six o'clock stint as guest speaker in the private lounge. Then, after dinner there was a trip scheduled for a private visit to the Basilica di San Marco, which evidently was an experience not to be missed.

He checked his messages, skimming through the notifications. A publisher was enquiring whether he'd be interested in writing his autobiography. His agent had updated him with a couple of upcoming TV appearances. A male 'fan' who'd recently complained that he'd worn the same azure-blue shirt twice in a month on TV was now asking him to donate it to him, unwashed, and complaining that the charcoal-grey shirt he'd worn on last week's show had been boring.

No pleasing some people.

There were other comments on his Instagram account, chiefly from male rugby fans and females keen for him to slide into their DMs.

There was also one from Arabella, one of his and Leon's friends: *Hey, you! Leon says he's going to introduce us to this new girlfriend of his when they get back – he looks pretty loved up in the background of that photo you were tagged in, so we're dying to know what she's like. Nice? Awful? You're the expert on women, so we trust your judgement. Do you like her?*

Jamie took a breath and gazed out of the window as a sleek white motorboat sped by in one direction while a longer blue boat chugged past in the other. To the left, several noisy seagulls were tussling over something on the deck of a fishing vessel.

Did he like her?

Do I like her?

There it was, the question he couldn't truthfully answer.

With a clatter of wings, one of the seagulls rose triumphantly into the air, a small fish clasped in its beak, while the others squawked in protest.

Choosing his words with care, he replied to Arabella: *No need to worry, she definitely isn't awful. You'll like her, I promise.*

Chapter 16

When those who'd been there before had told Fen a tour of the Basilica di San Marco was an unforgettable experience not to be missed, she had agreed to go along but her expectations hadn't been high. Obviously it would be impressive, but she hadn't imagined for one moment that it would be anything more than that.

How wrong could one person be? It was so, *so* much more.

There were no other tourists permitted in the cathedral during these private visits. If the basilica was wonderful from the outside, the interior effortlessly outdid it. The gold mosaics and the artwork painstakingly created and added to over the course of many centuries were extraordinary. The architecture was overwhelming, from the floor of inlaid marble and glass to the domed ceilings adorned with intricate paintings that took your breath away.

Coupled with so much stunning beauty, however, was the atmosphere of the place. It was the realisation that for over a thousand years, Venetians had been coming here during times of trouble and peace to worship and pray for those they loved and had lost. When the lighting ceremony took place, the burnished gold mosaics glowed more intensely and the colours in the paintings grew more vivid; it was as if the characters depicted were coming alive before her eyes.

When they were invited to explore, Leon turned to the right to more closely examine a painting that had evidently caught his eye. Fen followed several others making their way to the front of the church, where the high altar was adorned with the Pala d'Oro, an astonishing Byzantine altarpiece of gold and enamel studded with precious jewels.

Close up, the sight of it provoked an unexpected wave of emotion that caused a lump to expand in her throat. Overwhelmed by the beauty of the craftwork, the atmosphere and the sheer joy of being allowed to witness something so magical, she felt her eyes fill with hot tears. Which was totally embarrassing, because no one else appeared to be having this reaction. Attempting to move away, she squeezed between two other visitors and realised her breath was starting to judder in her lungs, as if an audible sob might be on its way out. Plus, it was threatening to be loud, which would be even more humiliating.

'You OK?'

It was Jamie. He'd noticed. Not much got past him.

'I'm fine.'

She'd kept her voice low, and he did too. 'You don't look fine.' He was frowning now. 'Something wrong? Is it to do with Leon?'

This was such a crazy idea that she did one of those undignified splutters that was half laughter, half sob.

'No! Although, kind of. Oh, help, and I don't have any tissues.' Fen gestured helplessly at the vaulted ceilings and the dazzling gold altarpiece. 'It's all so b-beautiful, everything's perfect, and I've found Leon and Disa's found Molly and it's the best holiday I've ever had. I've never been so happy and I don't know what I've done to deserve all of this and now I'm really crying and you must think I'm a complete *lunatic*.'

The words had come rushing out in a torrent and her cheeks were properly wet. Mortified, she wiped her face with both hands. 'It's this place, it's really got to me. I can't get over how people b-built something so incredible.'

Jamie's mouth had begun to twitch at the corners. Her breath catching in her throat, Fen whispered, 'Please don't make fun of me. I already feel stupid enough.'

And now he was laughing, but quietly. 'I'm not making fun of you, I'm just glad nothing's wrong. And I'm happy you're happy.' Producing a clean tissue from his pocket, he passed it to her then briefly rested his hand in the small of her back as a couple of the Australian guests edged past them. 'Cry as much as you like. I'm the same when I hear "Nessun Dorma". Sometimes these things get to you and there's no stopping it.'

His hand had only made contact with her spine for a moment; one second it was there, the next it was gone. But the sensation of his fingers against the fine cotton of her shirt remained, sending zip-zaps of adrenalin radiating outwards like the chrysanthemum burst of a firework. Fen's eyes widened and a tiny shiver went through her. Had he felt that too? Except of course he hadn't; all he'd done was politely shield her from being jostled. And now he was turning away, studying a statue, pointing it out to one of the other people on the tour.

Right, time to get a grip. At least the tears had stopped and her breathing was under control. The tsunami of emotion had swept her up, but now she was back to normal. And here came Leon.

'This place is out of this world,' he exclaimed. 'I've just taken sixteen photos of a pair of marble angels.' He paused. 'Are you all right? Your eyes look a bit pink.'

'It's made me all emotional. Jamie had to give me a tissue. Are *you* OK?' Because he'd winced while twisting sideways to duck out of the way of someone else's photo.

'Absolutely. It's only the bruises coming out.'

Jamie rejoined them, shaking his head. 'Going for the old sympathy vote, are you? Such an attention-seeker.'

'I've never broken any ribs.' Leon touched his left side and gingerly pressed it. 'What does it feel like?'

Jamie frowned. 'If you really think they're broken, you should see someone about it, get yourself checked out.'

Leon grinned. 'Are you calling me a wuss? Of course they're not broken. And I'm on holiday, aren't I? Definitely not trotting off to the hospital to be poked and prodded about.'

'Maybe you should,' said Fen.

'That's not going to happen. It isn't only rufty-tufty rugby players who can be big and brave, you know.' He landed a playful fist on Jamie's arm. 'No need to fuss. By tomorrow I'll be fine.'

The situation was getting trickier. No, scratch that. It was turning into a total nightmare and Jamie wasn't liking it one bit.

The private tour was over and everyone was making their way back along the waterfront to the ship. The night was still, the stars were out, and all around them in one of the most romantic cities in the world were couples, arm in arm and with their heads together, either walking along or sitting on benches, speaking earnestly, groping each other or kissing as if their lives depended on it.

Upon leaving the basilica, he'd found himself buttonholed by

Matt and Margot from Uttoxeter. Matt on his left was intent on talking rugby, while Margot on his right was bursting with questions about every celebrity he'd ever appeared with on TV. Their chatter was entertaining, but he was unable to enjoy the repartee as much as he normally would. Instead he found himself replying to them both on autopilot, his mind elsewhere. Up ahead were Leon and Fen, laughing, chatting non-stop and holding hands as they strolled along. Even from behind, you could sense their connection and the strength of feeling between the two of them.

As Jamie watched, Leon stopped walking and drew Fen against him, his free hand curling around her neck as he pulled her in for a lingering kiss.

There it was again, that specific sensation in the centre of his chest. He might not be able to describe the feeling, but he knew for sure he didn't like it.

He knew what it meant, though. He liked Fen Madden. More than liked her, more than he'd ever liked a woman before.

He wanted her, but couldn't have her.

Maybe if he'd been the one to meet her first . . .

Except he *had* met her first, outside that bar on Whiteladies Road, but he hadn't known it was her and she'd been nothing more than a figure in the shadows, giving him a brief lesson in good manners before watching him walk away.

It had been his big chance and he'd missed it. That was karma for you. If he'd changed his mind about going inside, had turned up at her super-keen friend's party, he would have seen her properly, spoken to her some more and got to know her better, then been intrigued enough to know he wanted to see her again. And again. The wheels of fate could have been set in motion and everything would be different now, because how he was beginning to feel about Fen was worlds apart from how he'd always felt about girlfriends in the past.

But none of that had happened, because he'd made the wrong decision, had metaphorically dropped the all-important ball.

And now there was nothing, absolutely *nothing*, he could do about it. He couldn't even try. Leon was his best friend and there was no way he could do that to him.

'Hello? You're miles away!' Margot was laughing and waving a hand in front of his face. 'Earth to Jamie!' She eyed him avidly. 'I was asking you what that comedian's like, the one you do the sports quiz with?'

'Sorry, I was thinking about the basilica.' Was using a place of worship as an excuse punishable by God? 'You mean Rick? He's a good guy, always fun to work with.' This wasn't remotely true, but it was his standard response to the question.

'Really?' Margot looked disappointed. 'My friend Geraldine met him once and she said he was really rude to her.'

Away from the cameras, being really rude to people was Rick's favourite thing, but Jamie wasn't going to fall into the trap of agreeing with her. Ahead of them, the kiss was now over and Leon and Fen were walking once more, her arm around his waist while his was at hip level, his hand tucked comfortably into the back pocket of her pink jeans.

Jamie looked away, recalling the moment in the church when he'd realised how overcome with emotion Fen was and had attempted to comfort her. It had only been the briefest of touches, but the effect on him had been electrifying, so much so that a surge of adrenalin had whipped through his body with such intensity that he'd wondered if it was even possible that Fen had felt it too.

He'd told himself that he hadn't meant to do it, but that was a lie; making voluntary physical contact with someone you liked was never really an accident, was it? Subconsciously, you felt compelled to touch them.

Which was something else he had to make sure he never did again. From now on, there needed to be zero touching. And yes, he could manage that, because in the long run it was the easier option. He couldn't describe the way he was feeling, but it had – *had* – to stop. Like an alcoholic realising he must never have another drink, because one would never be enough. It was called self-control.

Up ahead, Fen was now answering her phone. Seconds later, Leon turned and waved to attract Jamie's attention.

'Molly's managed to switch to an early shift, so shall we all meet up tomorrow evening?'

Did he want to? Not particularly, but what else would he do? It would be rude to refuse. He said, 'Up to you. I'm easy.'

Leon laughed. 'Well, we all know *that*.'

Margot, still at his side, gave him a hefty nudge. 'I don't know who this Molly is, but if you ask me, she's a lucky girl!'

Chapter 17

Heading up onto the busy sun deck at one o'clock on Friday, Jamie made his way over to the table for two occupied by Kayla's friend and said, 'Hi there, is this seat free?'

She looked up from the book she'd been reading. 'It is. And you don't have to worry, it's safe. Kayla's gone to meet her chap.'

'I saw her leaving the ship an hour ago. She doesn't seem to have been around much.'

'I know. She's completely crazy about her gondolier. Which lets you off the hook.' As he pulled out the spare chair, she added, 'And I promise not to talk to you about rugby.'

He laughed; this was why he'd chosen to join her. 'It's been a bit non-stop this morning. You're Hattie, yes?'

'That's right.'

'And the guy over there,' he pointed discreetly, 'is your ex?' It hadn't taken long for word to get around that Hattie's former husband and his current younger partner were also on the ship.

She nodded. 'For my sins.'

'What's the girlfriend like? Friendly?'

'Suzanne?' Hattie's tone was wry. 'She thinks I'm the frumpy older ex-wife. Not worth bothering with.'

'What? You're not frumpy.'

'Maybe not compared with other older ex-wives. But compared to her, I'm geriatric, overweight and out of shape. As she's pointed out to me more than once.'

Jamie shook his head, because this wasn't remotely true either. 'But I've seen you and your ex chatting together. It's good that you get on well.'

Hattie looked as if she was about to say something, then checked herself and nodded instead. The next moment, eyes sparkling, she blurted out, 'We do, actually. Better than his girlfriend realises. And I shouldn't have said that, but I couldn't help myself. I trust you, though, so please don't tell anyone. Even Kayla doesn't know.'

'You can absolutely trust me. Now I'm intrigued. So are the two of you having a thing?'

She grinned at his choice of words. 'You mean are we sleeping together? Absolutely not. But only because I'm saying no. I'm sure Guy would, like a shot.'

'And you aren't tempted?'

'It's more fun knowing he wants to. I know that probably makes me sound like a bad person,' said Hattie. 'But Suzanne keeps putting me down because she thinks I'm the keen one, desperate to be noticed. If she was friendlier, I'd be on her side.'

'She's coming over.' Jamie lowered his voice as Suzanne, in a barely-there olive-green bikini, sashayed towards them.

'Hello.' She greeted them both, then turned to Hattie. 'I don't know if you're aware how important it is to protect your skin, but you've been out here for over ninety minutes now and you haven't applied sunscreen.'

'I did it before I left the cabin.' Hattie smiled up at her.

'Exactly. So you really should be reapplying by now. And using factor fifty, with your skin. You don't want those wrinkles on your neck getting even worse.'

She sauntered off to the staircase, clearly aware that everyone else was admiring her sinuous body.

'Wow,' Jamie marvelled. 'I definitely think you should sleep with him now.'

'Probably not going to happen.' Hattie laughed. 'But I'll let you know if it does.' She indicated the watch on his left wrist. 'That's very nice. Vintage, too. Seventy years old, am I right?'

Impressed, he nodded. 'I bought it a couple of years ago. You know your watches, then?'

'I work in an antiques shop now, but I trained as a jeweller. My speciality was old watches and vintage jewellery. Yours is very special.' Checking her own, she said, 'Time for some lunch, then I'm off on the tour of the Fortuny Museum.'

'And I have another interview lined up in an hour.' Watching as she gathered up her bag, her book and her bottle of water, Jamie said, 'Nice to talk to you. See you again. Have fun.'

Hattie grinned. 'But not the naughty kind. Bye.'

Later that afternoon, back from her trip and going through the photos on her phone in the deliciously cool, almost empty bar, Hattie found herself being approached by Disa, as glamorous as ever in an emerald-green kaftan edged with silver thread.

'I have a big favour to ask.' Disa perched on the arm of the chair next to hers. 'Jamie tells me you're a jeweller. I wondered if you'd be an angel and take a look at a ring of mine. But if you can't or don't want to do it, please say. I'd completely understand.'

'Of course I can take a look. You wear beautiful jewellery – I was secretly admiring your tennis bracelet last night.' Hattie scanned the glittering rings on Disa's fingers. 'Which one is it?'

But as she reached for her handbag – as a jeweller, she never went anywhere without her loupe – she saw that Disa was taking a dark blue velvet ring box from her own bag.

'It's this one. If you could check it over, see what you think, I'd be grateful.'

Hattie opened the box and experienced the all-too-rare thrill of appreciation at the sight of a truly special item of jewellery.

'Well, well.' She fitted the loupe into her eye socket and took out the ring to study it under magnification. 'It's an old European-cut diamond.' Carefully examining it from all angles, she said, 'I'd estimate it at four carats. Accented by smaller single-cut diamonds. The colour of the central diamond is F or G, which is good. The cut is excellent. Clarity . . .' she studied it more intently, 'VS1.'

'That's interesting.' Disa nodded slowly. 'I took it to a guy not long ago who said the clarity wasn't that good. Nor the colour. He wanted to buy it from me, but I'd already decided I didn't like him, so I left the shop. Not that I was planning to sell it anyway.'

'What was his offer?' said Hattie, and shook her head when Disa told her.

'Thank goodness you didn't let it go for that. I can't give you an official valuation, but that was way too low. At the very least, it's worth twice as much.'

'That's really helpful.' Disa returned the ring to the velvet box and dropped it back into her bag. 'Thanks so much for letting me know.'

'My pleasure. It's a stunning ring.' Hattie wagged a finger at her. 'But for goodness' sake, don't have it rattling around in your bag like a lip balm. Make sure you keep it locked away in the safe.'

Disa smiled. 'Don't worry. I will.'

'She's gone,' said Guy.

'What?' Hattie had been on her way back to the cabin when he'd waylaid her in reception. 'Who's gone?' Oh no! His mother was in her eighties and frail; had she died?

'Suze.' He was visibly shell-shocked, clutching his phone. 'She told me she needed to meditate in peace in our cabin, so I spent an hour up on deck talking to Jamie about the World Cup. When I went back, she'd cleared all her stuff out. Packed everything into her case and left.'

Gone. No one was dead, though, which was good. Hattie rearranged her sad-death-of-an-elderly-relative expression.

'Without saying anything?'

'She's just sent me a video.' Guy thrust the phone at her and pressed play.

'Hello, Guy.' Suzanne's face filled the screen. She had recorded the message in their cabin. 'I'd apologise for doing it this way, but if I'd told you I was leaving, you might have tried to persuade me to stay.' Her tone was steady. 'I'm afraid I can't do that. The thing is, I think we both know this relationship of ours isn't going anywhere. You're great company, but as time has gone by it's become increasingly obvious we aren't as compatible as I'd hoped we could be. Your refusal to eat healthily is always going to bother me. And you're never going to embrace Pilates, are you? I thought at first I could cope with your lack of interest in all the things that are important to me. If I'm honest, I was hoping to convert you to my way of thinking.' A smile lifted the corners of her mouth and she shook her head ruefully. 'But no, I soon came to realise that was never going to happen.

'And don't think I haven't noticed the way you light up when you're around Hattie, either. That's been interesting to observe. I do wonder, though, if she feels the same way about you?' She paused, then went on, 'Anyway, that remains to be seen. But not by me. I'm giving you some space to see if you can work your magic on her, and am catching the next flight home to see my girls. So, I'll be off now. No hard feelings, Guy, and thanks for an entertaining few weeks.' She waved at the camera, then blew a kiss. 'Have a happy life. Bye!'

'Wow,' said Hattie.

'I *know*.'

'Are you upset?'

'Well, it was a shock. Obviously I wasn't expecting something like this to happen out of the blue, but isn't it really what I wanted? I knew she wasn't right for me. And after the other evening . . .' he nodded encouragingly, 'surely this is the best possible outcome?'

Was he serious?

He did appear to be. There was an unmistakable glint of hope in his eyes.

'You're unbelievable,' Hattie marvelled.

'Come on. We can have some fun, can't we?' The mischievous grin was back. 'You know you want to. Even Suze thinks we should give it a go.'

'What you *should* do,' Hattie told him, 'is speak to someone in charge of this ship. See if they can find a carpenter to pop down to your cabin. And get them to install a revolving door.'

Chapter 18

Some moments remained fixed in your mind for ever. Gazing at the newly familiar faces around her, Disa knew this would be one of them.

There was a party atmosphere at La Lanterna this evening, on the final night of their eventful week in Venice. Beneath the trees, glittering with strings of white fairy lights, the five of them sat together, eating and drinking and marvelling at the way the past few days had turned out.

'Well, this has been the best holiday of my life.' Disa raised a glass to Molly. 'I came out here hoping to meet you, but I had no idea if my plan would succeed, or that you'd turn out to be so perfect.'

'And you've been the best surprise ever. Both of you.' Molly blew her a kiss, then one to Fen.

'My week's been pretty average.' Leon shrugged. 'I mean, Venice is OK, apart from being a bit old and watery, but it's a shame I couldn't have met anyone half decent.'

'Same,' deadpanned Fen, next to him. 'Just think, if I'd played my cards right, I could have bagged myself a gorgeous Italian gondolier like Kayla.'

Disa was still laughing when Jamie raised his glass. 'Here's to all of us. It's been a superb week all round. And I'm glad I brought Leon along with me. I'm also glad he dropped his Scotch egg down that escalator.'

'I'm glad I caught it.' As Fen said it, Disa saw her squeeze Leon's knee.

'And I'm so glad I met all of you,' Molly chimed in. 'We mustn't lose touch. If any of you ever want to come back to Venice, you must stay with me. Whenever you want. I mean it.'

'And the same if you want to visit us in Bristol,' Disa told her. 'I hope you will. You'll always be welcome.'

Molly glanced in Jamie's direction. 'I'd love that. Thank you.'

They all clattered their glasses together and raised a toast to each other. Then the church bells began to ring out in the warm night air across the city. It was ten o'clock, their signal to leave; a Venetian masked ball was being held on the ship, and Jamie had promised to be there to celebrate with the rest of the guests.

'You three go on ahead,' Disa told them. 'I'll catch you up. I just want a few more minutes with Molly.'

When the two of them were alone, Disa said, 'This is going to make me sound like a terrible person.'

'Oh! Why?' Molly looked alarmed.

'Don't panic. I just needed to make sure you were . . . nice, I suppose. And you are,' she added hastily. 'You are! Which is why you absolutely deserve this.' Unzipping the cross-body bag she hadn't taken off all evening, she drew out an envelope and the blue velvet jewellery box. 'Here, take these. Maybe read the letter first.'

She'd kept it back upon first meeting Molly. Now she watched as Declan's daughter scanned the words her father had written to her. Having read them herself at least a dozen times, Disa now knew them off by heart:

Molly, my darling girl. I love you so much, and haven't seen you for so long. You might have forgotten all about me by now. Your mum has kept me updated on your progress and I know you're happy with your stepfather. But Yvette felt it would be easier, under the circumstances, if we had no further direct contact, and I felt I had to respect her wishes. I did tell her, however, that in that case I saw no reason to give you my late mother's engagement ring.

I'm so sorry, I should never have said that. Not my finest hour, and of course you must have it. Once you reach the age of eighteen, I very much hope you'll want to meet me, and when that happens, I shall pass it on to you, to do with as you wish. It's a Victorian diamond ring that you might not want to wear. If money would be more useful, feel free to sell it.

As I write this, you are fifteen years old. If you make contact three years from now, once you're eighteen, I'll be able to give you the ring along with this letter.

I do hope you will.

I'm sorry I haven't been able to be the father you deserve.

I love you so much.

Dad xxx

As Molly finished reading the words written in Declan's heartbreakingly familiar handwriting, Disa realised that tears were sliding down her own cheeks. She wiped them away with her napkin.

'Take a look.' She indicated the box.

Molly opened it, then gasped. 'And this belonged to Dad's mum? My grandmother?'

'It did.' Declan's mother, Elspeth, had been frankly terrifying. Disa, who wasn't easily scared, had found it hard to relax around her. Following Elspeth's death at the age of ninety-two, she'd left items of jewellery to various distant relatives. Disa had duly received an enamel brooch of a giraffe. When she'd asked Declan about this ring, he'd told her it had been sold a couple of years earlier to pay for his mother's new Bentley.

Another lie, of course, but at the time she hadn't questioned it.

'What was she like?' said Molly.

'Imagine Queen Victoria crossed with Margaret Thatcher.'

Molly tilted the ring this way and that, watching as the glow from the candles on the table caused the diamond to throw out rainbow sparks of light. She said slowly, 'I don't know anything about jewellery. But it looks . . . big.'

'It needs to be kept safe.' The restaurant's outdoor garden was still busy. Disa lowered her voice and gave her the ballpark figure of the ring's worth.

Molly, her eyes like saucers, clapped a hand over her mouth. '*No.*'

'Yes. He wanted you to have it. But it's yours to do whatever you want with. If selling it would be more useful, do that.'

'It's so much money.'

'You deserve it.'

'And you didn't even need to give it to me. You could have kept it for yourself.'

'I could. Except it wouldn't have been mine, would it?' Disa reached for her hand and gave it a reassuring squeeze. 'It belongs to you.'

★

Disa made her way back to the ship past the gently bobbing sleeping gondolas lined up at their poles along the edge of the Grand Canal. Before she'd left the restaurant, Molly had taken the ring inside to Rosa, the owner, who had locked it away in the safe. Tomorrow she would take it for a proper evaluation and consider its future.

A wiry grey cat emerged from the darkness and Disa bent to say hello. For a few seconds it weaved its way around her ankles, head raised so she could stroke it. The next moment it lost all interest and slunk off, melting back into the shadows in search of fresh entertainment.

Like so many men had a habit of doing, Disa thought drily as she watched the cat disappear.

Please God, don't let Leon do that to Fen. If he tried, he'd have her to answer to.

Happily, she didn't think he would.

'Swap! Swap!' Above the noise of the music, Raewyn bellowed so loudly in Jamie's left ear that she almost burst his eardrum. A retired head teacher from Melbourne, she had pretty much demanded he dance with her, and she wasn't the kind of person who tolerated insubordination. But now the song had come to an end and he was evidently being released. Behind his black and gold Venetian mask, he heaved an inward sigh of relief. Raewyn was vigorously tapping the shoulder of someone behind him and announcing firmly, 'Come on, swap with me, you're next on my list.'

Seconds later, it became apparent that the next victim on her list was Leon, who'd been dancing with Fen. And now Raewyn was pushing Fen towards Jamie, saying, 'There you go, your turn with this one.'

So much for the vow he'd made forty-eight hours earlier. It was proving to be a promise it simply wasn't possible to keep. Not without drawing unwanted attention to himself, at least. The dance floor was full of masked guests, Fen was in front of him waiting to be danced with, and . . . typical, the next song beginning to be played by the band was a slow one.

Of course it was.

In slight desperation, he said, 'If your feet are hurting, we could always sit down.'

But Fen was looking surprised, and Leon, a few feet away with Raewyn, called across at him, 'Mate! What are you, *ninety*?'

'I'm fine,' said Fen.

Right. Looked like he was going to have to get through the next few minutes. Thank goodness for the ornate mask covering at least some of his face. Placing one hand on Fen's tanned bare shoulder and resting the other as lightly as possible on her waist, he kept as much distance as he could between them without it looking ridiculous, and together they began to move around the dance floor in time with the music. Behind him, Jamie could hear Raewyn shouting to Leon about her plans to explore France, Spain and Morocco next. Someone else was singing 'la-la-la' out of tune, and he tried to concentrate on that. But the dream from the other night was still there, box-fresh in his mind. The more he tried to banish it, the more vividly it continued to haunt him.

He hadn't kissed her then, and was still deeply regretting it.

Risking a glance at her mouth, which was slightly open, he quickly looked away once more. The next moment, having forgotten to move his left foot in time, he found himself over-compensating and treading on her toe.

'Ouch,' Fen said mildly.

'Sorry, sorry. Wasn't concentrating.' *I was too busy thinking about that dream and your mouth.*

She looked amused. 'You know, you're so good at everything else, it's actually reassuring to find out you can't dance.'

It was his turn to say, 'Ouch. I *can* dance.'

'You can? No offence, but—'

'No offence always means you're about to say something offensive.'

Fen shrugged. 'Fine, you're a grown-up, you can take it. If you can dance, why are you touching me as if I'm covered in wasps? And why *are* you dancing like a human clothes-airer?'

It was the way she asked the questions, like a serious scientist, that made him burst out laughing and thankfully banish all thoughts of the dream.

For now, at least. 'Brutal.'

'But honest.'

'Careful, I might have to accidentally step on your other toe.' He was able to see the glint of mischief in her eyes through the eyeholes of her intricately painted pink mask topped with ostrich feathers. 'And I'm doing my best, OK? But maybe I get a bit shy when I have to dance. I'm better at rugby.'

'Shy!' Fen scoffed. 'I bet you've never been shy in your life.'

'You'd be surprised. It can happen to all of us.'

'But you're always meeting new people, and you're famous. Everyone loves you.'

Not quite everyone. 'That makes it worse. People expect more of you. Look.' He moved her around and pointed. 'There's Disa, dancing with the captain.' He paused. 'You'd think she'd have found a new man after all these years.'

'There have been a few contenders.' Fen deftly avoided his clumsy left foot again. 'None that have lasted long. Nothing more than a couple of months. Grandpa really was the only one for her.'

'You never know, someone else might come along, sweep her off her feet. Still plenty of time for that to happen. What's wrong?' said Jamie, because Fen had stopped dancing and was looking up at him as if he were a puzzle she couldn't work out.

'Nothing. Just . . . you. You're not anything like I expected.'

He felt his heart speed up. The mask made it that much harder to read her expression. 'What does that mean?'

'You're nicer than I thought you'd be.'

'I am? What did you think I'd be like?'

'OK, honestly? I was expecting you to be full of yourself. The important one. Always expecting to get your own way, and irritated when it doesn't happen. Like Elton John that time he lost his temper playing tennis because the wind wouldn't stop when he wanted it to.'

'Wow.' Also, how closely was she comparing him with Elton John?

'I know. Sorry.'

'You really thought that?'

'Well, yes. Because you're famous, I suppose. But the good news is, you aren't like that. Which is better!'

'In what way, exactly, am I better?'

'You don't act as if you're above everyone else. And you chat to everyone like you're really interested in what they have to say. You're friendly. And kind. They all love you here.' She gestured airily with her hand. 'That's it, really. Like I said, you're nicer than I was expecting. And I'm so glad you came on this ship.'

'Oh?' It was good to hear.

'Because if you hadn't, Leon wouldn't have been here either.

And I might never have met him. Which doesn't bear thinking about.'

The song was coming to an end. Jamie smiled. 'In that case, I'm glad to have been able to help. My job here is done. And I'm officially a nice person too.' Stepping back, he gave an ironic bow. 'The ultimate compliment. You've made my day.'

'She has?' Here came Leon, released by Raewyn and ready to reclaim Fen. 'What's been going on here?'

'Apparently I'm not as terrible a person as Fen thought I was.'

Grinning, Leon clapped him on the back. 'Don't go getting your hopes up, Hamilton. She still prefers me.'

He was speaking the truth. As the band struck up the next song, Leon whisked Fen off. From the corner of his eye, Jamie glimpsed a flash of spiky red and gold hair and turned to see Kayla making her way past in a purple mask, her usual beaming smile for once missing.

He nodded at her. 'Hi! Haven't seen you around much lately.'

'I know, thought I should be here tonight. Felt a bit guilty about leaving Hattie on her own this week.'

It was the last night of the cruise, the singer was now belting out Jamie's favourite George Michael song, and Fen had told him he was a nice person. Indicating the band, he held out a hand in invitation. 'I love this one. Fancy a dance?'

But instead of giving a squeal of delight and launching herself at him like an overexcited puppy, Kayla paused. Then she shook her head. 'No, thanks.'

What?

Behind the mask, something was evidently amiss. 'Is everything OK?'

She gave him a long look, then heaved a sigh. 'Not good, actually.'

'Do you want to talk about it?'

'Not really. You carry on, enjoy the rest of your evening. I'm fine.'

Chapter 19

'I can't understand it. Angelo said he'd call me and fix a time and place to meet up. He *promised*.' Up on the top deck, Kayla's hands trembled as she reached for her glass and almost knocked over an empty one that had been left next to it.

It had been obvious from the start that something like this would happen, but Hattie still felt desperately sorry for her. Poor Kayla had been ghosted on her last night here. Angelo had shown his true colours and she was devastated.

'It's so unfair,' Hattie said. 'Men are the pits.' Kayla's shoulders were hunched in despair and Hattie wished there was something – anything – she could do to make her feel better. All she knew was that she definitely wasn't allowed to say 'I could have told you this would happen.'

'I know *most* men are the pits. But I was so sure Angelo was different.' Miserably Kayla rubbed her hand down her face, smearing crimson lipstick across her chin. 'He said he loved me and I *believed* him. Oh hell, and now look who's here, coming over to make fun of me. Make him go away.'

There he was, appearing at the top of the staircase and heading in their direction, a silver and magenta mask pushed to the top of his head. Jumping up, Hattie hurried across to head him off at the pass.

'Hattie, I—'

'No, Guy, it's not a good time.' Firmly she shook her head. 'Please leave me alone.'

'But—'

'How many times have I told you? I'm not interested and I'm not going to change my mind, so do me a favour and give us some space, we just need to be—'

'Hats, will you let me *speak*?' He raised his arms in exasperation. 'I'm not here to beg you for sex! I came up looking for Kayla because there's some guy down on the dock asking for her.'

Hattie's mouth dropped open. 'What? Who is it?' *Surely not . . .*

At that moment, they heard a male voice calling out, 'Kay-laaa!'

Kayla's head jerked up and swivelled like a meerkat's. Leaping to her feet, she gasped, 'Oh my God,' then bellowed, '*Angelo?*' into the warm night air and hurtled across the deck.

'KAYLAAA!'

Hattie caught up with her as she reached the rails on the other side and gave a sob of joy and relief. Her voice breaking with emotion, she howled, 'ANGELO-O-O.'

And there he was, gazing up from the paved area beside the gangway, as good-looking as in the photos Kayla had proudly shown off. He was clutching a massive bunch of white flowers in one hand and supporting himself with a crutch on the other side; while his left leg was encased in a surgical boot.

'*Ti amo*, Kayla! I am so sorry, but I was in the 'ospital and my phone, eet died in the Canal Grande so I could not make a call to you, but now I am here!'

Together Kayla and Hattie raced down the staircase, into the reception area and off the ship. Tears streamed down Kayla's face as she threw herself into Angelo's outstretched arms, scattering white rose petals like confetti and almost knocking him off his feet.

'I was so worried! I thought you were dead! Then I thought you were alive but you didn't want to see me again, which was even *worse*.' She was covering his face with frantic kisses. 'What happened? Tell me everything!'

'A tourist, he pass out and fall into the canal.' Angelo's accent was strong, but his English was good. 'An old man. I dive in, and a motorboat came to 'elp too, but my leg got squashed between the boat and the side of the canal. It was trapped, but I manage to push the old man up out of the water and the wife was shouting and crying. Then *bouf*, the bone in my leg went crack. The man was rescue by the carabinieri and we were both taken to the 'ospital. And my phone was still in my pocket but 'e is dead. Anyway, I am 'ere now.' Tenderly he stroked Kayla's cheek. 'And so are you. I am so sorry I am late. I thought I would never see you again.'

'Me too. I'm so happy you're here. You have no idea.' Kayla saw the crimson lipstick marks transferred from her mouth to his face, and lovingly wiped them away with her thumbs.

'I buy you flowers.' He proffered the now battered bunch of white roses, then dug into his pocket for his wallet and took out a neatly folded wedge of sodden banknotes. 'And 'ere is all the money you lended me. I give it to you now so I do not forget. Sorry they are wet from the canal. My beautiful Kayla, I love you so much.'

'I love you more.'

Guy had come down from the top deck too. Standing beside

Hattie as they both watched Kayla and Angelo holding each other, he murmured, 'Sounds like he really means it.'

'Seems like he really does.' Hattie had noticed the tremor of deep emotion in Angelo's voice as he spoke to Kayla, as if she were the only woman in the world for him. She'd been wrong about him all along.

An arm slid around her waist, the hand coming to rest on her hip. Leaning in, Guy whispered into her ear, 'That could be us, you know.'

Honestly, any excuse. Maybe all those years ago she'd been a bit of a pushover, but that wasn't going to happen again. Slowly and deliberately, she removed his wandering hand. 'You don't give up, do you? It's never going to be us.'

Chapter 20

The Cotswolds

A week had passed since they'd returned from Venice, and now it was meet-the-parents day.

'You don't have to worry,' Leon told her. 'It's going to be fine. They'll like you.'

'OK.' But the mere fact that he'd used the word *like* rather than *love* was making Fen nervous, along with Jamie's cheerful 'Good luck' before he'd left for London on Wednesday evening. She definitely felt as if she was going to need it. Apart from anything else, their address was Hetherton Hall, Hetherton, for goodness' sake. It was giving out full-on *Bridgerton* vibes. What if they expected her to curtsey?

And now that they were on their way there, she felt as if she were bracing herself for the most important – and terrifying – job interview of her life.

Her head swivelled as Leon turned left instead of right. 'Isn't this the wrong direction?'

'Don't worry about it. I know the best route.'

Twenty minutes later, having left Bristol behind them and now winding their way along narrow country lanes, she still had no idea what was going on, until Leon pulled into a driveway. The first thing Fen noticed was a couple of outbuildings and an orange windsock. Then, finally revealing itself behind the buildings, she saw the blue and white helicopter on a helipad in the centre of the field.

'You're kidding.' It was the one Leon part-owned; he'd shown her photos of it on his phone.

'Thought we could arrive in style.' He grinned sheepishly. 'I wanted to impress you.'

'You already impress me. We could turn up on a tractor and I'd be happy.'

'I'm just showing off.' Reaching sideways, he planted a kiss on her mouth. 'Flying a helicopter is about the one thing I can do that Jamie can't. So, are you up for it?'

She curled her hand behind his neck and returned the kiss. Did he honestly think she'd say no? 'So long as you won't be showing off in a loop-the-loop kind of way, because I might not be so keen on that.'

'We'll give it a miss this time,' said Leon. 'I promise.'

He greeted his friend and fellow pilot up in the control tower, completed the pre-flight checks and made sure Fen was comfortable and secure in the seat beside him. Then they were off. Last week she'd taken a last, lingering look at Venice from the air as their plane had left Marco Polo airport and risen over the azure lagoon, and now she was enjoying another bird's-eye view, this time of the Cotswolds in all its green and golden glory as they flew above woodland, fields and toy-sized villages on their way to Hetherton, a few miles from Wotton-under-Edge.

Over the roar of the engine and the hypnotic *thud-thud-thud* of the helicopter's rotor blades, Leon spoke to her through his headset, pointing out the glistening lake where he and his friends had swum as teenagers, the escarpment he'd once tobogganed down in the snow, ending up smashing into the frozen stream at the bottom, and the llama farm where a llama had spat in his face, causing him to fall backwards off a wall and split his head open on a rock.

'I had to have seven stitches.' He tapped the back of his head.

'So collecting injuries isn't a new hobby. You're a liability.' Fen laughed through her own headset, because he was still suffering from assorted aches and pains and knocking back painkillers for the damage his body had sustained in Venice. But had he bothered to visit his GP and maybe considered getting sent for an X-ray? No, of course he hadn't. He wasn't a complainer, preferring to play down his symptoms instead.

'And there it is.' He pointed into the distance as the house he'd grown up in came into view ahead of them, nestling in the bowl of a verdant valley and bathed in sunlight. 'Home sweet home.'

It was certainly imposing. If only it could have been smaller. She held up her phone and took a series of photos as they approached and made their descent into a flat field at the bottom of the garden. Up on the terrace, his parents had now emerged to greet them.

Once again hearing Jamie's voice in her head wishing her luck, she wished this would stop feeling like a school exam she hadn't revised for.

Two hours later, she was wishing it could have been that, because at least an exam would have been over by now. But here she was, still stuck and unable to escape a seemingly endless ordeal amid the knowledge that she absolutely wasn't what Leon's parents had had in mind for him when it came to girlfriends.

Oh, they were unfailingly polite on the surface, but that almost made it worse. Afternoon tea had finally been served in the drawing room and the conversation was flowing like quick-setting cement. Greville Spencer-Carr had spoken at length about arable farming and weather systems. His wife, Hilary, having asked Fen where her family was from, had been visibly disappointed not to have heard of them. A further line of enquiry as to her favourite classical composers had come to a sticky end when, stupidly attempting to wing it, she'd pronounced the J in Janáček wrongly, only to see Greville wince and say, 'Ah yes, we watched a fascinating documentary on *Yanáček* the other week.'

It was while Hilary was talking about soil drainage and the impossibility of finding decent gardeners who knew what they were doing that Fen's knife slipped. In her hurry to catch it, the plate balanced on her knees tipped sideways and the two halves of the scone she'd been doing battle with dropped onto the antique Persian rug.

'Sorry!' Crumbs scattered everywhere. This was *so* much worse than a school exam. Hurriedly picking up the halves spread with butter and greengage jam, Fen managed to knock the edge of her teacup and sent tea slopping into the saucer.

'Don't worry about it, really. Accidents happen. I'll go and find a cloth.' Hilary smiled, nodded and swiftly rose to her feet.

Of course it had to happen while Leon was in the bathroom. After thirty seconds of clutching the dropped knife and scone-halves in awkward silence, Fen said to Greville, 'I'll just take these through to the kitchen.'

Before she could reach it, she heard Hilary in there, on the phone.

'. . . pretty girl, and of course Leon's besotted, but no, she just won't do.' There was a pause, followed by a quiet trill of laughter. 'It'll pass, I'm sure. Remember when he was five and completely obsessed with those Teletubby creatures? For a couple of months they were his whole world, then one morning the housekeeper found them kicked under the bed because he'd discovered Spider-Man. I can't imagine we'll be seeing this one again; he's only known her for a fortnight. And you understand what I'm saying, don't you? She might be a nice enough girl in her own way, but she isn't one of *us*.'

Frozen in the corridor, it occurred to Fen that since she could hardly return to the drawing room with the dropped and crumbling scone-halves, she didn't have much choice. Pushing open the door to the kitchen, she flashed a sunny smile at Leon's mother, tipped the pieces of scone into the bin and said cheerfully, 'Sorry to interrupt, I'll use tissues to clear up the spill, shall I? You carry on with your call.'

Hilary murmured, 'I have to go, Annabel,' and switched off the phone. Regarding Fen across the kitchen, she said, 'Sorry. Obviously you weren't meant to hear that.'

'Obviously.'

'I had no idea you were hiding behind the door, listening.'

'Trust me, it wasn't planned.'

Leon's mother shrugged. 'Nevertheless, you heard. But you have to understand, I'm simply being realistic. We have all this to protect.' She gestured around. 'Plenty of young women can be unscrupulous where men and money are concerned.'

'You mean me?'

'I don't know you. But potentially, yes.'

'The answer's no, you're wrong. But OK.'

'We also want to protect our son, of course, from being

targeted for the wrong reasons and ending up suffering heartbreak. Anyway, I'm glad you understand.' Hilary's smile was perfunctory. 'By the way, probably better not to mention this conversation to Leon. It would only upset him.'

'I imagine it would.' Fen nodded in agreement. 'But it's not going to put me off.' There was a roll of kitchen paper on one of the counter tops and she tore off a few sheets. 'I'll go and clear up the mess.'

The visit may have lasted under three hours, but it had felt more like thirty. As they took off from the field, Leon said, 'That went pretty well, then,' and Fen's spirits dropped, because he actually meant it. He went on, 'Sometimes they can be a bit funny about girlfriends, but not this time. They seemed to like you.'

She couldn't tell him; it would be too cruel. And now she understood why he chose to use the word *like* rather than *love*. But wow, if he thought his parents liked her, how had they treated previous girlfriends who'd had to endure turning up and being introduced to Hilary and Greville?

Whose grandfather, by the way, had made lavatories for a living.

'I liked them too.' It was the first lie she'd ever told him.

'Good, I'm glad.' Peering below them as they gained height, Leon leaned across and pointed down. 'See that wood, to the right of the lake? When I was eleven, I had my first kiss in there. Her name was Josephine Barber and her mum worked behind the bar at our local pub. She always gave us free crisps.'

Was poor Josephine warned off by Hilary too?

'How was the kiss? Was it mind-blowing?'

'Totally. Until ten minutes later, when I climbed an oak tree and fell out of it. Broke my collarbone.'

'Showing off again.' Fen smiled, but she'd noticed the fleeting grimace as he'd been reaching across to show her the wood.

'And your back still isn't better either. You really are going to have to get it looked at.'

'It'll sort itself out. These things always do. Hey, look at that hay barn down to the left.' He pointed again as they flew over it. 'That's where—'

'Nooo, don't tell me,' Fen interrupted, laughing. 'I really don't want to know what you got up to in there.'

Chapter 21

Bristol

Jamie had spent the last week up at Elstree Studios, recording a new sports quiz. The days had been long and the evenings in the hotel bar rowdily sociable.

Now, the rain was hammering on the roof of his car as he headed west down the motorway at midnight. By the time he arrived back in Clifton, Leon would most likely be fast asleep, and at a guess Fen would be there with him, because they were still at the can't-bear-to-be-separated phase and the Clifton duplex apartment was evidently far larger than Fen's basement flat in Redland.

But when he let himself in an hour later and pushed open the door to the living room, Fen was asleep under a spare duvet on the sofa.

Jamie paused, his breath catching in his throat at the unexpected sight of her, at the curve of her cheek and the sweep of her lashes beneath closed eyelids. Did this mean the two of them had had a monumental argument? Leon wasn't a snorer, so it couldn't be that. And if it was due to an argument, what had it been about? Surely not anything serious—

Sensing his presence, Fen's eyes snapped open, her head lifting from the pillow. 'Oh, it's you. Thank goodness.'

'What? Why?' He left his case by the door and moved closer. 'What's happened? Where's Leon?'

'Upstairs in bed.' Pulling herself into a sitting position, Fen rubbed her face and shook back her hair. 'I'm worried about him. Something's wrong but he won't do anything about it. Those bruises have gone, but he's in way more pain than before. It's like he's got flu and his whole body aches, but it doesn't seem like flu and he keeps saying it'll be better tomorrow. Except it's getting worse and he can't sleep properly, just groans all the time because every time he moves, he wakes himself up. He's not eating either. Why won't men ever admit they're ill? It's crazy, all he does is knock painkillers back like Smarties and tell me he's fine, when he so obviously *isn't* fine. You'll have to back me up, make him see sense . . .' She tailed off at the sound of footsteps slowly descending the stairs.

Leon appeared, looking drawn and visibly unwell. 'Thought I heard voices. How was London?'

'You look terrible.' Narrowing his eyes at him, Jamie came straight to the point. 'What's going on?'

'Don't you start. I'm OK, it's a pinched nerve in my back or something.' Leon grimaced as he bent to pick up a blister pack of painkillers from the coffee table. His jaw tightened when he turned it over and saw it was empty.

'You aren't OK. Look at you. And what's happened to your face?' Seeing him every day, Fen evidently hadn't noticed, but it was immediately apparent to Jamie, who'd been away for over a week, that Leon had lost weight.

'I'm not feeling great, that's all. Haven't been eating much.'

'Get your coat.'

With a flicker of humour, Leon said, 'Why? Have I pulled?'

'I'm taking you to A&E.'

'What? That's crazy, you can't do that.'

He could have a point. 'Have you even made an appointment to see your GP?'

'*No.*'

Fen said, 'I keep telling him to do it, but he won't.'

Leon was glaring at him. 'And no way am I turning up at A&E at two in the morning, so you can forget that. Whatever I might have, it isn't an accident or an emergency.'

'Fine, then.' Dammit, he was stubborn. 'But you still look like crap, and I'm taking you to the walk-in clinic first thing in the morning. Now go back to sleep,' Jamie instructed, 'and try not to die in the night.'

'You're such an old woman.' Leon managed a wry, unconvincing smile. 'Do us a favour, will you? Find me some ibuprofen and a few paracetamols. And I'll do my very best not to die.'

'You'd better not.' Jamie shook his head at him by way of warning.

'But if I do,' said Leon, 'you'll have the satisfaction of knowing you were right.'

Thirty-six hours later, feeling as if he were watching himself from a distance, Leon turned to Jamie and said, 'See? I told you we shouldn't have come here.'

From the very beginning of their friendship, a shared love of black humour had bound them together, but Jamie wasn't smiling now. Not at all. He was looking horrified and devastated, which was undoubtedly the correct reaction, but Leon found himself refusing to allow the significance of the consultant's sombre words to sink in.

Cancer. Metastases. Stage four. Not what we wanted to find.

He was probably in shock. All he knew was that he didn't want to be here in this hospital, having to listen to a complete stranger telling him something he definitely didn't want to hear.

'I'm so sorry.' The consultant sounded as if he meant it, but did he really? How many people had he said it to over the years? After a while, it had to become repetitive. Did that make it meaningless? Leon glanced at the box of tissues on the table next to him. Was he expected to cry? He shook his head, because no way was he going to do that. Was this even real? Maybe it was all a hallucination.

'I don't like it here. I want to go home now.' As he said this, he had a flashback to a recent party where his friends Ginny and Den had brought along their newborn son and Ginny had told everyone how she'd been nine centimetres dilated, legs up in stirrups and baby minutes away from being born, when she'd gripped the midwife's hand and shouted, 'I can't do this any more, make it stop, please just let me go *home.*'

His brain gave him a nudge, reminding him that he'd always blithely assumed he would one day have a family of his own, two or possibly three children if he was lucky . . .

Maybe this was his punishment for taking the future for granted, so much so that he'd spent weeks dismissing those occasional jabbing pains in his abdomen, the bouts of tiredness, the loss of appetite. Who, after all, would ever assume such vague symptoms could mean something so serious?

'And you will,' the consultant's tone was reassuring, 'as soon as we get your medication sorted and all the necessary arrangements have been made. We have people here who can help you with that. Now.' He turned to Jamie. 'You're listed in our records as the next of kin . . .'

Arriving at the hospital, it had been the easier option; Jamie had known he wouldn't want to worry his parents unnecessarily.

'Jamie's my oldest friend. My best friend,' Leon amended. Poor sod, he hadn't been expecting to have to deal with something like this.

'I'll do anything that needs doing.' Jamie was nodding at the consultant.

Feeling his head swim, as if his brain no longer belonged to him, Leon said, 'Except choose my coffin. If you put me in a purple coffin, I'll kill you.'

The consultant took this in his stride, evidently used to hearing inappropriate humour in times of stress. 'You'll need to let your family know.'

'I know.' Leon nodded; this was what he'd been dreading. 'I will.'

'And if you have any more questions at all, speak to the nurses on the ward. Or to any of the medical team.'

'Right.'

'I know it's a lot to take in.'

Leon indicated the beige wall behind the consultant's head. 'That painting up there is crooked. It's really annoying.'

He was definitely in shock.

The older man rose to his feet, then turned and carefully straightened the framed seascape. 'Better?'

Leon attempted to picture his future, such as it was. No wedding, no children, potentially no more holidays or birthdays or Christmases. No growing old or even middle-aged.

He nodded at the man who'd passed sentence on him and said, 'Much better. Thanks.'

But when the consultant had departed and it was just the two of them left in the room, Leon looked at Jamie and saw his own state of shock reflected back at him.

'So it looks like the show's over before it's even begun.' His voice sounded different, as if it no longer belonged to him. 'Fuck.'

'Fuck,' said Jamie.

Fen had spent most of the previous day at the hospital while Leon had been undergoing a slew of tests, and the last thing she wanted to do was leave him today, but she had a two-hour meeting arranged with a business owner who'd driven down from Sheffield to speak to her in person. Working as a remote personal assistant often meant never meeting your clients face to face, but this particular woman had insisted on it to discuss the potential arrangement. And the contract would be an important one, so postponing it hadn't been an option.

When she finally arrived back on the ward, the nurse at the desk said, 'He's outside in the garden with Jamie.'

But when she found them sitting together on a bench, with Leon's wheelchair parked close by, the looks on their faces when they saw her making her way towards them chilled her to the bone.

'What is it?' The creeping dread that had been steadily escalating over the last two days felt as if it was now closing around her throat in an iron grip.

Jamie rose to his feet, indicating for her to take his place. 'I'm going to grab a coffee. Give me a call if you need anything.'

When Jamie had left, Leon took her hand in his.

'What's happened?'

'I've seen Dr Emerson.'

'And?' *Don't want to hear this, don't want to hear it.*

After a long moment, he said, 'Think of really bad news. Then multiply it.' He swallowed audibly, unable to carry on, and she knew it was what they'd all been inwardly dreading.

Squeezing his hand, she blurted out, 'If it's cancer, we'll get through this. Millions of people have cancer and beat it. If anyone can, it's you, and I know the treatment can be rough, but we'll be with you every step of—'

'There isn't going to be any treatment.' This time his voice cracked with emotion, the words catching in his throat. 'Because there's nothing they can do.'

'No . . . *no*, that can't be right. There's always *something*.'

'He showed us the scan. It's everywhere.' He shook his head. 'In my pancreas, in my liver, in my bones. No surgery's going to help. Palliative care only, to keep me as comfortable as possible.'

It was the question she couldn't bear to hear the answer to, but it had to be asked. 'Did he say how long?'

'A couple of months, three if I'm lucky.' Leon closed his eyes for a second and said brokenly, '*If I'm lucky*, can you imagine? Shit, it doesn't feel real, I keep waiting to wake up and discover it was all a dream. This isn't the way my life was meant to go. I had *plans*, so many plans. And instead of ticking them off my list, someone up there's laughing at me for taking it all for granted, and sooner or later they're going to reach down and just . . . take my batteries out.'

Fen felt sick. Really sick. This couldn't be happening. But it *was*, and the next moment they were hugging, holding each other tightly while the world around them tilted on its axis and in the distance an aggrieved male driver blasted his horn and yelled violently, 'What the hell? I was *waiting* for that fucking space.'

How long did they cling together? She had no idea. Finally Leon croaked, 'I'm sorry. You don't deserve this.'

'Nor do you. No one does.' She could feel his warm breath on her neck, the tremor in his chest. 'And don't ever say sorry again.'

'I love you.' He touched the side of her face, and in the bright sunlight she saw the tinge of yellow in the whites of his eyes that hadn't been there last week. 'It's just so fucked up. I waited all these years to find you, then it finally happened. And now this.'

'But at least I'm here.'

'If I hadn't gone to Venice, you could be having a fantastic day now. Enjoying the weather, heading off out with friends for drinks in the sunshine on Princess Victoria Street, getting chatted up by good-looking guys . . .'

'Stop it.' She pressed a forefinger to his mouth. 'I'm never going to wish I hadn't met you.'

'I still wish I could wake up.'

'Have you told your mum and dad?'

'Not yet. They're coming in this evening.' He closed his eyes briefly and Fen's heart went out to him, and to his poor parents; it had to be hard enough coming to terms with what he'd only just found out himself, let alone having to break the news to everyone else.

'I should have made you see a doctor earlier.' A wave of guilt washed over her.

'You mean a week ago?' He shook his head. 'Don't even think it. By then it was already far too late. According to Dr Emerson, this thing's been flying under the radar for months. The MRI scan yesterday lit up like a Christmas tree.'

'But it only started after that guy smashed you into the wall.'

'Except it didn't, really. Everything was already there inside me, growing and spreading, but any symptoms back then were easy to ignore. *Fuck.*'

An old man with a walking stick was hobbling past several metres away. Shooting them a look of disgust, he growled, 'Language.'

'Sorry,' said Leon.

The man shook his head, muttered, 'Kids today,' and shuffled off.

Fen had just left the ward to get a can of Coke from the shop downstairs when Leon said abruptly, 'Should I finish with her?'

'What?' Jamie stared at him in utter disbelief. Was he mad? 'What are you talking about?'

'I just wonder if I should. To make things easier for her.' Leon shrugged helplessly. 'Like, let her off the hook to spare her all the shit to come.'

Jamie's heart went out to him. He shook his head slowly. 'Honestly? That's the stupidest idea you've ever had. You think Fen would *let* you do that to her? Do you actually imagine she'd breathe a sigh of relief and say, "Thank goodness, I can forget about him now, put it all behind me"? Because that's not the way these things happen. So don't even think about trying it. She loves you, you idiot, every bit as much as you love her.'

'OK.' The relief on Leon's face was immense. 'If you're sure.'

Jamie's throat tightened with the emotion he was having to work so hard to suppress. 'Of course I'm sure.'

Fen and Jamie left shortly before Leon's parents arrived. Yet another unthinkable ordeal lay ahead for him, as well as for Hilary and Greville. And after them came his friends, workmates, everyone else who knew him. In the coming days, the shock and grief would spread out in an ever-increasing circle, like the ripples on a lake.

Jamie walked alongside her to her car in the far corner of the hospital car park.

'He's being so brave.' Fen fumbled in her bag for her keys, which had to be in there somewhere. 'I don't know how he does it. I still can't believe it's happening.'

'I know. But that's Leon.' A message arrived on Jamie's phone and he glanced at it. 'Right, I've cancelled the trip to New Zealand.'

'The TV thing?' Landing the job had been a big deal, she knew. He'd been due to fly to Wellington ten days from now to begin almost a month of filming.

'I'm not going to leave him, am I?' There were violet shadows beneath his eyes. 'Not flying to the other side of the world while he's here going through this.'

Fen nodded; of course he wouldn't do that. Not for the first time, it occurred to her that she hadn't cried yet, which seemed inconceivable. She only had to see a TV ad about a lost puppy to dissolve into tears. Look at that evening in the Basilica di San Marco, when she'd been so embarrassingly overcome by the beauty of the place. But today, when you'd think they'd all be sobbing non-stop . . . nothing. Presumably because they were still in deep shock. It would happen in due course, she knew that. But not yet.

'Anyway, drive carefully,' Jamie ordered. For a second he hesitated, and Fen thought she might be about to receive a consoling hug, but instead he stepped back and awkwardly raised the hand holding his own car keys. 'I guess I'll see you tomorrow.'

'Yes.' A wave of helplessness swept over her. 'I just . . . don't know what to *do*.'

'There isn't anything you *can* do. Except be there for him.'

'It isn't enough.' Another wave, followed by a third larger one, like a gathering tsunami.

'It's what he wants. *You're* all he wants.' Jamie's gaze didn't falter. 'OK, I'm going to tell you something. When you left the ward this afternoon to get a drink from the machine, Leon asked me if I thought he should break up with you.'

Fen's jaw dropped. '*What?*'

'He thought he should tell you he didn't want to see you any more. To make things easier for you.'

'And he seriously imagined I'd *let* him do that?'

'I know. He was trying to help. I told him you wouldn't have any of it, that it was never going to happen.'

'Good. And did he believe you?'

Jamie nodded. 'He did. He was relieved to hear it.'

Oh, Leon. What must he be going through? It was an unimaginable situation to be in. Needing to be sure, Fen said, 'I asked him how long and he said two or three months. That's what the consultant told him, right?'

Jamie nodded. 'It's only an estimate.' He paused. 'You never know, it could be more.'

Two months. Or three. And if it could be more than that, it could also be less.

Fen opened her driver's door, unable to even look at him. 'Thanks. I'll see you tomorrow.'

The nightmare was so far no more than a few hours old.

It had only just begun.

Chapter 22

'For the rest of your life,' said Leon, 'every time you see a Scotch egg you'll think of me.'

It was five weeks since the brutal diagnosis, four and a half weeks since his release from hospital. The initial shock had sunk in and their new normal – which was the very definition of *abnormal* – was something they were slowly adjusting to, even as Leon's illness continued its inevitable progression.

'Every time I hear "I'm Still Standing" I'll think of you,' Fen countered, because the song lived rent-free in his head, prompting him several times each day to become Elton John and sing the words aloud, whether he was actually standing or confined to the sofa, or lying in the king-sized bed with its view over the Avon Gorge and Clifton Suspension Bridge.

'Good.' Leon gave a nod of satisfaction. 'My work here is done. Plus, every time you watch an episode of *Schitt's Creek* you'll think of me.' She'd introduced him to the show and he'd fallen in love with it; whenever his energy was depleted, the next episode had always been there, ready and waiting for him. When they'd reached the end, he'd been bereft and she had got him into *Fisk* instead.

'Every time I hear the name Ryan Reynolds I'll think of you,' Fen told him, because he'd watched the Deadpool films over and over too.

'It must be nice to be Ryan Reynolds. He's got everything.' Propped up against a pile of pillows on the bed, Leon gave her hand a squeeze. 'Except you.'

'I know, poor Ryan. I hear he cries himself to sleep at night.'

'And that makes me the lucky one.'

This was the way their conversations switched and turned, one moment teasing and flippant, the next heartbreakingly sad. From the way he was looking at her now, Fen knew they were due another twist. She mentally braced herself. 'What is it?'

'Staying here any longer isn't an option.' Leon gestured around the apartment. 'It's not practical.'

She'd been simultaneously expecting this and dreading it. Up here on the two highest levels of the four-storey building, the views might be spectacular but the number of stairs had always threatened to become a real issue. Leon's lung capacity was depleted, and yesterday he'd been too weak and exhausted to climb the stairs without stopping every few seconds to catch his breath.

'Would my place be easier?' But she already knew it wouldn't. The stone steps down to her basement flat were steep and tricky to navigate at the best of times, and Leon was already shaking his head. She blurted out, 'Or how about Disa's house? We could turn the dining room into a bedroom and—'

'My parents want me to move in with them.'

'Oh.' This was something else she'd been dreading. Each time Hilary and Greville arrived for a visit, they told her she could take a break and return once they'd left. Leon was their beloved only child and his diagnosis had absolutely floored them.

Understandably, they were devastated, and desperate to have him back at Hetherton Hall so they could take care of their son in the time he had left to him.

'I know.' He didn't need to explain. 'But it makes sense. There's plenty of room and no problem with stairs. They want me home with them so they can look after me. I can't say no.'

'Of course you can't. It'll be more comfortable. And I can still come and see you every day.'

He reached for her hand. 'You don't have to. Only if you really want to.'

'Oh well, I probably won't bother, then.'

'Come here.' He smiled and drew her in for a kiss. 'You know what I mean. Can't let the business slide. You need to keep it going.'

'Don't worry, I am. Have laptop, will travel.' Apart from the occasional in-person meeting with clients, she was able to work anywhere and had taken to doing so whenever Leon slept or was watching sport on TV. 'I'll be bringing it with me.'

'You could help me pack some clothes if you want. Jamie's going to be taking me tomorrow.'

So soon? Fen's heart sank; she desperately wanted to keep him to herself for a little longer. But that was selfish, not to mention impractical. Leon's needs were paramount, and of course his parents wanted him home with them. It went without saying that she and Jamie would carry on visiting him daily, but would his other Bristol-based friends still make the journey once he was living thirty-odd miles away?

As if reading her mind, Leon said, 'It's forty-five minutes in the car. Not too bad.' He paused to cover his mouth and cough painfully. 'But you don't have to come every day, you're allowed to take time off—'

'You're not getting rid of me that easily,' Fen cut in. 'I'm planning on pitching a tent outside your bedroom window.'

The coughing started up again; it had been steadily worsening over the past fortnight. He pressed his hand to his chest and waited until his breathing was once more under control, then looked at his watch. 'Time for more pills, then I'm going to have a doze before Jamie gets back. Early night tonight. Give my love to Disa.'

He looked pale and utterly exhausted. She didn't want to leave him, but Disa had booked a table at her favourite restaurant, firmly informing her that she needed a break.

'I will.' Each time Fen put her arms around him, the extent of his weight loss shocked her afresh. 'And I'll see you tomorrow. Let me know as soon as you're settled in and I'll be there.'

When she let herself out of the apartment ten minutes later, Leon had taken his meds and was asleep in front of the TV. Yet again, she reminded herself that what Hilary and Greville were having to endure was even more agonising than her own situation, however impossible that might seem. Less than two months ago, she hadn't known Leon even existed.

And now she didn't know how she was going to live without him for the rest of her life. How much worse must it be for them?

Jamie had cancelled as many of his commitments as possible, but had had an unavoidable meeting in Bath this afternoon. Never mind, he was nearly home now, driving across the last section of the Clifton Downs and rounding the final bend on Sion Hill—

What the hell?

But it wasn't just someone who looked like Leon. It *was* Leon, unbelievable though it seemed. When Fen had messaged him thirty minutes ago, it had been to let him know that Leon was fast asleep and she'd left a chicken casserole in the fridge for later.

Yet here he was, leaning against the railings of one of the houses maybe a hundred metres up from their own apartment. Jamie screeched to a halt, pulled up beside him and jumped out of the car. 'What's going on? What the hell are you *doing*?'

'Didn't I mention it? Training for my next triathlon.' Leon was catching his breath, clearly relieved to see him. 'Not going quite according to plan.'

'You absolute lunatic. What's this about?' Jamie opened the passenger door and ushered him into the car. Leon's striped shirt and faded jeans hung loose on his shrunken frame, but his hair was wet and he smelled of his favourite lime shower gel.

'I needed to get to the shops.'

'Are you out of your mind? You couldn't wait for me to get home? What if you'd fallen over in the shower?'

'But I didn't. And I didn't know if you'd be back in time. Still, you're here now. Knew you'd come in useful one day.'

'Where are we going?'

'Just do as you're told. Down here,' Leon instructed, 'then hang a left onto Caledonia Place.'

The woman who buzzed them into the jeweller's had served Jamie last Christmas when he'd gone in to buy a gold bangle for his mum. Her eyes lit up when she saw him again. 'Hello! Did your mother love her bangle?'

'She did, thanks.' He indicated Leon at his side. 'But I'm not the one buying today.'

'I'd like a chair if that's OK,' said Leon. 'And an engagement ring.'

Jamie's eyebrows shot up. He hadn't been expecting that. 'In the car, you said you wanted to buy Fen a pair of earrings.'

'Yes, well, I lied.' Leon lowered himself onto the chair the jeweller had swiftly placed in front of the glass-topped counter. 'You might have tried to tell me it wasn't a good idea.'

'Have you asked her to marry you?'

'Not yet. Going to do it tomorrow. Thought it could be a surprise. And if she turns me down,' said Leon, 'don't worry. I'll ask you instead.'

They left the shop fifteen minutes later, just before it closed. As the door was locked behind them, Jamie said, 'Uh-oh.'

Ten metres away, an officious-looking traffic warden was standing beside the car, which he'd left parked on double yellows. It wasn't in anyone's way, but that had never been a convincing argument, he'd found.

'Your vehicle, is it?' The warden looked up as they approached.

'It is. Sorry.' Jamie unlocked and opened the passenger door for Leon, then helped him in.

'My fault,' Leon told the man, subsiding with relief onto the seat and shaking his head apologetically. 'He had to park in a hurry and come into the shop to collect me because I couldn't make it on my own.'

The traffic warden had recognised him, Jamie realised, and was determined not to be impressed. But Leon was now coughing weakly into a handkerchief and appearing more unwell than ever, with a pale green sheen to his skin. Looking up at the man, who hadn't yet printed out the parking ticket, he croaked, 'I'm really sorry,' then turned to Jamie. 'And don't worry, I'll pay the fine.'

Jamie said, 'You don't have to.'

'Of course I do.' Leon held up the small bag containing the

ring box. 'If it weren't for you, I wouldn't be asking my girlfriend to marry me tomorrow, would I?'

'Are you serious?' The warden was taken aback. 'Is this the real deal?'

'It is. Want me to show you the ring?'

The man shook his head and raised both hands. 'Off you go. Try to park a bit less illegally in future.' He looked down at Leon in the passenger seat and added gruffly, 'Good luck, mate.'

When the warden had walked away down Regent Street, Jamie said, 'Well done.'

'I've never managed to talk my way out of a parking ticket before.' Leon gave him an ironic high-five. 'Turns out all you need to do is get stage four cancer.'

'Every cloud.'

'All we have to do now is wait till tomorrow.' Leon grinned at him. 'And for your sake hope she says yes.'

Chapter 23

The Cotswolds

'I love you.' Leon reached for Fen's hand. 'More than you'll ever know. And I know I'm not much of a catch, but you'd make me the happiest man in the world if you'd marry me.'

Had she misheard? Fen blinked. Or was it a joke? She waited for the punchline, then realised Leon was serious. He meant it.

'Really?'

'I know I'm supposed to get down on one knee, but if I tried it, you'd only have to lift me up again. And yes, really. It would mean a lot to me. OK, it'd mean everything.' He dipped his free hand into the pocket of his blue linen shirt and took out something that glinted in the sunlight. 'But you can say no if you want to. It's allowed.'

'How romantic,' Fen said with a faint smile.

'I know, sorry, I've messed up and got it in the wrong order. This has to be the worst proposal you've ever had. Fenna Marmite Madden, will you marry me?'

'I love you too, more than *you'll* ever know. And yes, of course

I'll marry you. But I have a confession.' Fen watched as he slipped the ring onto her finger. 'My middle name isn't Marmite. It's Marieke.'

'Disappointing.' For a moment Leon moved the ring back up to her knuckle, then slid it down once more. 'But I suppose I can get over it. I do love Marmite, though.'

There it was again, the ability to joke and make each other smile under the most difficult of circumstances. She'd learned that it was possible to be simultaneously happy and grieving for what they would soon lose. Like now. Taking Leon's face between her hands, Fen kissed him and kissed him for as long as she dared, because at any moment another coughing fit could begin.

'I love you. I can't believe you just did that. I had no idea.'

'And I can't believe you haven't even looked at the ring yet.'

'It couldn't be more beautiful if it tried.' She gazed, mesmerised, at the glittering solitaire diamond on a narrow platinum band, simple and elegant and absolutely the style she would have chosen for herself. 'And it fits. How did you manage that?'

He tapped the silver band she wore on the matching finger of her right hand. 'I tried this on last week when you took it off to make pastry. It exactly fitted my little finger.' He waggled the finger at her. 'Which obviously meant I had to cross off all the other names on my list, because the only person I could ask to marry me was you.'

They looked at each other without speaking. Fen imagined how she'd feel if he wasn't ill and they could expect to spend the next fifty or so years together. On the evening of their third day in Venice, he had gazed into her eyes and said, 'Hang on, have I found you? Are you my future wife?' And of course it had been a joke, but she clearly remembered thinking, *God, I hope so.*

A sharp knock at the door made her jump. In a low voice she said, 'What do your mum and dad think about it?'

'Leon,' his mother called with a trace of impatience. 'Time's up. We're coming in now.'

'No idea,' Leon murmured in Fen's ear. 'But I guess we're about to find out.'

The news went down as well as Fen had inwardly predicted. When everyone – Leon's parents, plus Jamie – had trooped into his room and he'd made his announcement, his mother had said baldly, 'But . . . why?'

'Because I love her,' Leon replied. 'And she loves me. And I want everyone to know that.'

Fen held her breath; could this be their cue to hug her? Perhaps even say something congratulatory?

Oh. Apparently not.

'Where did you get the ring?' Greville was looking confused.

'I bought it, Dad. Yesterday.'

'Well, that's nice.' Hilary managed a smile. 'Being engaged is fine. But there's no need to rush into anything.'

'Really?' Sitting up in bed, Leon raised his eyebrows. 'Under the circumstances, I'd have said there was every need.'

'Darling—' Hilary began, but Leon hadn't finished.

'Not much point in arranging to have a wedding next summer, is there?' He paused to cough, and flinched as the effort set off a spasm of pain in his left side. 'Or even this autumn.'

'But it takes time to organise these things.'

'A normal ceremony, maybe. Not the kind we need. I've already spoken to the registrar in Stroud. There are special arrangements that can be made in situations like ours, in fact—'

'Leon, this isn't a decision to be taken lightly,' Greville interjected.

'I've never been more serious about anything in my life.'

'There are aspects that need to be taken into consideration.'

'Are there?' Leon looked faux-surprised.

'You know what I'm talking about.'

'Fenna.' His mother turned to address Fen. 'I wonder if we could speak privately to our son. Maybe you and Jamie could take a walk around the garden, give us some time alone with Leon.'

Once outside, following a winding gravel path around the side of Hetherton Hall, Jamie said, 'I'm sorry they're putting you through this.'

Fenna shrugged. 'I guess it's to do with money.'

'Oh, I'm sure of it. There's a fair amount involved.'

'And they think that's why I want to marry him?' Even the thought of it made her feel sick. 'I'm not interested in any of that.'

'I know.' Jamie nodded.

'Except you don't know, do you? Not really. I could be desperate to get my hands on it, could have been planning this whole thing from day one.'

'Nobody could have planned for all this to happen.' His tone was bleak.

'I hate that they don't trust me, though.'

'They've always been like that. When I first started coming here, they were the same with me. *Careful.*' He put out his arm and yanked her sharply to the left as they approached a lily pond.

'What?' She almost lost her balance, stumbling against him before spotting the tiny khaki frog she'd so nearly stepped on. Squashing a frog was all she needed. She shuddered and moved away, breaking the contact of Jamie's hand on her arm. 'Thanks. Don't need to add murder to my list of crimes. It'd probably turn out to be Hilary's favourite frog.' She looked sideways at him. 'What should I do? Can I just sign a document or something, saying I don't want anything at all? Would that help, d'you think?'

'I can't see Leon letting that happen. We talked about this last night. He guessed his parents would pressure him to get a prenup, but he doesn't want one.'

'It's not going to make things easy for me.'

The frog was following them now, hopping along the path like something out of a Disney film. Fen bent down and gently touched it with a small stick, pointing it at the pond then nudging it again until it got the hint and landed with a *plop* in the water.

Her phone went *ting* and a message from Leon flashed up on the screen.

You can come back now. Xx

A few seconds later, a message arrived on Jamie's phone too, and with a wry smile he said, 'Snap.' But when he took the phone out of his pocket, they both saw the words on the screen saying: *Hiya! Fancy meeting up for a drink tonight at the Prince? I'm celebrating a promotion at work and the Moët's on me!!! See you at 7! Love, Zena xxx*

He put the phone away without replying, but it served as a brutal reminder to Fen that while she and Leon were going through hell, the rest of the world was carrying on as usual, as if nothing were amiss. Jamie was being discreet about it, but he was still socialising and meeting up with friends. Because life went on. It always had, always would. When Leon was no longer here, Jamie would obviously be devastated at first, but eventually one of his other friends would be promoted to best-friend status and would take Leon's place.

The realisation hit Fen like a prop forward crashing into her chest.

'What?' He saw the look on her face.

'Nothing. Have fun.'

'Is this about Zena?' He frowned. 'I'm not going to meet up with her.'

Which should have been good news, but it was too late now; she was picturing flirtation and laughter during a carefree get-together, and feeling like a tightly coiled spring about to explode.

'Why not?' She could hear the edge in her voice, knew she was probably being unfair. 'You may as well go out and have some fun. I mean, what's stopping you? Zena's looking forward to celebrating with you, so you shouldn't let her down. Anyway, Leon wants to see me. I expect his parents have been telling him to take the ring back and see if he can get a refund. What a great day this is turning out to be.'

She spun round and headed in the direction of the house, her throat clenching with unresolved anger and her eyes burning with unshed tears because this was the pits, *the absolute pits*, and after not having cried for weeks, the last straw had evidently just been broken along with her resolve, and how, *how* had it come to this? Her breath was catching in her throat, her shoulders were shaking. Leon was dying and the unfairness of it all was *unbearable*.

'Wait,' Jamie commanded, catching up and pulling her back round to face him. 'It's OK, don't cry.'

'It isn't OK. There's nothing OK about this. And I'm *not* crying . . .' But the last word came out as a strangled sob and the tears were already streaming down her face. Jamie shook his head slightly, and for a split second his grief mirrored her own. Then his arms came around her, drawing her against him, and the misplaced anger dissipated. Fen allowed herself to dissolve and be supported by him. All the emotions she'd been holding in for so long had finally been given the green light to escape, and she let it happen, racking sobs soaking the front of his navy polo shirt as she clung to him and felt the comfort of his hand rhythmically stroking her back. It was like being small again, sobbing over a grazed knee and being consoled by Disa.

'There you are,' Hilary announced behind them. 'What on earth's going on here?'

Oh, come on, did she seriously imagine . . .?

Fen swung round so Leon's mother could see the state of her; from past experience, she knew her face would be blotchy, her eyes bloodshot. Some people might be able to cry prettily, but it wasn't one of her particular talents.

'Not what you're thinking,' she said, her voice breaking with emotion. 'I love Leon with all my heart, he's just asked me to marry him, and you think all I'm interested in is his money. Which I'm not, except I can't prove it, although if you want me to sign a prenup, I will.' She took a shuddery gulp of air. 'I'll sign anything you want, but all *I* want is for him to be well again, and I can't make that happen.'

'Come back inside.' The strain was evident in Hilary's lined face. 'Leon has given us a talking-to. He wants us all to get along together, and I've promised him we will. Are you happy to do that?'

It probably wasn't what Hilary wanted, but a truce would make life so much easier. From now on, their shared goal was to make sure Leon had the happiest possible final weeks. Fen wiped her cheeks with her hands and nodded with relief. 'Yes, of course. Absolutely.'

'Good. And he wants to book the wedding at the register

office. He's called them, and they need you both to go over there this afternoon to set the wheels in motion. Twenty-eight days is the minimum length of notice by law.'

Twenty-eight days. Numbly, Fen nodded. Did they even have that long left together?

'He says it will give him something to look forward to,' Hilary continued, her tone bracing. 'Anyway, come along, we need to hurry up. He's getting dressed and Greville's loading the wheelchair into the car.' She surveyed Fen, her head tilted to one side. 'And I hope you've stopped crying now, because you really need to do something about your face. It's a mess.'

Chapter 24

Bristol

Jamie was in Clifton, on his way to pick up a couple of ready meals from the delicatessen, when he spotted Fen walking up the street ahead of him. As he watched, she stopped outside one of the shops and pressed a buzzer.

Approaching her, he saw that the door had been answered and she was speaking to a dark-haired woman standing in the doorway.

It was the bridal shop, he realised.

'I'm sorry, if you don't have an appointment, I'm afraid there's nothing I can do about it,' the woman was telling her. 'We can't let people simply wander in off the street and start trying on our gowns for fun.'

Fen didn't know he was there, listening. Jamie pretended to be studying a chandelier in the window of the antiques shop next door.

'I'm not wanting to try on dresses for fun. I'm getting married in a fortnight.'

At this, the woman in the doorway gave a bemused half-laugh, as if suspecting that it might be a joke. 'I'm afraid that doesn't give you nearly enough time – the waiting list for our initial appointments is far longer than that. You really haven't thought this through, have you? I can't imagine anyone's going to be able to help you at this stage. I honestly think your only option now is to postpone the wedding!'

'Right, sorry.' Fen looked utterly defeated. 'I didn't know I needed to make an appointment.'

'Fen,' said Jamie. 'I thought you were going dress shopping with Disa?'

Turning and realising for the first time that he was there, Fen shook her head. 'Oh, hi. Disa had to cancel. She's come down with tonsillitis.'

'And now you aren't even allowed to *look* at wedding dresses?'

'I know.' She shrugged helplessly. 'I had no idea it was going to be so difficult.'

The woman in the doorway had recognised him. In an instant, her whole demeanour changed. 'Well, I—'

'So now we have to postpone the wedding?' said Jamie.

'Look, if it's really important, I'm sure I can make an exception.' The woman shot a dazzling smile at him. 'I had no idea this was, you know, something to do with you!' Stepping back, she indicated with a sweeping gesture for them to enter the shop. 'Unless of course you're the lucky groom-to-be, in which case I don't think you'd be allowed in!'

Jamie looked at Fen, who gave the tiniest shake of her head. He smiled at the woman and said politely, 'I'm not the groom-to-be. And thanks for the offer, but I think we'll take our chances elsewhere.'

'So that's that,' Fen said when the door had closed. 'What are you doing here anyway?'

'On my way to the deli for some food.'

'I'll walk with you, pick up a few things to take to Leon.' She paused. 'He probably won't eat them, but you never know.'

Jamie nodded; the last fortnight hadn't been going well for Leon, who was now sleeping more, eating less and needing increasing doses of morphine to keep the pain in check. He was also struggling to cope with visitors who outstayed their welcome. Yesterday a group of friends from the flying club had turned up, and he had dozed off while they'd been making plans to take him up in the helicopter for what would most likely be his final flight.

By the end of the visit, it had become apparent to all of them that such a trip – climbing up into a two-seater Robinson R22 – would be too much for him.

Fuck, it was still unimaginable.

Jamie gave himself a mental shake; there was still plenty that needed doing, and time was running out.

'What are you going to do about the wedding dress?'

'Doesn't look like there's much I can do. It was Hilary who said I should have one; I wasn't that bothered anyway. I can always wear my pink and green flowery trouser suit.'

Hmm.

Ten minutes later, as they left the deli with their bags of food, Fen stopped outside the vintage clothes shop. 'I once bought a really superb velvet kimono from this place. Maybe they'll have something I could wear for the wedding. And don't think I didn't notice your face earlier when I mentioned my trouser suit.'

Jamie smiled, because of all the clothes he'd seen her in, the big-shouldered, short-legged, bright pink and peppermint-green outfit was the most . . . eclectic.

'Can I come in with you?'

'If you want to. Didn't have you down as a vintage kind of person.'

'Me neither. But I'll give it a try.'

It wasn't a shop he'd ever ventured into before, but the interior was an actual treasure trove of clothes on padded silk hangers, spectacular hats and accessories, and rainbow arrangements of scarves and jewellery. Fen knew the staff working in there and told them she wanted something for a special occasion. Jamie, seated in a peacock cane chair, watched as she tried on a series of outfits, emerging each time from the changing room and striking a pose, and in return receiving Shaz and Zoe's straight-from-the-hip verdicts.

'Eight out of ten,' Shaz announced. 'Nice, but I'm not sure about the stripes.'

'Pretty,' said Zoe, of a multicoloured flowery frock, 'but maybe too pretty. Seven out of ten.'

'Six for this one. It's a bit seventies disco queen,' said Shaz.

Zoe shook her head at the next one. 'Not your colour. Too yellow. Sorry, it's a four from me.'

In the end, it was Shaz who found and made Fen try on a silk bias-cut dress with an iridescent pearl sheen and handkerchief hem. Emerging from the changing room, Fen said with a sigh, 'I thought this could be the one, but it's miles too big.'

It was, but the women were already swarming around her, tightening it up with bulldog clips. 'You can get it made smaller! We have someone who does alterations but she's in Mallorca at the moment. Do you have anyone who could sort it for you?'

Fen shook her head. 'No.' She turned to look at Jamie. 'What do you think?'

It was a sleek, simple dress that, once it had been properly fitted to her body, would be exactly right for a register office wedding. Jamie nodded. 'Ten out of ten. This is the one. Leon will love it.'

They left the shop and sat down in a café to search online for someone to alter the dress. Twenty minutes and many phone calls later, they were discovering that waiting lists were a thing for dressmakers too.

'This is no good.' Fen finished her coffee and shoved her phone back into her bag. 'I'll find something in another shop.'

Switching to his contacts list and scrolling through, Jamie found what he was looking for. 'OK, this could be a long shot, but bear with me. Seeing as we're desperate, let's give it a try.'

'You take a call out of the blue from Jamie Hamilton,' Brendan O'Hara said cheerfully, 'and you tell him to get himself over here pronto. I mean, who could resist a request to help out the most famous ex-rugby player in Bristol?' He darted around Fen, who was standing on a slightly wobbly bench in the far-too-big dress, and deftly pinned folds of silk into place.

It wasn't quite the setting she'd anticipated, but beggars couldn't be choosers. They were in a tiny hut that smelled of mud and Lynx and teenage boys, while outside on the football pitch, two teams were playing a noisy after-school match with the score currently standing at 3–2.

At least Brendan appeared to know what he was doing. Fen obediently held out her arms and tried not to be ticklish as he pinned the bodice. In his seventies now, he had for decades volunteered at the school in south Bristol, looking after and maintaining the sports kits and equipment, and doing anything around the PE department that required upkeep. But his actual career, Jamie had explained to Fen as they'd made their way here, had been in tailoring, so although silk wedding dresses might not be what he was used to dealing with, he was still handy with a needle and thread, and willing to give this one a go.

'Don't you worry, m'darling,' Brendan continued now. 'I know I'm more used to sewing up torn shorts and jerseys these days, but I can get this sorted for you by the weekend.' Indicating Jamie, who was standing guard inside the doorway ensuring they weren't interrupted, he broke into a grin. 'I remember when this one got himself into a skirmish at school and one of the sleeves was ripped clean off his new blazer. By the time I'd sewn it back on, it was as good as new.'

'My mother never even found out,' said Jamie. He pulled a face. 'Just as well, seeing as she couldn't have afforded to buy another one.'

Fen raised her eyebrows at him. 'You got into a skirmish? I'm *shocked*.'

'Ah, there was a boy in his class who was being picked on something rotten,' Brendan explained. 'Jamie was standing up for the lad when the bullies decided to pile onto him instead. Six of them there were, what with them being a shower of cowards. But Jamie here was one of the good guys. Otherwise I'd never have sewn that sleeve back on for him.'

The shriek of a whistle signalling the end of the match made Fen jump and almost lose her balance on the rickety bench. Cheers and groans went up from the players outside, and she felt a sudden urge to clamp her arms around her chest. 'They're not going to burst in here, are they?' This hut was their changing room, after all. Their discarded school uniforms were scattered in untidy piles along the other benches.

'Jamie lad, hold back the hordes,' Brendan instructed. 'We'll be finished here in a couple of minutes.'

Although the situation now felt increasingly surreal, Fen remained standing on the bench while Jamie explained to the lads gathered outside the hut that they couldn't come in just yet. Their initial cries of protest turned to excitement as they realised who he was and began to bombard him with questions.

'My phone's in there, in my bag. Can I have a selfie with you when I get it back?'

'Will you sign my shirt?'

'My mum fancies you. D'you want her number?'

'What's it like being on the telly?'

'If you sign my arm, I could get it made into a tattoo.'

Brendan finished pinning the dress and unzipped it, then turned away as Fen carefully slid out of it and passed it over to him before climbing back into her own clothes at the speed of light.

Phew, done.

Then Jamie stepped aside and the boys burst into the hut, all intent on grabbing their phones out of their school bags and getting a selfie with Jamie Hamilton to show off to their friends and families.

As the selfie-taking continued, one lad gave Fen a puzzled look, then turned to Brendan. 'Why is she in here, sir?'

Fen said, 'He was helping me with my wedding dress.'

The boy glanced around the muddy hut and gave a disbelieving laugh, as if she'd just claimed to be Sabrina Carpenter. 'Yeah, right.'

What had started off as a depressingly unsuccessful outfit-buying trip had ended up an unexpectedly fun one, and now Fen's spirits had lifted. Jamie was driving her back across town and they were sharing a bag of cherry Haribos while laughing at a comedian on the radio. For a short while, the endless dread of what lay ahead had receded. It was purely temporary, she knew that; once he'd dropped her back to her own car, she would drive over to Hetherton Hall. Later, Jamie would arrive and she would leave to go home and hopefully get some sleep, so that at any time of the evening Leon would have someone with him if he woke up and wanted company. So far, she hadn't spent the night there, because Hilary liked to take the night shift, sitting at his bedside and keeping watch over him as he slept.

Her phone rang and her heart leapt because Leon's name was on the screen. Snatching it up, she put him on speaker. 'Hi, I'll be there by four, and guess what? I've found my dress for the wedding!'

But it wasn't Leon's voice on the phone. It was Hilary's.

'Leon's not doing so well. The doctor's visited and upped his meds. She says we should prepare ourselves for the worst.' She paused and took a breath. 'Anyway, I thought you should know. It's not looking good.'

Fen's palms were slippery with perspiration, her throat so tight she was unable to speak. If the last weeks had involved the sensation of falling off a cliff in slow motion, that feeling was suddenly speeding up in the most terrifying way possible.

Next to her, accelerating hard as the traffic lights ahead turned from green to amber, his knuckles white as he gripped the steering wheel, Jamie said loudly enough for Leon's mother to hear, 'Tell him we're on our way.'

Chapter 25

The Cotswolds

The room felt different now. When they'd first arrived, Hilary had been at Leon's bedside, sitting stiffly upright on a chair and wiping her eyes. Leon had been asleep, his breathing slow and heavy, his hair unnaturally tidy where his mother had combed it.

'I'll go and have a cup of tea,' she'd murmured. 'This is so awful.'

'You're exhausted. Get some rest,' Jamie had told her.

'We'll come and fetch you if anything changes,' Fen had added, her hand resting on Hilary's arm as their paths crossed.

And instead of moving away, Hilary had nodded and said with a ghost of a smile, 'Thank you.'

But that had been three hours ago. Now Leon opened his eyes. 'Hey. Where's Mum?'

'Catching up on some sleep.' Fen gently squeezed his hand. 'How are you feeling?'

'Like everything's happening without me. How long have you been here?'

'Since four.'

There was a clock on the chest of drawers opposite. Leon blinked at it. 'And now it's seven thirty. I'm sorry. This must be so bloody boring for you two. You don't have to stay.'

'Except we're not going anywhere,' Jamie said from the foot of the bed. 'So get used to it.'

A faint smile lifted the corners of Leon's mouth. 'Mate, this has to be seriously messing up your social life.'

'It is. And yet I'd still rather be here. Go figure.'

Leon put his hand up to his head. 'Must be the new 'do. Has my mother been brushing my hair again? It's like being back at infants' school.'

Fen leaned across and ruffled it into its natural state. 'There, that's better. You're back.'

'Probably not for long.' He stroked her wrist. 'Did you manage to find a dress?'

'I did!' There was no need to give him the convoluted version. 'It's being altered to fit me. You're going to love it.'

'If you're wearing it, I will.' Leon sucked in his breath as a wave of pain caught him unawares. 'God, Fen, it wasn't meant to happen like this. I love you so much.'

'I know.' Her throat began to ache with the effort of not giving in to her emotions. She was dimly aware of Jamie's footsteps behind her as he slipped out of the room to give them some privacy.

'Talk about terrible timing. I wish I could have met you years ago.'

'Better this way,' she told him, 'than never at all.'

'Really?'

'God, yes. You've definitely been worth it. Venice was the best week of my life.'

'Mine too.' With difficulty, he took a deep breath. 'I don't think I'm going to make the wedding. Do you think we should get it brought forward?'

It would mean being admitted to the local hospice, which she knew his parents were against. 'Do you want to?'

'I don't know any more. You decide.'

He was flat-out exhausted, that much was obvious. If he was too worn out to enjoy the day, was there really any point in going through with it? It wouldn't make any difference to the way she felt about him. Stroking her index finger along the line of his jaw, Fen said, 'If it's too much to think about, why don't we leave it for now and see how you feel in a day or two?'

He nodded, visibly relieved. 'You've made me so happy.'

'Same.'

'Want to come and lie next to me?'

'More than anything in the world.'

Slowly and with some difficulty, Leon edged himself over to make room. Taking great care, Fen kicked off her flip-flops and climbed onto the bed beside him. He tilted his head to face her and whispered, 'No funny business, mind. I'm not that kind of guy.'

'Just a cuddle, I promise.' She gently placed her arms around him and rested her head in the crook of his neck.

They fitted together so well. Leon trailed his fingers across her torso, then left his hand resting on her stomach and murmured, 'We could have had babies.'

Fen nodded, words beyond her now. Sometimes she could almost picture their family, two girls and a boy playing in the garden, their blonde hair gleaming bright in the sunshine, the boy's as tousled as Leon's, the girls' flying free behind them as they raced across the lawn.

'Will you look after Jamie when I'm gone? He's going to miss me.'

She couldn't imagine Jamie needing looking after, but nodded anyway. 'I will.'

'Love you.'

'Love you more.' *So much more.*

Leon's eyelids were closing. Reaching up, she pressed a kiss on the side of his mouth and felt his lips pucker up in return. 'God, what a shitshow,' he murmured. 'It's like watching a brilliant film, then discovering it has a really rubbish ending.'

'It's not the end yet.'

He reached for her left hand, his fingers tracing the outline of the diamond solitaire. 'Tired again. Don't go anywhere.'

'I won't.'

Fen waited until he'd drifted off once more and there was only the sound of his breathing in the makeshift bedroom that had become the world he now lived in. The windows were open. In the distance she could hear the sound of a tractor in a nearby field and the drone of a light aircraft overhead. Birds were singing in the trees. A warm breeze filtered into the room, bringing with it the scent of cut grass and roses from the garden. A pair of butterflies danced together, their creamy white wings bright against the dazzling blue of the sky. As Fen watched, one of them broke ranks and fluttered in through the window, then panicked and began bouncing off the glass before eventually managing to find its way out again to rejoin its mate.

A narrow escape; for a few frantic seconds they'd lost each other. Now they were back together and all was well once more.

Lucky them.

Fen exhaled. Then again, at this precise moment in time, would she want to be anywhere but here?

No, of course not.

Which in its own way made her lucky too.

Jamie turned the door handle in slow motion and silently pushed open the door. Two hours had passed since he'd left them alone in the room, and he knew the next round of Leon's painkillers was due.

The sight that greeted him turned his heart over. The lower angle of the setting sun meant it was now shining directly through the open window, bathing the bed in amber sunlight. And lying curled up there together in a tangle of white sheets were Leon and Fen, both fast asleep, looking more peaceful than he'd seen either of them looking for weeks.

Oh shit, unless that meant . . .

But no, even as the terrible thought crossed his mind, a small fly landed on Leon's bare ankle and his foot twitched in response. Not dead, thank God, just utterly relaxed and happy to be with Fen.

It was a heartbreakingly beautiful sight to behold. The love they shared had been wonderful to witness from day one. Turning away, Jamie left the room once more and carefully closed the door behind him. Having never experienced a connection of that intensity himself, he could only imagine how it felt.

It hadn't happened that night. The uneven decline continued for another seventy-two hours, and Leon was able to say whatever he wanted to say as weary acceptance ran hand in hand with the weakening of his body and the knowledge that the inevitable end was drawing near.

Fen stayed with him, and Hilary and Greville didn't object. Jamie came and went, letting himself into Fen's flat, collecting whatever she needed and bringing it to her at Hetherton Hall. On the third day, he'd arrived with the silk dress Brendan had finished altering, and when Leon was briefly awake, Fen unwrapped it and showed it to him.

'Go on then,' said Leon. 'Put it on.'

There had been no further mention of bringing the date of the wedding forward; no burning need in the end to be married. Fen changed out of her shirt and leggings and into the bias-cut dress the colour of mother-of-pearl. Touchingly, Hilary lent her a pearl choker and helped her to put her hair up in a topknot. When she made her entrance into Leon's room, the expression on his face was one she would always treasure and never forget.

'Look at you.' He drew her close when she joined him on the bed. The whites of his eyes might be properly yellow now as the liver failure took hold, and his skin held a waxen pallor, but that irrepressible smile still lit up his face. 'What did I ever do to deserve you?'

Fen said, 'You tricked me into thinking I was about to get my hands on a free Scotch egg.'

Leon died the following evening with everyone around him. His breathing slowed, he no longer responded with anything but the faintest of nods, and his eyes remained closed. At eight thirty he took his final breath while Hilary held one hand and Fen clasped the other.

Fen closed her eyes and listened to Hilary's stifled sobs.

It was all over.

It was also unimaginable, but life without Leon in it was only just beginning.

Opening her eyes, she turned her attention to Jamie on the

opposite side of the bed, his hand resting on Hilary's shaking shoulder. He looked devastated. If she felt like this after having known Leon for two months, how was it for Jamie, who'd been his best friend for thirteen years?

Chapter 26

Oxford

Hattie pushed open the door and emerged from the pub, to be greeted by a waggy-tailed brown and white terrier on a long lead, clearly hoping that she might have more snacks about her person than his owner, who was sitting at the nearest bench nursing a pint of beer.

She bent to say hello to the little dog, and apologised for not having anything for him to eat. Forgiving her, he carried on madly wagging his tail and dancing around her. Honestly, why couldn't more men be as lovely as dogs?

Moving away, so she could speak without being overheard, she took out her phone. Kayla picked up before the second ring.

'Just so you know,' said Hattie, 'I'm never going to forgive you for this.'

'Oh no, not again.' Kayla gave a snort of laughter. 'Another one telling you how much he still loves his ex?'

Hattie sighed. This was what had happened on the last date Kayla had persuaded her — against her better judgement — to go on, with Peter the bitter bathroom fitter. And it was all very well for Kayla to crack up laughing, but she wasn't the one currently trapped on yet another blind date from hell.

'This one's obsessed with his mum, for a change. And fish fingers. He's shown me the spreadsheet he's drawn up to demonstrate which ones are the best and worst, and why.'

'You can't blame me for that. He didn't mention it in his list of interests. Where are you now?'

'Outside the pub. We've ordered our food and he's gone to the loo, so I came out to give you a quick update. Oh, *no*.'

'No what?'

'I'll call you back.' Hattie stared at the sporty red Mazda that had just flashed its lights and slowed to a halt twenty yards up the road. As she watched, the car reversed until it was level with her. The next moment, the driver's door flew open and her ex-husband jumped out, beaming with delight. 'Hats! I mean, Hattie, it *is* you! What are you doing here?'

Not again. Did this mean he'd somehow arranged for this to happen? Had he persuaded Frank the fish-finger fanatic to match with her on the dating app for a laugh?

'What are *you* doing here?' she countered accusingly, and Guy spread his hands.

'I live up the road. This is my local pub. But if you're stalking me, that's fine, I really don't mind. In fact, I'm flattered.'

'Of course I'm not stalking you.' They'd chatted a fair bit online but she hadn't seen him in person since Venice.

'Ah, that's a shame. But you're looking well. Here on your own?'

'Actually I'm with a . . . friend.'

'A . . . friend?' He picked up on the hesitation, mimicking it and raising an eyebrow. 'Sounds interesting. Got yourself a new man?'

Just her luck; if only he could disappear in a puff of smoke. Hattie shook her head. 'No.'

'So this is getting mysterious.' His tone was playful. 'Now I'm intrigued.'

'Phew, you're out here,' exclaimed a voice behind her. And there was Frank, looking relieved. 'When I saw the table was empty, I was worried you'd done a runner and left me! I thought, *Not again!*'

Guy looked shocked. 'Has she run out on you before?'

'Not this one. There've been others, though.' Frank wiped imaginary sweat from his brow. 'Internet dating, it's a minefield.'

'So this is the first time you two have met?' said Guy. 'How's it going?'

'Really well so far.' Frank nodded enthusiastically.

'Really well?' Guy was visibly impressed. 'Excellent!'

'I was taking a call from a friend,' Hattie said hurriedly. 'We can go back inside now.' She narrowed her eyes at her ex-husband. 'Bye.'

Thirty minutes later, the terrible date was limping to its conclusion and even Frank had come to realise they weren't a match made in heaven. It was while he'd been reciting his long list of favourite coach trips and had caught her attempting to smother a yawn that he'd stopped and said accusingly, 'Aren't you even interested?'

And how was she meant to respond to that? As she prepared to do the polite thing and lie through her teeth, the door to the pub swung open, and there was Guy again. This time his arrival didn't seem like such a bad thing. Spotting them and making his way over, he said cheerfully, 'Thought I might have missed you. Still going well?'

'Not really,' said Frank. 'I think I'm boring her. It's usually what happens, no idea why.'

OK, maybe it would be helpful to tell him. Hattie swallowed her last mouthful of sticky toffee pudding. 'To be frank, er . . . Frank, I think the lists aren't the best idea.'

'My mum said that too. But I like making lists. It's kind of my hobby.' He paused. 'So do you two know each other?'

'We used to be married,' said Guy.

'Oh!' Frank looked alarmed.

'Don't worry, I'm not still in love with her. I just want what's best for my ex-wife.'

'I don't think I'm best for her.' Hastily taking out his wallet, Frank called across for their bill and said to Hattie, 'We're splitting it, right? Except you had two glasses of wine and I only had a shandy, so you'll need to pay the difference.'

When Frank had left, Guy said, 'I hope you're not too heartbroken.'

Hattie gave him a look. 'What are you doing back here?'

'Rescuing you. Also, offering you a lift home.'

'Why?'

'Because it's raining and the buses out here only run once an hour.' He paused. 'It's good to see you again. You're looking well. And I'm saying that in a friendly way, don't worry. Not trying to chat you up.'

On their last evening in Venice, he definitely *had* been trying to chat her up. Slightly miffed that he was no longer interested, Hattie said, 'Because you've found yourself a new lady friend?'

There was that twinkle in his eye. 'Let's say I'm keeping my options open. So, how about that lift home?'

She glanced out of the window. The rain was now hammering down, bouncing off the road like shrapnel. Her flat was a good half a mile from the bus stop, and of course she hadn't brought an umbrella with her. 'Go on then. Thanks.'

In the car, Guy said, 'So who'd've thought it, eh? Kayla and the gondolier, still going strong.'

'I know. He flew over here a fortnight ago. And Kayla's off to stay with him for four days next week. She's even taking evening classes in conversational Italian, so she can really get to know his parents. If that isn't true love, I don't know what is.'

'Good for her.'

'How about Suze? Any updates?'

'She's back together with her ex. Apparently their break was just a blip.' Guy tapped his fingers on the steering wheel as they pulled up at a junction. 'Which is fine by me.' He gave her a sidelong smile. 'Basically, I was an idiot. We weren't each other's type at all. When you know what you like, it makes sense to stick to it.'

Did that mean what she thought it meant? Was he hinting that maybe their own years apart had been a blip? Hattie guessed what would come next. But twenty minutes later, when he pulled up outside her flat, the expected invitation didn't happen.

'I'm sorry your date with Frank didn't work out.' He gave her arm a consoling pat. 'But don't give up. The right man's out there somewhere, waiting to meet you.'

A consoling pat? The cheek of it!

'Thanks for the lift.' She waited for him to at least kiss her on the cheek.

But there was no kiss and Guy's tone was brisk. 'No problem at all. Happy to help. Bye.'

Which had the effect of making her heart give a little flip of surprise and, yes, *pleasure* when he called her three days later.

'How's it going with you and Frank, then?' He sounded jovial. 'Engaged yet?'

'Not quite. I'm playing hard to get.'

He laughed. 'Listen, no worries if you're not interested, but there's a new Indian restaurant in town that's been getting some seriously good reviews. I wondered if you fancied giving it a go with me tomorrow night?'

Hattie took a breath; she and Guy had always loved Indian food and trying out new places to eat. Tomorrow evening she was free. And yesterday in her lunch hour she'd bought herself a new dress that flattered her figure no end.

Maybe a week ago she would have turned him down. But now it seemed like an offer she didn't even want to refuse, and without hesitating, she heard herself say, 'Sounds like fun! Why not?'

Bristol

Jamie's agent had called him yesterday and said, 'I know you'll probably say no, but the *Every Night Show* has had a last-minute cancellation for tomorrow and they'd love it if you could step in to chat about the new sports quiz.'

And Jamie, having discovered how bleak and empty the days were without Leon around to share them, had said, 'OK, may as well.'

Anything to take his mind off the current situation at home. The apartment had never been tidier nor felt more empty.

Now here he was, sitting in his dressing room, waiting for the popular live magazine-style TV show to start. He was due to appear in a few minutes, having been briefed earlier by Sadie Ingalls, the presenter who'd be interviewing him tonight.

But seven minutes later, diverting without warning from the subject of the sports quiz and the friendly rivalry between the teams, Sadie changed tack. 'Speaking of friendship, can I say how very sorry we all were to hear about the tragic death of your friend Leon Spencer-Carr.'

What? There'd been no warning that this would be mentioned. Then again, why shouldn't it be? Taken aback, Jamie said, 'Thanks. Yes. It's been a tough time.'

Sadie nodded sympathetically. 'I can't imagine how hard it must have been for you. And his family, of course. It all happened quite quickly, I believe.'

'It did. A couple of months ago we were in Venice and everything seemed fine. Then the symptoms began.' Jamie paused, cleared his throat. 'And it went downhill after that.'

'You and Leon shared a flat. He was your best and oldest friend.' Sadie's voice softened as she leaned towards him. 'You must be missing him terribly.'

'We're all missing him terribly.' He was on live television and the unexpected change of subject had caught him off guard. As he paused, realising his emotions were getting the better of him, he saw a blown-up photo appear on the screen to his left, of himself and Leon during their university years. The informal snap had been taken during a party at a scruffy student flat, and they were both brandishing bottles of lager, roaring with laughter at some shared joke.

His eyes filling with tears, he pictured Leon's reaction if he were still alive and could see him now; it was only too easy to imagine the amount of teasing that would ensue. Leon would find this hilarious.

'Oh no. I'm sorry, here . . .' Reaching beneath the desk in front of them, Sadie produced a box of tissues and offered it to him.

Jamie ignored the tissues, even as he felt a tear roll down his cheek and brushed it away. 'He was like a brother to me. I loved him, and he'd never let me forget this moment, he'd be wetting himself laughing. It's hard to think I'm never going to hear him taking the mickey out of me again. But I was lucky to have him as a best friend. And I'm going to miss him for ever.'

'Of course you will.' Sadie had taken one of the tissues for herself and was carefully dabbing beneath her eyes. 'And he was lucky to have you. Thank you so much for sharing those beautiful words with us. Listening to you, I'm sure I'm not the only one getting emotional right now . . .'

Oxford

The piece with Jamie ended and Sadie Ingalls moved the show smoothly on to the next segment, about the nation's favourite flavour of crisps. Five minutes ago, Hattie's doorbell had buzzed and she'd let Guy into the flat because he'd arrived a few minutes early and she was still deciding which shoes to wear depending on how far she might have to walk to the restaurant. The TV had still been on, and when Sadie had announced that their next guest was Jamie Hamilton, Guy had said, 'Hey, how about that? OK if we watch it? He might mention the Venice trip.'

Now, having sat together and taken in Jamie's interview in a state of shock, Hattie switched off the TV and turned to Guy in disbelief.

'Leon's *dead*. How can that be possible?' She felt the build-up of pressure in her chest, covered her face with both hands and began to sob, because Leon had been so cheerful and friendly whenever they'd seen him, and witnessing Jamie's genuine grief on the screen just now had been deeply affecting. 'I can't believe he's gone. And poor Fen . . . it doesn't bear thinking about.' Everyone on the ship had been aware of the brand-new love-at-first-sight relationship between Leon and Fen, and had delighted in seeing them together, both so giddy with joy at having found each other.

She turned to Guy, burying her wet face in his neck, and he wrapped his arms around her. Gruffly he said, 'It's a shock. He was a good lad. They thought they had the rest of their lives together. Shit, it just goes to show, we never know how long we have left.'

For the next hour, they absorbed the news, letting it sink in. Hattie kept tearing up each time it struck her afresh that Leon was gone. Guy was affected too, but just as when her father had first been diagnosed with his debilitating illness, eight years ago, he was the one doing the consoling. He'd taken charge this evening, cancelling their taxi and the restaurant reservation, comforting her while she sobbed and not minding at all that she'd got mascara stains on the front of his favourite shirt.

'Thanks. I forgot you were always good in a crisis.' She managed a weak smile as he held the mirror in front of her so she could clean away the streaky mess of make-up.

'I may not have many talents.' Guy took the sodden grey cotton-wool pad from her and replaced it with a clean one. 'But I do my best to help where I can.'

'I look terrible now.'

'No you don't.' He paused. 'You always look lovely to me.'

Hattie sniffed in a way that wasn't lovely at all. Since Venice, theirs had become a kind of see-sawing friendship, with Guy being the keener of the two and Hattie enjoying having the upper hand. But what she was struggling to admit, even to herself, was the fact that her own feelings were becoming increasingly muddled. She was liking him more, but scared of getting involved again. He'd been doing his best to prove to her that he was a changed person, a better man than before, but how could she trust him and believe it would last? Could a relationship that had fizzled and died a few years ago ever be successfully revived?

Having had nothing to eat since breakfast, Hattie winced as her stomach now rumbled. It felt wrong to be happening while they were still getting over the news about Leon.

But Guy said, 'Hey, we do need to eat. Do you want to go out?'

She shook her head. 'No.'

'Shall we order in?'

'I suppose.' It crossed her mind that in the old days, he would invariably have tried to change her mind, had never wanted to stay at home, whereas now he was definitely enjoying it more. It was as if he had got the endless need to be elsewhere out of his system. He'd already tried to explain this to her, and she'd struggled to trust him, but as time passed it was beginning to seem as if what he was saying might be true. Which was ironic in a way, seeing as these days she was finding herself enjoying going out so much more.

Maybe, just maybe, they could end up balancing the see-saw after all.

'Actually, I've had a better idea.' Guy rose to his feet now. 'Why don't I make you your favourite?'

Hattie sniffed again. Her favourite was a cheese soufflé, and when they'd been married, Guy had always done them for her on her birthday. Soufflés weren't the easiest, but he'd taught himself how to make them. She wasn't an enthusiastic cook herself, and it was years since she'd last had one.

'It's too much trouble. And I've run out of eggs.'

'That's why they have these things called shops,' said Guy. 'You wait here and I'll be back in ten minutes. Here, have another tissue in the meantime.'

Hattie wiped her eyes once more. The nicer he was to her, the more she wanted to cry.

Bristol

Sadie Ingalls had been in a corner of the green room, deep in conversation with her producer. Coming over to join Jamie as he accepted a glass of wine from one of the runners, she said, 'When you wake up tomorrow, you're going to find another two million women have fallen in love with you.'

'You mean because I made a prat of myself on national TV?'

'Because you were brave enough to show how you feel about losing your best friend. There's nothing more irresistible than a man who isn't afraid to reveal his emotions. And you were already attractive in the first place. The way you spoke about Leon tonight was quite a moment. It was extra special, and the reaction on social media has already taken off. Our show's never seen a response like it.'

Jamie said evenly, 'Great for you, then.'

'And for you too.'

His jaw tightened. 'Believe it or not, that isn't why I did it. It wasn't planned.'

Sadie looked horrified. 'I know that! Jamie, that's not what I meant *at all*. You've touched the hearts of millions of viewers,' she hastily explained. 'You're giving countless men permission to shed a tear in public and feel no shame about it. That is such a powerful gift. You're going to make a real difference, you know? Because what you did and what you said was so authentic.'

Jamie nodded, ashamed of himself for having overreacted. His emotions had been all over the place. He'd tried calling Fen immediately after the show, but she hadn't picked up or called back. 'OK. Sorry. It's been a tough couple of weeks.'

'Please, no need to apologise.' Sadie clutched his forearm. 'I know exactly what you're going through. I lost my closest friend when I was eighteen and it was devastating.'

'You did?'

'We're not here to talk about me. I just wish there was something I could do to make you feel better. But there is no magic solution. You have to make your own way through it, and eventually the pain lessens. You're able to remember the good times without wanting to yell at people when they compare your loss with the time their pet rat died.'

Jamie half smiled, because he'd already been subjected to similar comments, well-meaning but painful to endure. 'So true.'

'Look, I'm heading off soon, going to grab something to eat nearby before going home. If you don't have any plans, you'd be very welcome to join me.' Her eyes sparkled as she lowered her voice. 'But of course it's fine if you'd rather not.'

He paused, picturing himself in his smart but soulless hotel room, ordering room service and watching rubbish on the oversized TV opposite his bed. Or . . .

'I know a little restaurant not far from here,' said Sadie. 'Italian, fantastic food, fazzoletti with walnut butter to die for.'

Maybe this was what he needed, a bit of distraction with a smart, sympathetic woman, coupled with some fazzoletti. Whatever that might be.

He checked his phone once more. Still nothing from Fen. Finishing his glass of slightly warm Sauvignon Blanc, he nodded. 'Why not? Sounds good to me.'

Fen's sleep patterns were all over the place. Yesterday evening she'd fallen asleep on the sofa at six, then had woken disorientated at midnight to find her phone out of battery on the floor beside her and no sign of the charger cable anywhere.

If Leon still existed somewhere on another plane, was this what it felt like for him, completely helpless, with no phone and no way of contacting anyone he might be desperate to speak to?

But since she'd set the TV earlier to record Jamie's appearance on the *Every Night Show*, she curled up on the sofa she'd previously been sprawled across and watched his eyes fill with tears as he spoke simply but movingly about Leon.

Tears, so bloody many of them, where did they *come* from? Fen wiped her face with a crumpled tissue from her cardigan pocket; her body appeared to be a bath tap that never ran out of water. When she told herself that at some stage in the future she *would* stop crying twenty times a day, the prospect of that caused her to feel so guilty it only set her off again.

She rewatched the segment twice more, then dozed off and dreamt Leon was yelling for help in the middle of a lake, but no one would let her dive in and rescue him.

She got up and poured herself a bowl of muesli, before discovering too late that the milk was off.

Then she tried to drink a mug of black tea, which was almost as grim as the sour milk.

She watched three episodes of an old comedy series that failed to make her smile even once.

At five in the morning, she showered and dressed, then drove to the twenty-four-hour supermarket.

Arriving at the till to pay for her new charging cable, a litre of milk and a six-pack of paprika crisps, she unzipped her shoulder bag and saw, curled like a snake around her purse, the missing cable.

Typical, typical, *fucking typical*. To top it off, her eyes were now leaking again.

'You all right, love?' said a middle-aged man behind her.

'I'm OK.' Fen nodded wearily.

'Got the flu, have you? You want to get home and go back to bed.' Evidently trying to reassure her, he said, 'You look terrible!'

Which was always good to know.

Home again, she plugged in her phone and watched it come back to life. There had been two missed calls from Jamie yesterday evening, made shortly after the programme had ended. She wouldn't call him back yet, in case he was lucky enough to still be asleep.

It was scrolling through social media that brought home to her how affected the viewing audience had been by his appearance on the show. The pages were awash with crying and broken-heart emojis along with extravagant declarations of love for Jamie Hamilton. There were also very many comments ending with *RIP Leon*, posted by people who until last night had never even been aware of his existence, which was weird but in a strange way almost comforting, because at least they'd taken the trouble to type out his name.

Then her gaze fell on a post that said, *Phwoar, lucky Sadie!!!* and was followed by a link to the online gossip section of a massively popular news website. Fen clicked on the link and saw a short, excitable piece about Jamie's appearance on the show titled: 'Grieving Rugby Star Consoled By Sexy Sadie!'

The first couple of photos were screenshots of Jamie wiping his eyes on the show. The rest were of him and Sadie Ingalls emerging from a restaurant in the rain, huddled together beneath an umbrella and looking as if they couldn't get enough of each other.

As if they didn't have a care in the world.

Fen took a deep breath, scrolling down the page to see how many photos there were ... eleven, twelve, thirteen ... and in several of them you could see that Jamie was holding the umbrella in one hand while the other was around Sadie's waist. They were gazing into each other's eyes, clearly having the best time, and in one of the photos she was leaning into him, her hand pressed to his chest, murmuring into his ear while Jamie tipped his head back and laughed.

The accompanying piece did a good job of guessing what had been going on, as well as what could be about to happen. There was also a helpful red circle drawn on the final photo, indicating the gold foil top of a champagne bottle peeking out of Sadie's unzipped shoulder bag, leading the writer to conclude that they were most likely heading off somewhere more private so she could console Jamie in the traditional manner.

That was the great thing about being well known, wasn't it? If you were a good-looking rugby player and life was getting you down a bit, there was always an attractive woman only too happy to take your mind off it and cheer you up.

Lucky old Jamie. Must be nice to be so easily distracted. Swallowing with difficulty, Fen pressed the side button and switched off her phone.

Chapter 27

It was the day before the funeral. Fen had been waiting by Arrivals at Bristol airport for seven minutes when the opaque glass doors finally slid open and Molly came through. Arms stretched wide, she wrapped them around Fen. 'I still can't believe he's gone. How *are* you?'

'Doing OK.' Fen was used to saying it now, meaningless though the response was, because she'd never been less OK in her life. 'It's so good to see you. Thank you for coming. You didn't need to, but I'm glad you're here.'

They'd been messaging back and forth non-stop since Venice, but it was so much better to see her again in person. For several seconds they held each other tight and rocked in silence. Then Fen said, 'Come on, let's get out of here, I'm parked in the drop-off zone.' She took charge of Molly's wheelie cabin case and led the way out of the airport.

'How's Jamie?'

'He's OK too.'

Outside, in the world's most expensive car park, she was in the process of opening the boot of the car when a male voice behind her said mildly, 'Ow,' and Fen turned to see that the cabin case she'd let go of had rolled away of its own accord, careering into the calves of a man in the process of opening the rear passenger door of his dark green Mercedes. Before she had a chance to grab it, the case ricocheted off his legs and scooted towards the bodywork on the side of the car.

'I'm so sorry!' She launched herself at the case in the nick of time. 'I didn't know it was going to do that.'

'Jeez, what's the matter with you? Are you *stupid*?' A heavy-set man spilled out of the rear passenger seat, glaring at her in disgust. 'The case has *wheels*, lady, but you didn't stop to think it might roll off down the slope?'

'I was distracted.'

'You mean you couldn't be bothered to engage your brain? You British women don't have a single clue, do you?'

Fen's cheeks reddened. 'It was an accident.'

'It's fine,' said the man whose legs had borne the brunt of the case. Belatedly, she realised the gleaming Mercedes was a limo-for-hire and he was a professional chauffeur. 'No damage done.' He flashed a reassuring smile at her. 'Don't worry.'

The driver's kindness, contrasted with his passenger's rudeness, caused her to burst into tears.

'Jeez, this is all I need,' sneered the passenger. 'If I wanted to see a woman crying, I'd stay at home with my wife.'

When he'd thundered off with his own case, Molly said, 'What a charmer. Is he always that awful?'

'He's been that awful for the last three hundred miles.' The chauffeur, who had to be close to retirement age, shook his head. 'He's been a nightmare. I'm so sorry he upset you.'

Fen said ruefully, 'It wasn't him being horrible. It was you being nice that made me cry.'

He smiled and closed the boot of the Mercedes. 'Next time I won't say anything. Have a good journey, ladies. You take care.'

The Cotswolds

The ancient church was situated on the top of a hill just outside the village of Hetherton. It was a golden afternoon, the sky clear blue and the sun bouncing off the windscreens of the dozens of parked vehicles lining the narrow lanes leading up to it.

Wanting to spend the night alone, Fen had been collected this morning by Disa and Molly and brought here in Disa's car. She took a deep breath as they reached the lychgate on foot and saw the hundreds of people milling around in the churchyard. This was where she and Leon would have held their wedding if life had continued as they'd both expected it to. And here came Jamie, who would have been Leon's best man, making his way over to them through the throng. He was wearing a dark suit and white shirt, and his shoulder-length hair gleamed. Greeting each of them with a brief kiss on the cheek, he said to Molly, 'It's good of you to come all this way.'

'I had to. I mean, I know I didn't know him well, but I was kind of the reason he met Fen. And look how many people are here. He was so popular.'

Jamie nodded in agreement. 'Everyone loved him.'

'He was lucky to have you as a friend.' Molly's eyes glistened.

'I was the lucky one, to have him.' He turned to Fen. 'Hilary and Greville are in the front pew. You and I are right behind them. Steve and Kamal from the flying club are in charge of the audio equipment and everything's ready back at the hall for the reception afterwards, so you don't have to worry about a thing.' He paused and checked his watch. 'His parents have gone inside, so shall we follow them?'

Fen nodded, her mouth dry. She knew that Leon had arranged every detail of the service himself, with the help of Jamie and a couple of other friends. He'd planned it to come in at under sixty minutes, which meant in just over an hour it would be over. The coffin would then be taken to the crematorium for the committal, but that was to be attended by Hilary and Greville only, while everyone else headed to Hetherton Hall for the reception. If she really couldn't handle the jollity and laughter of the occasion as friends greeted each other and celebrated Leon's life, Fen knew she didn't have to stay; she was free to leave at any time.

Just an hour here in the church. She could do this.

Nodding at Jamie, she took the arm he was holding out to her. 'Let's go.'

The service began and afternoon sunlight streamed in through the stained-glass windows, splashing bright colours onto the front of Fen's plain charcoal-grey top. Her throat was too tight to even attempt to sing the opening hymn, but the number of people crammed into the church made up for it. Greville stood and read a passage from the Bible, then Hilary stumbled through an emotional poem that provoked several audible sobs.

Jamie reached for Fen's hand and gave it a squeeze as another of Leon's many friends paid tribute to him. Then, after more music, it was his turn to speak.

Taking his place at the head of the nave, he cleared his throat and began. 'Leon was the wittiest, cleverest, handsomest best friend anyone could wish for.' Pause. 'He wrote these words, by the way, and told me I had to say them.'

Everyone laughed.

'He also wanted me to tell you he was an excellent singer, a superlative helicopter pilot . . . and, it goes without saying, a world-class lover. Although anyone who's heard his attempts at karaoke might find the rest of his claims hard to believe.' Another pause for laughter, then he grew serious and spoke movingly about their instantaneous and enduring friendship, Leon's disastrous skills in the kitchen, his love of flying and his absolute lack of self-pity when faced with his devastating diagnosis.

You could have heard a pin drop in the church.

'He was braver than I could ever be,' Jamie concluded, and Fen saw the effort it was taking for him to keep his voice steady. 'He was my best friend, and my absolute hero. He also dealt with cancer like a boss, and I know none of us here will ever forget him. I'm so glad he met Fen. It was love at first sight for the two of them, and it was a privilege to be there to see it happen. When Fen chose Leon, she couldn't have chosen a better man. And they would have been together for ever. Sometimes life really isn't fair. However, Leon's might have been cut short, but he lived every minute of it to the full.' He paused and took another breath. 'I've already mentioned that he planned every aspect of this service. Including the finale, which we'll leave you with now.'

He nodded to someone at the back, then exhaled before stepping down and rejoining Fen in their pew.

For a few seconds there was absolute silence in the church. Then came the recorded sound of a helicopter engine being switched on, gradually growing louder and more intense as the power increased and the rotor blades spun faster and faster . . .

Then the pilot's voice sounded over the airwaves, and all the little hairs on the back of Fen's neck rose because it was Leon's voice, crackling slightly but unmistakably his, uttering the words:

'Hanbury Tower, this is GOLF-DELTA-KILO-ECHO-SIERRA requesting permission to lift and depart.'

The next moment, above the roar of the engine, a different voice responded. 'KILO-ECHO-SIERRA, this is Hanbury Tower. What is your departure direction and destination?'

Fen closed her eyes as Leon replied calmly, 'This is KILO-ECHO-SIERRA, my departure direction is vertical. My destination, sunlit uplands and beyond.'

The voice from the control tower spoke again. 'Roger, KILO-ECHO-SIERRA, you are cleared to lift and depart. Thank you for your visit.'

Everyone listened to the now-thunderous sound of the helicopter taking off and rising into the sky, the noise gradually fading as it flew higher and higher, until silence reigned once more.

Then the applause started, filling the church and growing in intensity as everyone rose to their feet, clapping wildly and visibly overcome with the emotion of it all.

This time beyond tears, Fen kept her eyes closed and said her own private goodbyes to Leon. Next to her, Jamie tilted his head and murmured, 'Couldn't ask for a better exit than that. What a way to go.'

By the time Leon's parents returned from the committal at the crematorium, the reception at Hetherton Hall was in full swing, the caterers serving drinks and bringing round endless plates of canapés.

Fen, standing back, watched the various groups of people shifting and re-forming, old friends greeting each other with delight and exchanging stories about Leon. How she wished he could have been here too, joining in and having the best time with them, some of whom he hadn't seen for years.

Jamie brought her another drink. 'He'd have loved this so much.'

'I know.' They were thinking the same thing at the same time. She wondered if he'd noticed that Molly had been monopolising him, making her feelings for him obvious, and lowered her voice. 'About Molly . . .'

He nodded at once. 'She's a great girl. But no.'

Leon's mother had been accepting condolences from a series of guests. As she excused herself and made to leave the drawing room, Fen took a gulp of wine. 'I need to have a quick word with Hilary.'

Jamie briefly rested a hand on her shoulder. 'Go ahead. I'll catch up with you in a bit.'

'What is it?' Hilary sounded exhausted when Fen followed her into the study a short distance down the panelled hallway.

'I'm not going to be staying very long, and after today we probably won't see each other again. So I came to say goodbye.'

'Oh. Right.' Hilary pressed a linen handkerchief to each eye in turn.

'And to give you this.' Fen removed the ring from her finger and placed it on the polished walnut desk.

Hilary looked at it, then at her, eyebrows fractionally raised. 'Why?'

'I'm not engaged any more. I can't carry on wearing it. And it wouldn't be fair to keep something that doesn't belong to me.'

'Leon gave it to you. It's yours.'

'I'd rather you had it.'

'Because you want to prove to us that you weren't with him for his money?'

Fen nodded. 'Yes.'

His heartbroken mother wiped her pink-rimmed eyes again. 'You didn't need to prove it. We knew. Not on that first day, but afterwards.'

'I loved him.'

'We knew that too. And I'm sorry we doubted you. Or thought you weren't right for him.'

'Thank you,' said Fen. 'Well, I'd better be getting back—'

'We were wrong. So wrong. And I want to thank *you* for making our boy happy.' Only too well aware that Hilary wasn't naturally the tactile type, Fen was touched to find herself caught up in a slightly awkward but still heartfelt hug. The next moment she felt the older woman's tears sliding down her own cheek and gave way to the pent-up emotion filling her chest. For several seconds they clung to each other, lost in grief, until the door burst open and a man Fen vaguely recognised as a co-worker of Leon's said, 'Fuck, sorry, thought this was the downstairs loo.'

It was twenty minutes later, while watching Molly make yet another valiant attempt at captivating Jamie, that Fen became aware of a slight commotion behind her and turned to see Sadie Ingalls making her entrance into the room.

Squeezing her way through the noisy throng, she reached Jamie and greeted him with a light kiss on the mouth before turning to Molly and saying, 'Sorry to interrupt, but I had to come. Hi, I'm Sadie.' She shook Molly's hand, then returned her attention to Jamie. 'How are you doing?'

'Not too bad. I wasn't expecting to see you here.'

'You weren't, but I couldn't let you go through this on your own. Managed to pull in a couple of favours and juggle my schedule. And I know I didn't get the chance to meet Leon, but I *feel* as if I knew him.' She tucked her hand into Jamie's and gazed up at him. 'Will you introduce me to Leon's family so I can offer my condolences? They won't mind that I've gate-crashed the reception, will they?'

All around the room, people were covertly admiring her elegant black silk jersey dress accessorised with silver necklaces, a dove-grey suede clutch and matching crimson-soled high heels. Her hair and make-up were immaculate, her air of confidence mesmerising. From this distance Fen might not be able to breathe in whatever scent she was wearing, but she guessed it would be exotic and expensive.

'Just when I thought I might stand a chance after all,' Molly said in an undertone, joining Fen after having been effortlessly cast aside while Sadie flashed her a dazzling smile and left the room with Jamie to seek out Hilary and Greville. 'God, she's glamorous. Did you notice the shoes?'

Ten minutes later, Sadie and Jamie were back. Fen, aware of them entering the drawing room, turned away to closely examine a framed painting on the wall behind her. *Don't bring her over here, don't bring her over here . . .*

Jamie brought her over. Of course he did.

'And you're Fen, Leon's fiancée. I'm *so* sorry for your loss.' Sadie was using her carefully modulated TV voice. 'It's such a tragedy, my heart breaks for you.' She enveloped Fen in a hug, and there was the cloud of exotic perfume, almost exactly as she'd imagined. 'You must be devastated. Poor darling.' Now she was stroking Fen's hair, as if she were a cat, and Fen's emotions were confused. She couldn't tell whether it felt strange or actually quite comforting and nice.

A flash went off over to the left, as someone took a photo of their VIP guest. Turning to glare at them, Jamie said, 'Really?'

'Don't let it bother you.' Sadie shook her head at him. 'They don't mean to be rude. Maybe we should go outside . . . look how stunning the grounds are. It was lovely to meet you.' She smiled at Fen, then at Molly. 'And you too, Milly. Take care.'

'You could come out with us,' Jamie offered, but it was now six o'clock and Fen had barely slept last night. She was wrung out and exhausted from having to smile and speak to people, many of whom she didn't even know. If Leon were here with her, she could probably power on through, but he wasn't and she had neither the energy nor the inclination. She and Jamie had supported each other up until now, but it was becoming apparent that he no longer needed her; from Sadie's body language and the way she behaved around him, their relationship had clearly moved on, providing him with the diversion he needed.

For Fen, the idea of getting intimate with another man any time soon was unthinkable, completely out of the question. But looking at Jamie and Sadie now, it seemed obvious that they were already sleeping together.

The thought of it made her feel a bit sick, because he was evidently finding it so easy to cheer himself up after the loss of the best friend he'd ever had.

'Thanks, but no,' she told him. 'I'm going to head home.'

Jamie looked concerned. 'Are you sure?'

'Honestly,' Sadie exclaimed. 'Is there anything worse than a man questioning a woman's decision? Of course she's sure! Look at her, she's on her last legs, poor lamb.' She wagged a playful finger at him. 'If she wants to leave, she's free to go!'

Fen nodded in weary agreement, the future revealing itself faster than expected. She and Jamie had only ever been connected via Leon, their common denominator. Now he was no longer here, there was nothing to keep them in contact. They would go their separate ways and live their own lives. She would see him on TV every now and again, and they might exchange a brief WhatsApp message at Christmas, but nothing more than that, because the link between them would have died along with Leon.

As for the lightning bolt of emotion that had so confusingly ambushed her out of the blue during their time in Venice . . . well, that had become the secret she could never reveal to another living soul. It was the source of her deepest shame.

She turned to Molly. 'If you and Disa want to stay longer, I can get a taxi.'

'Don't be daft. Disa's already said we'll leave together whenever you want.' Molly gave her a comforting squeeze. 'I'll let her know we're ready to go now.'

Chapter 28

Bristol

The next morning Disa was thinking about the funeral while unloading the dishwasher when the doorbell went. Since it was ten thirty and she was expecting a parcel, she made her way to the front door.

Except it wasn't Jonathan, her regular chatty postman. It was a woman she'd never met before in person.

But recognised at once.

'I know I told Molly I'd be here to pick her up at midday,' said Yvette. 'But I'm early.'

Disa's mouth was dry. She tried to swallow without it being obvious. 'Molly isn't here. She's gone over to Fen's.'

'I know. I called her. I've been sitting in my car for the last twenty minutes plucking up the courage to come and see you.' Yvette paused, took a breath. 'And if you want to shut the door in my face, you can. But I wanted to apologise for doing what I did, and also to thank you for everything you've done for Molly.'

Disa took in every detail of in-person Yvette, from her short light brown hair and topaz eyes to her slender frame and tanned limbs. She was wearing a simple pale green sundress, creased from where she'd been sitting in the car on the drive down from Birmingham. One blue bra strap was visible. On her feet were cream leather ballet slippers, and her perfume was light and citrusy. This was the woman Declan had loved and lied about for years. She and Disa were pretty much the same age. There was a chunky necklace of tawny wooden beads around her neck, the kind that Disa would never choose to wear, but other than that, their overall sense of style wasn't dissimilar.

Disa moved to the left and gestured for her erstwhile rival to follow her inside. 'I was going to invite you in anyway when you arrived to collect Molly.'

'You were?' Yvette's relief was palpable.

'It doesn't do to hate people when it's too late to change what happened. And I'm too old now to hold on to grudges.'

In the kitchen, Disa made coffee from the fancy machine she didn't always bother with, then led the way out to the back garden. They sat across from each other at the glass-topped table on cushioned wicker chairs.

'Thank you,' said Yvette. 'For everything. Molly told me you were wonderful.' She paused. 'Declan told me that, too.'

'I suppose it's better than being called an old harridan.'

'He never had a bad word to say about you.' She took another audible breath. 'He loved you so much. You were his number one, his first choice. I was always the runner-up.'

'He loved you too,' said Disa.

'But just that bit less.'

'Well, I'm glad you had real feelings for each other. Better than if he'd slept with other women for fun.'

'You must have been devastated when he died.'

An emerald dragonfly from next door's pond landed on the table between them, its transparent wings shimmering in the sunlight. For a crazy moment Disa wondered if it was Declan, reincarnated and here to beadily observe the meeting between the two women from his past life.

'I was devastated then, and when I first found out about you.'

'I'm so sorry,' said Yvette. 'If it helps at all, I hated being the other woman.'

Should she say it? Or keep it to herself? The dragonfly shifted position but didn't fly away. Its body suddenly reminded Disa of the time in Thailand that she'd bought Declan a shirt in that exact shade of iridescent blue-green.

Is it you?

The wings quivered for a moment, as if giving a silent signal. Did that mean yes? Good enough.

'Don't worry,' she said with a wry smile. 'I got my own back.'

Yvette looked bemused. 'Meaning?'

'I had a fling of my own.'

Are you listening, Declan? Do dragonflies even have ears? I really hope so.

'You did?' Yvette's topaz eyes widened.

'Oh yes. And I did it on purpose, to make myself feel better.'

'Did it work?'

'Absolutely. I felt . . . powerful. He was a very attractive man.'

'You're an attractive woman.'

'Thank you. But your confidence does take a dip when you know the man you love has been involved with someone else. Anyway,' Disa continued, 'I met him through work. He came into the office, wanting us to value his house and put it on the market. I volunteered to carry out the valuation. By the end of that visit, we knew we liked each other, and he invited me out to dinner. It was a few months after I'd found out what Declan had been getting up to behind my back. When I'd had invitations from men before, I'd always turned them down. This time I realised I didn't want to say no. But professionally it would have been wrong, so I had to explain that I couldn't see him if our company was selling his house.'

'What happened?' Yvette was leaning forward now, fully invested.

'He told me he'd use a different estate agency. And then he kissed me. Right there in his sitting room.' Disa smiled at the memory. 'Basically, I lost out on the sale, but I won the man.'

Yvette clapped her hands. 'My God, this is amazing! And how long did it last?'

'Ten weeks.' *Ten magical weeks.*

'Is that all? Why?'

'It was only ever going to be that long. The reason he was selling his house in Bristol was because he was moving to Spain. Knowing we had that time limit made it all the more magical. And when he left, it meant I could give myself fully to Declan again, but this time feeling more equal to him, not to mention better about myself. And he never knew.'

'So you didn't ever meet up with the other guy again?'

'Never.'

'You didn't try and find him online after Declan died?'

Disa shook her head. 'After Declan died, the only man I wanted was Declan.' As she said it, the dragonfly took flight and zipped off in a blur of wings like a tiny flying saucer, swooping over the hedge and into her neighbours' garden. At the same moment, they heard the sound of the front door opening, signalling Molly and Fen's arrival. 'I'd prefer it if the girls didn't know about this.'

'I won't breathe a word.'

'And just so you know, there was no sleeping together. Plenty of kissing and very much wanting to.' Disa's tone was rueful. 'But at the time, I couldn't quite bring myself to take that last step.'

'Bet you regretted it after he'd gone.' Yvette's eyes were bright with sympathy.

This was the woman who'd caused her so much unhappiness in the past. But now Disa could see how irresistible she'd been to Declan. Yvette was warm-hearted and principled in her own way. And Disa liked her too.

She looked at her and said, 'Damn right I did.'

Later that evening, alone in the house and with the TV failing to hold her attention, Disa found her thoughts sliding back to that time all those years ago. Had what she'd done really been so terrible? Back then, it had cheered her up no end. The memory of that first meeting with Marcus Rochester was as crystal clear in her mind as if it had happened yesterday. She'd been arranging the property brochures in the estate agent's window when she'd looked up and seen him smiling at her through the glass. And she'd smiled back, because it was a big part of her job to be nice to potential clients. The next moment, when he'd pushed open the door to the office and said hello, her heart had begun to beat faster, almost as if it knew before she did that this was no run-of-the-mill client. He was tall, he wore a well-cut navy suit and he gazed at her as if she were the woman he'd dreamt of meeting his whole life. Disa could still remember the scent of his aftershave and the exact way he'd looked at her as she had taken down his details. The attraction had been both instantaneous and mutual, but she had a husband, albeit an unfaithful one, so her reaction had remained entirely professional. Well, at least for the next thirty hours.

Oh, but the ten weeks that followed had been like living in a dream. It had actually made her understand why Declan had been unable to resist the chemistry that had drawn him to Yvette. But she *had* resisted the temptation to sleep with Marcus, and to his credit he had accepted that decision, hadn't tried to persuade her to change her mind. Although sometimes, in retrospect, she kind of wished he had.

Like now. Disa looked at her phone on the coffee table and briefly considered googling his name again. But no, she'd seen everything she'd needed to see the last time she'd given in to that particular temptation.

The last thing she needed was to have her secret hopes dashed all over again.

Fen had once read an observation made about grief: that when you were at home, all you wanted was to be out somewhere. And when you were out, you wished you could be back at home.

Well, it was true. The last few weeks since the funeral had proved it. Wherever she was, she wished she could be somewhere else, feeling less uncomfortable and perpetually out of place. People had sent sympathy cards and emails, and they'd been lovely to read but couldn't reduce the loss. She'd received a thoughtful letter from Hattie, who'd also been on the ship back in May and had witnessed her and Leon falling in love. Her friend Kayla, who'd had a fling with a gondolier at the time, was – to everyone's amazement – still seeing him, although apparently no one expected it to last. Hattie explained that she hadn't known Fen's address, but had sent Jamie a message on

Instagram in the hope that he'd see it, and he'd given it to her; she hoped this was all right.

Which it was, of course, although Fen was no longer replying to the messages Jamie sent her. It was easier; they led entirely different lives and had no reason to pretend to remain friends. The other week she'd accidentally come across a clip online of Sadie looking impossibly glamorous in slinky racing-green silk, being interviewed on the red carpet at some film premiere or other.

'Jamie couldn't make it this evening,' she told the female interviewer, 'otherwise he'd be with me. I'm here all on my own tonight!'

Hmm, I know the feeling.

'But everything's still going well with you two, is it?' The interviewer giggled. 'Because if it isn't, you can always send him my way!'

'Not a chance!' Sadie laughed. 'You know, it feels as though it's all thanks to his friend Leon that we're a couple now.' She pressed her hand to her chest and looked suitably serious. 'As if he deliberately brought us together.'

The clip was so annoying that Fen had watched it over and over, hating it more each time.

But this evening she was steering clear of social media and scrolling through online holiday brochures instead. Looking at the bright, inviting photos, she attempted to visualise herself in any of the settings: Paris . . . Copenhagen . . . Vienna . . . Sicily . . . Malta . . .

Her phone rang. She hesitated, then saw it was her best friend, in Amsterdam, and picked up without even bothering to push her fingers through her uncombed bedhead.

Tonia said, 'Wow, you're looking amazing. Off out somewhere special?'

'It's your own fault for making me take a video call.' Smiling, Fen brushed the biscuit crumbs off her pyjama top and realised for the first time that it was buttoned up wrongly. 'Anyway, enough about you. Show me the baby.'

Tonia swung the camera down to focus on her daughter Sonja, six weeks old, fast asleep in her Moses basket and looking more angelic than ever.

Her heart melting, Fen said, 'I've never met her, but I already love her.'

'You need to meet her,' said Tonia, as she did during each of their calls. 'Come on over, Fen. Stay with us. Keep me company while I change hundreds of nappies and lactate like a Friesian cow.'

Fen was tempted, as she was every time, but still reluctant to inflict herself and her current sadness on a happy family whose mood she could only bring down. Her friends might be pretending to want to see her, but what if she ended up losing them because she was such dull company? It was the reason she was rejecting every well-meaning invitation and keeping herself to herself.

'Please,' Tonia added. 'This is me asking nicely.'

'I can't.'

'You could if you wanted to.'

'You wouldn't want me to.' Fen sighed. 'Maybe later in the year.'

'OK, time for me to be stern and bossy now.' Tonia gave her a stern and bossy look. 'My daughter is never going to be six weeks old again. The longer you put it off, the more you're going to miss. We don't care if you're sad. It's allowed. You can have the top-floor bedroom, and if you find you can't stand the sight of us, you're free to spend as much time as you want up there, or out on your own. But please, please, *please* come and see Sonja, even if it's only for a couple of days. Because if you don't, it means we're all going to have to fly over and land ourselves on you. And I'm sure you'd hate that even more.'

Fen looked at the TV, paused halfway through an episode of *Friends* she knew practically off by heart, then at the half-full packet of custard creams on the coffee table. Why had she bought them when she didn't even much like custard creams? Then she glanced up at the swaying cobweb on the ceiling that had been there for over a month because she couldn't be bothered to stand on a chair and get it down.

'One more thing,' said Tonia. 'I know I didn't get the chance to meet Leon in person, only on FaceTime, but from what you've told me about him, I bet he'd want you to buy a ticket and get on the plane.'

'That's a low blow.'

'Sorry. That's how desperate I am.'

Fen hesitated. Was she going to do it?

'What's that?' Cupping a hand behind her ear, Tonia bent over the Moses basket. 'You think Auntie Fenna doesn't love you after all? In fact you're starting to think she hates you? Sweetheart, don't cry.'

'This is an even lower blow.' Fen shook her head. 'You should be ashamed of yourself.'

'And you should know by now, I have no shame.' Tonia flashed her an innocent smile. 'Let me know when you're due to land and we'll meet you at the airport.'

'Thanks.' She'd known it would have to happen eventually.

'Don't mention it.' Tonia's voice softened. 'And Fen? He'd be proud of you.'

Chapter 29

Amsterdam

It had been the right thing to do, as Fen's oldest friend was only too happy to remind her. Two days after that phone call, she had landed at Schiphol airport and been greeted by Tonia, Hendrik, two-year-old Sebastian and howling baby Sonja, who had melted her heart and magically stopped howling upon being plonked by her mother into Fen's arms.

That had been six weeks ago; it was now the first week of November, and to her own amazement she was still here, occupying the guest room on the top floor of their multi-level apartment in one of the prized seventeenth-century canalside houses on Herengracht, close to the heart of the city.

She hadn't expected to stay more than a few days, but Amsterdam's friendly inhabitants and serene beauty had given her the sense of escape she hadn't known she needed. Being here alone wouldn't have worked, but to be surrounded by the chaos of a happy family was a welcome distraction. She adored them all, and spent her time cuddling Sonja and playing endless silly games with Sebastian, shopping and reminiscing with Tonia, and taking the children in their double buggy for long walks around the city and to the Vondelpark. When a sticky-fingered toddler was shrieking with laughter and clinging to you like a koala, it turned out it was impossible to be too sad.

It was also close to impossible to get scrambled egg out of your hair. But hey, sometimes it was worth it. And slowly, gradually, she was beginning to feel better.

Having lain in bed for several minutes after waking, she now swung her legs over the side. Time to get up. She drew back the curtains and gazed out of the window at the hotel almost directly opposite on the other side of the canal. The leaves on the elm trees lining the narrow streets, turning shades of yellow, orange and raw umber, were beginning to drop into the water now, but were still bright in the misty morning sunshine. People were heading to work on foot or by bike, or walking their dogs, and a group of tourists outside the Ambassade were excitedly taking photos of themselves and each other, blocking the way of someone at the main entrance waiting to leave the hotel.

Moments later, a taxi drew up and the gaggle of tourists shifted to the left, allowing the person access to the vehicle. A thud of disbelief almost knocked the breath out of Fen's chest, because although he'd only been visible for a split second, she could have sworn the man was Jamie.

Unless her subconscious was playing tricks on her, making her think it was him. Because really, how likely was it that he was here in Amsterdam, just a few metres away on the other side of the canal?

The taxi moved off and Fen pressed her face to the window to watch it cross the bridge up ahead before disappearing from view. Her fingers were tingling and she felt light-headed with the unexpectedness of the sight of him. If it even was him, *which it probably wasn't.*

Reaching for her phone, she typed his name into Instagram on the hunt for clues, but the last photo had been posted three weeks ago and was of one of his rugby friends scoring an evidently winning try.

Next she checked Sadie Ingalls' recent posts, but they were all photos of Sadie wearing an assortment of stylish outfits during her attendance at various parties and social events.

The door swung open and Sebastian came racing into her bedroom, arms outstretched. Fen picked him up and was thoroughly kissed by someone with apricot jam all around his mouth.

'Fen! We go park?'

She loved that he was growing up bilingual but somehow always knew to speak to her in English.

'Yes, we'll go to the park.'

After an energetic morning chasing squirrels and trying to catch falling leaves in the Vondelpark – without success – Sebastian had fallen asleep next to Sonja in the double buggy. It was now midday. Perching on a bench next to them, Fen took out her phone and called Disa. It was always good to hear her voice and to catch up with all the gossip from home. Then it was her turn to update Disa with stories about Seb and Sonja and the new sights of Amsterdam she was still discovering.

'Oh,' she said finally, 'and the weirdest thing this morning. I thought I saw Jamie getting into a taxi outside the Ambassade.'

After a split second's hesitation, Disa said casually, 'Did you?'

Suddenly suspicious, Fen frowned. 'But that'd be crazy. It couldn't have been him.'

'Couldn't it?'

'What does *that* mean?'

'OK. It was Jamie. He came to see me the other evening.'

'He *did*?' In the buggy, Seb stirred, and Fen hastily lowered her voice. 'What for?'

'He wondered how you were doing. And I wondered why he wasn't asking you himself. Then he told me you'd blocked his number and weren't replying to his emails. Which of course I hadn't known about, so then I wondered why you'd done that.'

There was now far too much adrenalin swishing round Fen's body and she hadn't had time to prepare a reply.

'I don't know. I blocked quite a few numbers. It just got too much, people asking me how I was all the time, having to say the same stuff.'

'Oh, sweetheart. He was worried about you, that's all.'

'He was being polite. Anyway, so what's he doing here?'

'It's a quick visit. He was booked to fly over to do a TV show and knew you were there. So he thought it might be nice for the two of you to get together for a quick coffee.'

'You gave him my address?'

'No.' Disa sounded pleased with herself. 'I told him the name of my favourite hotel in Amsterdam.'

Fen exhaled; it *was* Disa's favourite place to stay whenever she visited the city to catch up with old friends. When Tonia and Hendrik had been searching for a new home, it was Disa who'd alerted them to the fact that this apartment had just gone on the market.

'He was booked into a different hotel, off Dam Square, but when I recommended the Ambassade, he decided to stay there instead. Which'll be handy if you do decide you'd like to meet up.'

A quiver ran down Fen's spine. 'Is he expecting to? But how?'

'He's busy recording the show now, but free this evening. Then he'll be flying home tomorrow. I said if he waited in the hotel bar from five until five thirty, I'd let you know and you could decide whether you wanted to see him.'

'From five to five thirty.'

'I thought earlier was better. Then if you don't turn up, he hasn't wasted the whole evening.' Disa was ever practical. 'He can go out and explore the city. Can you believe he's never even visited the red-light district?'

Fen shook her head; Disa was incorrigible. 'What if I'm busy from five till five thirty?'

'Are you?'

'No, but I might have been.'

'Does that mean you'll see him?'

'I don't know. I'll have to think about it.'

'Well, he'd very much like to see you,' Disa said gently. 'So I hope you do.'

Above the children's buggy, an amber leaf was drifting down from the horse chestnut tree overhead. As if in a cartoon, it twirled and landed on Sonja's face, causing her to wake and let out a high-pitched squawk of surprise.

'That's the baby,' said Fen. 'I'd better go.'

'He misses Leon as much as you do,' Disa reminded her.

'Waaaahhh.' Sonja gave a wail of outrage.

Fen nodded. 'I know.'

Chapter 30

Had he ever been in this situation before? Not that he could remember. Jamie genuinely didn't think he'd waited for someone wondering whether they were going to turn up.

Unless you counted Leon, who over the years had made a habit of dozing off on the sofa and arriving everywhere an hour later than everyone else.

But no woman had ever stood him up, which meant the not knowing was a whole new experience for him. And he was rapidly discovering he didn't like it. Was Fen on her way or not? It was twelve minutes past five and the doubt and uncertainty were expanding inside him like Styrofoam. He took a swallow of ice-cold lager, put the glass down on the table, then seconds later picked it up again. The sun was setting outside, and from where he was sitting, down here in the bar below pavement level, he could see people's legs as they walked past the high window. Were those Fen's legs in jeans? OK, no. What about those, approaching from the other direction? But again no, she would never wear a skirt like that. Maybe he'd be better off switching seats so he couldn't look out for her.

Next moment, the right legs came into view, tanned and slim and instantly recognisable as they paused outside the hotel then made their way down the flight of stone steps to the sliding glass doors at the bottom. And there she was, making her entrance and causing his heart to beat faster, with both relief and the joy of seeing her again after what had felt like far too long. Her curly blonde hair was longer, her face and body thinner, and she was wearing an above-the-knee pale blue jersey dress with a cream denim jacket and blue ankle boots.

Jumping to his feet to greet her, Jamie banged the side of the table with his leg and sent his drink flying, just managing to catch the glass before it hit the floor but not before it had tipped lager all over the tabletop and down the front of his dark grey trousers. *Fuck, what an idiot, and now everyone in the bar's staring at me.*

But in a way, it worked as an ice-breaker. Laughing, Fen pulled a pack of tissues from her oversized shoulder bag and stemmed the flow of lager dripping off the edge of the table. Two members of the bar staff swooped in with cloths and a third brought Jamie a fresh drink, then took Fen's order of a glass of Chenin blanc.

Finally calm was restored and they took their seats. Jamie said, 'Shall we start again? Thanks for coming. I was looking at all the legs going by, wondering if they were yours.' *Shut up, you're gabbling.* 'Anyway, it's good to see you.'

'You too.' Her eyes bright, Fen clinked her glass against his.

'I didn't know if you were going to stand me up.'

'I didn't know either.'

He shook his head, confused. 'Why?'

'I don't know, I suppose I just expected us to lose touch.'

'Well, you not replying to any of my messages is one way to make sure that happens.'

'Sorry.' Her cheeks grew pink. 'I thought the only thing we had in common was Leon. Once he'd gone, there was no reason to stay in contact. We live different lives. You'd go your way and I'd go mine.' She shrugged. 'I assumed that was what would happen.'

Her words cut him to the quick. 'You see, that didn't even occur to me. I thought we'd never lose touch.'

But Fen didn't reply; she was looking past him now at the rows and rows of books lining the walls of the bar. Since arriving here, Jamie had learned that the Ambassade was known as the writers' hotel, where novelists and non-fiction authors stayed when they came to Amsterdam. Every one of the books in the glass-fronted cases had been signed by its author, and he'd told himself he could pretend to study them with interest if Fen stood him up.

But that hadn't happened. She was here. The relief was enormous.

'I haven't been very sociable.' Fen turned back to him suddenly. 'I'm sorry. It's been a tricky few months. Would you like me to unblock your number?'

He broke into a smile. This was progress. 'I'd like that very much.'

She took out her phone and pressed a few buttons. 'There, done. Anyway, how have you been?'

'Carrying on as usual. Working. Getting used to the apartment being quieter and a lot less messy. Wishing it could be noisier and messier.' He paused. 'The Australia trip's been rescheduled for the end of November. How about you?'

'Same, I guess. Being here has been good for me. Spending time with the kids has kept me busy. And I'm still keeping the business running, obviously. But Tonia's hiring a full-time nanny to take over when she goes back to work. As soon as that happens, I'll be heading home.'

Jamie looked at her, taking in her pronounced cheekbones and thin arms. 'You've lost weight.'

'I know. It wasn't on purpose. I didn't feel like eating for a while, but it's getting better now.' She smiled. 'I'm loving the bitterballen here and the stroopwafels. They'll have me back to normal in no time.'

'Good.' He nodded, reassured. 'And the sleeping?'

'That's better as well. How about you?'

'Not too bad.'

'What's wrong? What are you looking at?'

Jamie shook his head. Behind her, a middle-aged woman had been holding up her phone, pretending to take selfies but actually taking photos of him. The flash had gone off over a dozen times. When Fen twisted round and saw what was going on, she said, 'Come on, why don't we finish our drinks and get out of here? It's too nice to stay inside anyway.'

How he appreciated her not making a fuss.

He put down his lager, still half full. If he wasn't drinking, he couldn't spill it again. 'Good idea. Let's go.'

Fen felt herself relaxing as soon as they were outside. The woman in the hotel had done them a favour. It was a magical evening, the air was still and unseasonably warm, and as they crossed the bridge, the sun, now setting low in the sky, turned the west-facing canal into a ribbon of gold.

It was also easier to chat walking along together side by side. She told Jamie all about Disa's argument with a garden designer who had the temerity to think his ideas were better than hers, and about the hapless car showroom manager who, when Disa had expressed interest in a top-of-the-range sports car, had said jovially, 'And is your husband OK with you spending this much money on a new runaround?'

Jamie whistled. 'I'd love to have been there. What did Disa say?'

'She told the guy she'd have to dig up her husband first, but then he'd say it was her own money, so what the hell business was it of his anyway?'

'I'd expect no less. And did she buy the car?'

'Of course not. She told him he was a silly boy who'd made a mistake he wouldn't forget in a hurry, and left. Went to another showroom and bought herself a bright red AMG instead.'

'Good for her,' said Jamie.

'She was so devastated after Declan died, I love that she's able to joke about him like that now.' Fen couldn't imagine being able to do it herself about Leon, but that was the thing about the passing of time; gradually scenarios that felt completely impossible became possible after all. Closing her fingers around the wrought-iron railings on the bridge, she watched as a narrowboat emerged from beneath it, and hastily changed the subject before she could get emotional. 'And how are things with you and Sadie? All good?'

At her side, Jamie shrugged. 'You know.'

'What does that mean?' She glanced at him. 'You're still seeing each other, aren't you?'

'Kind of. She's busy with work, and so am I. We occasionally meet up.'

'Wow, so romantic.'

He looked sideways at her for a moment before returning his attention to the next canal boat, this one full of camera-wielding tourists.

They began to walk again, kicking through fallen leaves. Fen said, 'Wouldn't it be better to be on your own?'

'Maybe.' His expression was inscrutable.

Next moment there was a whispery whoosh of tyres on tarmac and the high-pitched ringing of a bicycle bell. An arm shot round Fen's waist, whisking her back onto the pavement as a bearded man shot past on his bike, shaking his head at her stupidity.

'Oh God, I'm such an idiot.' Gasping for breath, Fen ricocheted off Jamie's chest and had to clutch at his other arm for support, before regaining her balance and leaping back. 'You'd think I'd be used to silent bicycles by now, but they still catch me out.'

What she kept to herself was that it had just happened again, the electric zing of adrenalin in response to the unexpected physical contact with him. It was the same zing as before, and she'd never wanted to experience it again. A vision of Leon shaking his head in pained resignation leapt into her brain, and she felt herself grow hot with shame.

Stop it, stop it, for heaven's sake get a grip.

'There's a café down by the Vondelpark that does the best almond cakes.' To divert her own attention, and this time remembering to look both ways, Fen set off across the road at top speed. 'I want to take some back for Tonia and Hendrik. You have to try them, they're out of this world.'

'If you insist,' said Jamie. 'I've never met an almond cake I didn't like.'

An hour later, they were still in the park, having watched earlier from their vantage point on a bench by the lake as the sun had finally disappeared and the sky had grown dark. Again, sitting beside Jamie was easier than facing him. As they chatted, they drank their takeaway coffees and finished the last slice of cake between them.

'Definitely the best.' Jamie licked his fingers, crumpled the paper bag into a tight ball and lobbed it with a rugby player's accuracy into the nearby bin.

They'd had two and a half slices each, all that had been left in the café.

'Told you. I'll have to buy them some more tomorrow.' Fen balled up her own paper bag and passed it to him. 'Come on, prove it wasn't a fluke.'

He took aim, threw it in the direction of the bin, and missed.

'Call yourself a rugby star?' She grinned. 'Useless.'

'I don't call myself a rugby star. It just used to be my job to play the game.' Jamie rose to collect the ball of paper, his hair falling forward as he bent down to retrieve it from the grass, and Fen averted her gaze from the frankly spectacular view of his shirt and jeans stretching across his shoulders and backside. Returning to sit beside her on the bench, he threw it again, and this time it went in.

'Fluke,' said Fen.

The next moment, a squirrel ran down the silvery trunk of a nearby tree, raced across the grass and leapt into the bin. They heard a rustle of paper, then it emerged triumphant with a French fry sticking out of its mouth.

'Looks like Winston Churchill.' Taking out his phone, Jamie snapped away before the squirrel shot back up the tree. He showed her the best shot and enlarged it. 'Want me to send this to you? Now I'm allowed to contact you again?'

It was a cute photo. 'Yes, please. Oh!' Reminded by the hair-style of a woman walking by, Fen produced her own phone. 'Forgot to tell you, I had the loveliest letter from one of the women on the Venice cruise. Remember Hattie and Kayla?'

'Kayla with the red and gold spiky hair? Quite keen on me until I got dumped in favour of a young gondolier?'

'That's the one.'

'And Hattie with the ex-husband who was also on the ship with his new woman, until she went back to her chap.' He looked pleased with himself. 'See? I do remember. Hattie told me when she messaged me on Instagram, asking for your address.'

'Yes, she told me as well. She and Guy saw the interview you did on TV and wanted to let us know how shocked and sorry they were to hear about Leon. She sent me a few photos too, taken on the ship, with me and Leon in them, and one of you and Leon on the dance floor. I'll send you that one. Her letter was wonderful, really long. It was so kind of her to make the effort to write it, because so many people don't know what to say so they end up not saying anything at all.'

'I know.' Jamie pulled a face and slowly nodded in agreement.

'Anyway, she said they'd wanted to do something positive, so they held a karaoke night in their local pub to raise money for a cancer charity in memory of Leon, and ended up making nearly four hundred pounds. Isn't that incredible? She sent me photos of that too, as well as a letter from the charity thanking them for their donation. Here they are, I put them all in an online album. Sorry, I should have sent them to you before.' She passed him the phone so he could see everything for himself. 'I did send copies to Hilary and Greville, but didn't hear back from them.'

The stars were starting to make themselves visible now in the sky. Fen waited for Jamie to finish studying the photos, then read Hattie's kind letter. As a PS, she'd concluded: *I know we only knew Leon for a short time, but he was one of those happy-go-lucky characters who always lit up a room (or a sun deck!). His light shone so brightly, it's still almost impossible to believe he's no longer here. If there are any other charity events held in his memory, please let us know, as we would really like to attend.*

At last, he looked up and handed back the phone. 'Yes, send me everything. I'll write back to her. I've been thinking about organising something, so . . .'

In the dim light, Fen saw the glimmer in his eyes as he got his emotions back under control. Her own throat was tight as she nodded in agreement. The normal thing to do now would be to comfort each other with a squeeze of the hand or even a reassuring hug, but she couldn't risk the *zing* happening again. Getting to her feet, she took a sip of lukewarm coffee before grimacing and dropping the cup into the bin. 'Shall we head back now?'

'Already?'

'I have some work I need to catch up on.' It was the excuse she'd prepared earlier. 'And you have an early flight home tomorrow.'

As they left the park and made their way over to the picturesque Nine Streets area of the city, where independent vintage and designer shops, café bars and restaurants lined the canals, Fen told him about the further messages she and Hattie had exchanged.

'Nobody thought for one second that Kayla's fling with her gondolier would last, but they're still going strong.'

'It's amazing.' Jamie nodded in agreement.

'Hattie says they're crazy about each other. Kayla's been selling loads of her belongings online to make money so she can fly to Venice every month. She's been teaching herself Italian and has met all of Angelo's family, who weren't sure at first, but now they love her. And Angelo's come over to Oxford too, to meet everyone. He was there at the karaoke night and they sang "You're the One" together. Brought the house down, apparently. It's just the maddest thing, the first time they clapped eyes on each other, they both knew. Everyone expected them to crash and burn, but they haven't. It was absolutely love at first sight,' Fen concluded. 'And it still is.'

Because six months later, Angelo was still here, she didn't say aloud. He wasn't dead. You could envy other people with happy lives and wonderful partners, but you couldn't resent them for it. Bitterness wasn't the way to go. Bitterness didn't make you feel better. This was something Disa had told her, and of course, as usual, she was right.

Everyone was allowed to be happy some of the time, but in this life there were never any guarantees. What you had one day could be snatched from your grasp the next. Tragedy was potentially only ever a split second away.

They arrived back on Herengracht an hour later. As they reached Tonia and Hendrik's house, Fen stopped walking and said, 'This is me.'

Jamie turned to face her, then looked up as a flock of birds swooped overhead. She sensed he was as unsure how to proceed as she was, seeing as she'd been careful to avoid any physical contact since the earlier close shave with the demon cyclist.

'Right.' He cleared his throat. 'Well, thanks for this evening. It was really good to see—'

The bottle-green front door flew open, stopping him in his tracks and making both of them jump.

'Yay, you're back!' Tonia gave a whoop of delight and skipped down the short flight of stone steps towards Jamie. 'Hello, I'm Tonia, so lovely to finally meet you – I've heard so much about you from Fen!'

Fen watched as she flung her arms around him. It was true, she'd talked about Jamie during the last few weeks. Thankfully, Tonia might have heard a fair amount about him, but she didn't know about the zings, because Fen hadn't mentioned those to anyone, not even her oldest friend in the world. Some things were far too shameful to admit.

But Jamie's temporary awkwardness had magically vanished. He was now kissing Tonia on both cheeks and telling her he'd heard all about her too, as effortlessly relaxed as he always was on TV. While she waited for the greetings to be over, Fen turned to admire the way the lights from the street lamps were reflected in the ripples on the water of the canal. Until she heard Tonia saying, 'Come on in, you must join us!'

'He can't.' Fen spun round. 'He has to be at the airport by seven.'

'Pfft, that's ages away,' Tonia scoffed. She turned back to Jamie. 'You're not going to leave us now, are you? We have Dutch beers and the best bitterballen, and the babies are in bed, I promise!'

'That's a lot of B's,' Jamie remarked. 'But yes, sounds great. Although Fen said she had work to do.'

'Sounds like some kind of feeble excuse to me.' Tonia turned to her. 'Didn't I say I'd like to meet him? How often do I get the chance to chat to someone famous?'

Fen knew when she was beaten. 'You met a Chuckle Brother once.'

'When I was sixteen, and only because he was buying a multipack of Hula Hoops in the supermarket.' Tonia dismissed the encounter with a shrug. 'Anyway, this one's better-looking.'

Fen said, 'How did you know we were back, anyway? Have you been peering out of the window for the last three hours?'

'Of course not. Remember when you first arrived and we didn't want you getting lost in the back streets so I installed that location app on your phone? I've been following you online all evening. How was the Vondelpark?'

She was impossible. She was also making her way up the steps, beckoning for Jamie to join her. And now he was looking back at Fen, saying, 'Is this OK with you? I won't stay long.'

What else could she do, other than shrug, say lightly, 'You're the one with the plane to catch,' and follow him into the house?

Chapter 31

Three hours later, Jamie was still with them, but now Fen was glad. Shortly after their arrival, Tonia had cornered her in the kitchen and said firmly, 'Hey, relax, everything's fine. We think he's great. And look, it's not as if you've been set up on some awful blind date, is it? He's just a *friend*.'

Somehow the blunt reminder had done the trick. It also helped that Tonia and Hendrik were outgoing, endlessly sociable and loved to host impromptu get-togethers. The drinks flowed, there was plenty of food, and within an hour the four of them had launched into a laughter-filled, fiercely competitive game of Pictionary.

For the first time in ages, Fen had found herself relaxing and genuinely having fun. By ten thirty, they'd moved on to Articulate, and an hour after that, it was charades. Having not had much to drink in recent months, Fen discovered she'd found the answer to a dilemma that had been bothering her before. Faced with the prospect of saying goodbye to Jamie on the doorstep earlier, she had decided a businesslike handshake would be the best way to go. But that had been several hours ago, and it was now glaringly obvious that this would be a ridiculous thing to do. Especially now, having proved themselves to be such a world-class team when it came to Pictionary and charades, if not Articulate, which they'd lost to their hosts. Who'd definitely cheated.

The remaining small-but-sensible part of Fen's brain reminded her she should probably stop drinking now if she didn't want a bone-crushing hangover in the morning. Knocking back the last half-glass of wine, she rose from the sofa, about to execute her genius plan. Beaming around at the three of them, she proudly announced, 'Just going to the bathroom,' and headed over to the door before turning and waggling her fingers at them. 'Back in a minute.'

As she left the living room, she heard Tonia say, 'God, I love her when she's like this!'

Two minutes later, Fen left the bathroom and tiptoed up the staircase to her own room, delighted with her plan because she'd *waved goodbye* without them even realising it had been her way of saying goodnight. See?

Total genius.

Hearing their laughter down in the living room, she silently closed the bedroom door behind her. The proximity-to-Jamie problem had been neatly averted, no zings had occurred and all she had to do now was go to sleep.

I am a genius.

The high-pitched yowl of a frisky cat woke Fen much later. It was still pitch black outside, far too early to *be* awake, and her head was letting her know the hangover had already begun, but some sixth sense was telling her there was something else amiss.

She lay there on her side realising she hadn't taken her make-up off, which was why her eyes felt gritty. That wasn't it, though. Lying still and trying to figure out the answer, she realised the bed appeared to not be as flat as it usually was, which was . . . weird.

Then she heard it, and her heart began to bounce against her ribcage, because that was the sound of breathing, and it wasn't coming from her.

What the hell? Surely not. But there was definitely someone here in this bed with her, and it was their weight that had fractionally altered the angle of the mattress. Was it . . . *Jamie*? She could hear his slow, regular breaths. Which meant he'd come to her room. The last part of the evening was distinctly hazy. Fen was frozen to the spot, her thoughts shooting into overdrive. Surely . . . *surely* she hadn't invited him to join her. Except if she had, did that mean anything more had happened?

No, of course not, she wouldn't have done that. And nor would Jamie. It had to be some kind of innocent mistake. Instead of heading back to his hotel, he'd most likely dozed off on the sofa, and rather than wake him up, Tonia and Hendrik had gone to bed, leaving him there. Then, when he'd woken sometime after that, in his sleepy stupor he must have come upstairs in search of somewhere more comfortable to crash out.

See? Completely innocent. No shenanigans had occurred. She'd been out for the count, and within seconds of sliding under the duvet, so had he.

Fen smiled to herself in the darkness. It was quite funny when you thought about it. He'd be embarrassed when he woke up and realised where he was. Now that she'd worked out how it had happened, she was actually enjoying the comedy aspect of the situation. Sharing a bed was always regarded as such an intimate thing to do, but compared with being squashed up against several complete strangers in an overcrowded Tube carriage, it wasn't even—

Movement. Beneath the duvet, he was shifting position. Fen held her breath, her eyes widening as his foot made contact with hers. It brushed against the back of her heel, then stayed there.

Well. How did *that* feel?

It was some time now since she'd shared a bed with anyone, and the conflicting emotions were swooping in. Guilt, because it wasn't Leon. And sadness, because it could never be Leon again. But there was also a weird kind of happiness adding into the mix, because lying in bed with another person, his bare foot resting against your own, was undeniably comforting, one of life's harmless pleasures. The sensation of physical contact was delicious. Yesterday she'd been mortified by the adrenalin rush she'd experienced when Jamie had pulled her against him, but that was because he'd been awake, and the last thing she needed was for him to become aware of how she'd felt.

Whereas this was completely different. He was fast asleep, his breathing still slow and peaceful. Concentrating all her attention on the sensation of their feet intertwining, Fen slowly, *so* slowly, adjusted the angle of her instep so the degree of contact could be increased. Closing her eyes, she found herself smiling again. This was fun. And foolproof too, because if Jamie did happen to wake up, all she had to do was pretend to have been asleep and completely unaware that he'd even been here in her bed.

Next, she shifted very slightly further onto her side, then froze as Jamie moved too, his arm sliding up and over until his hand came to rest on her waist.

She hadn't expected that to happen. But the sensation of his warm fingers against her torso, where the thin white pyjama top had ridden up, was even more incredible.

Then something weird happened. An echoey snuffling sound appeared to be emanating from the other side of the bed. What was going *on*?

The next moment, Jamie's breathing changed and he shifted beneath the duvet before muttering, 'Shh, it's OK, she'll go back to sleep.'

Except he didn't, because the voice Fen heard didn't belong to Jamie. Rolling over, she yanked the duvet away from the head buried beneath it and saw Tonia blinking up at her.

'What's going on?' Fen checked the other side of the bed. 'Where's the baby?'

'Sorry. Hendrik was snoring like a train. When he snores, I move into the spare room.' Reaching out for something on the bedside table, Tonia located the baby monitor and showed it to Fen. 'I brought this in here with me in case Sonja woke up. But fingers crossed she'll go back to sleep now, then we can too.'

'Waaaaahhh,' Sonja cried tinnily through the monitor.

'Or maybe not.' With a sigh, Tonia sat up and rubbed her eyes. 'I'll go and get her.'

It was ten to six. Fen went downstairs and made coffee, then they sat up in bed together while Tonia fed her daughter and they chatted companionably about last night.

'Was it rude of me to disappear?' said Fen.

'These things happen. I came to make sure you were OK. You were zonked out.'

'I was tired. What time did Jamie leave?'

'Not long after you left us.' Tonia lovingly stroked Sonja's silky blonde head. 'Isn't he great, though? And even better in real life than when you see him on TV.'

'I suppose.' Fen kept her tone casual. This might be her oldest friend, but still she couldn't bring herself to confess the muddled feelings – a confusing blend of forbidden attraction and overwhelming guilt – that made her friendship with Jamie so problematical. She knew that Tonia would be on her side, would loyally insist that it was nothing to be ashamed of and completely normal, what with Jamie being so fit . . . but that was beside the point. It was how *she* knew she felt about it that mattered. Plus, Tonia was her best friend so of course she'd shower her with reassuring reasons why it was all fine, but deep down she still might be secretly thinking: *You can't have loved Leon that much, can you? Not if you're getting all zingy with his best friend, you heartless tart.*

'He'll be over there getting ready to leave for the airport around now— Oh *noooo*.' Tonia was diverted by the ominous noise emerging from Sonja's nappy. 'We're going to have to change you!'

There were times when Sonja became slightly less irresistible. Fen wrinkled her nose. 'Less of the *we*.'

Tonia carted her smelly daughter off to the bathroom and Fen drew back the curtain, looking out of the window at the hotel opposite, its own elongated lit-up windows reflected in the glistening black water of the canal. There was a male figure standing outside the entrance with a carry-on case at his side, and she turned away, heart thumping.

Twenty seconds later, her phone lit up with a message: *Is that you over there at the window?*

OK, so he'd seen her. Fingers trembling slightly, she replied: *Might be. Who's asking?*

Was he . . . laughing? Looking up from his phone, he raised his free hand in greeting, then typed: *Someone you recently unblocked.*

Fen replied: *I could always do it again.*

The next words on the screen appeared: *Please don't.*

What he didn't know was that until thirty minutes ago, he'd been someone she'd thought she was in bed with, someone whose bare foot had tangled with hers and whose hand had curled around her waist.

He was definitely never going to find out about that.

She typed: *Sorry about crashing out last night. I was so tired.*

He replied: *No worries. Yesterday was fun. We must do it again soon.*

Fen took a shuddery breath, because it was something she knew she would want to do. But it was wrong, wrong, *wrong*.

And even if it wasn't wrong, it could never end well.

Headlights lit Jamie up as his taxi made its way along the narrow street towards him. She typed: *I'm going to back to sleep now. Have a good flight.*

Then switched off her phone and made her way downstairs to join Tonia and Sonja.

Six hours later, following a productive morning's work for a new business client in Sunderland whose appointment system for her dental practice had become hopelessly muddled, she stopped for a break and found herself scrolling through Instagram. She didn't follow Sadie Ingalls' account but had looked at it often enough for Instagram's algorithm to know she was interested. And there it was, popping up to playfully jiggle the knife between her ribs, a series of photos of Sadie and Jamie greeting each other at the airport.

Sadie had posted: *Ships – or planes – that pass in the night! Our schedules might be crazy, but as I arrived at Heathrow's Terminal 5 this morning heading for Copenhagen, I managed to meet up with Jamie on his way home from Amsterdam.*

Fen exhaled and switched off her phone. The moral of the story being, if you don't want to see something, don't go on Instagram. And if you really can't help being nosy, it serves you right.

Chapter 32

Bristol

It was the end of November. Jamie had spent the month calling in favours from pretty much everyone he knew, as had the rest of Leon's friends. Companies and celebrities from all over had contributed to the online auction he'd organised, which had already been running for the last six days.

Tonight, at ten o'clock, the final bids would be placed, the auction would come to an end and he would be able to announce the total amount raised for the cancer charity they'd chosen to support in Leon's name. To celebrate the success of the event – because it had already wildly exceeded all estimates – he was hosting a thank-you gathering here at the apartment for those who'd worked so hard to promote it, as the final hours and minutes counted down. A group of Leon's colleagues were on their way, along with many of Jamie's rugby friends, several of whom had auctioned themselves off to the highest bidders. Disa had been at her magical best, persuading local business owners to donate far bigger prizes than they'd planned to offer. Leon's fellow pilots at the flying club were auctioning helicopter rides, and various celebrities had stepped up, offering money-can't-buy experiences that had attracted mind-boggling bids.

The doorbell rang, heralding the arrival of the first guests, and Jamie experienced the usual flashback to the happy years he and Leon had lived here together, when each time a visitor pressed the bell, Leon would exclaim in world-weary fashion, 'Just tell my fans to leave me *alone*.'

He still missed his friend every day. What he wouldn't give to hear him saying it one more time.

Checking the video doorbell, he saw Hattie, Kayla, Guy, Molly and Fen crowding around the doorstep.

Fen, who he knew missed Leon every bit as much as he did. And the others, who might only have known him briefly during their time in Venice, but who'd formed a tight bond and worked hard together to help make this fundraiser a success. And now, jumping out of a taxi behind them, here came Sadie, who'd also achieved a miracle when she'd recently interviewed a pair of married Hollywood A-listers and charmed them into donating a week's stay in their glorious waterfront palazzo on the banks of Lake Como. It had been good of her to make the effort, following the gradual petering-out of their relationship. Having picked up on his lack of enthusiasm, Sadie had been the one to suggest that from now on they should just be friends, and he'd been delighted to agree that this was the right decision, especially since he was off to Australia next week.

But for now, it was an evening for celebrating their collective achievements. Jamie pressed the button to unlock the door, and moments later heard the first clatter of footsteps on the stairs.

Leon might be missing, but everyone else would be here because of him. It was still going to be a good night.

Molly gazed around the spacious living room, now noisy and crowded as the final hour of the online auction approached. Guy had taken over as MC and was standing in front of the window, with its iconic view of the lit-up Clifton Suspension Bridge. With his laptop on the table before him and a cordless microphone in his hand, he was updating the room as each new online bid was placed, to whoops and cheers from everyone gathered in the apartment, as well as occasional comedy groans when their own bids were exceeded.

She was glad she was here, and it was lovely to see everyone, but her secret wish had been that Jamie Hamilton might do a double-take when he clapped eyes on her again, come to his senses at last and realise that she was the one for him.

Except it hadn't happened. True, he had greeted her warmly with open arms and a kiss on each cheek, but this was how he'd greeted every female upon their arrival. Plus, an unexpected rain shower earlier had made her fringe go curly in not-a-good way, which had left her feeling less attractive than she'd hoped. Finally, because disappointments always came in threes, within ten minutes of getting here and while helping herself to a canapé, she'd been accidentally bumped from behind so a dollop of curried mayonnaise landed with a splat on the front of her brand-new white top.

'I'm *so* sorry, someone knocked into me,' Sadie Ingalls had trilled when Molly swung round in dismay, and if this had happened in a romcom it would have been because Jamie's girlfriend saw her as a threat and was determined to banjax the chances of her luring him away. Except the truth was, it *had* been an accident and why would his girlfriend be bothered anyway? Sadie was glamorous, stylish, famous . . . on a whole other level.

In the grand scheme of things, it wasn't important, Molly knew that, but in all honesty, the evening wasn't going as well as she'd hoped, and it was also really annoying when her fringe did this ridiculous—

'If it isn't my long-lost twin,' a voice announced over to her left.

Since the comment appeared to be aimed at her, she said, 'Sorry?' Surely Disa hadn't unearthed yet another long-lost relative for her to meet?

He regarded her with amusement, wild auburn hair falling into light blue eyes, a face full of freckles and crooked incisors visible as his grin widened.

'You and me. Twins.' He waited for her to get it, then pointed to his lime-green polo shirt. Molly's gaze slid down to the tomato-orange stain above the waistband of his jeans.

'Oh, right. I thought you were making fun of my hair. Which usually looks a *lot* better than this.' She shook her head and twanged one of the curls that had turned into a corkscrew over her left eyebrow.

He looked offended. 'Are you suggesting we both have terrible hair? Bit brutal. I think mine's superb.'

'Mine can be pretty good too.' He wasn't her type, but right now she didn't have anyone else to talk to. 'It just drives me mad when the rain sends it out of control and makes it go frizzy.'

'Frizzy. I love that word. So back to the thing we have in common.' He indicated the stain on his polo shirt again. 'This was one of those chicken parcels. When I bit into it, I didn't know it was full of red pepper puree.'

'At least you spilled it down yourself. Mine happened because someone knocked into me.'

'Who? Want me to have a stern word with them?'

'It was Sadie Ingalls.'

His lip curled. 'That monster? God, that's so typical of her. She'll have done it on purpose.'

Molly gaped. '*Really?*'

'No, of course not.' He laughed at the expression on her face. 'I've never met her. But everyone says she's nice. Anyway, hi. Handy.'

It was noisy in the room. He was holding his hand out towards her. Blinking, Molly said, 'What?'

'I'm introducing myself to you.' Gravely he added, 'It's an old-fashioned system but it has its uses. Saves that embarrassing moment years down the line when you have to admit you've never known my name. Andy McLennan. Andrew if we're being formal, or if you're my mum telling me off.' There was that grin again. 'Now it's your turn.'

'To tell you off?' Molly wagged a finger at him. 'Andrew, I can't believe you didn't take more care of that shirt of yours. If you'd used a napkin this would never have happened.'

He looked impressed. 'You sound exactly like her.'

'Now go and tidy your room.'

'Name,' he prompted.

'Molly Piper. Molly to my friends.'

'At last. Hello, Molly. And you live . . . where?'

'Venice.'

'Whoa.'

'But I'm moving back to the UK.'

'Phew, and there I was about to cross you off my list of top fantasy future girlfriends.' His eyes glinted with mischief as he mimed restoring her name to the list and giving it a giant tick.

A sparkly sensation began spreading across Molly's skin, across her shoulders and down her spine; he was quick and funny, and she was enjoying sparring with him. Leaning forward as if to check the list, she said, 'Have you spelled my name right?'

He showed her the imaginary chart. 'M-O-L-I, isn't that it? And will you be living in Bristol?'

'Gloucester. Why?'

'Just checking you're within my radius. You're in luck. I can manage Gloucester.'

She was feeling giddy, glad she'd come along now after a dodgy start. The initial certainty that he wasn't her type was unravelling at top speed. 'Won't your wife mind?'

'Not if we don't tell her.' Andy waited, then said, 'I'm not married. I think I may have been waiting my whole life to meet you.'

It was a joke, but what if there was a tiny bit of truth in there too? The sparkly sensation wasn't subsiding. 'How did you know Leon?'

'We worked for the same company. I know, financial services, I'm that riveting. But he was such a laugh and fun to work with. We were friends for years. Still miss the guy. That's why we're all here, isn't it? To remember him and raise money in his memory.' He pointed at her. 'Tell you what, if you agree to come out on a date with me, I'll add fifty pounds to the pot.'

'Is that all?'

'Fine. One hundred pounds.'

'I've never been so insulted in my life.' But it was hard to keep a straight face when fifty pence would have been enough. She would have paid him.

'Two hundred pounds,' said Andy, 'and that's my final offer.'

'Done.' Molly seized his hand and shook it. 'You have yourself a bargain.'

They gazed at each other as if neither of them could bear to tear their eyes away, two people surrounded by conversation and laughter as the rest of the world, unaware of what was happening, continued around them.

'Look at you two,' Fen exclaimed, coming up behind them. She turned to Andy. 'It did the trick, then?'

Molly said, 'What did the trick? The two hundred pounds?'

'He didn't know how to strike up a conversation with you. Then he saw the stain on your top and decided to get one to match.' Fen frowned. 'What two hundred pounds?'

'Doesn't matter.' To Molly's delight, Andy's pale, freckled face had turned pink.

'I did tell him it wouldn't work and not to waste a good polo shirt on you.'

Was she completely *mad*? 'What made you say that?'

'Because you've told me you only go for men with dark hair and dark eyes,' Fen reminded her. 'You said you'd only *ever* gone out with men like that. You showed me photos, and that's what they were all like . . . slick, well groomed, smartly dressed . . . That's why when Andy spotted you and said you were exactly his type, I had to warn him that he probably wasn't yours.' She gave Andy's arm an apologetic pat. 'No offence. Just being honest, didn't want you getting your hopes up.'

It was Molly's turn to blush. It was true, all true. As their friendship had deepened, she and Fen had discussed past boyfriends, what they'd liked and hadn't liked about them, and the eternal mystery of what it was about men that either provided the initial spark of attraction or acted as the ultimate turn-off. She'd shown Fen photos of the ones she'd been out with, and yes, without exception they'd been olive-skinned, with flashing Italianate eyes and the kind of glossy, straight, nearly black hair that gleamed in the sunshine. She might not have moved to Venice purely because there were so many handsome men there, but at the same time it had definitely been a plus point.

Andy was studying her now. 'Really? That's a shame. Oh well, gave it my best shot, can't say I didn't try.'

As he turned away, he raised his freckled arm to push a lock of tangled auburn hair out of his eyes, and a crystal-clear memory bounced into Molly's brain, of her pulling a face at Fen during one of their FaceTime calls and saying, 'Eurgh, this guy with pale skin and freckles tried to chat me up on a flight once. No way could I go out with someone like that.'

Now who was the monster?

'Please, I'm sorry, I didn't mean it,' Molly blurted out.

Andy shook his head at her. 'I think we all know you did.'

The passenger on the plane had had soft, pudgy arms. Andy's weren't pudgy at all. He also smelled irresistible, unlike the man on her flight, who'd had a nostril-shrivelling case of BO.

Molly held his gaze, desperate to make amends. 'OK, I might have meant it years ago, when I was young and stupid. And I know I used to like those kinds of men, but that was then and this is now. I've changed my mind.'

He raised an eyebrow. 'Well, that's a start. And it would have been great. Except now I know what you're really like, I've changed my mind too.'

Molly's hopes plummeted; it was like clinging to the edge of a mountain and feeling your fingers lose their grip.

'Andy,' Fen protested, 'be nice.'

'I am nice. I'm always nice. But it doesn't always work out in my favour.' He paused, then looked at Molly. 'So does that mean you would still want to have dinner with me tomorr—'

'YES!' Molly interrupted before he could finish. It came out as a high-pitched yelp that made Fen jump.

'Right. The only problem is, in view of recent events, I'm afraid I have to withdraw my bid of two hundred pounds.'

Nooo. Aloud, she said sadly, 'Oh.'

'This time I need *you* to bid to go out on a date with me.'

His eyes were bright with what she hoped was mischief, but was he joking or actually serious?

'Really?' she said.

'Really.'

'Fifty pounds?'

He frowned. 'I think I'm worth a lot more than that.'

'Eighty?'

'Eighty what?' said Hattie, joining them.

'Hi, I'm Andy. Molly's bidding to win a date with me, but she seems to think I'm only worth eighty pounds. Even though I'm sure we'd all agree it's for an excellent cause.'

'It is.' Hattie nodded vigorously. 'Can I join in? I'll bid a hundred.'

'Good for you.' Fen grinned. 'Any advance on one hundred?'

'Two hundred,' said Jamie, appearing next to Hattie. 'What am I bidding for?'

Andy gave him a sultry look. 'A date with me.'

'In that case, two hundred and fifty.'

'Hang on,' Molly protested. 'This isn't fair. Five minutes ago, I was the one up for auction.'

'Any further bids? No? So that makes me the winner.' Pulling his wallet out of his jeans pocket, Jamie peeled off a wad of notes.

'You've always had a thing for me, I knew it.' Andy gave him a stern look. 'But just so you know, I don't snog on the first date.'

'Tell you what, take the money and add it to the pot,' said

Jamie. 'And whoever else wants to go on a date with you can have you, with my blessing.'

'*Me*,' Molly blurted out. 'I will!'

'There you go, sorted, she's taken you off my hands.' Jamie clapped Andy on the back, then said to Molly, 'No kissing, mind. Not on a first date.'

Across the room, Guy was wielding his microphone and double-checking the running total online. 'So with seven minutes to go, the money's still rolling in. If you want to join the bidding, the link's right there on the screen, but you don't have much time left, so don't hang about, get your credit cards out.'

He was being filmed by another of Leon's friends and streamed live on Instagram. Molly said to Hattie, 'He's so good at doing that, makes it look easy.'

Hattie nodded. 'He loves it. Stick a mic in his hand and he's away. When we first met, he ran a mobile disco.'

'And does the fact that you're both here tonight mean you're back together?'

She grinned. 'People keep asking me that. They're all expecting it, but it isn't going to happen. We had a go at being married and it didn't work out. The last thing I want to do is mess things up again. Guy's fantastic company and we spend a lot of time together, but that's as far as it goes. We're better off as friends.'

'He's crazy about you, though. I was watching him earlier. His face lights up every time he looks at you.'

'Only because he wants me and can't have me.' Hattie lowered her voice. 'The thing is, I've never had the upper hand before. And now that I do have it, I've discovered I like it. So no, there's no way I'm going to give that up.'

They both watched as Guy, now joined by Jamie and Sadie

as well as a gaggle of boisterous England rugby players, began noisily counting down to the end of the online auction.

'You recommend it then?' Molly raised her voice to be heard above the escalating roar of the countdown. 'Right, sounds like a plan. I'm going to do it too.'

Back from the bar with fresh drinks, Andy said, 'Do what? To who?'

'Men. Treat 'em mean, keep 'em keen, and whatever happens, don't sleep with them. It's the way forward,' she told him with an angelic smile.

Hattie high-fived her. 'Works for me.'

Chapter 33

For Fen, it hadn't been the easiest evening to get through. The mood had been both upbeat and celebratory and a staggering amount of money had been raised, and if Leon had been here he would have loved every minute.

But he wasn't here, and it was at times like this that the reality and permanence of the loss hit home like a wrecking ball in the chest. Everyone had worked so hard to make the event a success, but she was worn out with smiling and pretending to be fine when on the inside all she wanted was to be alone.

Luckily there was a solution at hand. Finding Molly with Andy in the kitchen, she confided, 'I'm pretty tired, going to head home now. Will you be OK here?'

'I'll be fine. I have my key.' Molly patted her pocket, then gave her a hug. 'I'll see you later.'

Unable to face the inevitable wider round of goodbyes with well-meaning people trying to persuade her to stay longer, Fen made her escape and slipped away down the stairs, letting herself out of the front door and onto the frosted street, sparkling silver beneath the glow cast by the street lamps.

Breathing in the icy night air, she decided to walk towards the centre of Clifton village, where Ubers would be circling. It was always entertaining to be able to look in through the uncurtained windows of the ultra-desirable houses of Caledonia Place, lit up to reveal the lives of the people who lived in them, some happy and others maybe lonely . . .

Pausing, she heard the thin, plaintive wail of a sleepless baby in one upstairs bedroom, then the miaow of a black and white cat observing her with disdain as it stalked across the road in front of her. Fen gave it a disdainful look in return, then jumped as her phone suddenly rang in her bag.

'Where are you?' said Jamie. 'I looked everywhere and you'd gone.'

'You were busy talking to people.' The tumult of feelings was as confusing as ever; try as she might, they weren't going away.

'Are you in a cab?'

'I'm heading up to Regent Street, I'll get one there.'

'That's stupid, you should have arranged for it to pick you up from here.'

'Don't make a fuss, I'll be— WAAHH!' Not paying attention to the road, Fen's suede boot skidded on a heavy patch of frost, sending her crashing to the ground. 'AARGH . . . *noooo!*' The phone shot out of her hand and flew off to the right, disappearing from view. She let out a howl of despair and scrambled to her feet, unhurt but desperate to find it. If only she had her phone with her, she could seek it out with the help of its torch.

'What are you *doing?*' Sadie called out as Jamie raced down the stairs.

'Something's happened to Fen.'

'*What?*'

He left the house, headed down the hill and swung into Caledonia Place, his gaze switching from the enclosed private gardens on the left to the five-storey terraced Georgian properties on the right, listening intently for signs of a person in distress. The sound of Fen's shriek of horror over the phone had been cut off as the connection had ended, sending chills down his spine. He couldn't hear anything, but she had to still be somewhere around here, surely.

Breaking into a run, he crossed diagonally over to the other side of the street as a taxi drove past, his pulse racing because it was the not knowing that was causing his brain to go into overdrive.

The next moment he saw them: two legs sticking out from under the side of a grey van.

'Fen!'

One of the legs moved and his heart gave a gigantic thud of relief because she wasn't dead. As he drew closer, he heard her give a muffled triumphant cry of 'Got it!' before wriggling backwards out from beneath the van like a caterpillar.

Not attacked. Thank God.

'You gave me a fright.' Jamie shook his head. 'What happened?'

'I slipped on a patch of frost and went flying. So did my phone. But I managed to find it. And look at that,' she added, hastily scrambling to her feet before he could help her up. 'Not even broken, hooray!'

'I was worried, didn't know what was going on.'

'Sorry.' Shivering from the cold, she took a step back. 'I wasn't looking where I was going.'

'You shouldn't have been out here on your own in the first place.' He began walking alongside her. 'You never know who might be around.'

'True.' Fen nodded in agreement. 'Anyway, well done on tonight. You raised so much money. It was brilliant.'

'I wanted to get it done before heading off to Australia.' He paused. 'Maybe we could meet up again before I go?'

She hesitated. 'I'm pretty busy for the next few days.'

The mental backing-off was happening again; he could feel her withdrawing and longed to break through the barriers she was once more putting up. Touching her arm, he said, 'Look, it doesn't have to be like—'

'Hey, wait for me,' a voice called out behind them, and they both turned at the sound of high heels clattering along the pavement as Sadie caught up with them, swathed in her expensive new lilac suede coat. Catching her breath, she said cheerfully, 'Where are you two off to? Is this a secret assignation or can anyone join in?'

'I fell over and couldn't find my phone for a few minutes,' Fen explained. 'Jamie thought I was in trouble. But I'm fine, just getting a cab home. There's usually a couple hanging around outside the restaurants in the village.'

'Well, I'm glad you're OK. I'll walk with you,' Sadie said cheerfully.

When they reached Princess Victoria Street, there was a cab waiting on the corner. Sadie gave Fen a hug, then Fen hopped into the back seat and gave Jamie a little wave. 'Thanks for coming to find me. Have fun in Australia. Bye!'

It was now one in the morning, the raucous rugby players had finally departed and Clifton had fallen silent. Having left Jamie's apartment an hour earlier, Molly and Andy had made their way to the hotel across the road for one more drink before calling it a night.

Which had inevitably turned into a couple more drinks and a lot more playful repartee out on the heated terrace with its front-row view of the lit-up bridge stretched across the Avon Gorge.

Molly was buzzing; and to think if she hadn't been able to swap her shifts at La Lanterna, she'd have missed out on all this. *Imagine* . . .

But wasn't it bizarre, the way perceptions could shift and change? To begin with, her views on Andy had been decidedly mixed, then there'd been a gradual realisation that he was growing on her . . . and now, less than four hours later, she was discovering just how much she liked him.

Like, *really* liked him.

And no, she wasn't drunk, it was just that the progression from doubt and suspicion to full-on attraction felt almost magical. He lived in Thornbury, worked in the centre of Bristol, loved to drive, made her laugh and had changed her attitude to pale skin and freckles *for ever*.

'We're the last ones here,' Andy observed. 'I think the barman would probably be happy if we left now.'

When they reached the canopied front entrance of the hotel, he said, 'Well, I mustn't keep you any longer. I'll call you a cab to get you back to Fen's. Thank you for my date, it was awesome.' He took out his phone. 'And I'm going to say goodnight like an absolute gentleman because I know that's the right thing to do.'

Oh . . . 'Is it?'

He raised an eyebrow. 'Your grand plan, remember? To hold back, treat me mean and keep me keen? I'm going to be honest with you now. It's working.'

Molly caught her breath. 'Really?'

'Extremely well.' He gave her a wry nod, followed by an even more rueful smile, made all the more irresistible by those adorably pointed incisors. 'When can I see you again?'

Er . . . hello? Maybe now?

'I'm only here for the next three days.'

'Tomorrow, then? Or the next day?' Andy leaned closer and lowered his voice as the night porter walked past. 'You have no idea how much I want to kiss you right now. But no,' he held up a hand, 'I mustn't. Not allowed. I know.'

For heaven's sake, why had she ever started this ridiculous idea? It was all Hattie's fault. 'Maybe one kiss would be OK. Just a small one.'

He looked at her mouth. 'This is killing me. And you're not helping, saying something like that.'

Sod this for a game of soldiers. Molly pushed him up against the wall and leaned into him, her arms winding their way around his neck and her mouth finding his, giving him no time to protest. She felt his lips curve into a smile, then the thrilling sensation of his body pressing against hers while his tongue slid into her mouth. Oh yes, he definitely knew how to kiss . . .

'Wow,' Andy murmured when they eventually came up for air. 'And that was a small one? You are dangerous.'

She'd asked him earlier where he was spending the night, and he'd said, 'Not far from here.' Since she could hardly take him back to Fen's flat, she said, 'Where *are* you staying tonight?'

'Why?'

'Just . . . curious.'

'Here.'

'*What?*' She stared at him. 'Are you serious?'

In response, he took out his wallet, flipped it open and showed her the key card. Molly said, 'Why didn't you tell me before?'

The corners of his mouth twitched. 'You might have thought I was trying to . . . I don't know, seduce you.'

'That would have been the best news ever.'

'But you'd decided to play hard to get, remember.'

'That was Hattie's idea, not mine. I didn't want to do it at all.'

'You get better and better.' He kissed her again.

'Not that I sleep around,' Molly added hastily. 'It's been ages since the last time. I'm actually really pernickety.'

'I'm glad to hear that. Tell you what, why don't you send Fen a message letting her know where you are? Tell her you'll see her in the morning. Or the afternoon. Whenever.'

'Good plan.' She quickly did so and pressed send. Then Andy reached for her hand and led her back inside the hotel, across the marble-tiled reception area and into the lift.

When they reached his room, Molly sensed she was on the cusp of something important, possibly even life-changing. A quiver of anticipation ran down her spine.

'I've just thought of something,' she said as the door clicked open. 'Leon met Fen because of me. And now I've met you because of Leon.'

'Maybe he planned it this way. I wouldn't put it past him. Either way, if he's watching us now, I'm sure he'll take all the credit.'

The hotel room door closed with a discreet clunk behind them and the low-level lighting flickered on. Molly pulled a face. 'I really hope he isn't watching us now.'

'Good point. Leon?' Andy addressed the room in general. 'Well done, mate, good job, but if you could leave us alone for a bit, maybe go and spy on some other friends, that'd be appreciated. I think we can manage without you from here on.'

★

'You OK?' Guy briefly rested his hand on hers as they drove through the night back to Oxford.

Hattie nodded. 'Yes. Bit tired, that's all.' Since she had to be at work first thing in the morning, they hadn't been able to stay the night in Bristol despite Disa's offer to put them up. She glanced across at him. 'Thanks for driving tonight.'

'No problem. Why don't you try and get some sleep now? I promise not to sing.'

Hattie smiled; when he was like this, it was hard to maintain her upper-hand stance. Guy might still believe she had it, but even as she'd been telling Molly about it earlier, she'd known she wasn't being entirely truthful. As time went by, her attraction to Guy was becoming increasingly serious, which was a nice way to feel but also scary, because what if she let down her guard and it ended up going wrong again?

Then again, what if it didn't? What if, by continuing to doubt him when he promised her he'd changed, she was actually missing out?

'You can sing if you want to.' He had a good voice, had been the lead vocalist in a band back when they'd first met. A fortnight ago he'd been approached to join another well-regarded band specialising in weddings, but had turned down the offer. Sleepily, feeling her eyes begin to close now, Hattie said, 'Why did you say no to those people who wanted you in their band?'

Guy overtook a couple of articulated lorries as they continued to make their way smoothly up the darkened motorway. 'Because it would mean travelling to gigs most weekends. And I don't want to do that.' He waited a moment, then said simply, 'I'd rather spend my time with you.'

Chapter 34

It was the middle of December, a glitzy new restaurant had opened on Park Street, and Disa had been keen for them to try it. She arrived at Fen's flat in a swirl of faux-fur that exactly matched her ash-blonde hair. Having admired the kitchen Fen had recently finished redecorating in shades of deep blue and bronze, her attention was caught by the calendar on the wall.

'What does that say?' Disa wasn't wearing her reading glasses. 'Whose birthday is it tomorrow?'

It was cold outside. Ready to leave, Fen finished winding a cream wool scarf around her neck. 'Jamie's.'

'Is it really? But that isn't your writing. Who put it on your calendar?'

Fen's heart gave a squeeze at the memory. It had been the day after their return from Venice. Leon had turned up in the morning with a bag of hot breakfast baps, eager to see her again and to explore her flat. Since it was tiny, it hadn't taken long at all, but he'd paid appreciative attention to the paintings hung on the walls, the framed photos of Disa and Declan taken in years gone by, and the multicoloured glass chandelier she'd fallen in love with online and had saved up for for months. In the kitchen, spotting the calendar pinned up next to the window, he'd turned the pages until he reached October. Reaching for the ballpoint pen nestled in the bottom of an otherwise empty fruit bowl, he scrawled *Leon's birthday* with a flourish in the relevant square, then said, 'Not that you'll have a chance to forget it. I'll probably remind you most days.'

'Now what are you doing?'

He'd flipped over the next two pages. On the square belonging to the thirteenth of December, he wrote *Jamie's birthday*. He grinned. 'We don't want to forget his, either. He'd go spare if he didn't get his present from me.'

'What do you buy the man who has everything?'

'Exactly. That's why I always give him the same thing, every year without fail.'

Fen had started to laugh. 'You do? What is it?'

Back in the present day, Disa interrupted her train of thought. 'Have you posted the card off already?'

'What card?'

'The one for Jamie.'

'No. I wasn't planning on sending one.'

'Sweetheart, you must. Opening cards on your birthday is the best feeling; it lets you know people are thinking of you!'

Needless to say, Disa was a diehard card person. She sent gorgeous, carefully chosen ones and loved receiving them in return. Fen said, 'He'll have loads. He doesn't need one from me. Are we ready to go?'

But it came as no surprise two hours later, after lunch in the restaurant that had more than lived up to its promise, when Disa drifted – in that casual way she had – into one of the shops on

Park Street that happened to sell, among other things, quirky cards for every occasion.

'Now this is a good one,' she exclaimed, showing it to Fen then whisking it out of reach when she went to take it. 'No, you know him better than I do, you need to choose one yourself.'

'Fine.' Fen gave in with good grace and began to flip through the cards on the racks; she knew only too well that if she didn't buy one, Disa was quite capable of forging her signature and sending one to Jamie herself.

When Jamie emerged from the shower the next morning and heard the distant metallic *snap* of the letter box, he wrapped a towel around his hips and headed for the staircase to see what the postman had brought him.

But as he made his way down the stairs, the sight that greeted him stopped him in his tracks. There was an emerald-green envelope on the mat in the narrow hallway. And a single small potato.

Followed moments later by a second potato — *clunk* — dropping through the letter box and rolling across to the bottom stair. Then a third — *clunk* — and a — *clunk* — fourth.

He didn't know whether to laugh or well up at the sight of them, but he knew he needed to get to the door before the potato-dropper got away.

He pulled it open and there she was, bundled up against the cold in a pale yellow angora beanie hat, an oversized pink sweatshirt and a blue paisley gilet over grey leggings. There was one last potato in her hand.

Startled, she said, 'You weren't supposed to come to the door. I thought it was too early for you to be up.'

'I'm catching the train to London.'

'Oh, well . . .'

'No, no, please come in, before I get frostbite.'

'I don't want—'

'Just for two minutes.' Backing away, Jamie bent to pick up the card and the potatoes. 'You can't run away now.'

She followed him up the stairs. 'Well, happy birthday.'

'Thanks. Let me put some clothes on . . .' He dived into his bedroom, speedily swapped the bath towel for shorts and a T-shirt, and re-emerged to find her lining the potatoes up on the glass-topped coffee table in the living room.

'When I saw them dropping through the letter box, I thought for a split second it was him. Then I knew it had to be you.'

'He told me about it,' said Fen.

Jamie smiled. It had begun during their first year at uni, when the girl he'd been seeing had complained that she didn't know what to get him for his birthday. That evening, Leon had said, 'Right, serious question. What's your favourite thing in the world?'

Jamie remembered the moment. He'd been in the shared kitchen, demolishing a plate of sausage and chips and drinking warm Irn-Bru because someone else had made off with his last can of Coke. 'Apart from sex?'

'Apart from sex,' said Leon, 'because I'm definitely not giving you that for your birthday.'

'In that case, chips.' Jamie speared the best one on the plate with his fork and gave it a twirl, admiring its crispy golden exterior. 'Definitely chips.'

And every year since, Leon had presented him with potatoes, hiding them in his bed, or in the wardrobe, or scattered around the apartment waiting to be found. This morning, knowing there wouldn't be potatoes lurking in the shower or inside his shoes had been hard to cope with.

'You don't know how much this means to me. Really.' He wanted to give her a hug, but somewhere along the way, at Fen's instigation, they'd fallen into a pattern of avoiding physical contact. 'And a card as well?' This was something else he hadn't expected. Opening the envelope, he saw that it was potato-themed too. As a smile spread across his face, his phone dinged with a message.

Glancing at it on the table next to her, Fen said, 'That's your cab letting you know it's outside. I need to go.'

He'd missed her so much, didn't want the fleeting visit to be over. Without giving himself time to think, he said, 'Let's go out tonight.'

'What?' Fen looked stunned. 'But it's your birthday!'

'All the more reason.'

'I meant, surely you're already doing something? You'll be in London!'

'It's a flying visit. Lunchtime meeting, then straight back. Please.'

Another ding on his phone from the waiting taxi driver.

Still mystified, she said, 'I can't believe you don't have any other plans.'

'Only one. Kev and Annie are back in Bristol with the baby and I'm meeting them at eight o'clock in the bar at the Castle Hotel. But I could pick you up first, we'll see them for a couple of drinks and admire the baby, then head off out. How about that?' Jamie held his breath; it was the ideal plan. Fen knew and liked Kev and Annie, who'd both worked with Leon and had been about to become parents when she'd last seen them, at the charity night. She would love to meet their baby daughter.

Say yes, say yes, please say yes.

BEEEEEP. The cab driver was getting impatient downstairs.

Flustered and already backing in the direction of the door, Fen said, 'OK, but you really need to get dressed for work now. I'll tell the driver you'll be out in two minutes. And I'll see you tonight.'

Bingo. His birthday had just got a hundred times better.

She said yes.

Chapter 35

When Fen opened the door to him that evening, Jamie nodded and said simply, 'Wow. Look at you.'

He wasn't looking too bad himself, in a dark blue shirt and trousers, and a charcoal-grey suede jacket. This morning his hair had been wet from the shower and he'd hastily thrown on shorts and a T-shirt. Mind you, his time in Australia had given him a deep tan, and most women would have swooned at the sight of him then.

Not her, though. Swooning was something she was keeping a lid on. As time went by, keeping tight control over her emotions was something she was getting better at. Practice was on the way to making perfect. She had loved Leon so completely that the very idea of developing feelings towards another man after his death had been unthinkable. Which was why it had come as such a shock to her when meeting up with Jamie again in Amsterdam had caused her emotions to go into overdrive, like a washing machine on spin, reminding her of how it felt to be *alive*. Yes, those feelings had grown more intense during the time they'd spent together then. And yes, they did still insist on surging to the surface each time she saw him. But she was definitely learning how to squash them down again. What he didn't know couldn't embarrass her.

Deep breaths helped. So did imagining Jamie's reaction if he were to discover the effect he was having on her. The thought of his incredulous laughter was the best antidote of all.

He'd been Leon's best friend and he happened to be ridiculously attractive, but that was OK, she could get through this.

In the car on their way to the hotel, Jamie said, 'Thanks for saying yes to this, by the way. I thought you might come up with some reason why you couldn't make it.'

'I nearly did.' Fen kept her tone playful. 'But then I felt sorry for you. I still can't believe you didn't have anything else arranged for your birthday.'

'Honestly? Same. I did put out a few feelers, but everyone had other things planned. Apart from Kev and Annie. And now you. Which is fine with me.' He nodded to the left as they pulled up at traffic lights. 'M. T.'

Fen looked and laughed; it was a game he and Leon had always played when they were out and about. Anyone spotting someone who resembled a celebrity would announce the initials and the other one had to figure out who they meant. This one was easy; an elderly but upright woman with a rigid eighties hairstyle and a tweed skirt was clutching her handbag as she hurried along the pavement. 'Margaret Thatcher.'

He applauded. 'Well done. Now it's your turn.'

'Not fair.' It wasn't something you could do on command; it took time to spot a lookie-likie. But the next moment, like a miracle, she saw one waiting to cross the road. 'Oh, F. C.!'

Jamie's head swivelled from left to right, in a hurry to find the person before the lights changed. As the man crossed directly in front of the car, he turned and raised a hand to thank them, his long hair and beard gleaming white in the headlights. 'Got it.' Jamie grinned. 'Father Christmas.'

Without thinking, Fen raised her own hand and they exchanged a high-five, just as he and Leon had always done after a successful spot. And there it was, the explosive rush of adrenalin she'd briefly forgotten and that almost took her breath away.

'God, I've missed doing that,' said Jamie. He turned to look at her. 'Can we always play it? Keep the tradition alive?'

A warm glow spread through her. Yes, it was something she'd love to do, could see herself doing in the future. Nodding, she said, 'Sounds like a plan. Although I don't think my last one was a lookie-likie, pretty sure he was the real Santa.'

They reached the hotel's jam-packed car park and, true to form in Jamie-land, a Volvo pulled out as they arrived, allowing him to slide into the only available parking space.

'That never happens to anyone else, you know,' Fen pointed out.

He smiled. 'Leon used to tell me that too. He called it my superpower.'

'It must be fun,' Fen said lightly. 'Swanning through life, everything going your way.'

'Sometimes.' He shrugged. 'Not always.'

'How's Sadie?' She knew they didn't see each other that often, but once or twice they'd been photographed together. Not that she kept checking Instagram. Well, not more than a few times a week.

'We broke up.'

'I had no idea! I'm sorry!'

'I thought you knew.' Jamie shook his head. 'Don't sound so shocked. It was a mutual decision.'

'I thought you really liked her.'

'She was great. No big deal, though. Sometimes these things just peter out.'

'Got anyone else lined up?' Fen realised she was holding her breath.

Another shake of the head, followed by a rueful smile. For a moment he seemed about to say something else, then his phone went *tingggg* with a message.

Phones. They really knew how to pick their moments, didn't they? He checked the screen.

'It's from Kev, wanting to know why we're late. They're waiting for us in the Beaufort Bar. Come on, we'd better get going.'

'Here he is! Happy birthday!' Kev greeted them at the entrance to the bar, clapping Jamie on the back then turning to give Fen a big hug. 'And you brought Fen along too. Hello, lovely, come and meet Georgia while she isn't screaming her head off.'

Fen's heart melted at the sight of Annie holding baby Georgia. 'Look at her, she's like an angel!'

'Takes after me,' Kev said proudly.

'You wish,' said Jamie. 'She's a miniature Annie.'

'Here. Have a cuddle.' Annie deftly passed the baby over to Fen.

'She's perfect.' Gazing down in wonder at the big eyes and tiny starfish fingers, Fen stroked Georgia's velvet-soft head and shell-like ears. 'What a miracle. Look at her mouth!'

Two minutes later, clearly bursting with impatience, Jamie said, 'That's enough. My turn now.'

He held out his arms, and Fen, turning to face him, discovered it was a far more complicated manoeuvre than simply passing a bundle of washing to another person. She attempted to offer Georgia to him sideways, but her head needed supporting, her legs were scrunched up like a frog's and her body was so floppy but infinitely precious that before long their own arms were entangled, the baby was trapped between them and the unintended but unavoidable physical contact with Jamie was sending what felt like showers of sparks through her body. *Good grief, so much for thinking I had all that under control.*

'I know, it's tricky,' Annie sympathised as they finally managed to complete the awkward handover. 'Took us some getting used to at first!'

Approaching them, a waiter said discreetly, 'I'm afraid it's that time.'

'No problem.' Kev nodded, then explained, 'No babies allowed in the bar after eight. But it's fine, there's a place upstairs we can go.'

As they made their way through the wood-panelled reception hall, other guests noticed them. A chatty middle-aged American couple passed them on the sweeping staircase, and the woman gazed with delight at Jamie holding the baby in his arms before turning to Fen and saying, 'Honey, look at your husband and adorable baby! Did you ever see such a proud daddy in your life?'

Which could have been embarrassing, but what would be the point in correcting her? Fen smiled at the woman and Jamie, at her side, replied cheerfully, 'I am.'

They reached the first-floor landing and Annie said, 'Let me take her back from you now. They told us we can make ourselves comfortable in the Beaulieu Suite.' She expertly relieved Jamie of his charge and Kev pushed open the double doors at the entrance to the suite, which was in darkness.

Then the lights came on and a massive cheer went up as a couple of hundred people bellowed, 'SURPRISE!'

'Your faces,' Annie exclaimed with delight several minutes

later, 'when you and Jamie walked in together and the lights came on. So brilliant! Well, you'll see it for yourselves later, loads of people were videoing it. I can't believe we managed to pull it off; we were so scared he'd guess when everybody said they were too busy to see him on his birthday. And you'd have been invited too, but the rugby guys said you weren't really going out and wouldn't have wanted to come along . . . except you're here anyway! None of us had any idea you were seeing each other!'

Oh God . . .

'We really aren't, not at all. I was kind of the last resort tonight, that's all. And this is fantastic.' Hastily Fen gestured around the vast oak-panelled conference suite, its ceiling covered in silver and blue helium balloons. 'He had no idea it was happening. Well done, you.'

'It wasn't just us.' Annie touched her arm. 'Leon was the one who thought of it. He told Kev back in the summer and said it'd be a good thing to do, so Kev got in touch with the chaps from the rugby club and they organised it between them, putting out the word and getting everyone to invite Jamie's friends from all over. At one stage we thought we'd need to hire a bigger venue,' she said with a laugh, 'because so many people wanted to come!'

'I say. Look at you,' a voice behind her declared twenty minutes later, and Fen swung round in surprise, because of all the people here tonight, she hadn't expected to see Amanda.

Who still had no idea she was the one who'd given Jamie that stern telling-off on the evening of her own birthday party, way back in March.

'Hi!' Amanda sat down on the chair next to her. 'Fancy bumping into you here tonight – I love your shoes! And look,

I was so sorry to hear about your boyfriend. I did mean to send you a text, but you know how it is, don't you? You never know what to say.'

'That's OK, it's fine.' Fen nodded. 'I didn't know you'd be here either.'

'My cousin's going out with one of Jamie's rugby friends, so that's how I got to hear about it and bagged myself an invite,' Amanda explained. 'I told them I'd messaged Jamie on Instagram after Leon died, because I knew how devastated he must have been. Awful for him, losing his best friend like that. Where did you get your dress from? You've lost weight, by the look of you, lucky thing!'

Fen reminded herself that Amanda was only a friend-of-a-friend with a talent for blurting things out before thinking them through. She said, 'I'm starting to put it back on now.'

'That's a shame.' Amanda tilted her head sympathetically, then leaned in closer. 'So anyway, what's all this I've been hearing about you and Jamie?'

Startled, Fen said, 'What?'

'You know how word gets around. Jamie let slip that he'd met up with you in Amsterdam, and we all thought, ey up, is there something going on that we don't know about? Then tonight we couldn't believe it when the two of you walked in together! So is this some secret affair we weren't supposed to find out about and you're the reason he and Sadie Ingalls broke up? Because that would be *wild* and—'

'It isn't wild,' Fen finally managed to blurt out, because Amanda was a full-on gossip machine and once she got going there was no stopping her. 'It's not wild because there's nothing going on. *At all*,' she added firmly, and saw Amanda's expression change when she realised it was true.

'Really? Thank goodness for that! I was saying to my friends, it all seemed a bit unlikely. I mean, when your boyfriend only died a few months ago, you wouldn't want anyone else! You'd still be in pieces, wouldn't you?' Amanda shook her head sympathetically. 'What kind of woman would act as if nothing had even happened and just throw herself at the first guy to pay her a bit of attention? I suppose some might, but you definitely aren't the type to do that! It's not like losing an umbrella and just going out and buying yourself another one, is it?'

Amanda had gone back to her own group of friends, no doubt to reassure them there was no need to panic after all, Jamie Hamilton was still on the market. Jamie himself was being kept busy greeting everyone who'd turned up tonight to celebrate his birthday. Fen, putting on a show Meryl Streep would have been proud of, smiled and chatted with those people she knew, and even danced with two members of the rugby crowd as well as one of the pilots from the flying club, who was hopefully more skilled at flying helicopters.

Jamie was waiting for her when the pilot walked her off the dance floor. 'My turn next. Not with him,' he amended, grinning at Fen. 'With you.'

But Fen shook her head; there was only so much Oscar-worthy acting she could manage in one night. Apart from anything else, camera flashes were going off like fireworks as more and more people took photos and videos on their phones.

'Sorry, I'm going to have to bail.' She pressed her temple with the heel of her hand. 'Had my first migraine in years last week, and I think another one might be building up. My head's starting to pound and I'm feeling a bit sick.'

'Oh *no*.' Concerned, Jamie said, 'Look, I'll take you home.'

'No, you won't. This is your party and you can't leave.' She managed a reassuring smile. 'Honestly, I'm going to sneak away so I don't have to do the whole goodbye thing. I'll call a cab and be home in no time. But it's been so nice to see everyone. And good to know your friends weren't too busy to see you after all.'

'I feel bad abandoning you.' He raked his hair back from his forehead. 'But if you're sure. And I'll call you tomorrow.'

He was about to hug her, maybe even give her a goodnight kiss; she could sense it was on the verge of happening. Ducking out of the way in the nick of time, she said hastily, 'Right, I'm off while no one's looking. Bye!'

It was a restless night's sleep. At around three, Fen awoke with a start from a hideous dream in which she'd been standing in front of an audience of hundreds of people booing her because she was heartless and disgusting, and if Leon were watching her now he'd be appalled and wish he had never met her.

The next morning, she spent a long time composing the right message:

Hi, so glad you had a great birthday. My migraine has passed and my head is fine this morning, but I've had a good think about everything and have decided it's best if we cool our friendship. Nothing personal, it's just that seeing you makes me miss Leon more, which is hard to bear. Not your fault at all, and nothing either of us can do about it, so please don't try to change my mind. Thanks for everything, and for understanding. Fen

Her breath caught in her throat as she pressed send, then again twenty minutes later when Jamie's reply popped up on the screen:

OK.

Followed several minutes after that by:

Whatever's best for you. I understand. If you ever change your mind, let me know.

Fen's eyes grew hot and an aching sense of loneliness expanded inside her ribcage.

If only he knew how she really felt. He'd probably be appalled too.

Chapter 36

The Cotswolds

Winter had been and gone. It was now April, and spring had arrived in the Cotswolds. The trees were bursting with leaves once more, the sky was a dazzling shade of blue, and lambs were prancing in the fields.

Sunshine poured in through the long sash windows of Hetherton Hall, and Fen, perched on the edge of an uncomfortable leather sofa, wondered if Hilary and Greville really trusted her not to make off with the pair of Royal Doulton china figurines on the marble mantelpiece.

They could trust her. She wouldn't want them anyway. She still wasn't entirely sure why she was here, but the invitation from the Spencer-Carrs had arrived in the post last week and presumably had something to do with Leon. So of course she'd arrived on time and been shown into the drawing room by Greville, who informed her she was three minutes early and asked her to wait. Hilary would be downstairs in due course.

Thirty seconds later, she heard a car pull up outside. Crossing the room to peer out of the window, Fen was glad she had, because there was Jamie stepping out of a brand-new black Audi and crunching his way across the gravelled driveway.

It was good to have a bit of warning, to give her body time to get over its reaction to seeing him again in person for the first time in more than four months. She took a few deep breaths and willed herself to calm down. He was looking tanned, wearing a pale pink shirt and dark blue trousers, and his hair was a bit shorter than usual, though it still fell past his collar.

In the distance, the front doorbell rang and was answered. At three o'clock on the dot, Leon's parents and Jamie entered the drawing room together, both Hilary and Greville looking noticeably older and frailer than when she'd last seen them, at the funeral. Fen's heart went out to them; the months since Leon's death must have been even harder for them to bear than they had been for her.

'Thank you both for coming,' said Hilary when everyone was settled. 'Needless to say, this was Leon's idea. He asked me to organise today's meeting.' She took a breath. 'It's to do with his ashes.'

Of course it had been Leon's idea. He'd made sure to arrange every detail of his own funeral, so why stop there?

'OK.' Jamie nodded. 'And his plan is . . .?'

'We couldn't let you take them before now.' Hilary's voice grew unsteady and she reached instinctively for her husband's hand as she collected herself. 'I told him that, back then. But he was right, we can't keep him here with us for ever. And now's the time.' Her eyes glistened with tears. 'He wants the two of you to take his ashes to Venice and scatter them in the lagoon.'

Venice . . .

Silence fell, the only sound in the room the sombre tick of

the ornate walnut grandfather clock to the left of the fireplace.

Hilary looked at Jamie, then at Fen. 'We can't force you to go, obviously. But . . .'

'If it's what he wanted to happen,' Jamie said evenly, 'then of course we'll do it.' He paused. 'At least, I will.'

Fen clasped her hands together in her lap. More silence. But what other choice did she have? How many times had Leon told her that the week they'd spent together in Venice had been the happiest of his entire life?

How could she say no? And it made sense that he'd ask Jamie to go with her; he'd known she wouldn't want to do it alone.

She nodded at Leon's parents. 'Me too. Of course we will.'

It was a brief meeting, but one filled with emotion. For the first time, Greville shed a tear without embarrassment, and thanked them both in a quavery voice. Then he shook Jamie's hand before pulling Fen towards him and giving her an awkward whisky-scented hug.

Next, it was Hilary's turn to embrace first Jamie, then Fen. 'Thank you from me too,' she told them both. 'We're so grateful to you. I hope we won't lose touch.'

It was a sentiment that would have seemed unimaginable on the occasion of their first, fairly traumatic meeting, but Fen smiled and meant it when she replied, 'I hope so too.'

'I like your hair like that.' Hilary gave a nod of approval, reaching out to lightly touch her blonde curls.

'Thank you!'

'Not so sure about those earrings, though.'

Oh, Hilary, never change.

'I agree.' Good heavens, was that a flicker of affection she was experiencing for the older woman? Fen nodded and said gravely, 'I think they were a mistake.'

Bristol

Three weeks later, forty-eight hours before she was due to fly out to Venice, Fen arrived home from a long-overdue visit to the hairdresser's to find an unstamped envelope pushed through the letter box with her name scrawled across it in anonymous block capitals.

Ripping it open, she took out a second, smaller envelope. This time her heart gave a giant *bump*, because the handwriting of her name appeared to belong to Leon, and beneath it he'd added: *Yes, don't be shocked, it's from me.*

Her hands trembled as she unfolded the letter inside, written in blue ink on heavy deckle-edged cream notepaper printed with his parents' address, and began to read:

Fen (forever my perfect ten),

The worst part of dying is never getting to find out what happens next.

It's been a year now since we met. Obviously I hope you're still missing me, but not too much. (And just so you know, if you aren't missing me at all and have entirely moved on, you wouldn't have been sent this letter. So if you're reading these words, I'd like you to pay attention.)

I loved you and I know you loved me too, but you're allowed to be happy again. That you and Jamie are going to be scattering my ashes in Venice means the world to me. Thank you so much for agreeing to do this. I'd like it to happen on the first day, so once it's done you can relax, enjoy yourselves. You'll be in Venice, after all.

OK, this is from me to you, and I might be wrong, but in case I'm right, I want to say this. If you're holding back on getting involved with someone else because of me, don't let me stop you. Especially if it's someone I'd approve of and be happy to see you with. Like maybe Jamie.

There, I've said it. Are you laughing right now? If you have your eye on someone else, that's fine, ignore me. But the one thing I never did tell Jamie was how much I loved seeing the two of you together, getting on so well as friends. To begin with, I'll be honest, I wondered if I'd lose you to him, until I realised he'd never do that to me. But now I'm gone (such a weird thing to write!), and if there ever has been a spark between you, I want you to know that I'm all in favour. I had great taste when it came to choosing a best friend, and you had the best taste in boyfriends, so why not? The more I've thought about it, the more sense it makes. Jamie needs someone like you, and I think you'd be absolutely right for each other.

Anyway, feel free to ignore all of this if it isn't relevant. Just wanted to let you know that if it might be, I'll be cheering you on.

Whatever happens, be happy.

Give my love to Venice. And of course to you, always.

Leon xxxxx

Fen pressed the letter to her chest and exhaled slowly, because she could hear his voice so clearly in every word he'd written, and it was as if he'd known what had been keeping her trapped in a glass box all these months.

But now she'd been given permission to escape the box. If she wanted to.

It was the ultimate act of kindness and thoughtfulness.

She wondered who had delivered Leon's letter to her door. His mother?

Father?

One of his many friends?

Then a thought struck her . . .

Had it been Jamie himself?

And if it had been, did he have any idea what was in it?

Surely not . . .

No matter how early you arrived at an international airport, it always came as a surprise to discover how busy it was. The drop-off area outside the main terminal was full of cabs and cars, and trolleys piled high with luggage were being pushed in all directions.

'Thanks so much for doing this,' said Fen. Getting up at six in the morning wasn't her grandmother's favourite pastime, but Disa had insisted on driving her here today.

'Don't be silly, it's fine.' Disa slid the car smoothly into a parking space. 'I wonder if Jamie's beaten us to it?'

Jamie had been the star speaker last night at a sporting awards dinner in Exeter, and was making his own way up here this morning. Climbing out of Disa's car, Fen scanned the faces around them but didn't spot him. Flipping open the boot, she began lifting her case out, then lost her grip on the handle and let out a yelp of pain as one of her fingernails snapped backwards.

'Whoops, can I give you a hand with that?' The friendly voice came from behind her, and since Fen was now sucking the affected finger with its torn-off nail, she nodded gratefully and stepped back to let him take over.

It wasn't until the case was safely out of the car that she got a proper view of the man's face and exclaimed, 'Oh, hello, it's you!'

He looked at her for a second before recognition dawned and he broke into a smile. 'I remember now. We meet again.'

'Last time you had a horrendous customer,' Fen reminded him.

'Ha, I did. The *worst*.' He started to laugh. 'Luckily most of my clients are far nicer.'

'Hellooo?' Disa called, buzzing down her window. 'Is there a problem? Because it costs a ridiculous amount to stay here and—'

'Sorry, sorry.' Fen closed the boot with her free hand at the same moment Disa stuck her head out through the open window.

'Oh my *God*,' said the limo driver.

'OH MY GOD,' shouted Disa, as Jamie appeared in front of the car. But it wasn't Jamie she was looking at. Pushing open the driver's door and almost falling out of the car, she straightened up and stared at Fen's Good Samaritan. '*Marcus?*'

'Disa.' The man shook his head in disbelief. 'This is . . . Wow.'

'You're here on holiday?' Her voice didn't even sound like her own.

'I moved back to the UK two years ago.'

'You did? Right . . .' She was visibly shaken.

His own voice softened. 'You haven't changed a bit.'

'Nor have you. Are you here with your wife?'

'No wife. Still divorced. You?'

Disa straightened her shoulders. 'Declan died. Twelve years ago.'

'I'm so sorry.'

'I can't believe you're here.'

'In this ridiculously expensive drop-off zone,' he reminded her with a faint smile. 'Disa, it's so good to see you again. You have no idea.'

'Oh, Marcus. Same.'

He held out his arms and Disa flew into them. Their hug went on and on. At Fen's side, Jamie murmured, 'Do you know who he is?'

Fen whispered back, 'No.'

'Come on. We need to get your bag checked in. I've already dropped mine off.' Jamie reached for her suitcase and wheeled it across the road to the pedestrian pathway.

'Right, we're heading inside,' Fen called to Disa.

Breaking off her embrace with Marcus, Disa came hurrying over and wrapped her arms around her. 'Sorry, sorry, it's someone I haven't seen for years. He moved to Spain.' Her eyes bright, she stroked Fen's blonde curls. 'Light a candle for Leon for me, will you? And have a good time, sweetheart. I'll see you when you get back.'

When Fen and Jamie had disappeared from view, Marcus said, 'Can I hug you again now?'

'Yes, please.' Disa closed her eyes as he pulled her to him once more, and breathed in the scent of him. His neck smelled of Imperial Leather soap with a hint of Eau Sauvage.

'My client's going to be here any minute.'

Fen had relayed the story to her of the limo driver and his nightmare passenger. Disa said, 'I looked you up online a few years ago. You were living the high life in Marbella with a stunning Spanish woman called Lucia.' She'd seen photos of them attending a charity ball together. It wasn't what she'd wanted to find, but it had told her all she needed to know. 'And now you're back here in England working as a driver?' Something had evidently gone wrong in Spain.

He shook his head. 'What can I say? I lost all my money and she left me.'

Her heart went out to him, but he was already breaking into a fond smile.

'Not really. Lucia was my gardener, it was her sixtieth birthday and I discovered she'd never been to a ball, so I took her to one. We were friends, that's all. And the reason I moved back here was to see more of my grandchildren. Gave retirement a go, but discovered it didn't suit me, so I set up a limo service and employed a dozen or so drivers. Which was fine until I realised I envied them because they were getting out and about, having more fun than me. So a year ago I decided to join them, and it's given me a whole new lease of life. You meet all sorts and hear all kinds of stories.' He gazed at Disa. 'If I hadn't recognised your young friend, you might not have looked out of the car and we'd have missed each other completely. Imagine that.'

It didn't bear thinking about.

'She's my granddaughter.' He'd seen photos of her as a child. 'Fen.'

'Of course, I should have realised. I see the resemblance now.' He glanced over her shoulder. 'And here comes my client. I'm driving him back to Almondsbury. Quick, can you give me your number?'

He produced his phone and watched as Disa keyed it in.

'I'm free this evening,' she told him. 'If you are.'

The relief on his face was palpable. 'I thought you'd never ask.'

'You knew I would.' She felt as light as air, like Mary Poppins floating up into the sky. 'What time do you finish work?'

'Four.'

'Can you get to Stoke Bishop by five?'

Marcus nodded, fighting to keep a straight face. 'Don't you worry, I'll make sure I do.'

Back in her car, Disa watched as he chatted with his client, placing the cases in the boot of the Mercedes then holding the door open for the man to slide onto the back seat. And then they were gone.

If she'd stayed in bed this morning and let Fen catch a cab to the airport, none of this would have happened. But she'd done a good thing and it had paid off. Today, karma had rewarded her, big time.

Her heart was still thumping as if she'd run a mile. The fragility of fate was truly terrifying.

How on earth was she going to manage to wait until five?

Chapter 37

Venice

'Shall we get a coffee now?' said Fen once they'd cleared security and thoroughly explored the perfume section in duty-free.

Jamie wagged a finger at her. 'No. Needs to be champagne.'

She laughed. 'Really?'

'Has to be done. Orders from on high.' He pointed the same finger skywards. 'Well, from Leon.' Steering her towards the stairs, he said, 'Come on.'

'Are you going to drop a Scotch egg down the escalator?'

'No, don't worry.' He smiled and shook his head.

'What other orders did he give you?' She still had no idea if he'd had a letter sent to him, or if he'd been the one who'd delivered hers.

'He asked me to make all the arrangements. Paid a lump sum into my bank account a few weeks before he died and told me I'd get my instructions in due course. Which I did, through his solicitor.'

When they'd been served their glasses of Pol Roger, Jamie raised a toast. 'To Leon.'

Fen clinked her glass against his. 'To Leon.' There was no need to say any more than that.

Then Jamie added wryly, 'And thanks for all the paperwork.'

'Was there loads?' He'd been tasked, she knew, with making the necessary legal arrangements with the civil registry office for the ashes to be scattered at a particular point in the Venetian lagoon. It had sounded pretty complicated.

'A fair amount.' He shrugged. 'But what Leon wants, Leon gets. And it's all sorted now.'

'He's kept you busy. Which hotel are we booked into?'

'The Danieli.'

'Right. And does it look OK?'

'No need to worry.' Jamie's mouth twitched at the corners. 'I think it's quite nice.'

An hour later, as the plane left the ground and soared into the clear early-morning sky, Fen said, 'You know, two glasses of champagne for breakfast is definitely the way to go.'

Arriving at the Danieli by water taxi from the airport, she discovered that the hotel was indeed quite nice.

This was also the understatement of the year. The place was unbelievably glamorous. Her room overlooked the lagoon, glittering in the bright sunshine, and lunch was served in the Terrazza restaurant on the top floor, giving them an uninterrupted view of the bobbing row of gondolas tied up below them, as well as the ever-changing boat traffic criss-crossing the water that separated them from the smaller islands of Giudecca and San Giorgio Maggiore.

At two o'clock, Leon had decreed, it was time to take the

canister containing his ashes to the pre-booked water taxi waiting for them outside the hotel.

Tiny puffball clouds dotted the turquoise sky, and gulls were crying overhead. The speedboat bounced like a skimming stone across the water as they headed out into the lagoon. When they reached the appointed spot, seven hundred metres from the shore, the boat slowed to a halt and its driver waited in respectful silence while Jamie and Fen took it in turns to shake the ashes out of the container into the water. She'd worried there might be a breeze and they would end up flying back onto them, getting into their hair and clothes. But no, on this day of dream weather, there was no breeze at all. The pale grey ashes floated for a while, spreading out across the surface of the water, then gradually dispersed, began to sink and finally disappeared from view.

They'd said their goodbyes, shed a tear and done what they needed to do. Now it was time to make their way back to the hotel.

When they reached the dock, a larger boat drew up to the right of them as Fen was stepping out of their water taxi, causing it to lurch dramatically to the left. If Jamie hadn't grabbed her in time, she would have tumbled backwards.

'Don't worry, I've got you.' He steadied her until she'd regained her balance.

Fen caught her breath; he hadn't deliberately made contact. Thanks to his lightning reflexes, he'd saved her from landing flat on her back in the bottom of the boat. She hung on to his arm and took the driver's proffered hand in order to climb out onto the stone steps.

'OK?' said Jamie, behind her.

Fen turned, grateful for his speedy reaction. 'I am now.'

'Tired?'

He'd caught her trying not to yawn. She flapped a hand by way of apology. 'Sorry, didn't get much sleep last night. I think I need a nap.'

'You do that. Call me later, when you've woken up.' He gave her an assessing look. 'And if you don't feel up to going out this evening, just say the word. It's fine.'

But when Fen did wake up, almost four hours later, she felt much better. From her room, she could see the sun beginning to set over to the west, drenching the sky with shades of cranberry and orange. After a quick shower and a change of clothes, she guessed where Jamie would be and made her way up onto the terrace.

And there he was, chatting with an older couple seated at an adjacent table. Fen watched from a distance as they continued their conversation, the husband gesturing as he spoke and his wife laughing at something he'd said. The next moment, Jamie's hands began to move too, and after a few seconds Fen realised he wasn't randomly gesturing, he was signing. And now all three of them burst out laughing, and something flipped in her chest, because she'd never known he could do that, and it was revealing yet another unexpected side of him.

A few tables away, a group of elegant women were observing him too. One of them called out something in Italian that sounded admiring, and Jamie briefly acknowledged them with a nod and a smile before turning back to continue his conversation.

Then the older couple's food arrived, and he spotted Fen watching him from afar. Excusing himself, he made his way past the group of women towards her.

'Who was that you were chatting to?' said Fen as they headed down the staircase.

'Mary and Donald from Edinburgh, celebrating their wedding anniversary. It's their third time here in Venice.'

'And Mary's deaf?'

He nodded. 'She is.'

'You were signing with her. Like, actual proper signing.'

Jamie looked amused. 'It's the best way. She can't hear me if I shout at her.'

'But I didn't know you could do that!'

'There's lots about me you don't know. I'm full of surprises.'

'Like what?'

'I'm fluent in Russian.'

'Oh my God!'

'I can knit.'

'*What?*'

'And I can tell what you're thinking right now.'

Fen raised her eyebrows at him. 'I'm thinking you're a terrible liar.'

He grinned. 'And you'd be right. I can't speak Russian and I can't knit. But I was friendly with one of our neighbours at university and she had a young son who was deaf. I taught myself BSL so I could chat to him. I'm no expert, but I can get by.'

They'd left the hotel and begun to walk around the corner into St Mark's Square. 'It's a nice thing to do,' said Fen. 'I wonder where he is now?'

'We're still in touch. He's a neuroscience graduate working in a medical lab in London. Anyway.' Jamie paused for a moment to look at her. 'How are you feeling now? Better?'

'Much better. Kind of . . . lighter. Did you email those photos to Hilary and Greville?'

He had taken a couple of photographs of the scattered ashes

on the surface of the lagoon, with the sunny Venice skyline behind them, so they could see the beauty of Leon's final resting place. He nodded and steered her out of the path of a small girl chasing a pigeon. 'I did, and they messaged back to thank me.' Another pause. 'I'm glad you're feeling lighter.'

Fen smiled. 'Me too.'

They reached La Lanterna fifteen minutes later, and as they walked through the ornate iron gates, Molly greeted them with delight. Giving Fen a tight hug, she said, 'How are you? How did it go?'

It was her last fortnight working at the restaurant. Next weekend, Kayla was flying out to be with Angelo full-time. The following week would be spent here in the restaurant with Molly, learning the ropes and fine-tuning her Italian. Then Molly would return to the UK and move into the flat she'd bought in Gloucester, while Kayla and Angelo moved into her old apartment – small but completely adequate – in the Cannaregio district, a short walk from here. Angelo's mother, Ariana, hadn't been too happy at first at the idea of her beloved son living in sin with a spiky-haired divorcee from England, but miraculously Kayla had managed to win her over and persuade her that it was the only possible answer until they were married.

And yes, Molly and Andy were still going strong as well; since that first evening in Clifton, the relationship had been coming along in leaps and bounds, and Andy's wild auburn hair remained her favourite hair in the world.

'I'm fine,' Fen told her. 'And this afternoon was beautiful. It's all done, and Leon's where he wanted to be.'

'You're looking well.' Molly gave her a squeeze, then said cheerfully to Jamie, 'OK, before you start feeling left out, so are you. Come along, let's get you to your table. And just a heads-up,

Disa called an hour ago. She sends you both her love and says dinner's on her tonight, so feel free to go wild and order everything on the menu.'

'That's kind of her,' said Fen. 'She's so thoughtful.'

'To be honest, she sounded a bit tipsy. Or maybe, like, really happy. She was laughing a lot and sounding quite giddy. I asked her what she was up to this evening, and she said she could tell me but then she'd have to kill me.' Molly looked bemused. 'God knows what she meant by that.'

'Interesting.'

Molly's eyebrows shot up. 'D'you think she's met someone? And it has to be a massive secret, so that means it could be a celebrity. You never know with her!' Excitedly she grabbed Fen's hand. 'What if it's a royal? Or even better, Rod Stewart?'

Belatedly, Fen recalled the chance meeting at the airport earlier today. 'Hang on, she did bump into someone this morning, a guy she hadn't seen for years. I wonder if that could have something to do with it?' Then another thought occurred to her. 'You were with me the last time we saw him! Remember the really nice limo driver in the airport drop-off zone, the one with the really stroppy passenger?'

'Ooh,' breathed Molly, her eyes widening with interest.

'You never know,' Jamie said cheerfully, 'she could be seducing him as we speak.'

Bristol

Disa wasn't seducing Marcus yet, but she was definitely looking forward to something of that nature happening later.

What a day this was turning out to be. She still couldn't get over the way life might appear to be continuing along a pre-set pathway but at any moment it could take off and go corkscrewing in all sorts of different directions. Up until five p.m., she had been seized with panic that Marcus might have second thoughts and decide not to meet her after all; might block her from his phone and disappear for good. Even while she'd been trying on a dozen different outfits like a teenager, she was terrified he wouldn't turn up.

But he had, he had, he had. The doorbell had rung at *just* before five, and when she'd opened the door, there he was, brandishing a huge bouquet of ranunculus, roses and antirrhinums in one hand and a bottle of Bollinger in the other, and with the most enormous smile spread across his face.

When they'd finally finished kissing in the kitchen and she'd told him about her earlier panic, he'd said, 'Are you kidding? I've been counting the minutes. This is the best day of my life.'

And now, several hours on, they were still talking non-stop, catching up with every aspect of each other's lives, drinking champagne, discovering that last year they'd both attended performances of *Les Misérables* at the Bristol Hippodrome, *just twenty-four hours apart* . . .

Disa was still shaking her head at the realisation that they'd had another narrow miss, and goodness knows how many more since he'd been back in the Bristol area, when Marcus reached for her hand. He said, 'I really want us to carry on talking. I want to know everything about you. And apologies for being a bit forward, but do you think we could maybe also do something else that feels long overdue?'

There it was, the delicious quiver of anticipation down her spine that had been missing from her life for so long. Earlier, despite knowing she was in good nick for her age, she had briefly wondered if he would still find her physically attractive all these years on, but from the way he was looking at her now, any such doubts floated away. Tilting her head back as she finished the last inch of champagne in her glass, Disa kissed him again and traced teasing fingers down the side of his dear face. 'Oh, Mr Rochester, I thought you'd never ask.'

Chapter 38

Venice

Molly wasn't the only one who'd noticed the difference in Fen yesterday evening. It had been palpable. Now, lying in bed and watching as the veil of morning mist over the lagoon fought a losing battle with the sun, Jamie could only compare it with someone unexpectedly released from prison and finding themselves free once more.

But was it entirely down to the finality of scattering the ashes, or could it in part have been due to something else?

He had no idea, and under the circumstances it wasn't a question he'd felt able to put to her. It was one of those complicated situations where it just wouldn't be right.

Hauling himself into a sitting position and piling the pillows up behind him, he reached for his wallet on the ornate bedside table and took out the letter. Despite pretty much knowing it off by heart, he still felt the need to scan each word, searching for a hidden clue. It had definitely been written by Leon – that distinctive scrawl was recognisable a mile off – but what he didn't know was whether this was the only one he'd penned, or had Fen received one too?

And if she had, what had Leon said to her?

Unfolding the two sheets of deckle-edged writing paper bearing the Hetherton Hall address, Jamie began to reread it for maybe the twentieth time:

Hey mate,

How are you?

Time flies when you're having fun, and I'd love to know how everyone is. I have so many questions, but you can't give me the answers, can you?

Which is really annoying, because I want to know what you're up to, and if you've found a better best friend than me. And how is Fen?

(OK, still no bloody answers from you, so I guess I'll get on and say what I want to say.)

I always trusted you with Fen, completely. Could you have taken her away from me if you'd wanted to? Maybe you could, if you'd set your mind to it. But I also knew you'd never do it to me. And that meant a lot. Actually, it meant everything. Best of all, by some absolute miracle I managed to find the one woman who chose me rather than you.

I also knew you liked her as a person. So what I'm letting you know now is that if you still do, and if you have feelings of more than liking her, then it would make me happy if you two were to get together.

This isn't an order, by the way. I'm just saying if you were thinking you couldn't go ahead because of me, then don't worry. You can.

Only if you promise not to break her heart, though. You need to be completely sure your feelings are strong enough that that would never happen.

If I'm wrong about this and you've already found The One or you aren't interested, no worries. In that case, destroy this letter and don't mention it to Fen or to anyone else, ever.

Either way, all I want is for you both to be happy and to have great lives.

Right, that's me done, I've said my piece. The rest's up to you.

So long, mate.

He refolded the letter and slid it back into his wallet. Once again, no clues had miraculously revealed themselves. Would Leon have mentioned it if he'd said much the same to Fen? Or would he have thought it better not to, allowing her instead to make her own decisions? And once again, who had hand-delivered the letter to his address? Had that been Leon's parents?

The only thing he did know for sure was that there was no way he could be the one to make any kind of move. If Fen was even remotely interested in him – and she might not be, might be horrified by the very idea – the initial advance absolutely had to come from her.

It wasn't the usual order of things. Invariably, over the years, he'd known how women felt about him and had either shown his interest in return, or hadn't. But this was different; he was only too well aware of the strength of his own feelings for Fen. Last night, after their dinner at La Lanterna, followed by drinks with Molly, he'd been careful to maintain the appearance of platonic friendship, because that was the only way to go.

All he could do was be patient and hope the attraction he felt towards her might be returned.

And if it wasn't . . . well, he'd have to man up and get over himself. Being *just good friends* with Fen might not be what he most wanted, and it definitely wouldn't be easy, but it would undoubtedly be better than nothing at all.

The thing about Venice was that it was small enough to be walkable, but by four in the afternoon, Fen's feet were starting to ache. She and Jamie had walked many thousands of steps, taken countless photos, explored dozens of narrow back streets, stopped at espresso bars for tiny coffees and cicchetti, and searched the shops for velvet gloves for Disa because she'd seen some last year and regretted not buying them ever since.

Finally the gloves had been tracked down to a dazzlingly vibrant boutique not far from the Libreria Acqua Alta. Fen chose a parma-violet pair lined with emerald silk for Disa, and Jamie picked out a second gold-lined pair in a dazzling shade of peacock blue. But as he flipped open his wallet to take out his credit card, Fen caught a fleeting glimpse of deckle-edged cream writing paper tucked into one of the other pockets.

'What's wrong?' said Jamie.

'Nothing.'

'You squeaked like a mouse.'

Had she? 'I did?'

'You did this.' He imitated the squeak that had escaped from her throat. 'Like a mouse on helium.'

The elegant male shop assistant, holding out the card reader, said gravely, 'We 'ave no mouses in thees shop, madam.'

When they'd left the boutique, Jamie said, 'Was it his shoes? Did you see them?'

The shoes had been candyfloss pink with orange laces. For a split second Fen prevaricated; she could say it was the shoes. But no. 'I saw the edge of a letter in your wallet.'

He looked at her. 'So you got one too?'

'The other day.' She nodded. 'How did you get yours?'

'Hand-delivered. Dropped through the letter box while I was out.'

'Same.' Fen's heart began to clatter against her ribs. 'But I don't know who delivered it. I wondered if it was you.'

'Not me. Maybe Hilary. Or Greville.' He sidestepped a tourist videoing a shopfront crowded with Venetian masks. 'Or it could have been someone he worked with, like Andy. Who knows? Came as a bit of a shock, though, getting a letter from Leon out of the blue like that.'

Fen shrugged in agreement. 'Kind of a shock, but kind of lovely too. It felt like he was still thinking of me. Well, it must have been the same for you.'

Jamie slowly nodded, and it felt as if the air around them was bursting with unspoken questions neither of them could bring themselves to ask. The next moment, Fen heard someone saying his name. As she began to turn, a family of four materialised in front of them and the father of the group said, 'You're Jamie Hamilton!'

'I am,' Jamie agreed, and the man's wife exclaimed, 'Dave said it was you! I couldn't believe it – I thought he was winding me up, but it's actually true! You're our favourite!'

'That's always nice to hear.' He was smiling at them, shaking the man's outstretched hand.

'We were going to go to Torremolinos,' his wife trilled. 'But I said no, let's give Venice a whirl instead! See, Dave? Aren't you glad you listened to me now? If we'd gone to Spain like you wanted, we wouldn't have bumped into your favourite footballer, would we?'

'Rugby, you muppet,' said Dave, already taking his phone out.

He handed it to Fen, who was tasked with taking photos of Dave and Jamie together, both with and without the children, then of Jamie with Dave's wife, Donna, then a few more of the whole family with Jamie, followed by a final dozen or so because Donna hadn't had time to redo her lipstick before the first lot.

'Sorry about that,' said Jamie when he'd finally waved the family goodbye.

'Don't worry, you made their day.' The potentially emotional moment between them had passed and she'd had time to recover. 'You're a kind footballer who always has time for his fans.'

'Poor Donna, they aren't going to let her forget that in a hurry.'

'But you sent them away happy, and that's the main thing. They'll treasure those photos for ever.'

'Speaking of photos, we don't have any of us yet.' They were crossing one of the tiny bridges above a canal extending in the direction of the lagoon. Producing his own phone, Jamie said, 'Shall we? Unless you'd rather not.'

Fen only hesitated for a moment; it would be a shame not to take a couple of selfies on the bridge with the stretch of water behind them. 'Let's do it. Try not to look too ugly.'

He laughed. They turned their backs on the view and he held the phone out in front of them, his shirt-clad arm resting against her bare shoulder as with his other hand he took four quick photos with the right amount of scenery in the background. Then he said firmly, 'Never more than four,' and it was her turn to look at him, laughing, and say, 'Why?'

At that exact moment he said, 'Or maybe five,' and took one more photo.

'See?' Bringing up the final one, he showed it to her. 'The one you weren't expecting's always the best.'

He was right. Even with the sun bouncing off the screen, Fen could see how much more relaxed she was. The other photos were fine, but in the fifth one, the camera had managed to capture the look they'd exchanged as well as what felt like the easy unspoken connection between them.

And for the very first time it felt . . . fine. Not wrong, not embarrassing and not shameful.

'I'm looking fabulous,' she told Jamie. 'Shame about you.'

He grinned and gave her arm a nudge. 'I'm pretty good at tipping people off bridges.'

'Can you send me the photos so I can see them properly?'

He did so, and in her bag she heard the *ting* as they arrived on her phone. 'Thanks.'

Leaning against the balustrade, Jamie watched as a gondola emerged from beneath the bridge. Keeping his gaze fixed on the gondolier as he skilfully steered to the left to avoid another one approaching from the opposite direction, he said, 'So what did Leon say to you in his letter?'

A rush of heat ran through Fen's body, and she was glad he wasn't looking at her. When she hesitated, Jamie went on, 'Sorry, is that too personal? You don't have to tell me.'

He wanted to know because he was curious, just as she wanted to know what was in the letter Leon had written to him. But how could she tell him without putting herself – no, without putting *both of them* – in a potentially mortifying situation?

Just because Leon had decided something might be a good idea didn't mean Jamie felt the same way.

And that was if Leon had even mentioned it in Jamie's letter. He might well not have done. God, imagine telling Jamie the plan and seeing the look of dawning horror on his face.

'It was a wonderful letter. It sounded exactly like him.' Fen smiled, because each time she read it was like hearing his voice again. 'He hopes I'm still missing him, but not too much. And he wants me to be happy.' Two small children in the second gondola were waving madly up at her, and she waved back, glad of the distraction. 'He says I mustn't feel guilty . . . you know, if I meet someone else. Because it's OK to move on.'

Jamie slowly nodded. 'Of course it is. But good of him to say that. And has it helped, d'you think?'

She waved again, but this time at the driver of a small motor-boat, who hadn't waved at her first and who didn't wave back. 'I think it has. I mean, not that I've been going out on dates with dozens of men and feeling guilty about it.'

'Have you been out on any dates at all?'

The only man she'd been anywhere with was him, and none of those occasions had been a date. She shook her head. 'None. No men, no dates.'

'But when it does happen, you know you won't need to feel guilty. Also, why did you wave at that guy then?'

Bugger. 'I thought I recognised him from last year. But he didn't recognise me. So I probably didn't.' *Listen to me, improvising like a boss.* 'Anyway, what did he say to you?'

It was Jamie's turn to look mystified. 'Who?'

'Leon.'

'When?'

'When d'you think?' Fen gestured in the direction of the letter, which was in his wallet. Which was in the front pocket of his black trousers. Which was probably giving quite the wrong impression. 'When he wrote the letter!'

He visibly exhaled, probably with relief. 'Sorry. Couldn't work out what you meant. Um, pretty much the same kind of thing. Hang on, let me have a look at the map. We could be close to that sculpture park you wanted to visit.' Evidently keen to change the subject – *did that mean Leon had mentioned her and the prospect was truly appalling?* – he was now gazing intently at his phone. 'Here we are, it's called the Giardini della Marinaressa. If we follow this canal to the end and turn left, it's only a few hundred yards away. We can—' A reminder flashed up on the screen. 'Damn, I need to get back to the hotel for an interview over Zoom. Completely forgot, and it starts in ten minutes. We'll have to visit the sculptures tomorrow.'

Then again, how interested was he in looking at modern art, really? Fen said, 'You do your thing, I'll go to the gardens on my own. We'll catch up later after you've finished.'

'If you're sure. Sorry about this.' He was already turning in the direction of the hotel.

'Wait, is it for TV?'

Jamie stopped and nodded, and Fen beckoned to him. 'Come here, let me sort you out.'

He wasn't vain. It probably wouldn't have occurred to him to look in a mirror before beginning the Zoom call, but his dark hair was sticking out on one side from the sea breeze and the collar of his blue and white striped shirt was wonky. As he stood before her, she efficiently straightened his collar and smoothed down the wayward section of hair. 'There, that's better.'

He grinned. 'Will I do?'

'Have another quick check when you get back to your room. And try not to say *fuck* on TV.' She couldn't resist it; this was what Leon had always jokingly reminded him when Jamie had been about to appear on a live broadcast.

'Thanks. I'll do my best.' He laughed, then turned and headed off.

Leaving her experiencing a belated buzz of adrenalin at the

realisation that this was the first time she'd ever touched his hair. And his shirt collar.

But mainly his hair.

Cupping her hand over her nose and mouth, she breathed in to see if she could smell his shampoo, and was almost convinced she could.

The gardens were in the Castello district, situated next to a broad promenade running alongside the waterfront. Shaded by mature pines, the park was dotted with an assortment of modern sculptures, some abstract in design, others less so. There was a giant white rabbit clutching an equally enormous shiny turquoise egg, a smaller elephant with gold eyes and tusks. There was also an installation that could have been mistaken for a children's climbing frame, a brightly coloured globe on a plinth, and a terrifying mythical creature that was half warrior, half rhinoceros.

It was a small collection that didn't take long to explore. As she made her way along one of the narrow paths, Fen smiled at an elderly woman occupying a wooden bench, then belatedly realised there was a cat curled up on her lap. Without thinking, she exclaimed, 'What a beautiful cat!' Then hastily added, '*Scusi*, I mean . . . *bella gatto*?' Or was it *bellissima*? That was probably wrong too.

'It's all right, I'm British.' The woman nodded in response. 'And yes, he is beautiful. Thank you.'

She had a slight northern accent, Yorkshire at a guess, and was smoothing the cat's glossy black coat from head to tail, over and over with a bony hand. Fen said, 'Phew, my Italian's rubbish. Look at his face, though! What's his name?'

'Merlin.'

'He really is incredibly handsome. And that's such a good

name for him. Where are you from?' Busy gazing into Merlin's hypnotic pale green eyes, it took her a few seconds to realise the woman was struggling to control her emotions. It wasn't until she replied, 'York,' with a quaver in her voice, that Fen saw the tears rolling down her thin cheeks.

'Are you OK? Sorry, what a stupid question.' She spotted the shredded tissue in the woman's other hand and pulled a packet of fresh ones from her own bag. Offering it, she said, 'Is he ill?'

The woman shook her head wearily and accepted the pack of tissues with a trembling hand. 'It's not been the best day.'

How many times during the last year had Fen been overwhelmed with emotion and desperate for a kind word or even a sympathetic smile from a stranger? How often had people simply looked the other way and walked on by? She sat down on the bench next to the woman. 'Would it help to talk about it? Only if you want to. If you'd rather be on your own, I'll leave you in peace.'

'Bless you, love. That's kind of you. My name's Hannah, by the way.'

'And I'm Fen.'

'It's been just the two of us, you see. For the last five years.' Hannah carried on rhythmically stroking Merlin, who responded by pressing his sleek head into the curve of her palm. 'I took him in as a kitten. He's fit and well, and so loving. I'm the one who's ill.' Another tear leaked out. 'I'm not crying for myself, I promise. I just can't bear the thought of leaving him behind. And I've asked around, but there's no one willing to take him. The doctor at the hospital told me it's time to get my affairs in order, and I've done that already, but who's going to love Merlin when I'm gone? He won't know where I am, poor darling.' Her voice began to waver again, and she shook her head helplessly. 'I can't bear the idea of him searching for me . . . Every time I think of it, it b-breaks my h-h-heart.'

'I'm so sorry.' Fen embraced her and felt the woman's ribs judder as she sobbed in her arms. 'No wonder you're worried. But he's such a handsome boy, and there must be places that'll look after him until they can find someone—'

'I know, I know, but I want to know who'll be taking my place. Because what if they're not the right people for Merlin? OK, I know I'm being overdramatic and you probably think I'm ridiculous,' Hannah hiccuped, 'but he's all I care about. I *love* him.'

Fen hugged her tighter. 'Of course you do.'

Hannah's tears of despair dripped onto the front of Fen's dress as she fumbled for another tissue. 'I just love him *so much*.'

Chapter 39

Arriving back at the hotel, Fen found Jamie up on the terrace with a pot of coffee and a glass of water on the table in front of him and his sunglasses covering his eyes. When he didn't react to her approach, she bent down, peered in sideways behind the pitch-black lenses and saw that his eyes were closed.

Quietly pulling out the chair opposite, she settled down to watch him. His hands were loosely clasped across his stomach, a lock of dark hair had fallen over his tanned forehead, and his long legs were stretched out in front of him, crossed at the ankle. He was sleeping silently, thank goodness. Always nice to know he wasn't a snorer. Breathing in, Fen caught the faintest hint of his oh-so-familiar lemon and cedar aftershave. The memory of standing beside him on the bridge earlier came rushing back, their arms touching as they took selfies with the view of the canal behind them, and she experienced a sudden urge to smell his hair, or to bury her face in the V of his open shirt, inhaling the scent of the warm skin between his throat and collarbone.

OK, getting carried away now. Mustn't do either of those things, especially not up here on the busy roof terrace of the five-star Danieli. Instead she would make the most of the fact that Jamie was fast asleep, allowing her to relax and spend as long as she liked admiring the angles of his face, those high cheekbones and that chiselled jawline, the way the shirt stretched across his broad shoulders then tapered down to his waist. A couple of inches above the belt buckle there was a narrow gap between the mother-of-pearl shirt buttons, revealing a glint of dark hair and tanned skin. And then there were the legs, extended in her direction beneath the table. If she tilted her head, she could see his leather shoes less than a couple of inches from her own sandalled feet.

Did this count as ogling? She probably shouldn't be doing it. But who wouldn't want to ogle Jamie Hamilton while he was sleeping in the sunshine? She was only human after all. I mean, look at his *hands* . . .

Jamie woke up, ridiculously relieved to discover he'd dreamt it all. Having to stand by and watch while the hotel manager flirted outrageously with Fen, and even worse, Fen flirted back with him, had been almost unbearable. She hadn't even seemed to realise how wrong it was to be doing such a thing. When they'd turned to leave the hotel together and he'd asked her where she was going, she had replied cheerfully, 'I've made a new friend and we're off out for the evening. That's allowed, isn't it? Look, I'll maybe catch up with you tomorrow.'

Then off she'd gone with a spring in her step and clearly living her best life, with Vittorio, the visibly triumphant hotel manager.

Absolute bastard.

Except it hadn't happened, Jamie reminded himself. Thank God. His own brain had conjured up this scenario. Slowly opening his eyes, he orientated himself and realised he'd dozed off at his table up here on the roof terrace. Plus, he was no longer on his own; Fen had returned and was sitting opposite him.

More than that, thanks to the extra-dark lenses in his Ray-Bans, she had no idea that he was now awake, watching her watch him.

Careful not to move a muscle and give himself away, he saw the expression in her eyes as she silently, intently studied him, her gaze moving from his face to his torso, his arms, then down to his feet beneath the table before switching back to his face once more.

His heart began to race, because for the first time he felt he was seeing her genuine reaction towards him, without the veil of awareness that had always seemed to create a sense of distance before now. Amazing, *amazing*, and it made him want to smile with sheer relief, but the last thing he needed was to break the spell.

One of the waitresses approached their table, discreetly signalling to Fen to ask if she'd like a drink. In response, Fen shook her head and mouthed *thank you* before settling back on her chair to observe him once more.

And be observed in return.

Her eyes were bright, her cheeks tinged with pink from the sun. He loved the way that every time she moved her head, the blonde curls framing her face bobbed as if they were on springs. Like now, as her phone gave a discreet *ting* on the table and she leaned forward to look at it.

Then she pressed play, and although the volume was low, Jamie was just able to hear the voice note she'd been sent.

'Hi! He sounds like pure heaven. No wonder you fell in love

with him! Look, I'm at work now, but I'll be home by six, so FaceTime me then. I can't wait to meet him! OK, got to go, see you later. Byeee!'

What? The voice was female and sounded faintly familiar, but from here he couldn't figure out who it was. Talk about a roller coaster. Holding his breath, not even reacting to the fly that had landed on the back of his hand, Jamie watched as Fen beamed and sent back a voice note of her own.

'I promise you, he's gorgeous, *better* than pure heaven. Honestly, you won't believe it when you see him! I'll call you at six. Bye.'

Just as he'd been getting his hopes up. And that bloody fly was still on the back of his hand. He watched as Fen, now smiling to herself like a woman with the best secret in the world, fired off another message to someone else. Who, though? Disa, maybe. Or Molly, or Tonia in Amsterdam. Or the gorgeous, irresistible man she was evidently besotted with.

Taking a deep breath and flicking his hand to dislodge the fly at last, he raised his head as if seeing Fen for the first time and took off his Ray-Bans, blinking as the sun shone directly into his eyes. 'Hey, I didn't mean to fall asleep. Sorry, have you been waiting long?'

'Not too long.'

'Was I snoring?' He knew he didn't snore.

'Like a hippo.' She grinned and shook her head. 'No. How was your interview?'

'Great. Didn't swear once.'

'Well done, you.' Her tone was playful.

'Did you find the sculpture garden?'

'I did. And I met someone there.' Her face lit up and he braced himself for the worst. 'Honestly, wait till you hear, it was like it was meant to happen . . .'

When she'd finished telling him the story, Jamie exhaled with relief and said, 'Thank God for that.'

They arrived at the apartment behind the sculpture garden shortly before six. Fen rang the doorbell and they both heard the woman whose name he now knew was Hannah exclaim, 'Merlin, they're here!'

She opened the door with the cat cradled in her arms, and the introductions were made.

'Fen told me you were a rugby player. I've seen you on TV.' Clearly unwell but delighted to see them, Hannah welcomed him before leading the way slowly into her living room.

'And she showed me the photos of you and Merlin,' Jamie told her. 'He's a handsome boy.'

Better still, he was a cat.

Fen set up the video call and Kayla's face filled her phone screen, her eyes widening as she took her first proper look at Merlin on his owner's lap.

'Look at you! Merlin, you're my dream date! Can you swish your tail for me?'

Unbelievably, with one slow blink, Merlin gazed at Kayla's russet and gold spiky hair, and gave his black tail an actual swish.

'I love him,' Kayla declared, and now her eyes filled with tears, because back in February, her beloved elderly cat Bandit had died a week after his fourteenth birthday. Wiping her face with a tissue, she went on, 'I really do. And I'm coming out to Venice next weekend. I'd love to meet him properly then. Obviously it's up to you, and there's no hurry at all, but if you think I'd be good enough, I'd be so happy to look after him for you, once you're ready for me to take over.'

'Now you're making me cry too.' Hannah managed a watery

smile. 'I couldn't ask for anyone better. If Merlin has to have a new mum, I'd love it to be you.' She turned her attention back to the cat. 'How about that, sweetheart? Does it sound like the answer to all our prayers?'

Another tail-swish, followed by a contented purr.

Reaching over and stroking Merlin's head, Jamie said, 'Looks to me as if you two ladies have got yourselves a deal.'

Oxford

'Hattie?'

Absently, she said, 'Hang on a sec.' They were in Marks & Spencer's food hall and she was concentrating on the situation at hand. Much as she loved avocados, they weren't to be trusted; even those that looked ready could be tragically unripe, while others might look perfect but turn out to be well past their best. She peered suspiciously at the ones in front of her and—

'*Hattie!*'

At least she'd trained him at last to stop calling her *Hats*. Straightening up, she heard smothered giggles behind her and turned to see what Guy wanted.

Oh God, and there he was. Down on one knee.

'Hattie, I love you with all my heart. You mean everything to me. Will you make me the happiest man in the world and . . .'

'*Get up,*' she squeaked. '*Stop it.*'

'. . . say you'll marry me?' he continued, undeterred.

'Please don't do this. It's embarrassing.' Shoppers had stopped shopping and all around them people were turning to watch. Phones were being pulled out of pockets and held up to capture the moment.

Guy said, 'It's only embarrassing until you say yes.'

Was this partly her own fault? Since they'd taken to spending so much more time together, he'd found himself round at her flat having to tolerate the kind of films he'd once have run a mile from. At a guess, it was being forced against his better judgement to watch the *Mamma Mia!* ones that had had this unexpected side-effect. In his head, he now appeared to think he was Oxford's answer to Pierce Brosnan.

At least he wasn't singing, although she wouldn't put it past him. Imagine the horror. As if this wasn't agonising enough.

'Come on, love,' urged an older woman in a pink straw hat. 'Don't keep him waiting!'

Her friend nodded in agreement. 'That'll be killing his knee.'

'It's not doing it any favours,' Guy agreed with the kind of twinkle in his eye that older women especially loved. Returning his attention to Hattie, he gave her a deeply soulful look. 'My angel, I adore you. All I want is for us to be together for ever.'

'Aah,' sighed another woman. 'Isn't that romantic? Hurry up, though, cos my chap's waiting outside for me in the car and he's a grumpy sod.'

'Sounds like my old man.' A second woman gave a snort of laughter.

'I'm not a grumpy sod,' Guy told them. 'I promise. Hattie, please say you'll marry me, before my back gives out.'

Their audience was starting to grow impatient. On the defensive, Hattie blurted out, 'You mean marry you *again*? Do you even remember what happened last time?'

'Ooh . . .' The people around them promptly turned to stare at Guy, still with one knee on the hard floor and visibly starting to suffer. Pink Straw Hat said accusingly, 'What did you do to her?'

'Nothing! I just wasn't the best husband back then. But I've learned my lesson now. And I promise – absolutely *promise* – to make up for it. Hattie, if you say yes, you'll never regret it.'

They were still the centre of attention. If only she could be anywhere but here. What their audience didn't know was that it was the third time Guy had done this. The first proposal had happened in their local Italian restaurant, but on that occasion, thank God, it had been so noisy and busy that no one else had noticed. The second time had been on the evening of Guy's forty-third birthday, when he'd hired out his local pub for a party and had concluded his birthday speech with a heartfelt declaration of love and a proposal. She'd turned him down that time too, but everyone had made light of the moment and the whole thing had been passed off as a joke.

Had he really thought that trying it again, this time in the M&S food hall, would make it third time lucky? God, the temptation to turn and walk away, abandoning him here in the fruit and veg section, was almost overwhelming.

But even though he didn't know it yet, she secretly loved him, and she couldn't bring herself to do that to him. Moving away from the serried rows of avocados that were either overripe or underripe, she stepped forward and held out both hands to help him to his feet.

'Hooray!' Pink Straw Hat and her friend, jumping the gun a bit, began to cheer and applaud.

'Thank you,' Hattie told Guy. She gave him a quick hug and whispered in his ear, 'You're such an idiot. Can we get out of here now?'

'Is that a yes?' His face brightened with delight and he planted a quick kiss on her mouth as the rest of the assembled shoppers joined in with the clapping. The next moment, a uniformed supervisor appeared from nowhere with a bunch of pink and yellow roses and presented them to Hattie, saying, 'With very best wishes from all of us!'

Oh Lord, and over there by the bakery section was one of her nosiest and least favourite neighbours. Definitely time to go. Having thanked the supervisor, Hattie grabbed Guy's arm and hurried him out of the store.

'I can't believe you said yes,' he exclaimed as they reached the exit.

'I didn't. And please, I never want you to ask me to marry you again. I told you last time.' She shook her head at him. 'We're friends, that's all. We spend time together.'

'Quite a lot of time.'

'That's irrelevant.'

'I'd rather be with you than anyone else.'

'Also irrelevant.' Honestly, did he think this was easy for her? Although since he had no idea what a struggle it was, presumably he did. But that was the whole point, she just needed more time to make sure they both really had changed enough to make it work.

How much more time? Hopefully they were getting there. When it was right, she'd know for sure.

'We didn't get the avocados,' said Guy.

'Doesn't matter.' Smiling, Hattie tucked her arm companionably through his. 'Come on, let's go.'

Chapter 40

Venice

Jamie was working on his laptop in the Bar Dandolo on the ground floor of the hotel when he heard the sound of stilettos making their way into the bar behind him. Since he could tell the footsteps didn't belong to Fen, he finished replying to the Q&A that would appear in the *Sunday Times*. The final question was: *What is your favourite thing to do on a lazy Sunday?* to which there was obviously only one possible answer, although he probably wouldn't say it. Then again, it had been so long now since he'd had sex on a Sunday, or on any day of the week come to that, that he was in danger of forgetting how to do it. Instead he typed: *Go for a six-mile run.* (Obviously this was a lie.) *Massive roast dinner. Fall asleep on the sofa watching a Bond movie. When I wake up, I'll finish all the roast potatoes then head out to the gym—*

'Jamie? Oh my God, it *is* you. Jamie!'

The clip-clop of heels drew nearer and his heart sank, because sometimes an enthusiastic fan could be that bit *too* enthusiastic.

The next moment, the owner of the heels appeared from between two of the imposing marble pillars in the bar and, with arms spread wide, let out a shriek of delight.

'I knew it!' Almost sending his gin and tonic flying, she launched herself at him and Jamie's heart sank lower still, because it was that stalwart member of the Bath social scene, Bridget Harding.

He hadn't seen her for a while and had no idea what she was doing here in Venice, but from the way she was pressing herself against him, she hadn't changed a bit. Attempting to disentangle himself, he said, 'This is a surprise.'

'Understatement of the year! And I'd call it a brilliant surprise, because let me tell you, you're the answer to a single girl's prayer.'

Bridget was in her mid thirties, but he knew that in twenty years' time she'd still be calling herself a girl. Single and exuberant, she was endlessly sociable and well-meaning, yet often exhausting to be around. Rather than tell her he really wasn't the answer to her prayers, Jamie said, 'So what brings you to Venice? Who are you with?'

She gestured in dramatic despair. 'It's a nightmare. I'm stuck with my great-aunt Effie, who flew over from Canada and needed someone to travel around Italy with. You have no idea how awful it's been. We've had six days in Rome, four in Florence, and now we're here until Sunday. But all we're doing is endless sightseeing, because she wants to experience everything Italy has to offer, and my God, it's all so tedious! Everything we look at is so *old*. Then when we get back to whichever hotel we're in, Effie's worn out and all she wants to do is *sleep*.' Bridget was still clinging to him like a limpet, gazing up at him in mock-despair at the awfulness of the situation she'd found herself in. 'But now you're here, and I'm so happy to see you again. I mean, I know I can't drag you around all the ancient churches and stuff, but when Effie goes back to her room, we can at least get together and have some fun – it's always Prosecco o'clock around here!'

How Jamie wished he could be the kind of person able to announce bluntly that he wasn't interested, but his conscience always got the better of him. Moments later, while casting around for a polite way to put Bridget off, he glimpsed a splash of yellow and saw Fen chatting to one of the waiters at the entrance to the bar.

Last night, having discovered they were staying at the Danieli, Kayla had told them that Angelo's best friend, Matteo, worked here. That was the thing with the island being as small as it was; the Venetians who'd lived here all their lives tended to know each other.

Spotting Jamie, Fen began making her way over, weaving between the towering marble columns and the seating. She was wearing new cream espadrilles, and her flippy daffodil-yellow cotton dress swirled above her knees, showing off her tanned bare legs.

God, how he loved those legs.

Following the line of his gaze, one of her hands still resting on his arm, Bridget was proprietorial. 'Who's this, someone after a selfie? Honestly, it must drive you mad being pestered all the time by strangers.'

The solution came to Jamie in a flash. He waved at Fen and broke into a smile. 'She isn't a stranger,' he told Bridget. 'She's my girlfriend.'

Making her approach, Fen wondered who the tall brunette in the slinky white trouser suit might be. Someone Jamie knew, obviously. She was strikingly attractive, quite intense-looking, and appeared not overenthusiastic at the prospect of having her time with him interrupted. Fen hesitated; perhaps she'd be better off excusing herself and leaving them to it. She could always head back upstairs to her room.

Except Jamie seemed keen for her to join them, so maybe this was another of Angelo's many friends for her to meet. She made her way over.

'Here she is,' Jamie announced. 'I was about to send a search party up to our room! Sweetheart, this is Bridget Harding, an old friend from Bath. We haven't seen each other for ages. Bridget, this is Fen.'

Sweetheart? Our room? If only.

But since there was clearly a reason for it, Fen smiled brightly and said, 'Oh right. Hello! How nice to meet you!' She stuck out her hand and Bridget shook it as if it had been pulled out of a kitchen bin.

'Hi. I didn't know Jamie had been seeing someone.'

'We've been flying under the radar, keeping it to ourselves.' He gave Fen a conspiratorial smile and slid his arm around her. 'Haven't we, sweetheart?'

Zap went Fen's heart as he gave her waist an affectionate squeeze. It was the most delicious physical sensation since that time in Amsterdam when she'd thought their legs were entwined, until discovering the person she'd been in bed with was Tonia. But this – *this!* – was really happening and it felt better than winning the EuroMillions. Well, if she ever actually won the EuroMillions she might change her mind about that, but right now it definitely *felt* as if it would feel better.

And if Jamie had his reasons for doing what he was doing, who was she to refuse to play along with it?

'Just for now.' Fen nodded in happy agreement, leaning her

head against his shoulder like one half of a newly-in-love couple. 'It's been fun. Kind of like our secret. When we came to Venice, we didn't expect to bump into anyone we knew.'

'Not that it matters,' said Jamie. 'We're enjoying being together, the two of us, that's all.'

'I suppose it makes a change from your last relationship,' Bridget conceded. 'I spent most of last year in Canada, so I was a bit out of the loop, but I did see a fair amount of stuff online about you and Sadie Ingalls.' Her eyebrows lifted. 'So what happened there? We were all longing to know!'

It was an impertinent question, but Fen was too intrigued to mind; she'd wondered about it herself.

The next moment, the hand that had been around her waist slowly slid up her spine, causing her to take a quick intake of breath and feel all the little hairs rising to attention as his warm fingers stroked the sensitive nape of her neck.

If he only knew what he was doing . . .

'Nothing terrible happened,' said Jamie. 'Sadie was great.' He shrugged. 'She just wasn't Fen.'

'Right,' said Bridget. 'Lucky Fen.' Her phone began to ring in her tiny Chanel clutch bag and she pulled it out with a sigh. 'And unlucky me. Looks like Effie's woken up. I'd better go. I'll see you around.'

When she'd left the bar, Jamie gave Fen a crooked smile. 'Sorry about that.'

'No problem.' With Bridget's departure he'd dropped his hand and now the back of her neck felt bereft.

'It came out of nowhere, seemed like the best way to put her off. When Bridget wants something, she goes for it.'

'And she wants you,' said Fen. Because that much had been obvious.

'She's pretty full-on. If I'd said we were just friends, she'd have been making a play for me. It's happened before. Her father was one of the directors on the board of the rugby club. When it comes to never giving up, Bridget takes after him. I thought if I told her we were a couple, she'd hopefully leave us alone.'

Fen nodded; she was all in favour of that plan. 'Makes sense.'

'Sorry I couldn't give you any warning.'

'That's OK.' It was actually quite tricky, trying to sound casual and relaxed when the back of your neck was pining for more attention.

'You did brilliantly, by the way. Well done.'

'You should have seen me in my primary school nativity play. I was even more spectacular in that.'

'Were you Mary?'

'The turkey, actually.'

His mouth began to twitch. 'Interesting.'

'I was a natural.' She gave her arms a little flap to demonstrate just how brilliant she'd been, and did a turkey squawk that came out louder than planned, causing heads to turn around the bar. Whoops, lowering the tone in the Danieli.

But Jamie was laughing, and when he looked at her in the way he was looking at her now, it was nice to have another reason to account for the rush of colour to her cheeks.

'So if we bump into her around the hotel, we're going to have to do it again, make it look realistic.' He paused. 'I mean, if that's OK with you?'

Fen shrugged. 'It's fine. Has to look believable, doesn't it?'

Oh dear, poor me, however will I cope?

Chapter 41

The sun was a ball of melting fire hovering above the horizon. Before long it would sink into the water, and they were in prime position, well placed to witness it happening from their table on the front line of the wide terrace overlooking the lagoon.

It had been warm enough out here for Fen to be fine in her sleeveless dress during dinner, but the temperature was starting to drop; it would make sense to nip back to her room now and pick up her cardigan, rather than risk missing the spectacular setting of the sun. As soon as Jamie returned from his visit to the bathroom she would do it.

A minute later, he was back, but before she had a chance to open her mouth, he said in a low voice, 'Don't turn around whatever you do. They've just come up and ordered drinks. They're sitting at the back of the terrace. If Bridget catches your eye, she might ask if she can join us.'

'Right, got it.'

'We need to look as if we don't want to be disturbed.'

He was leaning sideways, pulling his chair closer, practically murmuring the words into her ear. Giving a tiny shiver of delight, Fen whispered stoically, 'Do what you have to do,' and really hoped it would involve more stroking of the back of her neck.

He said, 'You're being very brave.'

She nodded slowly. *See? This is my neck, right here.* 'I know.'

OK, so she definitely wasn't going to go back to her room to pick up her cardigan now.

The next twenty minutes had to rank among the very best of her life. Desperate not to break the spell, neither of them turned around for even a moment, although Fen was vividly aware of Bridget and her great-aunt sitting behind them. She could feel their presence, sense Bridget's gaze fixed unwaveringly on the back of her head and imagine her frustration at the sight of Jamie's arm lovingly draped around her shoulders. At times he adjusted his position, tilting his head closer to hers as they chatted, and lazily rubbing his hand between her shoulder blades or stroking the line of her collarbone with his thumb. It had been a toss-up which of these was her favourite, because they all provoked the most delicious reactions.

It finally occurred to her that the loving gestures could be looking a bit one-sided, so she whispered, 'Do you think I should be doing something too?'

'Might look more realistic.' Jamie nodded. 'Feel free.'

There was an offer she couldn't refuse. The only annoying thing was that she hadn't thought of it earlier. As the sun inched its way down to the horizon, turning the expanse of water to swathes of rippling silver and gold, Fen allowed her fingers to playfully caress his neck, then roam across his shoulders. When she laughed, she gave his arm an affectionate squeeze. When the breeze tousled his hair – God, she *loved* doing this – she smoothed it back into place. And when Jamie nudged the side of her leg with his own, she nudged his in return and kept her leg pressed against his.

The upside was that no cardigan was needed; her body was finding every second so unbelievably thrilling that it was creating its own heat.

The downside was that . . . nope, there were no downsides.

'Here comes the sunset.' Jamie raised his glass to hers as both the sky and the lagoon began to flood with colour. Moments later, he leaned forward to take an uninterrupted photo over the parapet. She might not have noticed anything was amiss if his knee hadn't been resting against hers and she'd felt it jerk with surprise.

'What is it?' She was leaning forward too, and Prosecco spilled from his tilted glass as he said urgently, 'Look up! Look at the sky!'

But some instinct made her look down instead, to the waterfront directly below them and the crowds making their way to and from St Mark's Square, at the water taxis bouncing over the waves and the row of gondolas tied up to their posts bobbing gently as they waited to be hired . . .

'The colours are *amazing*,' Jamie blurted out in a panic.

But it was too late, Fen had seen what he was so desperate for her not to see. One of the gondolas, having completed its journey down the Grand Canal, was being tied up at the wooden dock and the gondolier was helping its two passengers out onto dry land. The first passenger was a woman who looked to be in her eighties, and the second was—

'*Sky!*' shouted Jamie.

'Oh, look,' said Fen. 'There's Bridget.'

She turned to Jamie and saw the faint flush visible in his tanned face. Who'd have thought he was capable of that?

'Where? Ah, yes . . . so it is.' He shook his head in disbelief. 'That's . . . I mean, all this time we thought they were sitting behind us, and they weren't here on the terrace after all! I guess they must have changed their minds and decided to go for a gondola ride instead.' His voice was strained. 'I can't believe we didn't see them leave, but I suppose we were too busy admiring the view.'

Fen couldn't speak; she was doing her level best to keep a straight face, but the fact that he'd been caught out – and was mortified at having been caught out – was so . . .

Wonderful? Was that the word? Empowering, maybe? Jamie, who was never at a loss for words, was floundering now and becoming more embarrassed by the second. Tilting her head, fizzing with jubilation and relief, she said slowly, 'I suppose we must have been. That has to be the reason.'

Jamie nodded, took a hasty gulp of Prosecco and began to cough, which turned him even redder. He sat back and gazed down over the parapet, and they both watched as Bridget and her great-aunt made their way towards the entrance of the hotel.

After a few more seconds of silence, he shrugged and said almost under his breath, 'Busted. What an idiot.'

Fen was smiling now; she couldn't help it. 'Why?'

'You know why.' He raked his tanned fingers through his hair.

'I think I know why. But I'd like to hear it from you.'

'Are you laughing at me?'

'Maybe. Just a bit. But in a good way.'

'I'm embarrassed.'

'Look at the sunset now, before it disappears. We're always going to remember this evening.'

'The evening I made a complete fool of myself because I didn't know how to tell you how I was feeling.'

'*Was?* Past tense?'

'Past. Present. And future.' Jamie paused, took another gulp of Prosecco and this time didn't choke on it. Leaning to one side, he eased his wallet from his trouser pocket and removed the folded sheets of notepaper.

Taking a deep breath, he placed them on the table. 'Here you are. You can read it if you want.'

Fen met his gaze, and saw everything she'd ever wanted to see in his dark-lashed eyes, glowing silver-blue in the last reflected rays of the sun as it sank into the lagoon. Unzipping her handbag, she took out her own letter from Leon and handed it over.

'Let's both do it, shall we?'

They sat together in silence for the next two minutes, each reading the words Leon had written to the other. When they'd finished and put the letters away for safe keeping, Jamie said in a low voice, 'Just so you know, I would never have let you read that unless I was one hundred per cent sure. But I am.'

He nodded slowly, willing her to understand, his breathing bordering on unsteady. 'Everything he said. One hundred per cent, I promise.'

Light-headed with elation, because it may have been months since she'd first begun to feel the same way about him, but the strength of those emotions had rocketed in recent weeks, Fen saw the unspoken question in his eyes and reached for his hand. 'Me too. I can't quite believe this is happening, but me too.'

'Really?'

'Really.'

The relief in his voice was palpable. 'I hoped so, but I didn't know for sure.'

'Me neither. And I couldn't risk saying anything in case I was wrong.'

'Same. My God, this is incredible.' He gave a huge sigh of relief. 'I've never felt like this before, ever. You have no idea. Oh . . .'

'Oh what?' Fen swivelled sideways to see who'd caught his attention, but it was only the hotel manager, speaking to a nearby table of guests.

'I dreamt he chatted you up and you went off with him. Don't laugh. I've never been jealous before, didn't even know what it felt like.' He smiled ruefully. 'Turns out I didn't like it.'

'I promise not to run off with the hotel manager.' Fen's cheeks were starting to ache, she was so happy. And they hadn't even kissed yet. It was what she wanted to do more than anything; the urge to put her hands on either side of his face and hold his gaze for a blissful moment before closing the tiny distance between them and discovering how it felt to kiss that flawless mouth was overwhelming.

'Go on,' he murmured. 'Tell me what you're thinking right now.'

'I'm wondering what it would be like to kiss you.' Had she actually said it? Out loud? More laughter bubbled up. 'What are you thinking?'

'Funnily enough, much the same.' He was grinning too.

Here they were, in one of the most wildly romantic cities in the world, both longing to make that all-important first move she'd dreamt of for so long, but hyper-aware that it wouldn't be an appropriate thing to do. Because this was a luxurious five-star hotel, they were sitting on the busy rooftop terrace, and everyone else out here was enjoying their dinner or their post-dining cocktails. They probably wouldn't appreciate the kind of full-on demonstration that might ensue . . .

'Sir? Madam? Can I get you another drink?' Their attentive waiter materialised beside them, breaking the spell.

Fen looked at Jamie and Jamie looked back at her, a smile hovering on both their mouths, and he began to shake his head, to explain that they'd had enough, thank you very much, when Bridget appeared behind the waiter and gabbled, 'Jamie, you won't *believe* what happened to us! Emilio, could you bring our chairs up to this table so we can join them? Hello again!' She waggled her fingers at Fen and drew her companion forward. 'And this is my great-aunt Effie! Effie, these are the friends I told you about. You don't mind a bit of company, do you?'

Jamie said, 'Well—'

'Sorted!' Pulling up the first chair brought over by the obliging waiter, Bridget said rapidly, 'You sit down, Effie, I'll have the other one. Now brace yourselves, you two, and wait till you hear all about our wild adventure!'

Chapter 42

Without pausing for breath, Bridget launched with gusto into every last detail of the gondola trip, which had lasted a whole hour and had been *so* much more wobbly and precarious than either of them had expected, because the narrow side-stretches of water might have been calm, but once you ventured out into the middle of the Grand Canal, it was like trying to cross the Atlantic Ocean in a canoe.

According to Bridget and Effie, at least. Having ordered a bottle of wine to calm their nerves, they were knocking it back at a rate of knots while mimicking the violent sideways rocking of their gondola as it was buffeted on both sides by the wakes of the larger boats overtaking them. Effie cried, 'I thought we were gonna tip over at any moment – like, a million times over. I was so sure we were gonna end up in the drink!'

Was it wrong to think that would be too much to hope for? Fen was still nodding sympathetically, but they'd been gabbling non-stop for over ten minutes now, during which time she had exchanged many significant glances with Jamie. Except there was simply no way they could make their excuses and leave while the dramatic retelling was still going on.

Finally, Jamie managed to interject, 'But couldn't you have asked the gondolier to stop and let you out?'

'Are you crazy?' Effie shot him a look of disbelief. 'We paid over three hundred Canadian dollars for that trip and the guy refused to give us a refund, so no way was I gonna let him off that easy. Shysters, the lot of 'em.'

'Wait till you hear what she said to him,' Bridget exclaimed, topping up their glasses. 'When he said he wasn't going to give us our money back, Effie went ballistic and—'

'Oh no!' Fen checked her watch and let out a yelp of dismay. Clutching Jamie's arm, she said, 'I forgot to tell you, we're supposed to be meeting Molly at La Lanterna – it's her last night working there, so they're throwing her a big surprise leaving party and I absolutely promised we'd be there by eight!' She turned to Effie and Bridget. 'I'm *so* sorry, we're going to have to rush over there and grovel for being late. Effie, it's been good to meet you.' Reaching for Jamie's hand, she said breathlessly, 'Quick, we need to go!'

'Well done,' he said as they hurried down the staircase. 'I had no idea you were that good at lying.' He squeezed her hand. 'Although I'm glad you are. Now, your room or mine?'

'It wasn't a lie.' Fen shook her head. 'And we don't have time for any of that. We should have been there twenty minutes ago.'

Jamie looked at her, horrified. 'What? *Really?*'

His face. They'd reached their floor. Pushing him in the direction of the corridor that led to their rooms, buzzing with anticipation, Fen grinned and waved her key at him. 'Nope.'

★

Outside the window, a chorus of church bells began ringing out across the city into a clear starlit sky, chiming the hour. It was midnight, and over the course of the last three hours on this momentous night in Venice, Jamie knew his life had changed for good.

In both senses of the word. It was as if a heavy velvet curtain had been swept aside to reveal a future he'd secretly longed for but never dared to believe could ever happen. But now it had, it actually *had*, and Fen was everything he'd ever wanted in a partner wrapped up in one magical package. She was funny, she was brave, and just the sight of her face and the sound of her voice made him ridiculously happy. And if he'd thought she was irresistible before this evening . . . well, he now knew it for sure.

Even more than that, he was entirely aware that they both owed it all to Leon's decision to write the letters that had enabled them to admit their feelings to each other.

He owed Leon everything.

Next to him in the bed, Fen's left foot was resting against his ankle. He felt her wiggle her toes and smiled, shifting his position so he could tilt his head and see her face. 'What's that for?'

'Sorry, I was remembering the last time I did that to you. It felt unreal.'

'Erm, if you'd ever done that to me before, I'm pretty sure I'd have remembered.'

Fen pushed her blonde curls out of her eyes and twisted round to face him. 'It was that evening in Amsterdam when you came back to the house. And I didn't know how to say goodnight to you without giving myself away, so I went up to bed.'

He frowned. 'Now I'm really confused.'

'I woke up in the night and thought you were in bed with me. Our feet were touching. I wriggled my toes against your ankle. It was a massive thrill, and the thing was, you were fast asleep so I could keep on doing it.' She pulled a face. 'Until you woke up and I discovered it wasn't you under the duvet after all. It was Tonia.'

Jamie laughed. 'And she'd climbed into your bed because . . .?'

'Hendrik was snoring.'

'So you thought her feet were mine.'

'I know, I know, hers are a size five. But I wasn't concentrating, I was having too much fun to notice.'

'For your information, I don't snore.'

Fen's smile was playful. 'Definitely a point in your favour.'

Oh, that smile; it got to him every time. Her mouth, the particular curve of her upper lip, was irresistible. Yesterday had been the best evening of his life and today was on course to be even better. Drawing her closer, Jamie caressed her hairline behind her left ear, felt her quiver in response to his touch, and gave her another lingering kiss.

Finally drawing back, he said, 'Any other points in my favour?'

'Gosh, it's hard to think of any. You'll have to give me a minute.' Closing her eyes, she concentrated for a while, then said slowly, 'I quite like it when you do that thing to the back of my neck.'

'What, this thing?' He resumed stroking the warm skin, this time at the nape of her neck, and felt her reaction. 'You *quite* like it?'

'OK, I like it.' Her eyes opened, and the look she gave him sent a wave of adrenalin through his body. 'I think I might like it a lot.'

He breathed in the scent of her skin. 'I have other good points too, you know.'

Fen wrapped her arms around him and murmured, 'I already know that.'

'How are you feeling?' It was the question he hadn't put to her earlier, but it needed to be asked.

She met his gaze, understanding at once. 'You mean do I feel guilty? I thought I would. Kept waiting for it to happen. But I don't, not at all.'

He nodded, relieved. 'I know. Me neither. It's because of—'

'The letters. It really is. We don't need to feel bad because there's nothing to feel bad about.' Fen smiled as she said it. 'We aren't doing anything wrong. Leon's on our side.'

Chapter 43

Bristol

The house was ready. By seven o'clock this evening, it would be filled with friends, family and new neighbours. Fen, upstairs in the master bedroom, gazed out of the window. In the garden below, the lawn had been freshly mown, the pergola was awash with honeysuckle and the trees had been garlanded with solar lights that would cast a golden glow over the party once darkness had fallen.

Miraculously, this was their home now. They'd completed on the sale a week ago and moved in last Friday. Their first viewing had taken place back in March, on a blustery grey day in driving rain, and they had fallen in love with the place regardless, the upside to the rain being that the next time they visited in bright spring sunshine, they'd loved it fifty times more.

There had been a couple of hold-ups along the way, when the buying chain had wobbled and almost collapsed, but everyone involved had held their nerve and battled on through. And this was it, as Jamie had announced on Friday when he'd insisted on carrying her over the threshold. They'd found the house of their dreams and were going to live in it together for the rest of their lives. 'We'll throw a housewarming party next week,' he'd told her, 'to celebrate never having to do this again.'

Fen watched now as his car pulled onto the driveway and came to a halt. An unstoppable smile spread across her face as he climbed out. Watching him from a distance was still one of her favourite things to do and never failed to give her a thrill. A year ago, on that unforgettable night in Venice, they had begun their relationship in a dizzy whirl of love and sex and the certainty that they were meant to be together, but at the same time she had mentally braced herself for the possibility that it would end in failure, the feelings might peter out or they could gradually realise they weren't destined to be a couple after all.

But despite her hidden fears, that hadn't happened. Instead, the love, the friendship and the delight in each other's company had seemed to grow on an exponential scale. Every day, the idea of not being together for ever seemed more impossible. Plus, just look at him, he was perfect. OK, apart from when he tried to make scrambled eggs. He was rubbish at that.

The next moment, Jamie glanced up and saw her watching him. He broke into a grin and Fen's stomach did a swallow-dive of desire, because the last year had been the best year of her life and they still had so much more to look forward to.

Starting with tonight's party.

Thirty seconds later, she heard footsteps on the stairs and turned to see him appear in the bedroom doorway. Back from his meeting, he unbuttoned his shirt and shrugged it off, revealing that tanned, toned torso.

'Everything ready?'

Fen went towards him. 'Pretty much. The drinks have been

delivered. The caterers are setting up in the kitchen. It's all under control down there.'

His eyes sparked with amusement as she ran her fingers over his chest. 'Down where?'

'I meant the kitchen. But now you're giving me ideas.'

'Do you know how much I like it when you have ideas?' Lifting her effortlessly, he carried her across the room.

Fen kissed him on the mouth and didn't release her hold on him as he slowly lowered her onto the king-sized bed. So it seemed she had something else to look forward to before the party started . . .

By eight o'clock, the house and garden had filled up and the party was well under way.

'Look at you, and look at all of this.' Disa, glamorous in cobalt-blue silk, slipped her arm through Fen's and gestured around her at the happy gathering. 'We started all this when we booked that cruise.' Turning to Jamie, she added, 'And we chose that week despite you being on the ship, not because of it.'

Jamie said cheerfully, 'As Fen often likes to remind me.'

'If we'd gone a week later,' Fen told him, 'I might have met someone even better. He could be out there somewhere now, single and miserable, wondering why he hasn't found the love of his life yet.'

'Don't bother going looking for him.' Jamie shook his head at her. 'You're stuck with me now.'

'Same as this one's stuck with me.' Disa patted Marcus's arm.

'Make that three of them,' Molly announced, joining in the conversation with Andy at her side. 'He might try to escape, but I'm not letting it happen. By the way, Kayla says we need to have a video call in a bit so she doesn't miss out on seeing us all. And she'll have Merlin on her lap so we can admire him and tell him what a handsome boy he is.'

'We'll do that,' Fen promised. If Kayla hadn't entered that competition on the radio and won a Venetian cruise, she most certainly would never have met Angelo, nor married him and become Kayla Sartori, nor currently be days away from giving birth to their longed-for first child. It just went to show, when you looked back at the people they'd met and the friends they'd made during that magical week away, you could never predict the twists and turns life might take.

As she looked around her at the hundred-strong gathering, she could see guests greeting old friends and introducing them to other friends, new connections being made. Through the open French doors leading out into the garden, she spotted Molly's mum, Yvette, chatting away to one of their new neighbours. Over to their left, one of Jamie's old rugby player friends was deep in conversation with Leon's parents.

And there, at the very furthest end of the garden, were Hattie and Guy. Goodness knows what they were discussing, but whatever it was, given Guy's visible double-take, he'd definitely been caught by surprise . . .

'What?' Guy frowned, taken aback.

'It's been exactly a year since that day in the supermarket when you got down on one knee in front of all those people and proposed to me.'

'Has it? Phew, I thought you were about to tell me I'd forgotten your birthday. Which is in October,' he quickly added. 'The fourteenth. See? I still remember.'

He never had forgotten her birthday. Hattie said, 'That supermarket thing was so embarrassing.'

'I know. I said I was sorry.'

'A whole year since the last time you asked me to marry you.'

Guy nodded. 'You told me never to ask you again.'

'And I meant it.'

'Which is why I haven't.'

'I know. And I appreciate that. Guy?'

'What?'

'Will you marry me?'

He did another double-take. 'Sorry?'

'Oh dear. Bit awkward,' said Hattie. 'Does that mean no?'

'It means did you really just say that?'

'I did. But don't expect me to go down on one knee in front of everyone, because it's not happening.' She shook her head.

'Say it again,' said Guy.

'It's not happening.'

'Not that. The asking bit.'

Hattie smiled. 'Why, so you can turn me down and get your own back?'

'No. I want to see your face when you ask me.'

'Fine. Guy Franklyn McAllister, will you marry me?'

'I'd love to.'

'Good. That's settled then.'

'You wanted to be the one doing the asking, didn't you?'

'Maybe, but I also just needed to be sure. And now I am.' Hattie stepped forward, checked that no one else was watching and planted a quick kiss on his mouth. Fifteen years on from their first marriage, Guy had proven himself to be more mature and far better husband material than before. All he'd needed was time to grow up.

Guy said, 'Thank you,' and returned her kiss with an equally brief one of his own.

A young lad chasing after a toy helicopter screwed up his face in disgust as he hurtled past them. 'Eurgh, old people kissing. So gross.'

When the boy had raced back up the garden with his helicopter, Guy gave her a proper kiss and said with a smile, 'So wrong.'

It was one in the morning by the time the last few guests finally departed. When only Disa and Marcus were left, Disa signalled to him with a nod and a smile, and he headed outside, returning two minutes later with a parcel they'd evidently been keeping in the car.

'Little housewarming present for you both,' she said.

Fen took the large, flat package, wrapped in silver paper. 'You didn't need to do this.' She gave it a little shake. 'Is it chocolates?'

'No, but I hope you'll like it anyway.' Disa linked her arm through Marcus's and watched as Fen and Jamie tore off the wrapping and the cardboard packaging beneath. 'And I need to explain why I never showed it to you before.'

Jamie lifted the last of the packaging away, and Fen, lost for words, reached out to touch the simply framed photograph, enlarged to A2 size.

It had been taken in Venice two years ago; she could tell from what they were wearing that the scene had been captured, presumably by Disa, on the second night of their cruise. There'd been a whole group of newly acquainted guests socialising up on deck after dinner that evening. In the centre of the picture were Jamie, herself and Leon laughing together at something one of them had just said. Her heart gave a squeeze of love.

'I was showing Marcus a load of photos on my phone last week and this one came up,' Disa explained, 'but it didn't look like that then. Everyone was too far away, and there were a couple of other people spoiling it – one was completely blurred and another looked as if he had two heads. It was such a shame. Then Marcus took my phone and started working some kind of magic.'

'Your grandmother didn't realise photos could be edited like that.' Marcus gave Disa an affectionate look. 'All I had to do was expand the photo, lighten it up and delete the unwanted guests.'

'Black magic!' exclaimed Disa. 'If only you could do that to annoying people in real life!'

'It's called technology,' he told her with a smile. 'It only took a minute, and there you were, the three of you, looking as if you'd known each other for years.'

Disa said, 'I showed it to Hilary and Greville on my phone earlier. Hilary had a little weep and asked if she could have a copy. I said I'd get one blown up and framed for her too.'

Fen nodded, still moved beyond words, because Marcus had taken a messy, overcrowded photo and made it flawless, drawing you in and making you want to be there. Yet again, her grandmother had inadvertently created a bit of magic of her own. And yes, of course it had been Disa who had hand-delivered the letters Leon had written to her and Jamie. She'd admitted it as soon as they'd returned from that second eventful trip to Venice.

'Leon asked me to visit him when he knew he didn't have much time left. We had a long chat about the two of you,' she had told them both. 'I didn't read what he'd written, but I had a pretty good idea. And he trusted me to do the right thing. If it was obvious a year later that for one reason or another it wouldn't work out, you would never have seen them.'

Remembering those words now, Fen glanced at Jamie and a shiver ran down her spine. It didn't bear thinking about.

But luckily, there was no need to. She looked again at the framed photograph. 'It's beautiful. And I know exactly where we can hang it.' Pointing to a space on the living room wall next to the fireplace, she said, 'There, where everyone can see it as soon as they come through the door.'

'The three of you, looking so happy together,' said Disa. 'And you all loved each other so much.' Slipping an arm around Fen, she added, 'You just didn't know it yet.'

RAISING READERS
Books Build Bright Futures

Dear Reader,

We'd love your attention for one more page to tell you about the crisis in children's reading, and what we can all do.

Studies have shown that reading for fun is the **single biggest predictor of a child's future life chances** – more than family circumstance, parents' educational background or income. It improves academic results, mental health, wealth, communication skills, ambition and happiness.[1]

The number of children reading for fun is in rapid decline. Young people have a lot of competition for their time. In 2024, 1 in 10 children and young people in the UK aged 5 to 18 did not own a single book at home.[2]

Hachette works extensively with schools, libraries and literacy charities, but here are some ways we can all raise more readers:

- Reading to children for just 10 minutes a day makes a difference
- Don't give up if children aren't regular readers – there will be books for them!
- Visit bookshops and libraries to get recommendations
- Encourage them to listen to audiobooks
- Support school libraries
- Give books as gifts

There's a lot more information about how to encourage children to read on our website: **www.RaisingReaders.co.uk**

Thank you for reading.

---

[1] OECD, '21st-Century Readers: Developing Literacy Skills in a Digital World', 2021, https://www.oecd.org/en/publications/21st-century-readers_a83d84cb-en.html

[2] National Literacy Trust, 'Book Ownership in 2024', November 2024, https://literacytrust.org.uk/research-services/research-reports/book-ownership-in-2024